ᛚᚠ • ᛥᛁᛥ • ᚦᛖ • ᚹᚠᚦᛖᚱ • ᚴᚢᛗ • ᛖᛏᚠ • ᚦᛖ • ᚹᚠᚱᛁᛥ •
ᛏᚱᛖᛚᛁᛉ • ᚦᛖ • ᚷᛚᚠᚱᛁ • ᚠᚹ • ᚴᚺᛗᚹᛋ • • ᚺᛖ • ᚴᛖᛖ • ᚠᚹ
ᛥᛉ • ᚠᛏᛥ ᚠᛚᚠᛏ • ᚺᛗᛋ • ᚹᛗᚱᛋᛏ • ᚹᚠᚱᛥ • ᚠᚠᛋ ᚦᛖ
• ᛖᛗᛋᚲᛗᚱ • ᚠᚹ • ᛚᚢᚹ • • ᚺᛖ • ᚴᚠᛚᛗᛥ • ᛏᚠ • ᚦᛖ • ᛥᛗ
ᛥ • ᚠᛏᛥ • ᚦᛏ • ᛥᛁᛥ • ᛏᚠᛏ • ᚠᛏᛋᛗᚱ • • ᚺᛖ • ᚴᚠᛚᛗᛥ • ᛏ
ᚠ • ᚦᛖ • ᚠᛚᛥ • ᚷᚠᚠᛋ • ᚠᛏᛥ • ᚦᛏ • ᛥᛁᛥ • ᛏᚠᛏ • ᚺᛏᚱ • •
ᚦᛖ • ᚱᚢᛗᛏᛋ • ᚠᚹ • ᚦᛖ • ᛚᚠᛥ • ᛗᛗᛏ • ᛋᚲᚠᚴ • ᛏᚠ • ᚦᛖ
• ᚹᚠᚦᛖᚱ • • ᚹᚱᚢᛗ • ᚺᛗᛋ • ᚷᚺᚠᛋᛏ • ᚦᛏ • ᚱᛗᛥ • ᚦᛖ
• ᛗᛋᛗᛏᛋ • ᚠᚹ • ᛗᚠᛏ • • ᛚᚠ • ᛥᛁᛥ • ᚦᛖ • ᛚᚠᛥ • ᛚᛁᚹᛁᛉ
ᛏᛗᛥᛗᛗᛏᛏ • ᚠᚹ • ᛗᚠᛏᛋᛁᛏᛥ • ᚠᚹᛗᛚᛁᛏ • ᛁᛏ • ᚦᛖ • ᛒᚠ
ᛋᚠᛗ • ᚠᚹ • ᚦᛖ • ᚷᚱᛏᛏ • ᛋᛚᛁᚲ • • ᛚᚠ • ᚠᚠᛋ • ᛗᚠᛏ • ᛋᚠᚹ
ᛥᛉ • ᚹᚱᚢᛗ • ᚠᛒᚢᚹᚠᚠᛏ • • ᛚᚠ • ᛥᛁᛥ • ᚷᛏᛗᛋ • ᚠᚱᛋᚠᛏ
• ᛚᚢᛗ • ᛏᚠ • ᛒᛗ • ᚦᛖ • ᚹᚠᚦᛖᚱ • ᚠᚹ • ᚠᛚ • ᛗᛗᛏ • •

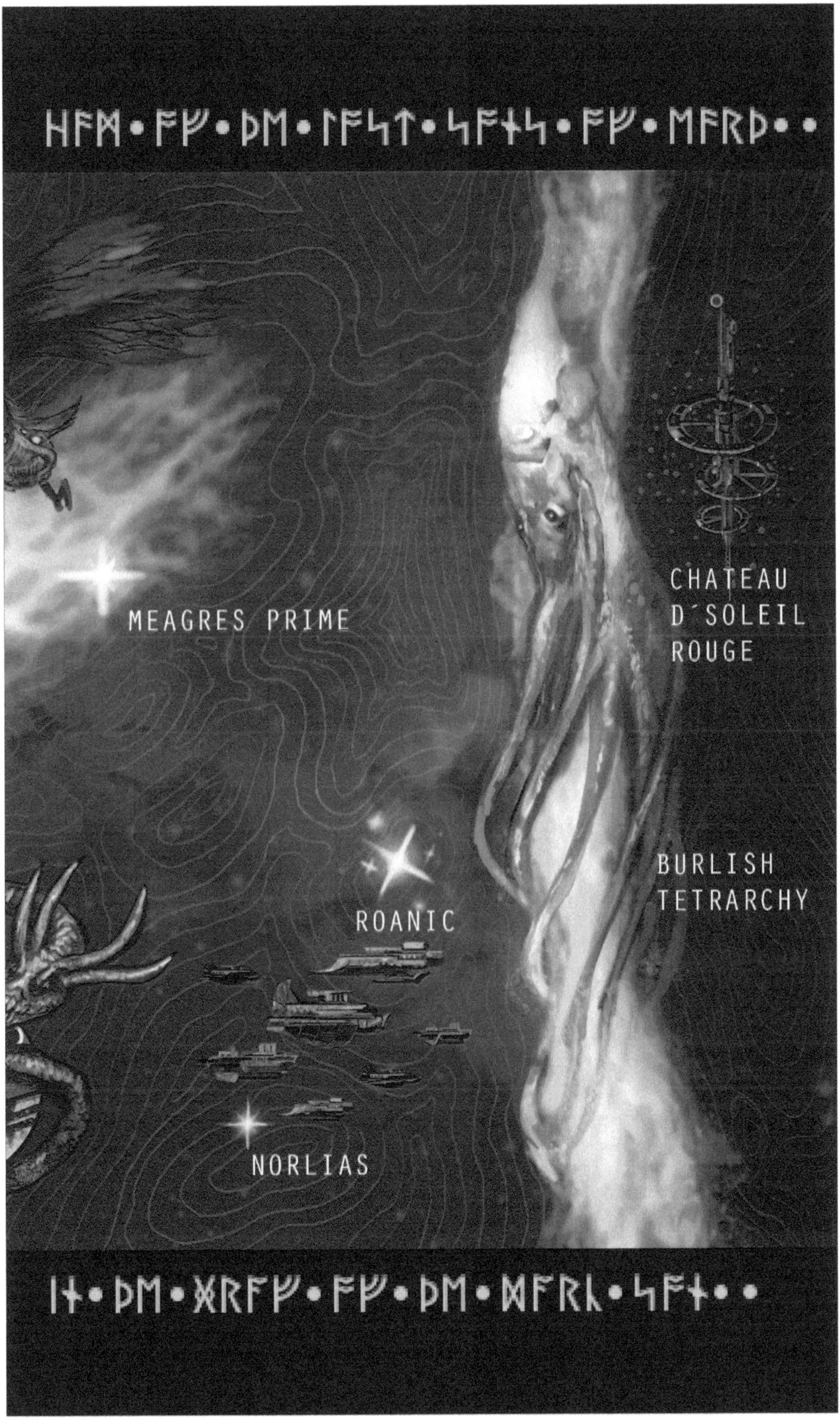
MEAGRES PRIME
CHATEAU
D´SOLEIL
ROUGE
BURLISH
TETRARCHY
ROANIC
NORLIAS

The Prisoner of the Red Sun Castle
By: Cal Parmain II
The Prisoner of the Red Sun Castle
Copyright 2014 by Cal Parmain II
© 2014 Cal Parmain II
All rights reserved.

Cover and Star Chart by Carlos Cara
Copyright 2014 by Cal Parmain II

Published in the United States of America
ISBN 978-0-692-25528-5
1. Science Fiction-Fiction.   2. Action and Adventure-Fiction

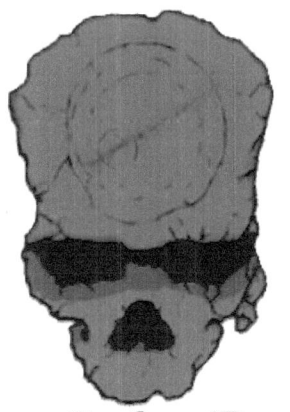

The Prisoner of the Red Sun Castle

By: Cal Parmain II

Contents

Chapter		Page

Histories and Additional Content

Preface to the First Printed Edition

This book is for my fellow dreamers, for starry-eyed boys who have awoken in the dawn of adulthood to find themselves mundane and dreary men. Our hero is much the same, a lost son of our modern age. These pages contain swashbuckling romance, a dash of vivid violence, and more than a little selfish revenge. To that end, this is a book of childish fantasy and is most certainly not meant to be mistaken for anything more than the pulpy Sci-Fi that it is. But, if like me, you grew up reading Burroughs, Howard, and Dumas, then it is my hope that you find some small enjoyment in the adventures of a lone assistant professor lost in alien skies.

It should be noted that the inspiration for much of the early plot for *The Prisoner of the Red Sun Castle* came from a far superior work written by a far superior author: Alexandre Dumas' *The Count of Monte Cristo*. If you are able to read Dumas, I strongly encourage you to do so. What I have taken from the master of French Romance is merely the foundation of adventure: an innocent man; a corrupt politician; a cruel, dark prison; and a wise, old teacher. What is left in Dumas' wondrous *Count* is purest revenge and exhilarating adventure unmatched in the written form.

Chapter I

James Orson

he sun appeared gray in the cloudy eye of the dead crow. The once-beautiful creature lay pressed into the pavement of the university parking lot. Its beak was cracked to the feathers. The tongue hung from the sharp tip, and the long, graceful wings were shattered and folded back against a pitiful body. It had been free once. Once that little lump of flesh had swum in the hot, wet air and feasted on the sky like a black god. But no more. Freedom was dead. Escape was impossible. A dead bird lay on the pavement surrounded by oblong pools of dirty rain.

The sun's heat spread across James Orson's body, thick and oppressive. He was sweltering in his sweater vest and jacket. He pulled the dull-red bowtie away from his throat and stared down at the corpse of the ruined bird. He could feel his stomach churning. Sweat began to bead on his forehead and drip down his face in disgusting tails of cool wetness. He imagined large, dark sweat stains covering his clothes. He felt sticky in his Oxford cloth shirt. He pulled on the off-white fabric. *Disgusting.* Freedom was dead.

Brakes screeched. A horn blasted.

"Get your fat ass out of the fucking road!" the young driver shouted, revving his engine aggressively.

Orson jumped back, startled, and muttered meekly to the ground, "Actually it's a privately owned parking area, not a road. You see, people have to walk-"

The horn blasted again.

"Get **out** of the way, asshole!' the driver repeated.

"Oh, s-sorry," James Orson stuttered, stepping aside.

The cheap, mass-produced sports car stormed past, crushing the bird's remains. Coagulated blood and sticky, black feathers splashed across Orson's khaki pants. The mess slid down his shins, leaving behind streaks of flesh and blood on the dull fabric. Bile rose quickly in his throat.

1

"Oh, god!" Orson spat in sweaty disgust shortly before vomiting in front of his fuel efficient, Korean-made economy car. In the distance the university clock tower struck seven o'clock.

The old Gothic Revival clock tower cast a crooked shadow over Stevenson Hall, home of the university's English department. Orson had hated it when he was an undergrad and he hated it even more as part of the faculty. The tower looked completely out of place next to the 'progressive', Art Deco inspired main building, and the clashing styles made the whole mess look ridiculous, something Orson attributed to the utter stupidity of bureaucrats chasing fads.

"Idiots," Orson grumbled to himself, passing under a large, blue banner.

Gold lettering was printed across an empty field of indigo, proudly display-ing the university's new motto, "*Gather together; for the Future!*" Orson hated that slogan. It reminded him of cheap commercials on late night television, as if an education were no more significant than a pair of new shoes or a fast food sandwich. Those words had no soul, in fact they seemed to him a void, a great hollowness, which gradually devoured the soul of every student, a terrible, thoughtless jamble of words conveying a broken concept of inept greed. Yet, if the rumors were true, the university had paid an enormous sum of money to a hot, new marketing firm to develop those five boring words. Orson shook his head. He thought of the ubiquitious *they*. *They* had an entire building filled with writers and struggling artists, and *they* chose to waste money on admen who wore suits that cost more than Orson's car. *They* never respected anyone. *They* were stupid, greedy bastards. Orson hated *them*.

Orson slumped through the bustling hall, dodging students. He recognized most of them from various entry level classes he'd been allowed to teach. More than once he was pressed roughly against the wall and had to wait for an open-ing to slip past. No one acknowledged his presence as they shoved by. After a brief struggle he made it to the back stairs. They were old, oaken things from the Eisenhower administration, sturdy and strong. The stairs had been here long before *they* were. *They* could never ruin that. It was why Orson loved those stairs. They gave him hope, reminded him that once things had been built to last. Kingdoms fall. Democracies fail. Stairs endure. Those old stairs were incorruptible. Orson ran his fingers along the smooth railing and started down.

There were only two people who used the basement stairwell. Orson met the other on the basement landing. The janitor was a very tall woman with thick, muscular thighs and massive breasts that made Orson uncomfortable. The janitor's curly, red hair was bunched up tightly under the plain, brown hat of her plain, brown uniform. Orson saw her coming and silently pressed himself against the wall to let her pass. Orson was sure she thought he was an asshole. He wanted to say, "Good morning! How are you?" and smile and introduce himself. Instead, he managed a muted, "Oh, e-excuse me," before spreading himself out farther like a bug on the wall.

The janitor remained silent as she passed. She had a mop and a bucket in her steely grasp and her face was twisted sourly. After she had disappeared up the next flight, Orson's heartbeat slowed down enough for him to quickly straighten his jacket and adjust his bowtie. His office was in the subbasement with the janitor's. They were the only two souls on the entire floor, and he'd been trying to introduce himself for three years. Orson shook his head, allowing himself an uncharacteristic, lighthearted smile. He felt sorry for whoever was responsible for that mess. More than once he'd heard the janitor rampaging through her office after cleaning up after a careless student. Orson smugly readjusted his tie and checked his briefcase. Then, as he looked down to straighten his paints, he remembered the gory mess dripping off of his shins. His heart caught in his chest and he struggle to remember if he'd remembered to clean his shoes before coming inside. *Idiot!* He shook his head worriedly as he continued down the stairs. He felt like an asshole.

As Orson reached the bottom of the final flight, his self-loathing had reached a critical focus that bordered on the masochistic. Yet, he forgot it all the moment his feet left the final step to the subbasement and he saw the old, metal door that read in faded, orange-red letters, "Warning: Keep Out."

Orson's stomach knotted with dread. The air was crisp with ozone, and the hairs on the back of his neck tingled his nerves. There had been a thunderstorm the night before. He could always tell. Orson mumbled impotent complaints about the idiotic, selfish administration as he opened the door to E.T.E.R.M.O.S.. Once-gleaming metal and cracked vacuum tubes filled the majority of the large, open space. Dull lights blinked prime colors through smoky glass, while slow clicks and stuttering machine noise chewed nonexistent data. The university's oldest computer system was active.

Something about that old machine left Orson uneasy. None of the faculty

3

knew much about it, aside from a few senile, old professors in the physics department. According to them, it had been built into the building's foundation back in the early fifties as part of a joint venture between the university and the Department of Defense, but, thanks to a tangled bureaucratic mess, the state-of-the-art computer system had taken so long to build that, by the time it was finally completed, E.T.E.R.M.O.S. was already obsolete. As a result, all relevant files were destroyed and all data cards burned. As might be expected, no one even remembered what the acronym stood for, let alone what function the machine was actually designed to perform. They would have just unplugged or disassembled the ancient thing, but it was apparently built directly into Stevenson Hall's power grid as a fail-safe. The old administration decided that it would be best to simply disconnect the data line and leave the sleeping beast to dream in dumb solitude.

Orson hated the damned thing. Every time it rained the master control unit would kick on, the lights would flash, and the whole place would smell of ozone for days. He was genuinely terrified that the rotting, primitive machine was going to explode one day and kill him. Of course, the administration assured him that E.T.E.R.M.O.S. was no more dangerous than an old VCR, but their distant assurances did little to reassure him and every month, for the first year of his employment, Orson had requested a new office. His requests were, at first, politely declined, then flat-out refused, and finally, completely ignored. He had long since given up.

Orson hurried past the stuttering relic. His office was in the back, next to the janitor's. Orson fumbled with his pockets searching for the fat, brass key to his office. He twisted it in the old lock and fought with the faded, pea-green door. Years in the humid basement had left the wood warped, making the door to Orson's office an hourly annoyance. A solid kick popped it out of the frame and the door burst open. Orson slinked into his office. It was a crummy, little room with no windows or much light at all, practically a prison cell. The walls were stained with age and the cheap, green paint was peeling back, revealing the original red underneath. A pair of exposed pipes made a makeshift book-shelf, where a weathered copy of *The Hobbit* leaned against the flaking metal. Beside it was *Peter Pan*, an English translation of *The Count of Monte Cristo* and a series of empty textbooks from his introductory classes. Orson dropped his briefcase into the ragged, old recliner by his door, hit the power button on his computer, and grabbed the mostly empty coffee pot from the shelf behind his desk. It was a Berne *Coffee Dominator*, the plastic had yellowed with age and a number of the swept, futuristic letters were missing from the side. It was almost as old as E.T.E.R.M.O.S. and probably just as dangerous. Orson hated it.

The bathroom was on the other side of the janitor's office. Luckily, the red-haired giantess was still occupied upstairs. Orson shuffled stealthily across the basement, doing his best to ignore the cacophonous E.T.E.R.M.O.S.. He put the coffee pot under the faucet and turned the knob. The pipes knocked loudly and sputtered a few sporadic bursts of brown water into the coffee-stained glass.

"Idiot." Orson muttered to himself. He emptied the sludge and rinsed the coffee pot with the clean water now pouring from the faucet.

As the coffee pot filled with water, Orson tried to ignore the old man in the mirror. He knew that he looked terrible. His shaggy, brown hair partially obscured his dull eyes, and there was an old scar on his round chin hidden behind a rough, patchy beard. He smiled ironically when he remembered that he was only twenty-nine years old. Orson's eyes drifted to himself and he sighed at the old man starring back at him. He returned to his office, and poured the water into his coffeemaker.

As the *Coffee Dominator* gurgled behind him, Orson pecked away at his computer, bringing up his email. There were five new messages, three from Professor Cullen marked urgent.

-Dorson, where are those papers? I need those grades by the 17th.

"Orson, my name is Orson," the assistant professor groaned before checking the next message.

-Dorson, what the hell are you doing down there? Get me those research papers ASAP.

"My name is in the email address!" Orson grumbled over his coffee. Before he could open his next message, his office phone rang.

"Assistant Professor **James Orson**, Stevenson Hall," Orson answered mechanically, "If it's about the pipes we already-"

"Dorson!"

Orson jumped in his seat. It was Professor Cullen.

"What's gotten into you? Russian Lit. starts in five hours!"

Orson instinctively nodded, dropping his eyes, "Yes, sir, I know that, sir. I put the graded papers in your mail box last night. I'm sure of-"

"You'd better be, Dorson. Don't forget, I'm meeting with the dean this afternoon." He paused to torture him. "I'd really like to recommend you for a staff position in the future, but I need to know that you're reliable. I need to know that you're a team player. Can I count on you?"

"Yes, sir."

"Say it, Dorson."

"You can count on me, sir." Orson nodded again to nobody.

"There's a good chap. Now then, about my laundry, tell them to take it easy on the starch. Last time my ties were like little broadswords."

Orson answered quickly, "I'll do that, sir. Anything else?"

"Nothing right now. Get back to work, Dorson. I'll call to let you know about lunch. I'm feeling like Mexican today."

"Yes, sir. I know this place down by-" CLICK. "Uh, okay then....“

Orson set the phone back in its cradle, and leaned back in his chair. He ran his fingers through his messy hair. On his wall, a faded kitten stared back at him. It was a gift from Elizabeth, a bad motivational poster.

"**You** hang in there," Orson grumbled.

Then he stared at the small, silver-framed picture on his desk. His eyes moved across the smiling blonde's face and his heart jumped. His fingertips brushed across the small, felt-covered box in his pocket and a dumb smile spread across his face. It didn't last long. He knew it was a pathetic ring. A small emerald was set in place of the customary diamond. It was Elizabeth's birthstone. He had promised himself that he'd replace it as soon as he could. Orson looked back at the portrait of his beloved Elizabeth, and he could feel a familiar, sickly blackness filling his chest. His own ghostly reflection caught his eyes. He felt worthless. A loud clanging next door told Orson that the janitor was back. He could hear her swearing loudly in a foreign tongue before returning briefly to broken English.

"God it damns! That shitty piece! Ne-berthel supthsweorth! Fuck mother! De ye show job done! That man! Ye yer nass wish! I kill his ass!"

Then Orson hear the janitor digging through her tool closet.

She swore loudly again, "Son of the bitch! Torgoth rieme **Cullen** ne-berthel nadirpagar!"

The janitor's shouts faded away, and Orson cautiously poked his head out of his office door. E.T.E.R.M.O.S. clicked away in the dark basement. He thought that he should talk to her. The janitor had been quiet for nearly a minute. Orson moved toward her door. He was trying to convince himself to knock. But what would he say? He'd never even had the courage to look her in the eyes. He never looked anyone in the eyes. Orson's hand dropped over the old knob. He wanted to open the door. He wanted to just turn the knob and open the door and smile and say, "Hi, are you okay?" He wanted to make himself do it. Orson stared at the heavy door. The robin's-egg-blue paint was chipped and flaking off, exposing the rough wood underneath. He couldn't do it. Orson raised his hand to knock instead, but just as his knuckles brushed against the door he heard the janitor talking to herself on the other side. Orson's courage evaporated, and his sweaty hand dropped to his side, defeated. He was about to turn back to his crummy, little office when he heard the sudden screech of the knob turning. The janitor's door slammed into Orson's face, knocking him to the ground.

The basement fell away and Orson slipped into an endless pool of blue water. Warmth surrounded him. No. Not water. He wasn't swimming or floating. His body wasn't wet. No. It was the sky. James Orson was flying. The air filled his lungs as he rose through the cloudless sky. The deep blue parted around his flesh. His body moved like a bird, like a great whale. Then there was no sky, no ground, no sun or stars. He dipped and fluttered through emptiness. Slowly all that he was bled away from him. It was like sand slipping through his fist. He was dead. It was glorious. An eternity of perfect blue filled the universe, spilling and splashing beyond its edges. The past, present, and future were as nothing. It was existence, freedom, and purity found in the utter perfection of nonexistence. It was paradise. Ruined.

A voice pierced the sky. "Are you okay?

Orson shook what had once been his head. "What?"

The matronly voice had touched something, a part of him he'd forgotten. He didn't want to remember. It was terrible. But he couldn't fight it. To fight was to acknowledge the coming of existence. The coming of hell.

"Ye are okay?" The blue began to fall away like painted sand.

"No," Orson muttered, "I'm fine."

The universe began to fill Orson's brain. Everything he had ever known poured into his consciousness like an ocean screaming with color. The blue was gone. Knowledge was terror. Life was real. Reality made him human. Orson was alive. He could feel the cold floor on his thighs. His head was lying on something warm and soft.

"Ye are ne okay."

Orson's eyes opened. Above his head he could see the janitor's face. She held him in her arms. His head was resting on her breasts.

"R-really, I'm fine," he answered, struggling to lean forward.

The janitor helped him to his feet.

"There es blood."

"What?" Orson muttered, raising a hand to his face. His lips were wet and tasted of copper. His nose was bleeding. "I don't- I..."

Sweat dripped from Orson's forehead. His stomach twisted in his belly. The world was spinning. His legs gave out under him, and he collapsed into the janitor's arms.

There were no dreams this time. There was no release. Orson simply slept. He awoke on a shabby, red couch in the janitor's office. His nostrils were stuffed with brown paper towel. The janitor was gone. Orson was alone. His head was foggy. He sat up, and pulled the bloody stoppers from his nose. Blood trickled after them. Wisely, he decided to stuff the paper towel back up his nostrils.

The janitor's office was unexpectedly well organized, with several tall shelves and two large cabinets. On the walls she had hung two documents yellowed with age. Orson stood carefully, mindful of his nose. He examined the strange print and the sweeping signature at the bottom. They could have been anything except English. The muted noise of his office phone pierced the fog. In a slight panic, Orson considered leaving a note for his rescuer. Then he left.

"Dorson! Where the hell have you been?" Professor Cullen's voice demanded through the phone, "I've been calling for the past half hour!"

"I had an accident, sir." Orson's fingertips touched his tender nose.

"An accident?"

Orson thought about the door and shivered. "I uh...fell, sir."

"Can you walk?"

"Yes, sir."

"Then, get your ass up here, Dorson, and bring those papers!"

"But I know they were in your mailbox," Orson muttered.

"Not those, you idiot! I need the retyped syllabi for my eleven o'clock class."

Orson had stayed up late finishing it. The copies were in his genuine imitation leather briefcase. He nodded again, "I'm on my way, sir."

Professor Cullen growled, "You've got five minutes."

Orson grabbed his briefcase and rushed out the door. He was half way up the stairs before he realized that he had hurt his knee when he had fainted. Each stair sent a new shock of pain through the wounded joint, and he limped his way up to Professor Cullen's fourth floor office.

Orson stopped at the beautiful, handcarven, oak door to catch his breath. His throat felt sticky and raw. His heart hammered in his chest. He knocked softly on the door.

"It's open."

Orson opened the door and stepped into Professor Cullen's office. It was a spacious room with a high ceiling. The walls were hung with pretentious 'artifacts' from Cullen's many trips to classical Europe, and there was a big window overlooking the university grounds. Orson limped onto the antique rug. He fumbled with the small stack of paper in his briefcase.

"Here you are, sir," he offered, finally.

Professor Cullen was in the corner, fiddling with his new cappuccino maker. It hissed loudly, releasing a puff of steam. He lifted the porcelain teacup to his mouth and slurped a little foam from the top.

"Just leave it on my desk, Dorson," Professor Cullen managed between careful sips. "Excellent cappuccino. I'd offer you a cup, but I've only just got the machine set right, you understand."

Orson answered quietly, "That's alright, sir. I need to get back."

On his way back to his crummy, little office in the subbasement Orson thought about how much he'd wanted a cappuccino.

Chapter II

The Disaster at Dinner

rson stared down at the checkered tablecloth. There was a dark stain at the bottom corner. He wondered what had left it. *A meatball maybe?* Orson glanced toward the kitchen. They were famous for their meatballs. *Well, maybe not famous.* He admitted to himself. *But people seem to like them.* Orson coughed softly.

"What could possibly be taking them so long?" Elizabeth asked, breaking the silence.

Her voice crashed Orson's meatball laden train of thought and he suddenly remembered where he was. The boom of distant thunder shook the quiet room. Rain slipped down the cool, painted glass of the restaurant window.

"I-I uhhh, I don't know," he stuttered. His mouth was dry. He took a sip of the cheap house red by his napkin, then offered meekly, "It could be anything really. You did special order the veal tortellini. They may be having problems in the kitchen..."

Elizabeth half-smiled. She was wearing the thin, black dress Orson had given her for their two year anniversary. He was wearing an old sweater vest with a small, faded stain on the bottom, poetically from a meatball. She was beautiful.

Orson took another drink of wine and cleared his throat. "There was a-actually something I wanted to-" His fingertips played with the little felt box in his pocket.

"James, why don't you find out what's taking so long," Elizabeth interrupted, nonchalantly.

Orson glanced down at the stained tablecloth again, then back up to Elizabeth. He pulled his hand out of his pocket and looked back toward the kitchen.

"I'm sure they're working as fast as they can," he said softly. "We've only been here half-an-hour."

Elizabeth looked past the dumpy assistant professor. She hadn't really been listening to him.

"We've been *waiting* for half-an-hour," she corrected him.

Orson nodded, "Uh, yes, but they are busy tonight, darling."

A waiter backed out of the kitchen carrying a platter of steaming entrees. Orson hoped it was theirs. His fingers played with the edge of the tablecloth. If it wasn't their food Elizabeth would make him talk to the kitchen. They'd probably think he was one of those annoying people, the sort that always act like they deserve the world and bother people. The waiter walked toward their table. Orson sat up and relief washed over him. He smiled dumbly to the waiter, but the man ignored him. He walked right past their table, stopping by a couple seated by the window. The goofy smile faded from Orson's face. He sank back into his chair, wondering how *those* two had gotten such a good table without a reservation.

Elizabeth sighed, and Orson risked a glance into her eyes. She wanted him to talk to the kitchen. She didn't have to say it. His heart sank. Orson looked back at the tablecloth, and took another sip of cheap wine. The fragrance filled his nostrils before he swallowed. It was rough and burned his throat. He hated the taste of alcohol. He didn't know why he'd ordered wine.

"I'll uh, I'll go see what's taking so long," Orson muttered as he quietly left the table.

He dodged another waiter and with a series of subdued apologies made his way through the maze of tables. He waited by the door for their waiter. The couples seated at the nearby tables talked in suddenly hushed voices as if he'd come specifically to listen in on their inane conversations. Orson pulled at his red bow tie. It was choking him. Finally, he got up the courage to peer through the little window. He saw their waiter. A young man in his early twenties was leaning against the back wall, laughing with the dishwasher. Orson gave him a timid wave. The waiter pretended to have not noticed him. Orson waved again. The waiter turned his back toward the door. Orson stepped away from the kitchen. He wondered if he could sneak back to his table. Elizabeth might believe him if he told her he had asked. He could tell her there had been an un-expected accident, and they had to start over on her tortellini. *Yes, she would believe that.* Orson tentatively looked back at his table. Elizabeth was watching him. Orson's stomach knotted. It wouldn't work. He'd have to go in there.

Orson pushed open the door to the kitchen. A gentle gust of heat and steam pushed past his face. He cleared his throat.

"Um, excuse me?" he asked timidly.

No one seemed to hear him.

Orson tried again, this time a little louder. "Excuse me?"

Still nothing. Orson looked back to Elizabeth. She gestured forward with her hands. Orson shook his head. He was sure customers weren't allowed in the kitchen. His stomach knotted tighter.

"Can I help you?"

Orson jumped back. Another waiter had come to the door.

"Can I help you with something, sir?" the waiter asked again.

Orson instinctively shook his head, then remembered why he had come to the kitchen.

"Ah, yes, actually," he nodded. "I was just wondering if you could tell me when our dinner might be ready."

The waiter answered quickly, "I'll go check. What did you order?"

"The veal tortellini and the spaghetti with meatballs."

The waiter nodded, "I'll be right back."

He went into the kitchen. Orson stepped away from the door. It hadn't been so bad. He adjusted his sweater vest and brushed some stray crumbs off of his pants. The waiter returned.

"There was a *small* problem. We're out of meatballs. I can have the kitchen prepare something else for you?"

Orson sighed, "Yeah, okay. I'll just have the ravioli then."

The waiter nodded, "Very good. I'll notify the kitchen and your food should be right out."

"Thank you," Orson answered nervously.

He walked back toward the table, fidgeting with the ring box in his pocket. He'd really been looking forward to the meatballs. He loved their meatballs.

"Dorson!"

Orson's heart jumped and his chest tightened.

"Dorson, what the hell are you doing here?" Professor Cullen demanded from behind him.

Orson froze. Professor Cullen had asked him to stay late to finish grading his coursework. Orson had lied, telling him that his grandmother had died and that he was needed at the funeral. It didn't seem that dishonest considering that he had, in fact, worked through her actual funeral last year.

"I guess the funeral ended early."

Orson stumbled with the words. "Y-yes, sir. I mean the funeral was just a short-"

Professor Cullen looked past him to the beautiful woman sitting at his table. He smiled knowingly.

"Dorson? I didn't know you had it in you." He laughed a little too long.

"I know I said I couldn't work tonight, but this is...you see it's our two year anniversary and I was, that is, I'm *going* to ask-"

Professor Cullen laughed again. "You're kidding? What are *you* doing with a woman like that?" He shook his head, then glanced down at his expensive, Italian watch. "You can have another hour. After that, I expect you back at Stevenson."

Orson sank, at once crushed and relieved.

"Yes, sir," he nodded in defeat.

"Professor? Hey, Cully?" Orson recognized the high, nasal voice. He'd tried to teach her basic composition the previous semester. She was currently enrolled in Professor Cullen's advanced History of Russian Literature class. "I thought you were going to take me to The Black Dahlia after this?"

The older professor's eyes grew suddenly wide. He quickly turned to his companion, "Candi, why don't you go back to the table. We'll leave shortly." He turned back to Orson and smiled. "I'm currently tutoring her in the finer points of Russian culture." Somehow, his smile had become an arrogant smirk. He knew Orson wouldn't say a word. "She's very **enthusiastic**." Then, he was cold. "Finish up here, Dorson, then get your pudgy ass back to the university."

Professor Cullen left with his student. Orson walked silently back to his table. He dropped into his seat, and mumbled, "Our food will be right out."

Elizabeth smiled. Orson tried not to look at her. She was so beautiful. Orson ran his fingers across his pocket, feeling the bulge left by the ring box. He knew he'd have to do it soon. He felt sick.

"What was that about?" she asked gently.

Orson shook his head, "Nothing. It was my boss."

"Was that Professor Cullen?"

Orson nodded, "Yes. I uh...I have to go back tonight. There's a lot of work I have to do."

"Can't they get someone else? Why does it always have to be you?"

"Because I'm the new guy. I have to prove-"

"Prove what, James? You've been there for two years. You're not the new guy anymore."

"Three actually, and well, I wasn't really on the faculty..." Orson stared down at the stain. He felt the ring in his pocket. He looked into Elizabeth's eyes.

"I love you," he blurted out.

Elizabeth smiled, "What?"

"I love you," Orson stumbled on, "and well, you know that Doctor Higgins is retiring in the spring, and they're looking for a replacement, and Professor Cullen has a lot of pull with the dean."

"James," Elizabeth smiled curiously, "what are you trying to say?"

Orson reached into his pocket. His hand found the ring box and he pulled it out as he left his seat. Just as he was about to kneel beside the table, his foot caught on his chair. Orson tumbled forward, dropping the ring. He scrambled on the ground looking for the little black box.

Elizabeth gasped in terror, "James, what are you doing?"

Just then Orson found the ring box. He raised himself up on his knee and opened the box. His heart was hammering in his chest. He stared up into his beloved's eyes and lost his voice.

"I...I..." Orson struggled to find the words, "Um...W-will you...marry-"

Elizabeth was shaking her head slowly back and forth. There were tears in her eyes.

"I can't," she mouthed softly, "I just can't."

Orson stared blankly. He struggle to find words.

"Why...not?" he asked meekly.

Elizabeth sniffled, "Why did you have to ask me that?"

Orson didn't know why she was crying. She should have been happy.

He shook his head, "because...I love you."

Elizabeth gasped, "Why couldn't you just wait? Why did you have to ask me tonight?"

She stood up, and half-ran to the door. She could barely walk in those tall heels, but Orson didn't have the strength to chase her. Outside, the rain was pouring down. Thunder boomed. Orson's arms fell limp at his side. He couldn't breathe. Every person in the restaurant was staring at him. He wanted to die. The darkness was choking him. He wanted the lightning to rip him apart. Behind him, their waiter loudly cleared his throat.

"Sir, your food is ready."

Chapter III

Exodus

he rain came down in thick sheets. Lightning split the sky. Thunder shook the darkness. Orson drove slowly. He was nearly blind and the road was slick. In the passenger seat beside him lay two untouched entrees hidden within a garish pair of tinfoil swans. They had cost him half a week's salary. There was a line of stop lights and intersections between the restaurant and the university. Orson hit every red light. He turned on his radio. Heavy Metal fought the thunder.

"God damn it," Orson spat at himself.

His grip tightened on the steering wheel. He wondered why he had ever been stupid enough to think a woman like Elizabeth would want to marry **him.** Her grandfather had been a senator. *Damn it!* It was so clear to him now. Elizabeth, that wonderful, beautiful woman, had just been waiting with him until she found the man she wanted to spend the rest of her life with. He was just keeping her company.

"Stupid!" Orson beat his hand against his thigh.

The street was abandoned, empty of everything but the storm. Overhead the dark clouds flashed with lightning. The music wasn't helping anymore. Orson turned it off. He looked over at the sparkling swans while he waited out the latest red light. He loved Elizabeth. He *loved* her. Orson remembered how her hair looked after a shower, dark and wet. He remembered the way her breasts swayed when she walked. He felt like crying. He thought about never seeing her again. He wanted to die. Orson beat his head against the steering wheel and wished he could slip away. He wished that everything that he was might just disintegrate into nothing. He was alone in the rain. The streets were empty.

Thunder, louder and more fierce than he had ever heard it, shook Orson's car. The dark clouds shimmered with a broken afterglow. Orson's heart clenched in his chest. The hollow wind threw water at the little car from the side. Above, a circle of green light shone softly. Orson drove back to the university. He had work to do.

It was almost nine o'clock by the time Orson made it back to the parking lot. This time he pulled up to the front, and with a self-satisfied smile he parked in the despicable Professor Cullen's reserved space. There was a small, stone walkway leading from the faculty parking lot to Stevenson Hall. It was partially shielded from the rain by a series of strategically planted trees. Unfortunately for Orson, the wind was blowing so hard that the rain was coming at him from the side. He leaned against the wind and fought his way inside the old building. He dripped a line of rain all the way down the stairs.

As Orson reached the bottom of the last flight of stairs and opened the door to the subbasement he remembered what he had never forgotten in his three years at the university. E.T.E.R.M.O.S. practically cackled with electricity. The room flickered with light. Orson stopped, his hand still on the door. The hairs on the back of his neck stood up, prickly and nervous. He stared at E.T.E.R.M.O.S. with reverence and fear. Then Orson remembered what had happened at the restaurant and suddenly he didn't care. Suddenly, he felt quite silly.

Orson let the door close behind him and marched toward his pea green door. He twisted the key in the lock, kicked the door, and entered his office. He threw his coat onto the back of the old easy chair by his door and dropped his briefcase beside his desk. Then he dumped the soggy coffee from the *Coffee Dominator* and replaced the filter. He grabbed the pot and set toward the door. His phone rang. It had to be the asshole. Orson let it ring. He wrenched open his door and filled the coffee pot in the bathroom sink. E.T.E.R.M.O.S. roared. It shook with light and noise. The air was crisp and flat. Orson ignored it. He stomped back to his office and slammed his door. Then he emptied the water into the reservoir and flicked the on switch. The *Coffee Dominator* gurgled with indignation. Orson dropped into his chair. The phone rang again. Orson smiled. *It was all for her anyway.* Everything he had been working for had lost its meaning. He didn't care. It had all been for Elizabeth. Orson's smile was gone. He laughed. Tears slid down his face. He laughed. His heart was break-ing. He laughed. Then, Orson beat his fist against his desk and his laughter broke. Then, he cried. It wasn't a reserved thing. It wasn't quiet. It was pitiful and childish. Orson cried as if for the very first time. He wailed. His face fell into his hands and he writhed in his flesh. A grown man cried, empty and bro-ken.

It was dark in Orson's office. The soft glow of his computer monitor illumi-nated his emotionless face. He typed away, occasionally taking a slow sip from his chintzy "World's Best Boyfriend" mug. He had been working for three hours, but he was nearly finished. He took another sip of cheap coffee. The phone rang again, the first time in hours. Orson answered it mechanically.

"Assistant Professor James Orson, Stevenson Hall. If it's about the pipes we already-"

It was Elizabeth's voice, wet with tears.

"James?" she said with as much composure as she could affect.

Orson was still very much numb. "Elizabeth?" he inquired.

Elizabeth paused to remember what she had spent the night discovering. When she finally spoke her voice was timid.

"I'm sorry, James. I'm sorry. It's just...James, I just don't know anything any-more. When you asked me that...I didn't know what to do."

Orson tried to ignore the fresh wound. He took a sip of coffee as if it would make him seem more nonchalant to the ghosts from dinner.

"That's okay," he answered. His voice shook ever so slightly. "It was too soon. I shouldn't have-"

"James, I'm pregnant!"

The chintzy little mug shattered against the floor.

"What? When! How!" Orson shook with terror and rotten happiness.

"I found out last week. Doctor Humphrey says I'm about two months along. It's why I've been so tired lately. And last week when I was sick in your car."

Orson's breath was shallow and fast. He stared at the cat poster on his wall. *Hang in there.* He couldn't speak.

Elizabeth went on, "I didn't know if I was even keeping it and tonight at dinner it just, it really scared me. I'm not even thirty for Christ's sake. I'm not ready to be a mother. And I didn't know what kind of a father you'd be-"

18

"You're pregnant!"

"James, listen to me! I *will* marry you..."

Orson stood over his desk, "What?"

"Yes. I'll marry you."

"You'll marry me?"

"James, I love you."

"You'll marry me!"

"Yes, James."

"I'm going to be a father?"

"Yes, James." Elizabeth's voice was like a beaming smile.

"You're going to be a mother?"

"Yes, James! Yes!"

"I'm coming over! I'm leaving right now!"

"But what about your work?"

"To hell with my work, I'm going to be a father!" Orson almost laughed.

He was going to be a father. How absurd! How magnificent! Orson dropped the receiver into the cradle. He saved his work, shut down his computer, and switched off the coffeemaker. He snatched his coat from the chair and grabbed the door knob. He turned it hard and pressed forward. It was jammed again. The rain had caused the building to swell. Orson kicked the frame and yanked back on the door. It popped out and Orson practically leapt out of his office. For perhaps the first time in his life James Orson was really, truly happy.

In the dark skies, miles above the suddenly ecstatic assistant professor, a charge had been building in the clouds, like the quiet spark of a dead god being roused from decades of slumber. The storm raged and crackled. All around lightning fell. The earth shook with thunder. The spark grew greater and greater. Then, in a moment of soul searing beauty, the inconceivable power of the storm found a path through the air. It split the sky in a ribbon of light and fury. Lightning ripped through Stevenson Hall's ancient wiring, flashing through miles of cable, and filled E.T.E.R.M.O.S. with blistering light.

James Orson landed just outside of his office with a broad smile across his face and happiness overflowing in his chest. In one moment of glorious eternity the overstressed capacitors filled to the very brim, and E.T.E.R.M.O.S. overloaded. The soon-to-be-father's eyes grew wide. Light and heat poured through

19

every atom in his body. His hands shielded his face. The pain was hellish and complete. His flesh withered in the roaring electrical storm. His death-scream echoed one word, a name.

"Elizabeth!"

Her name left his lips as they were turned to ash. Then an explosion shattered his bones and scattered James Orson like dust.

Outside, the shock wave lightly shook the little Korean economy car, and the two tinfoil swans fell against each other in a silent embrace. The rain fell on a cold and empty world.

Chapter IV

Chaos

Immortality is a desperate illusion. For all the beauty of life, and all the brilliance of fire, nothing can ever burn eternal. Every man will die; every life is finite; every day will end, not in spite of the beginning, but because of it. Know that the universe is mortal and burns toward a slow, quiet cold. Beyond the primal fundament of space, time can have no meaning. In the end, nothing that is matter *can* matter. All that has ever existed, or ever will, has been held within an æternal idea bleeding through insignificant physicality like drops of cheap, red wine on a weathered, white tablecloth. Nothing breeds nothing in a universe held in the bosom of absurd reality.

The transcendental spark cries from darkness, *Then what is one man against Æternity! Against the unimaginable whole! What is the value of nothing weighed against everything!* And the darkness answers *nothing*. Weep for nothing.

James Orson wasn't cold. He wasn't lonely or sad. James Orson was nothing. If such a thing can be imagined to exist, James Orson was nonexistence. Lost in the infinite absurdity of all, he was only that he wasn't. There was no time. There was no space. James Orson was beyond the universe, cradled in an idea. The night sky stretched past the old horizon burning in the bleak darkness of æternity, and a great empty everything waited in the howling silence of deep quiet.

James Orson was dead.

Chapter V

The Birth of James Orson

n the eleventh millennium of the Holy Celestial Calendar of Man, the chaotic dual-galaxy of Avoromedia is divided. Born from a lost age of fear and absolute desolation, it is a dark renaissance for mankind. Corruption and malevolence stir in the distant dark of worlds now forgotten, and the majority of sentient life exists as blind vassals in the service of decrepit kings and cruel emperors. Petty politics lumber through ancient bureaucratic systems while border skirmishes feed upon the old lords of dead stars. Of the thirteen Old Houses of the First Father, only nine remain, united under the banner of Man. The Hundred-Year King, Nero, is a grim skeleton, a dark reflection of mortal fear and twisted hubris. He sits atop a black throne at the heart of the Great Purple Nebula. In his realm, the Kingdom of Man, all serve the will of the mythical Allfather, the protoman, all serve the call of blood. In this dark age, all are slaves.

It is the fifth anniversary of the imprisonment of the traitorous Winter Count, condemned terrorist and madman, hero of the revolutionary cause. To those poor souls who dare to cry for social reform and revolution, there are no more heroes, there are no more gods. For these wretched few, there are only the sad remains of men long broken in the tyrannical machine. Many have died. The future stands at the brink of an abyss. And it is here that fate pulls the Godslayer from the infinite womb of mother Chaos.

It is at this moment that James Orson is born.

*****

Cradled in the vast expanse of night, a lone shadow bathes in the light of an unnamed, red giant star. It is an old ship and the hull groans against the push of the undersized engines. *The Red Diver* is listed in the Corsican Registry as a cargo vessel under license of the Free Captains Trade Union. Pirates and cannibals haunt the Blind, the name given to the uncharted expanse at the edge of the Burlish boarder, and so it is unusual for an older vessel to travel into those unregistered systems. But this day is the stuff of history. *The Diver* has sailed the quiet stars for months, waiting for a single moment in time. Connected to the ship is twenty kilometers of high-strength cable lined with solar collectors. They float like sleeping devils in the roaring light of a distant hell.

In the bloated belly of the hundred-meter-long ship would-be-revolutionaries all hold their breath as salvaged and stolen machines hum with power. A dozen men and women work frantically, checking and double checking wires and tubes. Everything feeds into a central structure at the heart of which is suspended a sort of proto-womb. A white-bearded man directs their actions. He reminds them of the importance of their work. "Death to The Usurper!" he shouts. Red starlight pours through the large, impractical view-ports, imbuing the writhing machinery with a spirit of mysticism. "Death to the slave! Death to the **betrayers!**" His voice bleeds desperate zealotism. "Remember our brothers! Remember our daughters and **sons!**" The zealot's eyes betray deep, ignored pain.

A gentle warning penetrates the hull. It's time. The zealot's eyes roar with release. He laughs.

One-hundred-million kilometers away, a solar flare burns across the surface of the red god. It takes only a moment before the ribbon tears across the darkness. *The Diver's* energy tether glitters in the starlight. Then it is slammed with the unimaginable energy of the screaming star. The alarms howl. The ship twists in the river of power, pulling hard to port.

The White-bearded Zealot shouts "Hold together! Hold together!"

Lightning screams through the void beyond. It writhes and howls across the surface of the hull.

"We're almost there!"

In the writhing chaos a strange emptiness bursts into existence, like a pocket of calm in the heart of a storm. It is within the proto-womb. The howling star pours energy into the growing calm.

"It's working brothers! Our savior comes!"

A second flare rages up from the star's surface. The monitor screams and flashes with light.

"Zevron! There's a second flare!"

"What?!" The zealot's eyes are wild. So much is at stake.

"We have to abort the sequence!"

Rage flashes within the zealot's empty eyes, "NO!"

"It's going to be here in six minutes!"

"Then we have six minutes to live, brother!"

"We'll die!"

"It is a glorious thing to die for freedom, brother! Hold position!"

The old ship twists and groans. It won't last much longer. The proto-womb pulses with calm darkness. Its surface shimmers. The outer layer begins to bulge. It grows with every passing second. Then the darkness bursts, sending out waves of ethereal lightning flittering through the air. Glittering bursts of light expose the skeletal form of a man.

"E~L~I~Z~A~B~E~T~H!"

The man screams through the thin membrane surrounding the proto-womb. The outer flesh of the womb stretches tight across his skeletal face. His voice is hollow and empty. It twists back on itself. It is not a human sound.

A technician stands by the proto-womb. He shouts triumphantly, "We've got him, Zevron!"

The zealot cackles with joy. Five years for this moment! Five years of false leads and botched salvage missions. Five years of failure. The zealot stares down at the womb, and his eyes brim with tears. Then he remembers the second flare.

"Haste! Haste! Detach the tether and get *The Diver* out of here!"

There is a flurry of activity as the crew prepares for the jump. *The Red Diver*'s reaction engines ignite. Metal groans as the ship begins to move. It's slow at first. The speed builds as the engines warm up.

"Hold on, my brothers!"

Five seconds later and the ship's main drive kicks in. The lights blue-shift as a bubble of ultra-thin space forms. A secondary bubble grows within the first, encapsulating The Red Diver and her crew. The ship rockets forward. The reaction engines die, and *The Red Diver* is gone. The energy tether floats, abandoned, in empty space.

Chapter VI

The Man from Earth

rson awoke raw. His mind was aware of nothing but pain. Light and voices filled his senses to bursting. His voice screamed in silence. His every muscle was absolutely fatigued. In sleep he was nothing and longed for nothing. Awake, he longed only for the darkness of sleep. His eyelids did little to filter the heat, white hot and overwhelming. It poured into his brain like water filling a sieve. He fought against the impossible weight of his flesh to shield his eyes from the pain. Thoughts raced through his consciousness. Vague images began to regain lost form. He knew that he was man with a name. He knew an assistant professor. He knew a man named Homer. He knew the names Hamlet and Iago. Then his mind seized on the memory of a beautiful woman. He thought of an unborn child, and he was sad, though he did not know why.

"That's not him."

"I am well aware of that, Master Zevron."

"Then, who in the nine hells did we get!"

"I don't know."

"For Father's sake, where did he **come** from!"

"There is no knowing. Everything was right. The machine was tuned to the Comte's resonance. We had more than enough power."

"Then what went wrong?"

"I don't know."

"Is Noël still in the Château?"

"He must be. Whatever we did...I don't think we got anywhere near him."

The voice of the one called Zevron wavered for a moment. It was hope muddied with fear. "Did the Blood-Fathers detect anything?"

"There was a bastion waiting outside the Eye of Winter, but I don't think they felt anything. Surely, we would have known by now."

There was a long pause before the voices spoke again.

"Is he awake?"

"He should be shortly. Physically he's...well he's alive. I don't know what I expected your little machine to do, but he's nearly fully recovered. Still, we don't have any of the medical supplies he needs on *The Diver*."

That seemed to surprise Zevron. "Already? You're sure he's of Man?"

"I don't know. I think so. He isn't from the fallen tribes, and he doesn't have the rack for a K'ruukta. I suppose he might be from the Burlish Tetrarchy. He's got the nose a Southern Burl."

Zevron sighed, "Let me know as soon as he's awake. We need to talk."

"Have it your way. As far I'm concerned, it's a miracle his heart's beating."

Orson's grip on the words began to slip. The light was finally fading. Only the rough, scraping sensation of the cloth draped across his nude body remained. It was painful to an extreme, like sandpaper being dragged across raw flesh. Light. Heat. Sound. Pain was compounded by pain. Orson could feel himself receding into a black spot in the very back of his head. Then he was gone.

When Orson awoke again, the pain was gone and in its absence he felt nothing. He was empty somehow. His eyes opened to soft, white light. He had been lain by the voices in what looked like a medical room aboard a submarine. The walls were dingy white-metal, and there was little wasted space. The bed was small, but not uncomfortable.

"So, you're awake."

A tall, thin man leaned against the doorway. He had short, dark hair and wore a small, sharp goatee. His voice was happy and lighthearted.

Orson stared for a moment before finding the right words in the storm, "Who are you?"

The thin man laughed, "I was just about to ask you the same." He stepped inside the small room. "I am Chazalle Logramme Leveque the Fourth, and I am your friend. So call me Chaz."

Orson asked the first question ready in his mind. "Where am I?"

The thin man smiled, and Orson noticed a thin parcel in his hand. It looked like a letter.

"Well . . . you are in the hull of a merchant class cargo ship. We are four days off the Port of Hellespont in Corsica, safely back in the lands of Man."

Orson pulled the air into his lungs. It was cold and stuffy, like the air in an old basement or forgotten cellar. Orson wanted to beat his hands against his rebellious skull. His head felt heavy and he was dizzy. He struggled to find more words.

"Corsica?" he asked, finally. "South of Italy? How did I get out here?"

Now it was the thin man's turn to look surprised.

"EE-taly?" he asked with narrow eyes. His voice was dismissive. "I do not know of that land. How is it that you do not know of the Silver Dragon, the great trade city, Corsica?" Then a shrewd smile curved across his thin, pale lips and his eyes grew wider than an ox's. "Ah, you *are* from Urth, aren't you?"

That seemed so strange a question to Orson. He nodded instantly.

"Of course, I'm from Earth. Where are you from? Where are we?"

The thin man laughed loudly. Then catching himself, he looked around to see if anyone had heard him. He got very quiet and whispered, "I know. You are from Urth. They have told us nothing, especially me. Do you know how the rebels fair within the Shroud? I am new to the cause, but my heart is stout." His face became very heroic. "I am from Angers. I have seen firsthand the cruelty of the Usurper. My father is an old fool. He thinks his position will save him. He does not see that Nero's lust for power has already overgrown his sense of self-preservation. He cares not for the realm, only for himself. Perhaps, one day the Usurper's hunger will turn on the Nobility itself, fed all fat on the slaughter of his lies, and the so called Nobles shall devour their own legs from under the body politic. The Black Brothers will not save him then," He scowled adding, "Even a 'Noble' magistrate will have cause to worry on that dark day"

Orson wrapped the cloth around his waist and sat up on the small table. He looked down, at the feet of the thin man, and answered honestly.

"I don't know anything about any usurper."

The thin man nodded quickly. He had played this dodging game with the revolutionaries before and considered himself no child to the ways of espionage.

"You are right. Now is not the time." His eyes narrowed and he glanced back to the door. "Though we are now aboard the truest vessel in the fleet, the Bastard King's reach must not be underestimated. We must be cautious if we are to survive."

Orson, knowing nothing outside of himself, nodded. "Yes," he repeated, "We must be cautious."

The thin man smiled. "The old medic put your clothes in the corner. We can speak later. Have faith my brother!"

Then he left. Orson sat for a moment at the edge of the table, gathering his thoughts. He ran his hands over the top of his bald head. He had so many questions. The thin man had said they were on a ship, and seemed surprised to learn that Orson was from Earth. *Why should that be surprising?* He wondered. Orson hopped down from the table, and felt his legs buckle. He could barely stand. His joints hurt and the muscles in his legs burned. He limped across the room and found the clothes left for him in the corner. It was a pair of trousers, a shirt, a vest, and a pair of leather boots. His limbs were heavy and sore. Orson dressed himself with slow deliberate movements. All the while, a word was screaming, broken in his mind. He was disconnected. His brain was noisy. He didn't feel alive. He was a puppet of flesh and bone.

As his numb fingers twisted the laces on his borrowed boots, Orson drifted through the current of his mind. Deep in the darkness he found an old memory. He was a child tying his shoes in the rain. *It was raining* **that** *night too*. Orson was afraid of the rain. He was afraid because the rain always stirred the monster sleeping in the subbasement. The monster that would kill him one day. The monster that *had* killed

James Orson! The lost assistant professor remembered everything. He closed his eyes. His heart was racing and breaking in the same overwhelming moment. Life was screaming through his bones. He was so in love and so alone. He was going to be a father. Orson smiled in defiance of the tears streaming down his face. He was going to be a father. Where was he? Where was Elizabeth? He couldn't breathe. Orson's lungs wouldn't hold air. They caught in his chest. He was gasping, dizzy. Then he fell forward, off the low bed, and crashed down to the floor. His heart was cold, and it was ripping in half at the very core of his being. He felt so hollow. He writhed. He whimpered. He tried to ignore the emptiness swallowing his soul. It was as if everything he had gained in the knowledge of himself was collapsing inward. The singularity of his existence was overwhelming. He held his head and wept. Lost.

He cried until he had no more sadness left with which to fill his empty soul.

When it was over Orson wiped his eyes and stared into the corner. He was stone now. A hollow thing, without the fire of life. He asked the one question that mattered.

Orson closed his red, swollen eyes and mumbled, "Where am I?"

The words gave his wasted body strength, and Orson pushed himself up off the floor. He felt so cold. His face was tender, and he touched it gently with his fingers. His patchy beard was gone. He had a beard once. Orson remembered that he had hair once too. His hands roamed over his head. It was gone now. All of it, even his eyebrows. The thought occurred to him that he had been shaved. Though he did not know why.

Orson leaned against the wall, and tried to make sense of what little of himself he had left. He thought perhaps he had been kidnapped. He'd read stories about old sailors disappearing in Oregon. They were sold as slaves in Shanghai. But, those were only stories. Orson rubbed his tired face. He had to get back. He pulled himself up. He had to escape.

Orson limped to the door. To his surprise, it was unlocked and the hatch opened with a gentle pull. Outside, a group of unfamiliar voices trailed off down one end of the corridor. Orson cautiously stepped out of the little medical room. The corridor in which he found himself was narrower than he'd imagined, though not cramped. He had never been on a boat before and had no idea how to find his way to the surface. Orson's mind reeled at the thought. What if they were still at sea? Orson contemplated being lost in alien waters. He would need to find a lifeboat if he was going to escape. But what if he was miles from the shore, in the open ocean? Orson beat his palm against his head and cursed the static growling in his hears. He couldn't focus. He beat his head again and suddenly noticed that the ship was not rocking or moving with the waves of the ocean. *The ship must still be docked.* Orson thought. *There's time.* He chose a direction at random and followed the corridor.

The boat was larger than Orson had expected. Every twenty or so feet the thin corridor was interrupted by an air-tight hatch, like something on a Cold War submarine. After five of these, Orson could see a set of stairs leading up to the next level. They had to lead to the surface. At the top of the stairs, there was another corridor. Orson followed it to the end where another set of stairs took him up to a closed hatch. He had followed the open corridor as far as it led.

Here, Orson hesitated. Until this moment all the doors had been open to him. This door alone was closed. He knew that on the other side there could be anything. It could be the surface and escape, or it might be the door to the kitchen. The static finally cleared in his head and in that sudden calm it occurred to Orson that he could not hear the waves crashing against the hull. The boat was suddenly silent and, more disturbing, absolutely still. He felt no movement. They couldn't be in water. Orson was seized by the sudden, urgent need to open the hatch.

He wrenched open the stiff lock and pushed the door. As the heavy, balanced metal swung forward, Orson's world was shattered. In the room beyond, a small crew of six men sat at recessed consoles before control panels blinking with neon light. A white-bearded man stood on a small, elevated platform between them. He leaned on the railing, staring longingly out of a large viewport. The window, which encompassed the majority of the far wall, looked out over an infinite expanse of stars. Galaxies danced in distant corners, stars burned in the darkness, and in the center of it all a great nebula stretched across a vast twinkling nightscape.

Zevron had been giving orders to his crew. "We're getting close to the border of Man," he stated before sighing. "Caught between Scylla and the Whirlpool. That bastion hasn't moved in weeks." He clicked his tongue, "How far are we from Antibes?"

The nearest crewman answered quickly, "If the stellar winds remain at our backs, we can make Antibes in twelve more days."

Zevron nodded, scratching his beard, "We'll need to resupply before that. Where is the nearest port?"

After a short pause the crewman answered, "The nearest independent port is south of Large, in the Duchy of Rorialus."

Zevron shook his head, "The last thing we need is some bored Psugian playing hedge knight, demanding to see our manifest. Where else?"

The other crewman answered, "There's a small smuggler's port near the Horn. If we use full burn we can gain the port in a day."

Zevron shrugged, "Make it happen."

The crewmen nodded, "Yes, Captain."

At the word "Captain", Zevron laughed. It was a lighthearted, heavy laugh at the absurdity of being shown such blind respect. His eyes were a cool, cloudy blue, like the sky after a storm. His hair was long and draped carelessly across his face. He brushed it back when he turned to leave. When his eyes met Orson's, he smiled.

"I thought thou was dead."

Orson didn't answer. He was still staring at the black sky outside the viewport.

Zevron shook his head, "Can thou speak or are thou Burlish?"

Orson had never been skilled in the art of conversation, and here he was at the edge of forever, his mouth dumb and his mind simply overwhelmed. He stood in the very essence of bad science fiction. He said the only words left to his tongue, "Where am I?"

Zevron laughed again. "Oh, man," he smiled, "Are thou alright?"

Orson answered stiffly, "Where am I? How did I get here?"

Zevron shook his head, "Thine accent is killing me, man. Thou sounds worse than that kid, Chaz. Where are thou from?"

Orson shook his head. "I don't have an accent! Am I in space?"

"Well, yeah," Zevron smiled deeply and warmly. Then his broad eyes narrowed as he recognized the confusion in Orson's face, "Oh, man. Do I have a story for thee..."

Orson was sitting on a small cot in a corner of the cargo hold. A large stack of various boxed freight made a near perfect enclosure, giving him some small measure of privacy. Zevron had given Orson a very brief tour of the ship, before showing him to his "quarters".

"It was a total blow-out," he had explained with a relaxed sigh, "Thou aren't the guy we were after, thou knowst. Hells, thou aren't even supposed to be here at all. We're not really sure what happened, but thou're supposed to be dead, I think. It's just crazy."

"I don't understand. What does that mean?" Orson asked, numbly.

"Right...uh, thou was brought here through a kind of ultra-dimensional packet machine. We grabbed thine body with...a sort of musical tone matrix or something. But, what we did to bring thee here, it never quite finished, I guess. Harmonics or something. Thou see, we nearly ran into some bad people...thou were, uh..." Zevron had scratched at his beard, "dead, man. Just...well not alive. Anyway, I don't know where thou're from, but thou probably really wants to get back there, and thou probably wants us to use the machine to put thee

31

back. Thing is, we couldn't send thee home that way if we wanted to. The uh **machine** it **pulls** things through the universe, well...not really but thou gets the idea. It's a one way trip, man. We'll have to take thee home the long way, if we can even find it, that is."

"I'm from Earth. It's in the Sol system. It's got nine planets orbiting it. You're humans! You evolved on Earth...how do you not know where it is?"

Zevron merely shook his head and laughed, "Urth? No kidding? Well, that's progress I guess." He had been carrying a book with him. It was bound in aged, white leather. He gave it to Orson. "Here. This is one of the oldest books in the galaxy, and it's my favorite. This is a first edition from the Bertrum Library," he offered, smiling once more before turning away, "Consider it a small token of apology."

Then Zevron left. Orson wondered what the apparent captain had meant. He couldn't shake the feeling that no one really knew what or where "Earth" was. Lying back on his cot, Orson brought the book closer. It looked very old. The leather was well worn and smelled of pipe tobacco. He opened the cover and a strange smile curled his lips. Orson was holding a copy of the *Odyssey*. An oddly appropriate gift for a lost man. Orson delicately thumbed through the old pages, looking for his favorite scenes, but this *Odyssey* was different than he remembered. It read like a bad translation. It followed the story, but the prose was all wrong. Orson continued to carefully thumb through the book. Scene after scene followed the same pattern. It wasn't Homer. It was very reminiscent of the *Odyssey* Orson remembered, but it wasn't Homer. Finally, Orson turned back to the first page.

The Red Diver sailed through dark, star-filled space. In the distance, the great purple nebula glowed bright with the light of the young giant star, Meagres Prime. The binary white dwarfs, Tyran and Nobul, danced at the edge. Orson lay in his little cot, quietly judging every missed comma and typo in the imposter *Odyssey*, while the crew was busy going about their usual duties. In the captain's quarters, Zevron sat at his desk, writing a letter of introduction, addressed to an old friend, a rebel sympathizer from Urth named Gin Crawley.

Gin was a wiry old man with a false leg. He was trustworthy and honorable. He'd done work for the cause before and, in the right circumstances, he could perform genuine magic. It seemed to the formerly Noble outcast that such a man just might do to get their mistake home.

Zevron dropped his pen across the parchment, and his seemingly carefree smile vanished. His thoughts had brushed the darker depths of his own insecurity and he wondered how he could have failed again. *Are thou dead, old friend?* He thought, letting his weight fall back in his chair. Zevron pulled a rough hand across his face, and he thought of the mistakes of his past. He had always blamed himself for the tragedy at the Winter Gate.

After the death of his son and only heir, Zevron had lost himself in wine and debauchery. He had left his house doubly disgraced, abandoning his wife and brothers, and had been living like an animal at the smugglers' asteroid when the disgraced Comte d'Noël had found him, drunk in the gutter, and brought him back to himself. It had been a member of Zevron's secret rebellion who had betrayed the Winter Count, a man whom he had personally recommended. The price of that rotten fellow's loyalty had been a handful of tarnished silver from a spiteful lover. Zevron often lay awake at night, imaging the nightmarish horrors visited upon his friend in the notorious Château d'Soliel Rouge. They called the watchmen there the Dead Guard, heartless things in hydraulic armor with empty faces concealed behind crooked masks. The commandant there was said to be a monster himself, a veteran of the old psychic war. *Every monster was once a man.* Zevron felt a terrible sliver of pain from the thought of his lost son. *He had such an innocent smile before they took him.* Zevron swore another oath of revenge, and returned bitterly to his letter.

In the dead of the night, the ship was quiet. Down in the cargo bay, by the engines, Orson lay awake. He missed Elizabeth. He longed to feel the weight of her lying on his chest, and smell her hair. The heavy pulse of the engines carried the weight of condensing space, and the deep pressure was like an invisible heartbeat. Orson closed his eyes and lost himself in the breath of the universe. Eventually, the man from Earth slept.

"Is not so good to sleep so late as this, my friend."

Orson was sprawled across his cot; his leg dangling over the side, his *Odyssey* open across his chest. He raised an arm to shield his eyes from the light. He recognized the voice.

Orson sat up, answering, "You're the man from the hospital, aren't you?"

The thin man bowed with a flourish and smiled, "Chazalle Logramme

Leveque the Fourth, at your service, dear friend. Or so I would wish... For now, I fear, *I* must ask for *your* service."

"What do you need?" Orson asked. His brow lowered incredulously.

The thin man shook his head with a lighthearted smile, "Nothing of great labor. I have learned that my father is ill. We disagree on the matter of his estate, and I must be present at his passing. I will be disembarking this fine vessel shortly, however I have been entrusted with a letter which must be made delivered."

"What sort of letter?" Orson asked.

The thin man smiled, "It is nothing scandalous." At that he held up a thin piece of folded parchment to the light, showing that it was indeed a simple letter. "You see, my friend, an old shipmate ask me to deliver this letter to his father in Antibes. I promise him 'on my father's grave'...Imagine the irony."

"What do you want me to do, exactly?"

"Soon this ship will make port in Antibes. I know that you are still...confused, but I am sure you will find your way off the docks to King's Row. The man you are looking for to deliver the letter is Jacques Roliequire. He lives at twenty-one south on The Spiced Road. It is just off the King's Row. Do this for me because I am your friend, and because we are brothers. And, *our* brothers are many. Help me, and I promise you we will get you back to Urth."

Orson eyed the letter suspiciously, "It's just a letter then?"

The thin man smiled, "Just a letter, my brother."

"Why can't you send it in the post? There must be some sort of mail service here."

The thin man shook his head and pulled the letter against his chest in an exaggerated gesture, "This letter is far too important to my poor friend. It is besides, the starsea is these days far too dangerous for little courier ships such as carries letters. What if it should be lost? I could not bear it."

Orson stared at the letter for a moment before moving his gaze to the thin man's eyes. They were small things, like the eyes of a gambler or of a smooth-talking raccoon. Orson, of course, couldn't see anything. Finally, he let his eyes drop.

"Alright. I'll deliver your letter."

The thin man smiled broadly and wrapped Orson in an exuberant hug. It was something ridiculous and exaggerated, the sort of thing lovers do in old movies. The thin man squeezed Orson briefly, then, with a kiss on the cheek, he released him, stuffing the letter into his hand.

Then the thin man said through his smile, "You are saving my life. Truly. Aw!" he sighed, "I hate that I must leave this ship. She has been a good mother." In an act of expert drama, he put his hands into his pockets. Then, feeling his purse, he smiled with kindness, "I am sorry I must leave, brother, but take this for the trouble." He tossed the little leather pouch onto the cot beside Orson. "You may need it when you get to Antibes. These starseas are treacherous."

Then, the thin man left. Orson didn't believe he could help him get home, but his request had been small and seemed genuine. Orson's eyes were drawn to the purse left behind. He wasn't a greedy man, but he was a scholar and as such was prone to curiosity. Orson reached for the pouch and held its weight in his hand. He gave it soft toss to better judge its contents. It jingled. Orson tucked the entrusted letter into his inner vest pocket to free his other hand. Then, he opened the smooth, little bag and felt inside. It was cold. *Coins?* Orson had expected space travelers to use some form of futuristic, digital currency, like money cards or credit chips. He pulled one of the heavy discs from the pouch and examined it closer. It seemed to be made of silver and had been pressed with the image of a man on a throne seated before an exploding star. The man's face was grim and cruel, his crown sharp on his skull-like head. Orson opened the bag wide and stared inside. There had to be more than a dozen coins in the little purse. He played his fingertips about the metal for a moment, enjoying the feel and weight of it. He'd never seen a real silver coin before, not like these. They had been hand-pressed, and each coin had small, unique imperfections that proved its authenticity. Orson dropped the coin back into the purse and hid it against the wall in his little corner of the cargo hold, more out of habit than distrust.

Satisfied that his treasure was well hidden, Orson tried to return to the *Odyssey*. But the cargo bay was empty, and without the constant noise of human activity his mind kept drifting back to his last night on Earth, the night he died. Orson used to treasure solitude, but, now, it was almost unbearable. It was in the quiet stillness that he remembered the details of his life most clearly. He didn't want to think about it. He didn't want to acknowledge the fear of being lost. It was something terrible, something wrapped around his whole existence, waiting to crush him in its darkness. Orson pushed it away. He read the same passage over and over. The words were less than echoes. He wanted to be home. He wanted to read the real Homer; he wanted burned meatballs; he wanted bad essays; he wanted bitter coffee and stale toast; but, more than anything, Orson wanted to lay his head on Elizabeth's chest and be home, warm in his bed. He missed those fleeting weekend mornings when he would wake up to her wrapped around him. He was going to be a father. *Would have been*. Orson set the book on the cot and stood. He felt the pressure all around him. He shouldn't have to be alone. He wanted out. He wanted to be home. He needed to speak to the captain.

Orson started walking without thinking. He was headed up to the command room with the great star-filled window. He didn't know what he would say. He didn't know what he needed to say. He knew only that he needed to say *something*.

Orson stood outside the door for a long time. He felt sick with embarrassment. He just wanted to be home, but he was frozen. He couldn't act. Then, with an act of uncharacteristic bravery, Orson's hand suddenly gripped the cold metal of the airlock. His heart surged at the audacity of it, but he still couldn't bring himself to intrude. He invented empty excuses, all of them very convincing. *It's a command room after all*. He told himself. *They would probably be angry*. Slowly, his courage evaporated, until he gave up and walked back down the stairs. Orson felt so empty, yet, he couldn't return to the emptier stillness of his cot. So, he slouched against the wall and waited.

The growl of his stomach told Orson that he had been waiting too long. He wished he would have brought the faux Odyssey. At least then he could pretend to read it. That would have been something. Orson let his head fall and ran his fingers over his scalp. He felt insignificant.

"Waiting for someone?" Zevron asked with his usual kindhearted smile.

His voice distracted Orson just long enough for him to escape his self-pity. He answered in a practiced voice he thought sounded aloof. "Yes, *you* actually."

"Me?" Zevron laughed, "What for?"

"I was just hoping you might tell me where we're going."

Zevron nodded his head. This caused several strands of gray hair to fall across his weathered face. He pushed them back

"Come with me," he answered.

He led Orson back up the stairs and into the control room. The small crew was busy going through their docking checklist. Zevron stopped at his place in the center of the room, leaning on the railing. *The Red Diver* was approaching a large asteroid. All around them great hunks of ice, hundreds of kilometers tall, floated like dreaming monsters. Lights poured from various points on the asteroid, scattering in the icy prisms around it. The entire area was bursting with beauty. Zevron pointed to the glowing nebula in the distance.

"That's where we're headed. We'll make it in about two weeks if we're lucky."

"What is it?" Orson asked dumbly.

Zevron turned back to Orson and leaned against the railing. He crossed his arms and sighed. "The less thou knows about what we're doing here, the safer it is for thee. There are some really bad guys out there who would kill thee just for being here with us. Now, I know thou didn't mean to wind up on this ship, and I would love to get thee home, but the work we're doing here is far too important. We've got to try again. No mistakes this time. When we make port at Antibes, I'll see that thou're transferred to another ship that has the time to get thee back to whatever lost star thou comes from."

Orson didn't know what to say. He just shook his head and said the first thing that came to his lips, "I want to go home."

Zevron put his hand on Orson's shoulder. He sighed and his deep eyes showed the honesty in his voice.

"We'll get thee home. I promise."

Chapter VII

Scylla

or the next several days, Orson rarely left his little corner in the cargo hold. He wrestled with fear and loneliness, but the thought of home was always on his mind. With the supplies gained at the smugglers' port they wouldn't need to stop again until they reached Antibes. Orson read the *Odyssey* cover to cover. He found an odd solace in that familiar journey. The clever Odysseus always survived, just as Orson hoped he would survive. In his heart, Orson wished for cyclopes and sirens, anything but the claustrophobic walls of space travel. The stars seemed so empty from Orson's prison in the cargo hold.

On the fifth day of the journey to Antibes, Orson was torn from the first real sleep he'd managed since arriving on the strange ship by frantic screams echoing through the hold. Orson sat up with a start. He could feel the engines groaning through the metal. His hair began to stand on end. Then the alarms started. Everywhere red light flashed and sirens screeched from the walls. Zevron's voice came over the communication system, broken and distorted.

"BRO~ERS, THEY'VE FouND US. DEST~OY it ALL! TheY ~ST NOT KNOW What WE haVE DOnE HERE! ALL IS noT LOST. WHERE ~VE failed THE OTHERS WILL BE VICTORIOUS. I ~ SO SORRY."

Then the speaker went silent, and the alarms cut out. Only the orange-red glow of emergency lighting remained. The engines stopped struggling, and the ship was dead in space. The screams continued more frantically. They were like the shrieks of drowning rats. The floor shook violently under Orson's feet. For a moment the screams were silent, and that silence was more terrible by far. Bewilderment and horror spread wide through their mute voices. They all knew death was coming, but they dared not think of it. Then the entire ship was thrown by such a powerful force that every free body was thrown to the ground. Orson's little corner was toppled, and the freight came crashing down around him. By sheer luck, two large containers fell together, forming a brace that held the rest up, and Orson escaped being crushed. Everything was chaos.

Orson crawled along the cramped floor, holding his *Odyssey* tightly in his hand.

A woman screamed somewhere, "They're going to take us! It's a Blood Inquisition!" A man shouted for her to shut her mouth, but she kept crying out, "They're going to peel the flesh from our skulls! They said we were safe!"

Then the voice was silent. All around, Orson could hear the crew pushing and shoving, fighting their way to the life boats. They couldn't know that there was no escape.

Finally, Orson found his way out. The hold was nearly empty. Everyone had abandoned their duties and fled, save one. A lean, bespectacled man dressed in an old, tattered lab coat worked frantically at the machine which had brought Orson to this strange place. Orson couldn't guess what he was doing. He only knew that he had to get away. He should have left with Chazelle at the smuggler's port. He had money, and he could-*the silver!* Orson turned back to the mess behind him. It was lost. He *had* money.

A heavy, metallic voice surged through the com system. "*ZEVRON, HEIR OF HOUSE BERTRUM, YOU HAVE BEEN FOUND IN VIOLATION OF THE DIVINE PROVIDENCE OF MAN. YOU HAVE DENIED YOUR BLOOD TAX. YOU HAVE SULLIED YOUR NOBLE HANDS WITH LABOR, AND YOU HAVE SIRED AN IMPURITY. YOUR LIFE, YOUR NAME, AND YOUR HERETIC SHIP ARE FORFEIT.*"

Zevron's voice shouted back in the distance, "Plow you, you rotting plowing corpses!"

The inhuman voice laughed. It was hollow and it was terrifying. "*BERTRUM TOR BERTRUM NAL, YOU **WILL** BE PURIFIED.*"

Orson's heart was racing. Fear assaulted his mind, and his hands froze. He couldn't focus. His fingers were numb and he was so lightheaded that he couldn't stand straight. He felt his body fall back on the toppled freight behind him.

"They're just trying to scare you!" The man working at the machine had finished. He was hurrying over. "We've got to get out of here. We've got three minutes until the hold opens and this whole mess is dumped into the void."

Orson was terrified. His legs felt like wobbly stilts.

"The lifeboats are stalled. They always get the lifeboats first. Those self-righteous cannibals will be nearly done with the others by now. When they're finished with the old man they'll do one last sweep of the ship before ejecting the core. They're only after Zevron. They'll leave after that. If we can hide until then, I can rig a lifeboat and with a little luck we'll drift back into the shipping lanes." Then he noticed Orson's pale face. "Hells," he sighed gruffly. "It's their voices. They make you sick. Look, I can help you, but you **need** to stand up. I need you to move. We don't have time."

Orson just nodded blankly. His skin tingled and he had to force himself to stand.

"Now, move your feet!" The last crewman pulled Orson to his feet, "There's a reason why Zevron bought this Vinici wreck. There's a series of smuggling compartments in the forward mess. If we hurry we can make it. Now, let's go!"

Orson nodded again. Then he was stumbling after the other man. The stairs leaving the hold felt to Orson's fear-weakened legs like the last few steps to the top of a mountain. He stumbled through the bulkhead, almost falling. The last crewman closed the door behind them and twisted the airlock tight. Stumbling down the corridor, Orson heard the roar of air rushing out of the cargo hold as the loading door opened. Then the floor shuddered lightly. A small explosive had detonated behind the machine. There was a loud lurch of metal and then one last, loud clunk as the machine was flung out into space.

Orson fell against the wall. He couldn't stand anymore.

The last crewman grabbed his arm, "We've got to move. They'll be down here soon. Come on. Get up!"

Heavy, grating footsteps lumbered down the stairs at the end of the corridor. A massive metal boot came down first, followed by the unbelievably broad body of an armored giant.

The last crewman pulled Orson through the nearest door, and roughly twisted the airlock. His breathing was ragged and he was noticeably shaken. His fear had reason. Everyone knew the stories. The Blood-Fathers of the Blackfallow order were renowned for their macabre savagery.

The last crewman spoke quickly and in a near-whisper, "I don't think it saw us."

The Blood-Father's lumbering footsteps came closer and closer. The floor shook with every step. Then, they stopped. Orson could hear metal scrape against metal. His chest was tight. His heart was beating faster and faster. The man beside him motioned for Orson to be silent as he loosed a long knife from his boot. Then there was the loud groan of twisting metal, and the door was ripped away. The metal giant covered the entire opening. The monster wore an intricate open-faced helm. He bent low to enter and Orson saw his face. It was the face of old man stretched far too tight across a misshapen skull. Tubes and twisting wires perforated his exposed flesh, and his eyes were murky gray. Those empty eyes stared into the room and Orson's blood froze in his veins. The giant's gauntlets were covered in dried blood. The talon-like tips were wet.

Suddenly, as the giant stepped through the door, the last crewman leapt at him with a roar.

"You won't have **me** you bloody ghoul!"

He had his knife in his hand, and he knew his enemy. He plunged the blade deep into the exposed flesh at the giant's neck, twisting it about in the wires and tubes. The monster made no sound. He simply grabbed the last crewman's body in his hands and tore him in half. Blood covered the floor and walls. Gore dripped to the ground. Orson couldn't move. He was more frightened than he had ever been in his life. The giant looked down at him.

"COME WITH ME. NO RESISTANCE."

Orson stared blankly. His mind could not comprehend what he was experiencing. He had never before seen a man die. The last crewman's blood covered Orson face and his clothes. His head nodded mechanically. Then he spoke.

"P-please, don't kill me." There were tears in his eyes, and he felt like a child standing before a rabid animal, "Please. I'll do whatever you want."

The giant's face was empty and emotionless.

"THOSE WHO OBEY THE FATHER'S WILL SHALL SERVE. HERETICS SHALL BE PUNISHED. THE TAINT SHALL NOT BE TOLERATED."

Orson shook his head. His voice was desperate, "I'm not a heretic. I don't even belong here. I just want to go home. Earth. I'm from Earth! I just want to go home..."

The giant stared at him with those milky eyes. They were the raven eyes of a corpse too long in the sun.

"YOU ARE FROM URTH?"

Orson nodded, "Yes, I'm from Earth."

The giant's brow furrowed.

"YOU ARE INNOCENT?"

Orson nodded, again, "Yes. I don't know anyone. I don't belong here."

"WINTER SON, YOU SHALL FOLLOW. IF YOU RUN I WILL KILL YOU."

The giant led Orson up the stairs. As they moved through the ship, Orson saw more of the cybernetic giants. They were accompanied by black robed men of normal, more human, stature. When they turned his way Orson gasped at the sight of the lumpy flesh hidden under the monkish hoods. Most were deformed in various, grotesque fashions, all had the same empty gaze as the monster leading him. The hooded men had prisoners of their own, crewmen Orson had come to recognize. Zevron's people had been good to him. Orson felt sick. His heart raced. He didn't want to die.

The surviving crew were led through a large hole that had been gouged through the side of the ship. The Blood-Father's had hauled the ship close to their own and simply cut their way in. It was crude but effective. In the great, cavernous room beyond, all of the prisoners were led past a central figure, a Blood-Father more imposing than all the others. He wore an elaborate set of golden armor. The chest was inlaid with a set of winged children, his left shoulder was covered by a large, pointed pauldron, and his great winged helm covered his gray eyes. This commander spoke to each of the black-robed men in turn, casting his doom upon the prisoners.

Orson was led before this one.

"KNEEL."

Orson dropped to his knees.

The bloody giant raised his massive gauntlet to his chest, "IN THE FATHER'S NAME."

The golden giant nodded. "IN THE FATHER'S NAME" Then he passed his empty gaze down to Orson. "THIS ONE IS NOT OF THE HERETICS?"

Orson's giant answered, "HE CLAIMS TO BE FROM URTH."

"URTH?"

"YES. HE CLAIMS TO BE INNOCENT OF THE CORRUPTION."

"DO YOU BELIEVE HIM, BROTHER JACQUEIRE?"

"I BELIEVE THE BLOOD, LOW FATHER."

The golden giant smiled. It looked grotesque pulled across the monster's dead jaw, "YOU ARE, AS ALWAYS, WISE, BROTHER JACQUEIRE." Then he nodded, "HE WILL SEE THE LORD HIGH MASTER, AND THEN WE WILL KNOW IF THIS *MAN* IS OF URTH."

The giant led Orson deep into the heart of the alien ship and left him in the darkness of an empty cell.

Chapter VIII

The Trial

s Jon Baptis Logramme Leveque sat at the little desk in the corner of his suite, he was filled with desire. His mind poured forth the light, airy castles of future lives. He desired money, and he desired power, and he needed name and title, but, most of all, he desired to leave his current post. He needed to get away from the rotting, old ship. It was the size of a city and over a thousand years old. Everything was falling apart. He needed to get out. *Soon.*

M. Leveque smiled into the mirror hanging on the wall behind the desk. His meeting last month with Baroness d'Trille of the House of Man had ended in a satisfactory agreement. In a year they would likely wed, and he would gain shared control of her father's holdings in the Rede. She had a decent face. It was even quite pleasing in some light, and he enjoyed the way it had flushed red when he had described to her the case he had overseen concerning the capture of the heretic Stensan Gromwelle. It was so...exciting. She had gasped quite beautifully at his excellent, even poetic, description of the man's pleas for leniency that had followed his sorrowful cries of innocence. He had been lying, obviously. It was always the eyes that gave them away. The innocent man was merely afraid and confused, the guilty man was always terrified. Leveque smiled at himself again. He could always tell. He was never wrong. Then his smile faded. He thought of the Blood-Fathers. Their large, ruined forms always left him unnerved. There was nothing in *their* eyes. Monsieur Leveque furrowed his brow. He had spent almost a year in the position of chief inquisitor for the Blackfallow order, yet, even now, he felt an uneasy chill in his spine at the thought of those monstrous, twisted men. Their devotion to the Father was...inspiring, even if it was a bit morbid. Chief Inquisitor Leveque now thought of all the heretics he had sent to be purified. In the end, they had all confessed their sins. In the end, they had all died slowly.

At the door to the arbitory, Chief Inquisitor Leveque met with Low Inquisitor Tiberius. It was the very same golden-armored giant that had overseen Orson's capture. In the safety of the great bastion ship *Fraternity* the low inquisitor did not wear his glorious helm. His pale head was marked by disease and necrosis. A half dozen greasy strands of wispy, gray hair hung in empty patches from his scalp. Strips of shaped metal held his fractured skull in one piece and knots of wires and tubing crossed deep into his neck, connecting it to the too-broad body beneath. M. Leveque discretely pulled his scented handkerchief to his nose as he approached. In all his time at his post he had never quite gotten used to the rotting stench of the behemoths. He struggled to hold his composure, but spoke with practiced precision.

"I have read His Lordship's letter. You are to be commended, Low Inquisitor Tiberius. This man in your custody is obviously of interest to the heretics. What have you learned from his conspirators?"

The great Tiberius acknowledged the chief inquisitor with a slight bow.

"MY LORD HIGH MASTER, CHIEF INQUISITOR. WE HAVE LEARNED VERY LITTLE. THE PRISONER PROCLAIMS INNOCENCE. THE HERETIC CREW TELLS US NOTHING. IT SEEMS THAT THEY TRULY DO NOT KNOW THIS MAN."

"Can their testament be trusted? Have they been *purified* yet?" He meant, 'have you ripped out their tongues.'

"THEY HAVE. OUR DATAHEADS HAVE EXPLORED THEIR GREY. FIVE WERE FIT FOR THE CORE. THEY DID NOT LIE."

The core? M. Leveque shuddered imperceptibly at the thought. *A bundle of severed heads connected to an ancient, organic computer.* M. Leveque sighed. He had grown tired of the savagery of the Blackfallows. There were other ways to obtain answers. Dead men can't talk. *And apparently dead men can't listen either.*

"What do you know about the prisoner?" he asked, masking his frustration behind an empty scowl.

"HIS NAME IS JAMES ORSON. HE IS 29 YEARS OLD. HE CLAIMS TO BE FROM THE LOST PLANET, URTH. YET, HE ALSO CLAIMS TO HAVE NO KNOWLEDGE OF ARRIVING ON THE HERETIC

VESSEL OR OF PASSING THROUGH THE DESTROYED GATE. HE CLAIMS ABSOLUTE INNOCENCE."

"Don't they always, *Low* Inquisitor? Blood will tell..." Chief Inquisitor Leveque added with a self-satisfied smirk as he entered the chamber.

It was a medium sized room. Unlike the rest of the ship, the walls here were lined with old, polished wood. The chief inquisitor's bench was elevated above the rest of the room, and a small fireplace glowed with the flickering light of magnetically suspended plasma. Monsieur Leveque took his seat at his bench, and, after first arranging his robes, examined the packet of collected evidence. There were only two items: a wrinkled, blood-stained letter and a worn copy of *The Odyssey. Curious.* The chief inquisitor mused to himself as he opened the book and slowly turned through the pages. He had never understood the heretics' love of the old books. They were so boring. Finally, he signaled for the prisoner to be brought in.

James Orson was restrained with thick, heavy chains. He was escorted by a pair of the mysterious, black-robed men. These two had the empty, gray eyes of the others and their misshapen flesh was pasty and pale. They secured his chains to the floor, and left. Orson looked dreadful. His face had become shallow and was wet with sweat. His body was bruised and dirty. He was slouched and his beard had started to show. It had been a week since he had been brought aboard *Fraternity*.

The chief inquisitor looked into his panicked eyes, and he knew instantly that the pitiful, little man was indeed innocent.

"James Orson," Chief Inquisitor Leveque began in his most respectably empty voice. He raised the packet dramatically. "We have absolute evidence that you are a heretic and a member of a conspiracy against the Crown, the Realm, and the Father. If you confess now you will be spared the torture of purification. Tell us of your contact with the treasonous Bertrum tor Bertrum nal, otherwise known as the heretic *Zevron d'Bertrum.* Leave out nothing. We are already aware of the full extent of your treachery."

Orson was filled with fear. He shook his head in wonder, and his voice was a whimper.

"I don't know anything. I didn't do anything. I don't know how I got here or what happened. I'm innocent. I just want to go home. They said something about a...a machine, like a teleporter or something. I told you already, I don't know what they did. I told you **everything**!"

The chief inquisitor was surprised by this obvious lie. *Teleporter, indeed! Ridiculous.* He was beginning to doubt his instincts. Clearly the miserable fellow before him was either an excellent liar or a complete imbecile. "You mistake me for a great fool, monsieur. It is not merely an issue of impracticality, what you describe is an impossibility."

"I swear it! They said a machine brought me here. I think they wanted somebody else. Some imprisoned count or something...You have to believe me! I just want to go home. I don't know anything about those people. I wasn't there long enough to know anything."

The Winter Count! The chief inquisitor shook his head in disbelief. *Preposterous.* No man had ever escaped Château d'Soleil Rouge. The heretics were clearly getting desperate. *What could they possibly hope to gain from this oafish man's abduction? The old pervert might as well be dead.* After a long pause, the chief inquisitor spoke, "Monsieur Orson, I believe in your innocence, and I believe that you have been unjustly treated. If you are indeed an outsider, then you are not fully aware of the scope of my king's power. It is, in a word, limitless. The United Kingdom of Man covers nearly a million stars. If your home is among them, you will be restored to it. That is my word on the matter. Now, tell me, do you have any enemies? It would seem that you are the unfortunate victim of an abduction. I don't yet know what the heretics hoped to gain from this...*ploy,* but surely these elaborate lies demonstrate to you their crooked nature. You have no reason to trust them. Speak."

Orson gazed down at the heavy chains pulling into his wrists. He tried to think of enemies. He wasn't important enough for enemies. He was just a man. A boring, stupid, fat man.

"I don't know of any enemies, sir. I'm just an assistant professor at a crappy, little university. I'm nobody. I don't even have tenure!"

The chief inquisitor shook his head, "We all have enemies. It is whether they are known that makes all the difference. Is there no one who might harbor a secret grudge against you, then?" As the chief inquisitor spoke he casually opened the sealed letter. He read the first line and his blood ran cold. "Where did you get this letter?" he asked, suddenly.

"One of the crew, the uh...the heretics, gave it to me. He said his name was Chaz something."

The chief inquisitor's heart clenched at the mention of his nephew's name. His future was crumbling at his feet. His reputation would be forever tarnished as a result of a *tantrum* thrown by a stupid, spoiled child.

Orson continued, "He said it was a letter for a friend's father on Spice Road in Antides, I think his name was-"

"Jacques Roliequire," The chief inquisitor finished for him coldly. Then he feigned a friendly smile. "It says so right here in this letter. Did you read this?"

Orson shook his head. "No, sir. I thought it was just a goodbye letter. I don't like to pry into personal matters."

The chief inquisitor spoke quickly, "Do you swear to me that you have no knowledge of what this letter contains?"

"I do, sir."

"This *letter* is a work of treason. Do you understand? It is death to anyone associated with it. I believe that you are innocent in the entirety. Do you believe that I am your friend?"

"Yes, sir, I do."

"Good," The chief inquisitor rose from his seat and walked over to the fireplace, "This letter is the only evidence against you. Watch me now." He threw the letter into the whispering line of suspended plasma. Star fire slowly engulfed the yellow paper, burning away all hope of James Orson's freedom. "I have just destroyed the only proof of your deception. When you leave this room, say nothing to anyone. Trust only me. I will see that you are restored to your home as soon as is possible."

For the first time since his arrival in this strange, frightening world Orson's heart filled with happiness and hope.

"Thank you, sir! Thank you!" His eyes brimmed with tears, "I thought I was going to die..."

Monsieur Leveque signaled the guards to return. The commanding guard approached the chief inquisitor. M. Leveque leaned closer and whispered a series of commands. The guard nodded, and as they released the prisoner's chains from the floor, the chief inquisitor said, "I am your friend, James Orson. Remember what I have said."

Orson smiled broadly. Tears streamed down his cheeks.

"I will. I swear it. I will!"

Then he was gone. After the guards had left and the doors were closed tight, Jon Baptis Logramme Leveque turned his back on the court. His heart quivered in his chest, and he had to brace himself on his chair to prevent his body from collapsing. His dreams had traveled so close to the pit that it had shaken him to his very soul. For all of his planning and careful maneuvering that one, little scrap of paper could have utterly destroyed him. M. Leveque cast his gaze to the fire, as if to reassure himself that the letter was indeed burned. The price of his restored ambition had been high. An innocent man was about to die.

Chapter IX

The Château d'Soleil Rouge

he guards led Orson from the court of the chief inquisitor. His heart was heavy and light. It grasped desperately at any emotion. One moment he was irrepressibly glad, the next his mind was twisting with terror. He was alive, and he had been promised his freedom...but he was lost. Elizabeth wasn't there. He was alone. Orson felt the weight of the chains pulling down on his wrists.

"Aren't you going to take these off?" he asked hopefully.

The guards remained silent. They had been forbidden to speak to the prisoner.

"Where are we going?" Orson tried again.

The guards were silent still. Orson thought to continue questioning them, but it didn't seem worth the effort. Instead, he hung his head and followed, trusting them to lead him to his freedom.

Eventually, they brought him to a small, dark cell. They put him in the center of the room, and Orson waited. The robed guards closed the door behind them and locked it tight. They had taken his shoes for some reason, and his bare feet felt cold on the hard floor. Fear crept at Orson from every side, but he remembered the Chief Inquisitor's promise. *Freedom. Home.* Orson stared at the thin strip of light coming from under the door and thought first of the comfy chair in his office, and then of Elizabeth's smile. His chest was a bleeding crater.

Though hours had passed, Orson knew in his heart that the guards would return shortly to release him. He didn't move. He stared at the light under the door and dreamt of the life that would surely be restored to him. He thought of his mistakes and of the changes he would make. He swore to be a better man.

In the darkness of the void, day and night had no meaning. There was no sense of time. Hours passed, then a day. Still, Orson waited for the guards to return with his savior, the Chief Inquisitor. He hadn't said a word. His heart twisted back on itself again and again. Hope and despair played at the edge of his mind. He wanted to cry out, but he had been instructed to remain quiet. His legs had grown sore. His back ached. Yet, he remained standing, as if moving from the spot where they had placed him might void his promised freedom. He stared at the light under the door and listened for the voice of the Chief Inquisitor outside. But his voice did not come. Dark thoughts began to creep into Orson's mind and he began to wish that he had been killed, ripped apart like the last crewman. He knew they were stupid thoughts to have, after all, he was about to be freed. When the guards slid his meal under the door, Orson found that he could wait no longer.

He shouted, "Is anyone coming to see me?" There was no answer but the sound of the footsteps fading down the hall. "Is the Chief Inquisitor coming?" Orson cried out, pleading for hope.

He was left in the dark silence of his cell. Finally, Orson let his legs collapse beneath him, and he sat on the cold, hard floor. He felt weak, but he couldn't bring himself to eat. He reminded himself that there would time to eat when he was free and on his way home. Sleep pulled his eyes closed, but Orson refused. He wanted to be awake when they came for him.

Eventually, they did come. It was the next morning when the guards finally opened the door to his cell. They were surprised to find the prisoner's dinner untouched, and they kicked it to the side as they entered.

"Stand up."

Orson's face pulled into a desperate smile. *I am your friend.* He reminded himself of the Chief Inquisitor's words as he pushed his tired body off the ground and waited for them to remove his heavy chains. But they were not removed.

"Follow me."

The guards took hold of Orson's arms and led him out of the little cell. Relief washed over the lost assistant professor as he crossed the threshold. He knew he was going to freedom. It had been days since he had eaten and he was dizzy from hunger. The guards pushed him forward, marching him down the corridor. The old passage was well lit and projected an air of dark nobility like the ruins of an ancient Roman temple reclaimed by the wild forest. Their footsteps echoed in the emptiness. A bundle of small pipes ran along the bottom of the wall, where occasional cracks hissed steam in little bursts. Despite the apparent effort made to keep the ship clean, it was in an obvious state of disrepair. The guards took Orson down another corridor that led to a large, circular airlock. With a soft gust of pressurized air, the lock opened and the door pushed outward. Another guard stepped out. He nodded to the first two.

"Is this the prisoner?"

The guard on Orson's right produced a sealed scroll. He handed it to the new guard, "Our orders."

Orson smiled, knowing that it was the order for his release.

The new guard took the scroll. "As the Father commands."

Orson looked to his new guard and asked, "Where are we going?"

The guards were silent. His new guard grabbed his arm roughly and led him through the airlock. A small ship was docked on the other side. The interior was less than four meters wide. It was bare and spartan. The guard led Orson to a plain metal seat connected to the wall. He chained Orson in and returned to close the airlock. There was a separate door inside the ship. The silent guard closed the inner door and sealed the lock.

Orson sat quietly. Once more his eyes dropped down to the heavy chains around his wrists. The metal had rubbed his flesh raw. Small patches of bare skin dripped little dots of blood onto the floor. The sight of his own blood brought unspeakable terror to his heart, though he fought it. He kept reminding himself of the Chief Inquisitor's words. *Trust only me.* He had to. Orson tried to rub his bloodied wrists. He told himself that it was all part of the Chief Inquisitor's plan. It had to be. They were going to free him soon.

Orson sat in the chair for two days. He ate sparingly. The food they brought him consisted of black gruel and a half-loaf of ashen bread. He reminded himself again and again that he would soon be free. He had to be. With that hope, he could endure anything. *Trust only me.* Orson did not even know remember his savior's name. *I am your friend.* The guards refused to talk.

On the third day, Orson was jostled from his light sleep by the ship's sudden negative acceleration. His breath caught in his chest when it ended. Minutes passed before the loud sound of twisting and locking machinery reverberated through the hull. They had reached their destination. The guard checked the seal on the airlock before releasing the inside lock and opening the door. Orson could see a great, empty room bathed in red light. It looked like a large docking area. He smiled again. Then the guard returned and unchained him from the chair. As he did so, he pulled carelessly on the heavy chains and they dug savagely into Orson's raw wrists.

"Get up." The guard commanded.

Orson struggled to stand. The guard pulled him up by his arm.

"Follow me," he growled.

Orson did as he was told, and the guard led him through the door and off the little ship. Outside, Orson found himself suddenly weightless. The guard's magnetic boots clanked loudly as he walked, dragging Orson's floating body along behind him. They passed through a tall archway and into an elevator. As the door closed, the red light was replaced with calm blue. The guard pressed a button and after a few moments a green indicator light came on. Orson felt himself falling. Gravity returned and he was on his knees. Then, the elevator sounded with a soft beep and the door opened to red light again. The air here was clean and fresh. The guard shoved Orson forward and they stepped into an artificial forest. There was grass under their feet and there were large trees all around them. The ceiling was dozens of meters tall, and a vast window ran the full size and length of the outer wall from the floor to the lofty ceiling. Outside, across the vast darkness of space, a great, red star rose above the horizon of an alien world, burning with brilliant fire like a god. It was breathtaking.

"Is this the new one?"

The rough voice had come from a short, balding man dressed in a militaristic uniform. His shoulders were very broad, making him appear stocky, and he held his weight on his left leg. He had been enjoying a smoke from a black ivory pipe carved in the shape of a bearded man. The smoke flowed around him like the gentle folds of an old garment. Orson's guard produced his orders. He held them out to the balding man.

"It is, Monsieur Commandant," he answered crisply.

The short, balding man clenched his pipe in his teeth then snatched the scroll from the lesser soldier. He broke the seal and unrolled the scroll, scanning it briefly before nodding his head. Orson had to speak. Fear was gobbling up the last of his hope. He raised his chained wrists to his new captor.

"Am I going to be freed now?"

The commandant raised a bushy eyebrow. His eyes stabbed into Orson's heart. "Where do you think you are, boy?"

"I don't know." Orson answered pitifully.

The commandant drew a mouthful of smoke from his pipe. It was difficult to discern if he was insulted or merely surprised. He took the pipe in his hand and let the smoke pour from his mouth and nose in a sad, billowing mass. "Then, you have my deepest sympathies, for you are a prisoner at the Château d'Soleil Rouge. Cheer, poor fellow. You will not suffer those chains much longer. A cell awaits. "

"What?" Orson asked. The floor was falling out from underneath him. His heart fluttered in his chest. "I'm not supposed to be here. I'm supposed to be free. I'm...I..."

And then all the strength left his body and James Orson hit the floor in a pile of numb flesh. He had fainted.

The Château d'Soleil Rouge was indeed deserving of such fear and panic, though, had Orson known the full, frightful history of that cursed place, he might never have endured the years that would come. The Château d'Soleil Rouge was an ancient space station, older than any mere citizen of Man could possibly know. It was a relic of the Old World, lost a dozen times over in the chaos of an endless war, and had floated, abandoned and forgotten, in the void above the bloated, red sun for uncounted millennia. Untold men had died within her cruel walls, such that the stain of their blood could never be cleaned. If such a thing could be done to the dark places of the world, then that grim castle was surely cursed, and if there were intrinsic humanity in the dumb stars, it would have remained forgotten. But that dark place was brought screaming into the new world by a band of lowly spice traders and heretics blindly fleeing from a bastion fleet. Their stardrives had malfunctioned in transit, and had left them stranded in uncharted space. When the Blood-Fathers came for the men, they found them in a celestial mass grave, hiding within the walls of a perfect prison, ready victims of that savage place.

The old King of Man wasted little time converting the newly discovered Château d'Soleil Rouge into a prison of incredible cruelty. The space station had been built as a massive three-stage centrifuge. The rotation of the first ring, located nearest the center, generated just under one g of force. This area was reserved for the guards' quarters and the commandant's house. It was an open space with more than three meters of fertile soil acting as the floor. In the long, forgotten years of the château's derelict journey around the lost planet, a great forest had grown in that soil, and so it had come to be known merely as "The Forest". The second ring, spaced farther out, was called "The Rind". It generated roughly two g's, and was where most of the prisoners were kept. The higher gravity made these dangerous men far more manageable. At this level and in "The Pit", the guards wore suits of hydraulic armor which allowed them to move about with relative ease. The Pit was the third ring of the château. The rotation there generated just over three g's. Unlike the other sections of the ancient space station, most of the outer ring was badly damaged. There were large gaps in the structure, scorched black and showing the bare framework beneath. The Pit was reserved for political prisoners, men who had so grievously wounded the Nobility as to deserve a painful death. The cells there were black holes of isolation, literal and figurative pits. There was no hope. There was no escape. None survived long. And it was there, in that hell, that James Orson awoke.

A loud noise had brought the lost assistant professor back with a whimper. His eyes felt like they were being pushed into the back of his skull. His chest was almost too heavy to move. He struggled to breathe, and his heart hammered in his chest. He tried to scream, but he could not find the air. His eyes opened to the darkness of his cell and he gasped, crawling along the ground like a dying beast.

"h-hel-p me. i-i...c-an't br-eathe," Orson spit in rasping syllables.

Loud footsteps thundered against the ground. The sound of moving machinery screeched through the heavy metal door. There was a small latch at the bottom which opened suddenly. Orson's dinner was shoved through, and the latch was slammed closed.

"p-lea-se. wh-ere am...i?"

The guard said nothing. Orson heard footsteps moving away from the door. He couldn't move. He rolled onto his back and fought to sustain his breathing. It was so hard. He struggled. *Help me. Help me. help me* The darkness was closing in. His vision was shaking. There was nothing in his head now, nothing but the struggle, nothing but the need to keep moving air in and out of his lungs. Every moment Orson had one desire. His mouth screamed dumbly, *Make it stop! Please! Make it stop!* The darkness was becoming irresistible. It was too much, the pain too great. Orson wanted to let it end. He closed his eyes and fell away.

When Orson awoke again his cell was bathed in the light of the red sun. A small, thick window, high on his wall, provided his cell's only illumination. Orson coughed and found that he could breathe again. His chest hurt, his lungs burned, and he gasped like a man at the end of a marathon, but he could breathe. It was like being on a roller-coaster perpetually trapped at the lowest point. Orson shoved hard against the cold floor. He managed to sit up and the struggle was suddenly worse. The blood left his head and he felt incredibly dizzy. He wanted to vomit, though his stomach was empty. He tried to scream again and found that he at last had a voice.

"Help me!" he gasped with all his strength. "I'm innocent! I don't belong here! Help!"

There was no response. He tried again and again, until his voice was hoarse and his heart raced. Eventually, he gave up, and sat in his dark cell. It was then that Orson noticed the small pool of water in the shadowy corner of the room. There was a small cup half submerged in the little pool. He crawled toward the water and reached out to it. As he gripped the immensely heavy, little cup he saw that the pool was fed by a small broken pipe in the wall. The water was very cold, the cup far too heavy in his hands.

The hours passed slowly and when the ringing finally left Orson's ears he could almost hear the absence of all sound. He sat staring at the door. The only other light that entered his cell was from the cracks under that door. Orson's eyes slowly adjusted to the darkness. His mind dwelt now, not on the suffering of his body, but on his loneliness. The absence of all sound was like the loss of life. Orson crawled to the back of his cell and leaned against the wall. Sitting in the shadows, Orson's thoughts returned to death. A broken smile stretched across his face.

Orson only knew the coming of the morning by the mechanical march of the guard returning to give the prisoner his morning meal. The impossibly heavy latch opened and the guard prepared to drop the gruel and bread onto Orson's metal plate. He saw that it was untouched and the latch slammed down. He left without a word.

For the next two days Orson refused to eat, only drinking enough to avoid the pain of dehydration. On the third day, when the turnkey lifted the latch to discover the three-day-old meal, the faceless man's agitation was palpable. The Pit was always emptying faster than he liked. Only a single prisoner had lasted longer than a year. The turnkey beat on the door, startling Orson.

"Eat," he growled.

Orson lifted his head in the dark, "Let me speak to the man in charge."

"The Commandant is busy. Eat. If yeh die I lose the three silver price for yer keepin'."

Orson shook his head in desperate disbelief, "No. Let me speak to your commandant. I need to speak with him."

"The Commandant does not speak to prisoners. Now, eat."

"Something went wrong. There was a mistake. I don't belong here. Let me speak to your commandant." Orson's voice was tired and strained from the effort of speaking.

"No one may see the Commandant. I don't have the authority. EAT."

Orson's sallow eyes drifted down to his plate. It had begun to spoil.

"If you don't have the authority then promise me that you'll try."

The guard grumbled loudly. Then shouted back, "Ask for something else."

"What?"

"Ask for books or a blanket. Ask for something else."

Orson shook his head to the ghosts in his cell. "I don't want anything else. I just need to talk to your commandant."

The turnkey was quiet for a moment. Eventually he answered, "The Commandant conducts prisoner evaluations once a year. He came only last week. If you live long enough you will see him."

Orson crawled across the cold floor and grabbed the plate in his hands. He could survive a year. He had to. Orson put his hands into the spoiled gruel and began to eat. The taste was awful, and he had to soak the bread in water, but he forced it down. When he had finished the turnkey put fresh food on his plate, and closed the latch.

Orson crawled back to the corner of his cell and sat in the darkness. *A year!* Tears began to cloud his eyes. He tried to fight it. There was a great missing piece in his heart and he tried not to feel it. He thought of a night in a restaurant on a planet called Earth. He tried to remember Elizabeth's face. He knew she was beautiful. He knew that he loved her more than anything in his life. He knew that he needed her. He missed meatballs. He missed grading papers. He missed being able to stand and breathe without pain. Finally, Orson cried. He was an empty shell. More than anything, more than even his freedom, he wanted to die. Tears fell with the weight of lead. Orson dreamt of emptiness.

Chapter X

Darkness in the Red Cell

n the months that followed, Orson was consumed by the thought of the end of his year of suffering. He used his impossibly heavy cup to scratch lines into the corner of his cell. Every mark brought him hope. Every mark brought him horror. That unexplainable heaviness was always there pushing him down. Gravity seemed so much harsher there. Everything was so hard. It was a struggle just to stand and breathe. Orson's mind chased his fading memories like ghosts in closing fog. He longed for answers. His stomach was twisted and nauseous. His joints ached constantly. The simple act of living was slowly becoming agony. But, more than all the physical struggle of his imprisonment, Orson was weighed down by loneliness. The Turnkey hadn't spoken to him since he had begun eating. The silence blurred his mind. Every morning his thoughts drifted to his own sadness. Every morning twisted his heart with a present absence. In short time the lost assistant professor had forgotten his comfy chair and even the taste of meatballs dripping with marinara, but his sorrow did not fade, rather it had become oddly focused on a singular loss, and to him it was like a deep wound being probed with cruel metal. He knew that if he could only escape for a moment he might forget the pain.

At first, Orson spoke aloud just to drive away the silence. He told himself long stories and recited what he could remember of his favorite books. Homer, Dumas, and Tolkien, they were all within him. He brought them out to fight the whispering emptiness consuming his mind. But, soon even those great stories were gone. In the end he had forgotten all but himself. So, Orson began to speak his memories, down to the most mundane detail, in the hope that he might save himself. One word above all had become a treasure on his lips, "Elizabeth." He said her name often. It brought tears and laughter.

Orson closed his eyes, "I love you." He longed to kiss her forehead, to feel the warmth of her flesh on his lips and whisper the words to her deep eyes. "I love you." Tears rolled down Orson face. "I love you." He stared at the wall and tried to remember her face. He couldn't remember her nose. It was such a beautiful nose. Orson beat his fists against his head. He rubbed his bruised eyes and clenched his teeth. Why couldn't he remember her face!

After three months he stopped even talking to himself. It was too hard, and it hurt to breathe. His meals came twice a day. There was nothing but the distance of the walls. His mind was growing gray. There was nothing. He watched the wall and tried to remember her face. He knew that he loved her, that he must have loved her, that he *could* love. Always he marked the wall. In a year he would be free. He should be free. There must have been a mistake. They thought he was someone else. They would come and get him soon. Of course, it would only be a few more days. He needn't wait the whole year. Why was he so tired? WHERE THE HELL WAS HE!

Time passed. Now, Orson rarely moved. He merely lay against the wall, staring at the shadows in the dark. He wanted to die. He waited hours for his meals, not from hunger but because they were the only things that happened during the long days of nothing. It wasn't so hard to move anymore and breathing was no longer the struggle it had once been, but Orson rarely spoke to the darkness anymore. His voice had already gone, and he had nothing left to speak, not even his memories. He had become empty, and he clawed at his head in silent agony. Now, Orson's memories brought him nothing but pain. In his cell he was powerless. All of his desire and anxiety had led to nothing, *could* lead to nothing. He was empty clay, and his emptiness was angst. His hair had grown long, his beard had hidden his face, and in the months of dawn-light and creeping darkness his eyes had begun to glow like the small, black eyes of a boar. He stared out from under a thick mask of matted of hair and his lips mimicked the words, "I love you" in a grim mockery of prayer. He had come to know genuine hatred.

Orson passed his days in disconnected sadness and impotent rage until one morning, as he finished scratching his cup across the wall, he found himself consumed by a feeling of absolute sickness and terror. There was something so important about that day, something that he must not know, must not see. It was a secret he should not remember. It had been whispered over a phone. He tried not to count the lines that marked the days. He should **not know** what day it was. It was something terrifying, far more so than the lumbering monsters that had imprisoned him. He didn't want to see it, but there was a pocket of joy in all that sadness and anger, hope that a piece of him would not die, and in the end Orson had to remember. Elizabeth had been two months pregnant when he left. It was his seventh month in hell. Their child would have been born.

When the Turnkey came that day to give the prisoner his morning meal, Orson howled. He screamed and wailed. He screamed for the commandant. He screamed for help. He screamed her name over and over. While he had somewhat adapted to the weight of his prison, and moving and breathing were no longer the impossible tasks they had once been, Orson's strength was nonetheless quickly exhausted. When he could stand and howl no more, he sat by the doorway and scratched at the floor, screaming sporadically when he found the air. For the next week Orson was mad. He sat and dreamed in utter silence, until the mechanical sound of the Turnkey lumbering down the hall shook him from his lie, then all at once he would rise up, full of power again and howl like an animal. He would beat his fists against the iron door until the bones of his knuckles showed and his skin hung from the rough metal in patches. In the weight of the red cell the door was an impossible barrier. Yet, lost in his madness, Orson would try to tear it down. His muscles would strain and his joints would scream. Still he would pound and push against the door.

"Let me out!" Orson cried in desperation. Months of cruel silence had left his voice hoarse and terrible. It had become the raspy bark of an animal. "Let me out! I'm a father! I'm a father! God damn it! Don't you hear me! My daughter needs me! Please! Please…"

His howling voice cracked and his rage trailed off in weeping tears. He sank to the ground clawing at the door in despair. His blood dripped down to little pools on the cold floor. The Turnkey ignored him.

Orson was losing his mind. He had tried so hard to keep it, to save himself from the nothing. He wanted to be strong like the heroes in prison movies and old books. Like all the men he idolized. The heroes never cried. Orson wiped the tears from his cheeks. He couldn't die. He couldn't let himself lose his mind. *Stop being so stupid. You can make it.* Orson's eyes drifted to the dripping water in the corner of his cell. The water splashed in the little, clear pool, and it was like a bullet ripping through his skull. All at once, he remembered a girl coming out of the shower in his crummy apartment. She was beautiful, truly, stunningly beautiful. He saw the adorable way she painted her toenails on the edge of his bed. He remembered the line of her legs, the curve of her hips. He remembered her soft patch of hair and how it tickled his nose. He remembered kissing the little belly button, just a little too high on her belly. He remembered the gentle swell of her breasts, the nipples like dark cherries resting on a dollop of cream. Then Orson remembered her face. She laughed with her eyes, and he wept. How could he ever have forgotten that face? Orson began to laugh through desperate tears. It was a small, terrible thing, and it grew into a wild howl. To the Turnkey, just finishing his rounds for the night, it was a sound far more terrifying than all of the screams and wailing cries. He had heard it only once before, and it was the sound of a man losing his soul.

Orson crawled over to the small pool of water and stared at his reflection. A madman stared back at him. *Is that really my face?* He wondered. He had forgotten everything. At that moment, Orson knew he would be free. Tears rolled down his cheeks.

The prisoner accepted his fate, and once more passed his days in silence. It was no longer difficult for Orson to breathe or move in the dark cell, though his joints always ached. Still, Orson chose to sit in the center of that frightful room like a monk in meditation. He moved only to collect his food, and to scratch another tally in the corner of his cell each morning. He was a good prisoner. His face was empty. He would soon be free.

When the prisoner's first year came to an end, he was sitting in his usual place, waiting for the Turnkey to arrive with his breakfast. He was late. Orson didn't know how he knew, but the Turnkey was late. Finally, he heard the low hydraulic shamble coming down the hall. When he raised the slot at the bottom of the door, the prisoner spoke.

"The year is ended. When will I see the commandant?"

The Turnkey slid the prisoner's morning meal through the hole with his usual detached effort.

Orson bent low and said again, "You told me I'd see the commandant. It's been a year."

The Turnkey was genuinely surprised. So much so that he chuckled to himself. It was a rough laugh and not at all how it had sounded in his head.

Somehow the prisoner had lasted a year. No one lasted a year, save the old man. The Turnkey smirked again. Then, he reached into the pouch at his side and, bending down, dropped another small loaf of black bread onto the prisoner's dish.

Orson was surprised. It occurred to him that the Turnkey may want to fatten his prisoners up a bit before the commandant saw them. That gave him hope.

"About the commandant," Orson asked, his voice an unintentional growl, "when will I-"

The Turnkey interrupted him with a rough sigh. If Orson could have seen his face, he would have seen a tired scowl, "He's not coming. Don' yeh un'erstand? The Commandant doesn' see prisoners."

Orson's blood turned to ice. His fingers and toes tingled. He was dizzy and his stomach turned.

"You said one year!" Orson growled, "You said I just had to make it through one year! I'm not supposed to be here! I'm innocent! I didn't do anything! I just want to see my daughter!"

"Stop cryin' now," the Turnkey answered. "There's nothin' I can do. I've asked four times already. The Commandant is not an easy man. If I ke'p bothering him with the mad requests of a single prisoner, he'll put **me** in one of these pits."

The prisoner shrank back. He was never going to see his daughter. He would never again kiss Elizabeth's nose. Tears rolled down his ragged cheeks. Orson mouthed, "I love you." The prisoner wiped his eyes and called out to the Turnkey.

"I've been in this...fucking cell for a year! I've slept on the floor like an animal! Why? What have I done? I need to know. What did I do wrong? Why do I have to be here! I don't know! I never did anything to anyone. I was safe! Goddamn it! I was safe...I didn't even live...Just tell me what I did. Just tell me how long I have to be here. I don't care how long it is...just tell me!"

"I don' know," the Turnkey answered truthfully. His voice was low. "Only the Commandant knows about the prisoners. I jus' keep yeh fed."

"How long do they usually keep prisoners down here?"

The Turnkey answered grimly, "Till they die."

Then he left. The prisoner stood for a while in the center of his cell. He thought about all the time he'd wasted in his life when he had never seemed to have quite enough. He thought of late nights in his cramped office and missed dinners with the most beautiful woman in the world. He thought about digital monsters he'd slain while the cool wind caressed the summer world. He thought again about trading his past for a future that would never exist. He thought about the book he was going to write one day. He thought about the life he was always waiting to start, and then he knew that he had traded his life for absolutely nothing. He smiled, and it was a terrible, broken smile. Horror gripped his heart at the very thought of **it**. He didn't want to. He didn't *want* to want to. When the horror passed, the prisoner felt only a comfortable despair. Every joint in his body ached. They always ached. Now, the pain was just a distraction. He hardly felt it. Time had slipped by like water through the dumb hands of a blissful child.

The prisoner found a sad peace in his brokenness. It no longer hurt to think of his past. He was alone, severed from the whole. No one was left to speak his name. All that he was, all of himself, was in the present. He knelt on the cold floor. It seemed so rough and hard now. The weight of his body pushed harder on his knees than it should have. The prisoner thought once more about Elizabeth's smile, that radiant, beautiful warmth. A kiss on his chin. A deep hug. Orson felt the tears. More than anything he wished he had said goodbye. She deserved a goodbye. His lips mouthed the words "I love you" one last time. Then, the prisoner threw back his head, and with all the force left in his body he drove his head into the floor. For a moment the world was empty, and then it all burned in a bright, nebulous explosion of pain. The prisoner did it again. And again. And again. Blood sprayed wildly from the wound, flowing over his face. The floor was slick and wet. With one, last effort the prisoner drove his fractured skull into the floor of his cell. Then, he was nothing. Blood pooled all around his twitching flesh in the darkness of his cell.

Chapter XI

The Old Man of the Château

rson was not dead. Despite all the violence and blood slowly spilling from his broken mind, James Orson was only *nearly* dead. Of course, he was not the first prisoner to lose his mind in the terrible cells of the third ring, though he was, perhaps, the first to literally do so all over the floor. He was discovered not long after his nihilistic outburst by another prisoner, an old man, who had once been a proud nobleman of high standing held in the benevolent esteem of the Crown of Man. But, no more. There was a reason why the third ring was called *l'fosse de désespoir* by those wretched souls who had been charged with guarding the cursed Pit over the years. *The Château d'Soleil Rouge* was where undesirables were sent to die. The Kingdom of Man was a civilized society, after all, and civilized societies do not execute their prisoners. Execution creates martyrs, and martyrs are immortal. It was far better to let the traitors and heretics die of natural causes in an unnatural hell.

As for the old man, his name was Gaston Ferdinando Comte d'Noël, Noble d'Sang Immortel, but he was better known as the Winter Count, and as for how he came to be imprisoned in this most terrible of places, that was almost entirely a matter of madness.

It was in the fall of the year eleven-thousand and fifty-one of the Holy Celestial Calendar. The Comte d'Noël was a man of a mere forty-seven years, and he was desperately in love. The object of his affection was the lovely Ambrosine d'fleurs. She was the daughter of the third holder of the Norlian Duchy. It was a small system but, being home to the gas giant Gran Tramore and its fifty-seven mineral-rich moons, it was a title of remarkable wealth. This made the hand of the Lady d'fleurs especially desirable, a fact that was not lost on her ambitious father, the self-titled Seigneur Horisali. But the Comte had no interests in Norlian wealth, nor in the great fortune of the vast lunar mines. He merely sought a balm to ease the scorching loneliness of his heart. Despite all evidence to the contrary the much-beloved Comte lived a life of quiet sadness. So, the Comte d'Noël had negotiated a reasonable price for the hand of his beloved Ambrosine, an arrangement which had ensured that the grandchildren of Seigneur Horisali would have a proper title. This ensured the general happiness of all parties involved, with the small exception of Ambrosine herself, who, being twelve, felt unready to abandon the bright laughter of her short, happy childhood for the dull, pet-like existence of a comtesse. But there was quite a lot the innocent, young Ambrosine did not yet know about her husband to be.

The Comte d'Noël was a man of many passions. He was a respected hunter, a gifted fencer, a champion wrestler, an accomplished cellist, and a well-known tulip fancier. This was, of course, all well-known. What was less known was that he had long been the anonymous author of a series of scandalous works known as the *Lettres Interdites*, the most recent of which was entitled *Ambrosine*, and concerned the unfortunate abduction and subsequent rape and general debasement of the eleven-year-old daughter of the laughably pompous seigneur of a small duchy. Naturally, this publication was unknown to Seigneur Horisali, who might have taken great offense to the subject matter. These secret writings of the Comte d'Noël had long been outlawed by the Crown of Man as immoral works, dangerous to the minds and souls of the peasantry and especially dangerous to the vulnerable hearts of the worthy and grand-tempered Nobility. This had a great deal to do with the publication of *L'assujettissement des Plumes*, a thinly veiled satire of the aging aristocracy.

The reward for the discovery of the anonymous author's identity was a moderately substantial sum of silver and, more importantly, the favor of the Regent of Man. The Regent had been particularly incensed by the aforementioned *L'assujettissement des Plumes*, which included a short chronicle of the sexual deviancy of an elderly regent of a crumbling imperium, including an act of sodomy involving two large hunting hounds and a Norlian beagle.

It should be noted that, outside of his deviant writings, the Comte d'Noël was regarded as a man of unimpeachable moral standing, possessing of a fiery intellect and of a fine judgmental mind with a great evenness of temper. In short, he was a gentleman of the first order. A fact that was very much lost on the Regent and the rest of the wounded upper-class.

It was on the morning of the first sun-day of the Deepertide of eleven-thousand and fifty-one that Ambrosine's father approached her about her upcoming wedding. She had been reading in the solarium, as she was fond of doing during the brief months preceding the Star-frost when the skies shimmered with the light of the titanic gas-giant, Gran Tramore. Her father's estate was on the outer hemisphere of the Great Moon of Gran Tramore. It was a large moon, with a mass just under that of the Earth, and was tidally locked with the gas giant. As a result of the Great Moon's peculiar orbit, the outer hemisphere was a Mediterranean paradise, a lush world filled with long coasts and shallow seas teaming with vivid color and life of all kinds. The inner hemisphere, however, was quite different. It was gifted with scant few hours of sunlight, and was home to the Shadow Lands and the Infinite Forrest, where the trees grew upward for kilometers, stretching taller and taller upon the shoulders of their wooden ancestors to gain what little light was available. There, life was wild and savage. It was rumored that great apes lived in those dark boughs and impossible cats with arms like men and teeth like daggers.

But none of this was known to the innocent, young Ambrosine and, as her father approached, she carefully closed her book and gave him a pouting smile.

He returned her smile nervously, "Darling, you must stop this. The Comte's ship arrived in Nötté this morning. You must put an end to all of this pouting. There is simply nothing to be done..." The seigneur paused, searching for something to say that might sweeten his daughter, "And you'll like him quite well. He's a **generous** man."

Ambrosine's fingers played on the edges of her book's worn, leather binding. She held it close to her heart and leaned against the large window. Her eyes sparkled with the hope of forbidden futures, and she stared out across the distant waters that danced along the glowing sands of the Coast of Norla.

"I don't want to be married. I just want to be me. I hate you, father." Her voice was soft and mostly empty. She thought she meant it.

Seigneur Horisali frowned.

"I know, Ambrosine. But, you must understand. Someday you will **have** to be married. It is far better that we choose now while there are so many options. The comte is a good man."

"Your comte is old and fat!"

"Ambrosine!"

With that she leapt from her cushioned seat and ran quickly from the room. Seigneur Horisali was left furious and alone. He sighed, rubbing his thin, wrinkled brow. His gaze drifted out the window. The water was a deep blue. To the common eyes of the seigneur it was empty, without beauty or meaning. Yet his Noble heart searched always for purpose, for a meaning beyond. His eyes narrowed and he smiled. There was a smudge on the window. Seigneur Horisali beat his fist against this thigh and shouted out for a servant. Ambrosine was already too far away to hear the poor boy's cries as her father lashed him. She was running blissfully up the tall staircase to her room.

Ambrosine just wanted to finish reading her book. It was strange book and it sent electric shivers through her stomach, though she didn't know why. What she did know was that she did not want to marry a comte. She wanted to marry a man like the powerful, noble-hearted and, most importantly, *classless* savages in her book. She mounted the last steps and ran down the long hall, positively bursting through the door to her chamber. She closed the heavy, wooden door behind her and tossed the thick, leather shell to the ground. Then, she hid herself away in the corner of her room to finish reading *Ambrosine*.

The Comte arrived later that night. There was a small reception held on the northern balcony. The blue star, Norlias, was sinking past the great orb of Gran Tramore, and the moons glimmered like many-faceted gems in the dusky sky. The Comte was seated at the great table beside his betrothed. His smile was deep and wonderful. Despite her greatest efforts to remain indifferent, Ambrosine found her eyes glancing up at her comte's rough, handsome face. He was dressed in a fine, blue frock coat with ivory frills at the broad cuffs. His long, black hair fell across his face as he laughed and when he reached for his dinner knife *his* Ambrosine felt her little heart twitch. His movements seemed so deliberate and powerful. She blushed as she imagined such powerful movements. She suddenly felt very warm. The gentle sea breeze kissed her cheeks and she almost forgot that she was supposed to be unhappy. Her eyes drifted down the table. She caught her father's smile and she remembered to frown. Seigneur Horisali did his best to hide his disappointment.

"Wine, sir?" their elderly wine steward asked.

The seigneur nodded sourly. The kind, old wine steward was very careful to gently tilt the bottle. He was well aware of his master's temper. Unfortunately, just as the gentle steward was finishing a perfect pour, a bout of arthritic pain seized the joints in his hand. The old man fought with all of his strength to steady his hand and for a moment he thought he'd bested the pain, but, just as he began to withdraw the bottle, he slipped ever so slightly and a drop of blood-red nectar splashed across Seigneur Horisali's lily white cuffs. The wine steward's heart froze. The seigneur was furious. His brow furrowed and his eyes burned like fire into the heart of the gentle, old fellow. The steward's voice shook as he answered the seigneur's gaze.

"I apo-pologize, sir. Please let me-"

"Enough!" Seigneur Horisali hissed quietly. "Leave my table, you withered, old man!"

The wine steward bowed reverently and hastily left the balcony. After he had gone, the seigneur motioned for another servant. He whispered into the thin man's ear, gesturing with his hands. Then the servant nodded and left. A cruel smile played at the lips of Seigneur Horisali. Later that night the wine steward would have his legs broken at the knee, and he would be discharged from the seigneur's service. He would die three weeks later from infection.

Ambrosine was happy. Perhaps more than that, she was in love. Her comte had been so unlike her expectations. The wedding was two weeks away, yet every morning she found herself waking with a tremor in her chest. She loved her comte. She smiled at herself in her mirror as she gently brushed her hair. Soon she would be married. She thought about her comte's powerful movements and blushed again. She couldn't wait to be his wife. There was a soft knock at the door to her chambers.

"Little miss, er *Madam*," her servant, Rodger, corrected himself. "Your intended husband, monsieur Gaston Ferdinando, Comte d'Noël, Noble d'Sang Immortel would like to request your presence at his breakfast. He is waiting for you on the southern beach."

Ambrosine giggled as she hurried to the door. The wedding couldn't come soon enough. Every moment the young Ambrosine spent with her comte the more she came to love him. It was as if his black eyes could pierce her flesh down to her very soul. He saw her, not as she wanted to be seen, but as she truly was. He was incredible.

As for the Comte, he was quite taken with Ambrosine as well. As might be guessed by his rather eccentric writings, the Comte d'Noël was not an innocent sort of fellow. He was, in fact, quite worldly and given to all manner of depravity. It was for this reason that he found his life so hollow and detestable, and why he was so deeply in love with Ambrosine.

He had first seen her at the annual birthday feast held at his winter estate at Flanders. Her father had come unannounced, without a proper invitation, and, what's worse, dressed in the previous year's fashion. Such presumptuous behavior was not to be taken lightly and in more formal circles the seigneur would have been stripped and lashed before the Noble Assembly, but the Comte d'Noël was never one to take such things seriously. To a mind like his, physical pain was never quite so attractive as the eyes of a man humiliated. The Comte merely made room for the gaudy, self-titled 'seigneur' at the showman's table where he could sit with the rest of the lower-class 'entertainment'. At first the seigneur and his daughter had felt mildly insulted by the Comte's generosity, but as the Comte's revelries drew on and the tables mixed, Seigneur Horisali forgot his wounded pride and came to enjoy his host's party. This was in no small part the result of the seigneur's taste for the Comte's winterwine, of which he had imbibed a large quantity. The twice fortified spirit had quite an interesting effect on the seigneur. Aside from staining his mouth a dark shade of purple, he was overcome with the most jovial sensations. It was just before the hour of midnight that Seigneur Horisali leapt up onto the broad table and began to dance. Young Ambrosine was mortified. She slouched in her chair and drooped her head, trying to hide behind her thick, blonde curls.

Meanwhile the Comte dealt with other annoyances. A lady of the court sat in his lap licking his ear. Her heavy, milk-full breasts strained against her loosely fastened corset as she softly suggested a less tasteful alternative to the cook's pie. The Comte's false smile hid his boredom. He had tasted all this 'lady' had to offer. He had twisted her body in the agony of his pleasure and had seen her eyes grow dull. She was without spark, and her mind had become overly full. Her skilled tongue wrapped around his earlobe, and her hand gently played at the front of his trousers. A sudden commotion in the fool's corner woke the Comte from this boring work. A tall troubadour was shouting at the pompous seigneur. Apparently, the man had been dancing on the table and had kicked a goblet of wine into the troubadour's lap, ruining his white frock and his marigold waistcoat. The seigneur was too drunk to properly apologize and could no longer stand on his own. He leaned against the table to steady himself.

"I d...did no sh...shuch thing," the Seigneur explained in his inebriated eloquence. "I merely knock'et it over. It wash an inoshent mishtake."

"That is false and thou dost well know it, sir!" the troubadour countered furiously.

There was a small crowd forming around them now. The Seigneur was about to speak when he noticed the curious faces and hidden laughter. His face became stone. He straightened himself up and pulled a deep breath into his lungs.

"Do you know whom you are talking to, fool." He spat sternly. "I am the seigneur of the Duchy of Norlia. My holdings produce an annual income of two-hundred millions of shilver shovereigns. If...if you pershist in these outrageous accusations I...I shall be forshed to..."

While the crowd's eyes were on the drunken fool, the Comte's own silvery eyes were drawn to the huddled form trying to hide in her seat beside her father. The little girl looked so innocent. Her bright eyes, dripping with silent tears, made his heart twitch. He *remembered* that look. Her cheeks were a deep crimson, flushed with humiliation and genuine sadness. Her pain was...real. The Comte smiled. It was the first time in ages that he had felt anything in his withered and corrupted heart. The trash in his lap mistook his amusement for interest and laughed coquettishly in his ear. It was just enough to shake him from nirvana. *The damned wretch!* The Comte frowned. He shoved the women from his lap and stood with violent quickness. Then he made his way to the source of the commotion.

The seigneur was just finishing his speech, "...if you pershist in these outrageous accusations I...I shall be forshed to have the matter brought before the magishtrate."

The troubadour was quite confused, and rightly so, after all there were no magistrates in Flanders, nor anywhere within the Shroud of Winter. The seigneur was showing his ignorance, much to the mortification of his daughter. Her total social annihilation was averted when the Comte interrupted.

"What is this **noise** in the midst of my celebration?" the Comte announced loudly, sauntering through the crowd, "It is not **proper.** Where are the *smiles*?"

The troubadour was the first to speak. His voice was low and his tone was quiet and submissive. "I beg thy pardon, Comte."

"Lord Gildaruene, what tragedy hath befallen thy waistcoat?" the Comte asked, assuming a lighthearted air.

Lord Gildaruene answered with a mixture of fear and restrained outrage. "This bufoo...*gentleman*," he corrected himself quickly, "intentionally kicked my cup from the table to make room for his *dancing*. He hath no concept of Station. Nor Order, nor Bloodright."

"Sir d'Norlia, is this true?" The Comte inquired, affecting a convincing look of genuine concern.

The Seigneur focused intensely on standing straight and released the table to anchor his hands on his waistcoat. He carefully formed his words. "It is not, Count."

The Comte smiled broadly, "Well, that's a relief isn't it, Lord Gildaruene. It would seem that thou wast mistaken after all."

"But, Thy Grace, I-" Lord Gildaruene quickly interjected.

"Was quite mistaken." The Comte's smile had vanished.

Lord Gildaruene nodded with nervous laughter. "Ah, yes. Too much wine I'm afraid."

The Comte smiled again, "Happens to the best of us." Then he turned back to his uninvited guest. "It is quite late, Seigneur. Wouldest thou and thy child care to join me for a drink on the balcony?"

It was very cold that night. The great, blue thunderclouds were beginning to descend from the upper atmosphere, and the sky was burning up a purple dream. The Seigneur enjoyed two more glasses of winterwine before he passed out on an overstuffed armchair. His innocent, perfect, little daughter was already slouched on the couch, deep in sleep. The Comte stared down at her in wonder. He ran his hand gently over her hair and Ambrosine snuggled into the couch. Of all the people in the galaxy, it seemed to him that she most deserved happiness. The Comte briefly considered carrying her up to his room and ravishing her to rid himself of the incessant irritation of the feelings stirring within his heart like long forgotten roots stirring from their winter slumber in the cruel rain of spring, but she was too beautiful and empty. The thought of destroying such a beautiful nothing seemed somehow monstrous to him. Instead, the Comte called his servants and had his guests taken to their lodgings. The next day the seigneur had a terrible headache, and his daughter was quite sure she hated all of the false trappings of Nobility. As for the Comte, it had been a very small thing and the seigneur's visit lasted only a short time, but it was enough to ignite an obsession in the heart of the much-traveled and world-weary Comte d'Noël.

So it was that he now waited on the southern shores for his much beloved Ambrosine. He casually ate a small Norlisian salad lightly tossed with olive oil. It was delicious. The sea breeze gently brushed his silvered, black hair in sparkled waves. His eyes followed the coast to the purple stars at the edge of the pale horizon. The Comte sipped from a small cup of Christmas coffee, and breathed deeply of the crisp air. It was much thicker than the atmosphere of his home.

Ambrosine was stopped by the Comte's man as she approached his table. Her servant, Roger, stood nervously behind her.

"I have come at the Comte's request," She answered with the simple eloquence of youth.

The Comte's man nodded with a subdued smile and returned to his master.

"Sir," the Comte's man spoke gently so as to preserve his master's tranquility, "the young lady d'fleurs has arrived. She has brought her servant."

The Comte let his cup settle onto the saucer and placed it back on the table. He wiped his lips with his napkin and relaxed in his chair. In the distant sky two large birds fought over a fish. His eyes saw back to the cold night when she had fallen asleep on his balcony. He permitted himself to smile.

"The servant may not follow. Escort her to my table."

The Comte's man nodded. He returned to Ambrosine.

"Thou mayst follow me."

Ambrosine smiled. She stepped forward and her servant followed closely. The Comte's man raised his hand and his brow furrowed.

"I apologize if I was unclear. The Comte wishes to see his betrothed. **Thou** mayest wait here."

Panic briefly surfaced in the servant's eyes. Ambrosine nodded with an innocent smile. "Of course. Wait here, Roger. I shan't be long."

She then followed the Comte's man.

"Good morning, mademoiselle," the Comte said rising to his feet. He gestured for Ambrosine to sit.

"Thank you, my Lord." She bowed and sat in the pillowed seat.

The Comte gestured to his man and Ambrosine was quickly served a freshly prepared summer salad with a croissant and a small glass of sweet, morning wine. It was a delicate blue and sparkled in the morning light. The Comte then sat and resumed sipping his coffee. Ambrosine nervously picked at her salad. She glanced up at her comte.

"I was thinking about our...*wedding.*"

The Comte smiled. In the distance a large bird fell from the sky. The other had torn out his throat. The haggard victor vanished into the light of the rising star carrying its prize.

"That is only natural," the Comte answered. "I liketh thee very much, Ambrosine. Thou art very beautiful."

"Really?" She smiled sheepishly.

The Comte turned his attention back to his betrothed and nodded. "Absolutely." He let his eyes run along her lithe body. "From thy slender, little legs, to thy tight, little breasts, thou art like a newly budding flower greeting the summer air, eager to be cut."

The young girl blushed deeply. She couldn't believe **her** comte had said that. She smiled and took a nibble from her croissant. Finally she glanced up. Her eyes met the Comte's. Her heart fluttered, and her chest felt warm.

She answered his gaze with a quiet, "Thank you."

Ambrosine left brunch feeling a sense of subdued pleasure at her comte's boldness. He reminded her of the men from her book. He was like a walking fiction. She had never met another man like him and, though she was reluctant to admit it, she was already in love with the Comte d'Noël.

That night as she retreated to her favorite place, the west study, her heart was a chalice overspilling the brim with fulfillment and hope. Her mind painted lives she and her comte would live. She blushed often.

"Young Miss, I think it might be best if you retire early this evening," her servant said, outside the warm, book-filled study. "Tomorrow is very important. You must not appear tired when you see His Lordship d'Noël. There is still much to do in preparation for your wedding and I believe-"

"I am aware of what my father desires, Roger." Ambrosine interrupted. "I desire to spend some time reading before I go to my bed. If you can't keep my father out of your thoughts, then you will have to wait out here in the drafty hallway."

She then turned around and, marching inside, she promptly shut tight the door. Roger was flabbergasted. He sighed and slouched against the wall. Inside, Ambrosine made herself quite comfortable. She seated herself on a large leather couch in front of the great, stone fireplace. The fire flickered warmly. Ambrosine glanced back at the door, then quickly around the room. She was indeed alone. At last she relaxed and opened her favorite book, *Ambrosine*. She turned to her favorite page and began to read in crimson wonder.

Outside, Roger pulled at his black bow-tie and began practicing excuses for her father. He was mumbling these lies to himself when the Comte approached. He was dressed in his evening jacket and was smoking a thin cigar. He smiled in that peculiar way of his that made one wonder if it was indeed a smile.

"Is my wife in there?" he asked with a gentle puff of smoke.

Roger quickly straightened his back, and drew himself up with his breath.

"The **Lady** Ambrosine is reading before going to bed," he answered.

"Isn't it a bit late for reading?"

"The lady has many eccentricities. What she enjoys is not yet your business."

The Comte's smile changed only slightly but it was enough to terrify Ambrosine's servant.

"I'm sure it is not. And in any case I have many eccentricities myself. Still, I think I will joineth her none the less." His eyes were fierce and serene. The smoke rose about his face like the breath of an old dragon.

Roger said nothing as the Comte opened the door.

Ambrosine was completely engrossed in her book. She was approaching a particularly terrible scene were her namesake was subjected to an especially juicy debasement by a group of corrupted monks when she heard the door open. Her heart seized and she quickly closed her book before poking her head cautiously over the tall back of the couch.

"I said to stay out in..." Her voice shrank when she saw her comte.

"I'm sure thou wouldn't mind some company," his fierce eyes smiled behind a swirl of gray smoke.

"Of course not, my lord," she answered, her face growing red with embarrassment.

The Comte rounded the couch and sat on the opposite side. He drew a long puff of smoke through his cigar. The tip blazed briefly red.

Smoke poured from his mouth, "Tis cold tonight."

He stared into the fire watching embers fall from the larger immolation.

Ambrosine answered quietly, "It always gets cold this time of year."

She grasped her book tightly. In her haste she had failed to notice that the false cover had slipped down. It was slight, but it was enough for the author to recognize his printed work. The Comte smiled.

"What art thou reading?" he asked. The firelight shone in his silvery eyes.

Ambrosine blushed dark red again.

"Just a boring book about...*needlework*. Nothing that would interest a great comte such as yourself."

"Needlework?" the Comte asked. He eyes twinkled with his hidden smile.

She nodded.

The Comte continued, "I think thou mayst be wrong, dear girl. That happens to be of great interest to me at the moment. In fact, I am in need of thy newly gained expertise."

Ambrosine's heart sank, "You are?"

"Yes. This morning I happened to tear a hole in my favorite pair of socks."

Ambrosine was stunned by her bad luck, "Your socks?"

"Yes," the Comte continued. He drew on his cigar again.

Ambrosine hid the book at her side, "Well...that's...a problem. Because I only know...how to...mend stockings! They're completely different you see."

"Of course." The Comte nodded. "Tell me, how did thou likest chapter thirty-seven? I felt that the author was far too conservative with the main character's reaction to the innkeeper's...less cleanly demands."

Ambrosine's face discovered a completely new shade of red. Her eyes grew wide then she glanced up at the Comte.

"How did you know?"

The Comte laughed gently, then pulled another mouthful of smoke from his cigar.

"Thou should beeth more careful," he said, nodding subtly to her book.

Ambrosine glanced down at her secret treasure, then pulled it quickly back to her chest. "It's not what you think. I found a maid reading it and I said it was wrong and that I would throw it away and I haven't even really read it."

The Comte interrupted her with a laugh. "I should be sorely disappointed if it is indeed not what I think it to be." Then, sliding closer to Ambrosine, he whispered, "I happen to be a fan of that particular book myself."

"You're not going to tell my father then?"

"Absolutely not."

Ambrosine smiled, then bounced a little closer to the Comte.

"I've read it three times already." She confided.

"Really?" the Comte smiled, clearly pleased with himself.

"It's just so...I don't know, but nobody here acts like that. They're always bowing and asking permission to do everything and sometimes I just want to get away from it."

The Comte nodded, "I know precisely how thou feels. That book is a fine escape. After all, I wrote it."

"You?" Ambrosine asked. Her eyes were like small, empty beacons.

The Comte nodded. "Of course. I'm glad thou likest my work."

Ambrosine looked toward the fire, and her voice became quiet.

"Sometimes I don't want to be treated like a princess. I'm not made of glass. Everyone is so afraid that I'm going to shatter into a million pieces if they touch me." She turned to her comte. To his surprise, her eyes had become wet and red with tears. "I'm not going to break."

The Comte d'Noël was surprised by himself. His heart was filled with pity. He wrapped his arms around the young girl and held her to his chest. Her little body shuddered with tears. For a very brief moment he felt monstrous. Then, he felt her little hand on his thigh. Her face rose and she pressed her lips into his.

"I'm not going to break," she said again, pressing her face against his chest.

He stroked her hair and said reassuringly, "I know."

Outside, the perfidious Roger, supposed faithful servant of Ambrosine, had gone.

The next week went surprisingly well. The day of their wedding feast arrived without incident, and with every passing day Ambrosine had come to love her comte more and more. She knew that he was a strong man and honest.

She loved him immensely. And as for her comte, despite his overwhelming desire, the debauched Comte d'Noël had not touched his bride to be, aside from their first, heartfelt kiss. It was surprising to him, but he found himself developing deep feelings for the girl, and he genuinely believed that he had come to love her. As he prepared for the feast thrown by the girl's oafish father, his thoughts were not of the sumptuous movements of the girl's tight, little body, or of her impending debasement, but rather of her smile and the way her nose scrunched up when she laughed. He checked his cravat once more in the mirror and found himself strangely overcome with a sense of wholeness he had never known. He was truly in love.

Seigneur Horisali had spared little expense to ensure that his daughter's wedding would be as grand as any affair before seen in the Noble houses of Man. The great solarium had been decorated in white, and the bottoms of the trees gilded in platinum and gold. Gran Tramore filled the sky and beyond, the shimmering planet, Norlias, shone like a beacon. Together, the titanic presence of the two heavenly bodies bathed the whole of the affair in otherworldly light.

The Comte d'Noël was seated beside his Ambrosine. He wore a white uniform with accents of blue and gold. At his side, his ceremonial wedding blade shimmered in its ivory sheath, like polished silver. He smiled broadly to the assembled guests. The seigneur had insisted that he invite every Old House to be in attendance, and such was the reputation of the Comte d'Noël that no name was absent.

Seigneur Horisali sat uncomfortably in his seat by the groom. He finished another glass of wine and motioned for the wine steward. The old man had been replaced by a stout young fellow with olive skin and dark hair. He was quick enough that the seigneur's attention never left his own stormy thoughts. His brow had remained low all day, as did the wine in his glass. The seigneur's mood was gray despite his great social victory, and his gaze was drawn by the slightest noise or laughter to the great doors at the entrance. Had the Comte not succumb to the sleepy venom of true and contented love he might have been better prepared for the treachery that was to follow. But he was not, and the doomed comte smiled to his beloved and stood to toast his soon-to-be father-in-law, lost in stupid bliss.

"I am overcome by Seigneur Horisali's generosity," the Comte remarked to the Assembly of Nobles, briefly raising his glass. "I knew the Seigneur to beeth a man of impeccable moral standing from the very first moment I saw him. I first met the Seigneur last year at my annual birthday celebration, where he arrived uninvited and entered unannounced." Laughter rolled through the guests.

Seigneur Horisali laughed through his teeth. He was mortified. His eyes blazed past his false smile. All regret bled from his heart. His mind leapt to twisted joy at the thought of the hells into which he would soon plunge that arrogant bastard.

Suddenly, the solarium doors were thrown open, and two impossibly large men entered. They were so broad that they had to enter single-file, and their armor bore the insignia of the Blackfallows. Behind the Blood-Fathers came ten soldiers of Man, and their leader, a tall, stern woman. She stood at just less than two meters and wore a blue and white military uniform. Her blonde hair was cut short with little style and it jutted out at odd angles. She stopped just inside the solarium, brandishing a crisp scroll. Her men raised their weapons, taking aim at the groom.

She raised the scroll toward the groom and exclaimed, "Gaston Ferdinando Comte d'Noël, Noble d'Sang Immortel! I, Lieutenant Kristopher, arrest you in the name of the Father. Come quietly and you shall be treated justly!"

The Comte nodded with a smile, and believing the lieutenant's presence to be an elaborate joke of some sort, he presented himself immediately.

"And of what crime, may I ask, am I charged with?" he laughed lightly.

The lieutenant nodded to the behemoth on her right who quickly pressed the Comte's wrists into heavy chains.

Then she unfurled the scroll and read, "Gaston Ferdinando Comte d'Noël, Noble d'Sang Immortel, you are charged with sedition against the Crown and the living blood of the Father, the Holy King, Nero. You are also charged with slander and defamation of Noble character."

"What?" the Comte answered, not finding the humor in what was surely a joke. His voice was suddenly serious, "I believe this *jape* has lost its color."

Ambrosine cried out as her Comte was led away. Her father remained slouched in his seat with his nose in a glass of wine and a cruel smile at his red-stained lips.

Chapter XII

Sanctuary

rson's eyes rolled open and the lost assistant professor awoke to incredible pain. It radiated from the wound in his forehead, cold and hot. Nausea assaulted Orson's mind and he thought he would vomit. If not for his empty stomach, he certainly would have. In time, the pain bled away, leaving behind only the hollow shell of a man lost outside of time.

Orson remembered everything. He had not lost himself after all, but neither had he been granted that brief reprieve of delusionment and confusion which might comfort the life-term prisoner in the first few moments of his awakening. Orson awoke and knew that he was still in hell. Tears flowed down his bruised face. The prisoner was dead. It had been the first true happiness he had known since his imprisonment. He brought up his bloody hands and dragged them across his eyes, smearing his face with deep crimson. His hair was a sticky mess, and his fingertips searched blindly for the wound. It was there, bound tight with expert stitching.

Orson forced his body up and, leaning his back against the wall, he stretched out his feet with detached numbness and stared at his cell. His eyes were drawn to the pool of dried blood at the center. There was a large mark where Orson had been dragged away from the door and on either side was a set of bare foot prints. The Turnkey must have saved his life. Orson smiled. He imagined that bastard panicking at the thought of finally losing the silver he earned for his keeping. Orson chuckled sardonically. Then, the smile faded. Something wasn't right. Orson's eyes scanned the walls, then returned to the blood. There was the smear moving away from the center, and the footprints... Orson's eyes shot to the door. It hadn't been opened. His meal(whether it had been his breakfast or dinner he could not tell) had been left in the corner by the pool of water. Panic pulled at Orson's heart as he contemplated the impossible reality. Someone else had been in his cell! *Not a guard. Not a guard! A man.* Perhaps it had been a fellow prisoner. The thought was so strange that Orson could not resist it. His eyes burned across the walls, one question above all in his brain: *How?* He dragged himself along the wall until he found his answer. A small panel in the wall of his cell had been removed and replaced. Though every precaution had been taken when seating the panel back into its place, the invisible alteration shone like a beacon to eyes which had for so long looked upon those walls and no others. Orson wanted to laugh, but pain split his skull. He growled to no one and beat the wound like a savage.

"No!" he shouted in a guttural moan. "No," he threatened the wound.

Orson focused on his breath. He felt nauseous and weak. He was so thirsty. He closed his eyes and laid his head on the floor of his cell. His skull throbbed along the wound. He wished he had the courage to try again, but he did not. Orson no longer had the strength to move. He let himself lie on the floor, until, finally, he slipped from consciousness. When he awoke there was more food in the corner. Hunger gnawed at his belly, and thirst twisted his stomach. He crawled to the water in the corner and filled his hands in the cold pool, drinking deeply. After several large gulps he turned his attention to the food. It was soft and almost rotten, but he was starving. Orson ate what he could and then he slept.

He awoke to the sound of grating metal, like rats scurrying within the walls of his cell. The work was careful and nearly silent, but long months of solitude had made Orson's hearing as acute as a wild beast's. His eyes opened in a burst and shone like amber jewels in the thin band of red sunlight pouring into his cell. The Other was coming! Orson's heart beat fast in his chest. He braced himself on the floor and his hand knocked his cup to the side. The quiet sound of the falling cup was a screeching cacophony. The walls were silent. Instinctively, Orson shut his eyes and feigned sleep. He waited in the silent stillness. Moments passed slowly. Still there was nothing. It was as if the Other could feel his excitement, as if he somehow knew the suicide was awake. Orson's exhausted mind conjured laughter, and then the sound of the Turnkey's hydraulic armor was scraping outside his cell. He knew it was a lie, but it was enough for Orson to question his ears. It was possible the first sound had been an hallucination as well. Orson waited.

Time crawled onward until he felt lost between the waking world and the world of dreams. His wound burned and throbbed. Sleep dragged him down, but he resisted. He focused on the pain, fighting to stay awake. His efforts were rewarded when the scurrying finally resumed. He listened as the panel was carefully removed and gently lowered to the ground.

Hushed gasps and heavy breathing told him that the Other was no more comfortable in the heavy gravity of the lower cells than he was himself. Careful footsteps moved in a stealthy shamble to his cell door. Orson knew that he mustn't let the Other know he was awake, yet some part of him needed to see. He had to look upon another face. Orson permitted himself a quick glance to the door. An old man dressed in dirty rags bent to remove his morning meal. The old man's back was broad and densely muscled, and his legs were like those of a bison or some other great beast of burden. His hair was long and gray. Before the Other turned back, Orson resumed his imitation of sleep. He heard the Other mumbling to himself as he placed the new food with the rest, and then he came back to Orson's body. He stopped over the wounded man, and with deliberate quickness he brushed aside Orson's matted hair to examine the wound. He clicked his tongue, and Orson could hear him rustling through a satchel. Then Orson felt coldness on his wound and pain surged through it. The Other had poured alcohol on his wound. Strength instantly returned to Orson's limbs and in a flash he had grasped the Other's wrist in his iron grip.

Orson roared an incomprehensible question, then his mind found words almost lost, like all the others in his tortured brain, and he tried again. "W-wo arrr yu?"

The old man had the steely gray eyes of a wolf. Thick, gray stubble hid his once-handsome face. He smiled broadly and deeply.

"Thou're not dead," the old man almost laughed.

Orson insisted again, his voice more human, "Who are you?"

The old man shook his head in surprise, "I am the man who has just saved thy life. Therefore, who art **thou** to so savagely grasp thy savior and make demands of him?"

Orson relaxed his grip and sank back down.

"My name is...*James*. I am James Orson. And I'm lost. I've been here for so long. Alone. I just want to go home. I'm a father. I-I was going to be married. I just want to know where I am."

Tears formed at the edges of Orson eyes. Whether they were from the sorrows of his past or from the overwhelming joy of speaking to another soul for the first time in so long, he did not know.

The old man watched him for a moment before his face softened and he sat down beside Orson and shook his head.

"How long hast thou been here?" he asked.

Orson looked to the marks on his wall. "A year," he sighed. It was a pitiful thing like watching a man die.

The old man stroked his chin, "I remember my first year. It was much the same. Thou hast my sympathy, boy. They put us here so they won't have to kill us themselves. A man will fight a tyrant, and a man will fight a despot, but a man cannot and will not fight *justice*." The old man's eyes had drifted to the cell door. For a brief moment Orson could see the weight in his eyes. "Even when justice is a cruel masque. **Don't help them.**" His gaze fell on Orson again. "Don't hurt thyself. Thou must stay alive, if only to spite the crooked bastards."

"You don't understand," Orson answered.

The old man looked fiercely into his eyes, "Thou had a family? People who loved thou? A woman? A man, perhaps? Thou wast happy for the first time in thy damned life and they took it away. They took *thee* away. They locked thou up, and never read thou thy charges. That's the history of every man at the Château d'Soleil Rouge. Thou art not as alone as thou wouldest think."

As he said this the old man's eyes began to drift away. He looked through tons of metal and rock, through time itself, to a moment of pure happiness, a library and a kiss. Then it was gone. The old man knew he would die alone. He smiled to himself as if to say, "No. I know where I am going to die and it is not here." He didn't believe it.

The old man turned his sight away from his soul and spoke again to Orson. "It is the gravity that makes it so hard here. Space is twice as thick here as it is on my home. No, no." The old man sighed to himself. "Where is my mind? Not space here. I forget. We're *spinning*. My home is one and a half standard units. This place." He paused for a moment, pulling the thick air into his lungs. "Is just over three units. The Commandant was quite pleased to inform me of this when I arrived. Thou should feel flattered. If thou'rt here then thou'st done something terrible to a truly terrible person." The old man chuckled, pleased with himself.

Orson didn't smile. He asked, "What did you do?"

The old man's eyes twinkled with hatred, "I wrote a book."

"Oh," Orson said quietly, then he asked the most important question, "Why did you save me?"

The old man answered, "I didn't save thee. I saved myself." He sighed. "If they found thee dead they might search thy cell. They might find my tunnels. I have the worst sense of direction...This place...it does something to thy mind. I was looking for blankets. Thou knowest, of course, thou hasn't asked me how I got into thy 'impenetrable' cell. This place wasn't always a prison. And it is very old. These cells were the old living quarters. The château is older than anything I can imagine. Hells, it may even be older than the Allfather." The old man scratched his hairy cheek. "If thou believeth in such things. I had no idea this place still existed. I thought it lost millennia ago in the Great Cataclysm. Perhaps I have been wrong all these years and the Bloodwar was not a lie after all...But this place has been here a long time. I have often wondered...when did **they** find it? How long has it been the silent hell of so many? All these years it has laid here in the darkness, an imperfect prison. No. It has been a guillotine of unimaginable coldness. Hidden away in the corpse debris of a destroyed planet." The old man laughed sardonically. "It does explain the failure of the K'ruukta Revolution. I'd bet money their so-called 'king' died here. Fool stags. Escape is impossible. This starsea is a chaotic nightmare, impossible to navigate without precise charts." Then he looked away into the shadows of the opposite wall. "I have been here for five years. I have dreamed of so many lives..."

Orson cleared his throat in an attempt to regain his human voice, "How did you survive for so long?"

"Hope," he answered flatly. "I found the old maintenance lines early in my first year. That saved me. I was...close to where thou art now. The lines run all over this level in a maze, most collapsed long ago, but I searched them all." The old man smiled to himself. "Half of this place is in ruins. Eventually, I found a path to an abandoned section of the second ring. It is much easier up there. I have endured by sleeping in a small sanctuary in the second ring, but I must be careful. If they were to suspect that I may leave my cell I would surely be moved to more secure lodgings, and if that were to happen I would lose all that I have been working toward." The old man paused for a moment as if he were making a final judgment. He looked again at Orson and continued, "I have been building a vessel!" His steely eyes practically burned at the thought of escape. "I have the containment hull finished. It is little more than a raft now, but it is quite large enough for the both us. For the past year I've lacked only propulsion. I'd almost given up on it until, quite by accident, I discovered a peculiar property of a certain, abundant cloth. The old blankets here are made of a fabric which when unwoven may be fashioned into solar collectors that can function as sails. I even used threads of this fabric to close thy wound." Orson touched the burning stitching.

"But, didn't you say it was impossible to navigate without charts?" Orson interrupted.

The old man frowned, "Perhaps it is. Or perhaps our vessel shall be small enough to avoid the unavoidable debris. There is all of the void waiting for us out there. There is only darkness within these walls. Perhaps we **shall** die."

Only a moment passed between those words and the next, but in that moment Orson let his eyes drift away from the old man. He looked back at the dried blood on the floor. The old man's eyes shot through all such shadows, they tore through their metal hell, through the glittering blackness, and through the dewy gray web of years. His vision rested not on stone and cold metal, but gentleness and love. He was looking at his bride, at real emotions. He was looking at a heart that could feel and soul that might bleed. He spoke with the voice of absolute authority.

"But we shall not die **here**!"

Then the thunder of hope left his voice and the old man glanced back to the bloodied fool sitting beside him.

"Thou art not alone. Come with me," he offered. "Take the chance. If thy choice is between certain death and uncertain life then it is no choice." The light of the red sun poured through the window, rising above the cell door. The old man stood. "It is morning and I must return to my cell. I will come for thou after the turnkey has made his rounds."

Then the old man left, and Orson was alone again. There, in the quiet darkness of the red cell, he once more took the stock of his life, of the days unlived, and of the hours squandered for a future that would never be. He felt the same deep regret. He had wasted so much on empty dreams.

Orson did not sleep that night. His mysterious guest had promised to return as soon as the Turnkey had come and gone with their morning meal. He waited through the rest of the morning, alone with his thoughts.

True to his word, the old man returned sometime after the Turnkey had left. He removed the access panel and gestured for Orson to follow. The tunnel led to a maze of rusted maintenance ducts. A series of hand grips ran along the wall, presumably to allow movement in micro gravity should the revolution of the château's arms cease. There were countless connecting pathways, most of which were completely collapsed. After nearly a quarter of an hour they came to a small bulkhead. The access portal was a once-brilliant orange, now dulled.

"Here it is." The old man said quickly. It was the first he had spoken since the night before.

Orson took a moment to catch his breath and rest his body. He leaned against the wall panting, "Where are we going?"

The old man smiled, "Sanctuary!"

He twisted the lock and opened the portal. Beyond was a hanging ladder made from a long, metal rope with flat bars every so often for steps. The old man leapt up the ladder. It was fixed to the floor but swayed as he moved. Orson stared for a moment, debating whether or not he should follow. Bright light poured through the tunnel above. The old man was slowly moving upward. Finally, Orson wiped the sweat from his eyes, took a deep breath, and began to climb.

It was harder than anything he'd tried before. He could barely move. The muscles of his legs were quickly exhausted. His thighs burned and his body seemed impossibly heavy. But after a few minutes Orson forgot all of that. The metal walls ended and a semi-clear tube of swaying plastic stretched out into space. Orson pushed himself to climb higher, faster. It had been so long since he had seen anything but the dull, gray walls of his prison. He climbed up out of the third ring and saw a vast cosmos swirling around him. Great asteroids and floating mountains danced amongst scattered glaciers, surrounded by a tempest of debris and scrap metal, while a million kilometers at their feet a red sun was rising over a massive, storm-shrouded planet. Above and below were the rotating centrifugal arms of an enormous space station, the Château d'Soleil Rouge. Orson was dangling above the outermost ring and climbing toward the second, spinning around with the motion of the arms. The higher he got, the faster he was spinning. The effect was immensely nauseating.

"Keep thine eyes up!" The old man shouted down.

Orson did as the old man commanded and slowly climbed the rocking ladder. It was difficult work, and Orson had to stop several times to rest, but at last he reached the second ring. He climbed through the access portal and collapsed onto the floor. To his surprise and relief the air was lighter and, for the first time in over a year, he could breathe without straining. The old man offered him a water pouch sewn from the same silvery fabric he used for everything else. Orson took a deep drink. He relaxed his body and it was then that he noticed the absence of pain in his joints.

"Where are we?" he gasped.

The old man sat beside him and laughed. "We're in The Rind. Can thou feel that?" He flitted his fingers in the air. "The gravity is lower here. It's how I've stayed alive this long. They don't know this place still has life support." The old man laughed again. "It took me years to realize that they don't actually know how to use anything on this relic. All of this technology is wasted on those backwards fools. As long as we're back in time for breakfast they won't know that we've gone. My sanctuary is in the next room. There's nothing else, unfortunately. This area suffered heavy damage, and there's no way out to the rest of the ring. All of the other tunnels have been collapsed."

The old man stood up and offered Orson his hand. He took it quickly, and they walked into the old man's secret room.

The Sanctuary was an open room of surprising size. At the center, surrounded by twisted bits of scrap metal, was the old man's raft. It was made from the shattered remains of an escape pod patched with the same clear plastic material of the long tunnel. The room ended abruptly at a thick, transparent door on the far side, more than large enough to accommodate the craft. For now, the emergency door acted like a great window and the whole of the room was bathed in the red light of the sun. The area beyond was wreckage. Just outside, the château's metal frame had been sheared off at the adjoining section, leaving nothing but cluttered space. Beyond that was a tempest of whirling metal, a great graveyard of ancient spaceships, and beyond that debris field was a vast asteroid belt. Below, the planet loomed; giant, beautiful, and sublime. Orson turned his attention away from the great window. In the far corner was a hammock made from a silver blanket, and in the adjacent corner was a large, makeshift carboy full of fermenting wine. The last corner was occupied by a small table and two chairs. There was a candle on the table for when the château's orbit took them behind the planet and the room was left in darkness. Beside the lone candle was a book.

"This is your sanctuary?" Orson asked.

"It is." The old man answered. He walked toward the table and set his heavy satchel down beside it. "Come," he motioned. "Sit. It's time we shared a drink. I would like to know the man to whom I am trusting my life."

Orson followed him.

"Where did all of this come from?" he asked.

The old man procured two metal cups from a locker below the table, and took a tall, metal cylinder from another. He then set the cups on the table and with a twist of his wrist opened the cylinder. As the old man poured wine into each glass he answered Orson's question.

"It was mostly here waiting for me. I believe this room was some sort of pantry for the ancient kitchens. Though there isn't much left." The old man sealed the wine cylinder and, setting it on the table, he lifted a glass to his lips, "Luckily, a substantial amount of canned beets survived." The old man took a deep draught from the cup and his face twitched. "Very good!" he coughed. Then he motioned to Orson again, "Sit."

Orson did as he was asked. The old man set a cup before Orson, and poured himself another. It was so strange to sit in a chair again. It had been a year since he had last felt human. Orson tried to get comfortable. Sitting in a chair felt wrong now, artificial in some way. He gave up on comfort and took a sip of his wine. It was shockingly bitter and burned his throat. He took another drink and coughed himself.

"My name is James Orson. I don't know where I am, or why I'm here. I'm an assistant professor. I work in a small office in the basement of a cheap, little university. I'm from a planet called Earth, and I'm a father. I just want to go home. I was supposed to be married. I had an entire life..."

The old man stared thoughtfully at Orson, sipping his wine.

"How did thou arrive here, James Orson?" he asked.

Orson stared at his own cup, "I don't know. I don't remember anything. I was in my office, and then I was on board a spaceship. It was some kind of accident or something. There was this man named Zevron."

"Zevron, thou sayest?" The old man's eyes sparked.

Orson nodded, "Yeah, do you know him?"

The old man leaned back in his chair, "I did."

Orson continued, "He told me that they were trying to get someone else, but that something went wrong with their machine and it pulled me through space to their ship. A few weeks later we were on our way to some spaceport when we were attacked by these giant cyborg monsters and these...these creepy, bald monks. They kept asking me over and over if I knew the Count of Noel or Christmas or something, and poking me with needles and they wouldn't shut up." Orson laughed. It was disgusting and melancholic. "Maybe the bastards were looking for Santa Claus out here! I told them I don't know anything. I told them everything. They wouldn't stop poking me and hurting me...Who the hell am I to know anything, anyway! They said they could take it from me if I didn't talk to them. Finally, they dragged me to this magistrate or judge." Orson took another drink. "I told him the same thing. I told him I was lost and scared. He said he believed me. I think he really did. He said I didn't need to worry, and that I should trust him. He said they'd take me home. Then they sent me here. There must have been some stupid mistake somewhere. I've seen bureaucracy fail like this. It happens all the time. It was a nightmare at the university. I used to get the wrong mail a few times a week...If I could just talk to the man in charge, maybe...maybe he would understand."

"I too believe thee, James Orson," the old man's eyes were like fire and he rose from his chair, "And more than that, I believe thou wast betrayed!"

Orson stared down at his disgusting wine. That was just what the magistrate had said to him...Orson let his mind drift into the cup, wondering what happened after he was dragged away. What had changed his fate? What had gone wrong? What could he have done? He knew that he didn't deserve it. He didn't deserve anything that had happened to him. No. He *deserved* a family. He'd worked hard. He'd been a good man. He deserved love. He'd *earned* it. Finally, Orson looked away from everything and asked a question himself.

"So, you think I was betrayed. It doesn't matter. I haven't **been here** long enough to do anything to anyone! WHY? Why the hell would anyone do this to me, put me through this? I'm a nobody. I was always a nobody. I never did anything in my worthless life, but **I** was betrayed? By **whom**! Who would betray me? I'm not worth it."

The old man countered, "Thou clearly art to someone."

Orson took a long drink from his cup, and the old man continued.

"Didst thou tell me everything that hast happened? Thou left nothing out?"

Orson raised his eyes from his cup, "I had a letter."

The old man's face twisted, "A letter thou sayst?"

Orson's thoughts had suddenly grasped a lost thread. He chased it through his mind. It led to a series of memories he'd forgotten. He had a letter and it was a dark letter from a spy. Orson's eyes grew wide at the memory. "Yes! When I first woke up here, I was on that ship and a man there, this skinny, little man, he gave me a letter for his friend. They found it in my pocket! His name was...I don't remember."

The old man nodded, "I see. What happened with this letter?"

Orson let his head fall into his hand. *STUPID! FAT, STUPID MAN!* His head shook back and forth. His blood was cold. "He burned it...he burned the letter!"

"Who burned the letter?"

"The magistrate," Orson answered trembling. His mouth was dry and he felt faint. "He said it was the only proof..."

The old man's face was a cruel scowl. There was quiet fury in his eyes. He knew he was not alone, "Thou never read this letter?"

Orson shook his head, "No. No, I didn't. It was sealed."

"Then, thou hast no idea what was written within?"

Orson fell back in his chair, numb. He felt sick.

The old man leaned forward, "Then how dost thou know what the letter contained? Thou wast lied to and betrayed by the very magistrate that promised thee thy freedom. Thy life was stolen, and thou wast sent here to die."

Orson felt himself falling again. Horror was building in his heart. Orson spoke in a whisper, "I can't remember his name."

The old man sat back in his chair, adding, "That thin-blooded, little bastard, the Commandant, would know."

Orson looked up from the growing void in his soul, "What?"

The old man's voice was flat and clear, "He keeps records of all prisoners: arrival dates, deaths, and, of course, a list of charges and judgments. Thy magistrate's name will be on the order that condemned thee here." The old man's face twisted bitterly, "If thou needest a reason to live, if thou canst think of no other," his eyes blazed with fury, "live for revenge."

Chapter XIII

Four Years

here was silence. Orson stared at his wine, consumed with sullenness and self-loathing. He felt like a blind fool.

Eventually, the old man roused him from his pity and led Orson down the long ladder, back to his cell. When the old man had gone Orson replaced the panel in his wall and sat in the darkest corner. There was so much noise in his head that it was almost impossible to separate a single thought, like all the strings on a violin screaming at once in dissonance. He knew he had been a fool. He knew that his trial had been a lie and that the men he had trusted had all betrayed him. It was too much. Orson let his eyes roam the dark corners of his world, a small cell in a space station orbiting a broken planet far above a dying sun. He pulled on his wild beard with absent habit and smiled. It was like a desperate scream. Orson raised his fingers to play with the swollen sutures on his head. It was painful and he could not resist pushing on the wound cruelly, punishing his stupidity. It was bad, but it was something. It made him feel. He wasn't alone anymore and, for whatever reason, he didn't want to die. Orson suddenly remembered how very tired he was. His bones ached. He was hungry. Finally, Orson left his wound alone and went to his food.

The old man did not return the next day, nor the next, nor even the day after that. If not for the presence of the secret tunnel, Orson might have believed himself to have hallucinated the entire ordeal. Alone again, his mind was finally organizing those terrible thoughts. He sat in the dark and felt a spark in the withered hollow of his heart. He thought of all the men who had betrayed him living their happy lives. There was a small fire in his heart now. He could see those devils kissing their daughters. He could see them cozy in their soft beds, warm and loved. The fire was growing. The darkness in Orson's cell was giving way to the red light rising from the great star. It burned through his window, chasing away the darkness. But Orson had his own fire now. He stood suddenly. Against all the power of hell, he stood, and he began to pace the confines of his cell. His eyes fell on the corner with the desperate marks where had first counted his days. Orson stopped. He remembered the old man's words. *Live for revenge.*

"No!" Orson shouted to no one. "I will not die here! Goddamn you! I will not die! My name is James Orson and I am a man! I am alive! I won't bend for you! I won't break for you! I WILL KILL YOU!"

His gaze fell now to the door of his cell and, for the first time, his thoughts focused, not on the return to his home, but on murder and blood. He felt his muscles grow tight and his dim eyes sharpen. When he had first accepted that he would never return to his home, it had nearly killed him, but he did not need those empty dreams to sustain him now. He did not need those lies. The shadows were no longer smiles and kisses. They were no longer beautiful. They were no longer Elizabeth and his daughter. The prisoner dreamt of violence in the shadows. Orson had found his voice again, only now he would speak of terror. He closed his eyes and felt a dark nihilism stirring in his heart. Orson could no longer fight it. He no longer wanted to fight it.

He screwed tight his eyes and shouted, "No!" Then he whispered to the shadows his promise. "My name is James Orson. I was an assistant professor. I was a husband. I was a father. Once, I was a prisoner. Today, I am an executioner."

These words were a new prayer, a dark promise, one he would he repeat often in the coming years. Again his laughter echoed through the empty halls of hell, sending shivers up the Turnkey's armored spine. Orson had finally and truly broken.

Nearly a week after their first conversation, the old man returned. This time he came just after Orson had finished his breakfast.

"Father curse you!" Orson heard hissed through the wall.

Orson set down his bowl and listened. His heart surged when he heard more hushed curses. Blood rushed through him, and he stood. Then he heard banging and scraping as the old man threw himself against the hidden panel, forcing it open. The metal fell hard to the floor, and the old man leaned against the tunnel wall, breathing heavily. He took a long draft from his wine pouch before motioning to Orson to get up and follow him. Orson nodded and together they silently made their way up to the old man's sanctuary.

"We must be careful," the old man began as they finally left the third ring, "Never let them know thou art gone. Always stay for breakfast. Always return for supper. Never forget to replace the access panel."

Orson didn't answer. He was too out of breath. With difficulty, he managed an affirmative grunt.

The old man pulled himself over the threshold and sprawled out on the ground. Orson did the same. The old man took another long draught from his wine pouch and waited for his heartbeat to catch up with him. He seemed much more fatigued than the last time, more worn. Orson closed his eyes and let his head fall back. Blood was rushing through his veins and his wound was throbbing, but it was the most comfortable he'd been in days. His breath was coming without struggle or pain.

The old man laughed, and Orson did the same.

"Welcome back," he smiled. Then, with a grunt, he was on his feet. "Come, my friend. Breakfast is waiting."

The old man's sanctuary was exactly as Orson remembered it. Though, one of the chairs in the corner had been moved and was being used to hold up a long section of silver fabric. The escape raft had been fitted with silver rope and strips of the silver fabric were stretched out beside it. The old man had been busy.

Orson followed his new companion to the table where he promptly shook a pile of fabric from the extra chair and set it down for his guest.

"Thou'll have to forgive the mess," he smiled. "I just finished the launch chute, and I'm in the process of measuring the sails. I estimate we'll need another fifteen meters. We're close now. Very close."

Orson and the old man sat at the table. The old man poured them both a cup of beet wine and prepared to enjoy some rare conversation. Talking was always awkward for Orson. There was so much in his mind, yet so little on his tongue. Still, he was glad for the company.

The old man began with a smile, "The sail is proving more difficult to fashion alone than I had expected," his smile began to fade, "It is good that I found thee, or I should never be free from this hell. It is a two man job, not just making the sails. I shall likely need thy strength to launch the ship as well. I've been struggling with my lack of materials. We'll need to begin searching for more blankets."

Orson nodded and took a sip from his wine, "I'm glad to help if I can."

"Thou can." The old man smiled.

Orson nodded again, "I can."

The old man took a long drink from his cup. At first they discussed the old man's plans for the ship and where he had searched for blankets and where the dead-ends were, but soon they had exhausted such conversation and began to genuinely talk, and eventually their talk turned, as it often does with two lonely prisoners, to their old lives. Orson told a joke about his old coffee maker, and then he told the old man about his job at the university; about teaching classes and grading poorly written essays, about Professor Cullen and about Elizabeth. The old man laughed quietly between long sips from his wine. When Orson recalled his lost child, the laughter stopped and there were tears. His gaze fell to his cup and his voice cracked ever so slightly. Perhaps it was loneliness, but the old man was moved more deeply than he had known was still possible. When it was over the old man sat back in his chair and, taking one final drink, he emptied his cup and stood dramatically.

"James Orson, thou shalt become my student."

Orson sipped on his wine, suppressing a grimace before asking, "What?"

"I shall teach thee everything I have learned in my many years. Thou art lost in my world, and I owe this life much. It has been very good to me until recently. So, I shall instruct thee."

Orson nodded slowly, "In what way?"

The old man smiled obviously, "I shall instruct thee on how to be a man."

Orson smiled harmlessly, "Ah, I see." He nodded and finished his drink. He felt like a very pitiful man, indeed.

The following months passed faster than any Orson could remember. He and the old man spent every available moment either working on their ship, or searching the ruined paths of the Château d'Soleil Rouge for materials. The old man was true to his word, and provided Orson with a thorough education. Their lessons were constant and ubiquitous. While they crawled through the deep dark of forgotten catacombs the old man told the sordid histories of the thirteen Houses of the First Father which had preceded the kingdoms, empires, and republics of the galaxy, and while they patched their escape ship's hull he told Orson of the ancient Cult of the Father and of the secret book which sup-posedly held the one true history; later, as they sewed the solar sails by the red light of the dying star, the old man unraveled the tangled spider's web of the Nobility, from royal gossip to their almost fetishistic obsession with caste, line-age, and blood purity. Orson was a born scholar, and there was always more to learn. The old man taught his student much of society and wealth, how to ne-gotiate with the lowest of pirates and how to charm their beautiful daughters, and using two thin, metal rods, he even trained Orson in the finer points of fencing(Which seemed an ironic necessity given the destructive power of most rifles and sidearms, but, projectile weapons, as the old man explained, were use-less aboard a ship in transit. One misplaced shot could damage the hull integrity, destabilize the shields, or worse, destroy the entire ship, if one were unlucky enough to shoot the spacial condenser in operation.). When it grew late in the evenings, the two men would take their supper by the great window overlooking the stormy planet below. Not wasting even this time, the old man would instruct him in the runic language of the starcharts, and the basic strate-gies of ship to ship combat. Orson's hammock was beside the old man's and he would often fall asleep listening to the rhetoric of the old philosophers of Noël.

Three years passed. Their escape vessel was nearly finished, and Orson had made himself quite at home in his former hell. He spent little time in his old cell, except to return for his scheduled meals. Time had changed him, inside and out. He was nimble in the deepest part of the third ring, and could traverse the darkness of the tunnels merely by instinct. He moved through the claustro-phobic maze like a salamander, delving into the deepest, most unknown, depths of the Château d'Soleil Rouge. His body had grown strong and quick, and his mind had been sharpened by the old man's tutelage to a razor's edge. He had even acquired a taste for the old man's loathsome beet wine. In short, James Orson had become accustomed to his hell.

It was just after breakfast. Orson and the old man sat at their table, discuss-ing their plans. They had been stockpiling supplies for months and the ship was full of stale bread, canned beets, and wine. The next morning they would launch their vessel and seek their fates outside of the cruel metal bosom of the Château d'Soleil Rouge.

"Thou hast got to keep those shiny eyes open, Boar," The old man started, "there's so much debris out there. We've got enough fuel left in the navigation thrusters to avoid three, maybe four, big ones. The mag shields will keep the hull safe from the smaller bits, but we can't open those sails until we're clear. It'll be at least a day."

Orson nodded with a smile. Boar was the old man's nickname for him. It had started because his hair was always in a state of wildness and his face was hidden behind his long beard. Of course the old man wasn't much better, but he at least tried to keep a respectable face with his makeshift razor. He had fashioned it from a bit of scrap and sharpened it on an old stone in the ruined kitchen. Orson, however, found the old man's razor a bit too unreliable. He had developed a healthy fear of such things in his youth, when he had nearly impaled his chin with his father's straight razor during his first attempt at shaving. It was the origin of his scar. So, Orson was the hairy Boar, and the old man...he was always the Old Man.

Orson answered, "And the planet's gravity?"

"We've been through this, stupid Boar," the Old Man sighed with a smile, "it's going to pull us down and toss us back into the void. If we're very lucking, we'll be thrown clear of the debris field and we won't die."

Orson smiled. "If we're lucky!" he laughed raising his cup before taking a very long drink.

The Old Man laughed with him. Then their smiles faded and the Old Man's voice was entirely more serious.

"Dost thine heart still burn for revenge?" he asked.

Orson stared at his wine. There was never a quiet moment when his mind did not briefly turn to the circumstances of his imprisonment, when he did not think about his lost life. Over the years he had forgotten the difference between the miracle of his arrival in the new world and the injustice of his betrayal. He only knew the loss.

Finally, he answered, "Yes. It is a wound that never heals."

The Old Man's smile was a cruel thing. "Good. Draw strength from it. Let that corruption be the path to thy redemption."

They finished their wine in deep gulps and their conversation left the dangerous topic of revenge and settled back on the familiar comfort of their future lives.

"I am not entirely without wealth or friends," the Old Man began with a favorite, well-worn topic. "I was always a careful man. Careful men plan for impossible disaster. I've hidden away enough of my family's silver to live quite a comfortable life. There's enough for both of us, my friend. Even if thou art a hairy boar," the Old Man laughed, "thou art still my brother."

Orson smiled at that and nodded. "That I am."

The Old Man continued, "The silver is in my family's winter home. It is as much as a fortress. True, it is outside of the Shroud of Winter, but there is no one left, save myself, who knows the location. It was built on a lost planetoid with an unusually dense core. Its circumference is miniscule yet the gravity is as thick as home." The Old Man smiled at the memory. "An island in space. Her star is a small thing, just a burning dwarf. Yet it is close enough to warm the whole of the planetoid to just below freezing. It is a beautiful place with high mountain peaks and vast forests blanketed in snow. My home is maintained by a village of custodians who have lived on my families land for over three-hundred years...the absence of their lord must be very confusing for them." The Old Man paused briefly to take a drink. "But my secret is safe. There, we may hide from this corrupt world and live out our remaining days in peace and happiness."

Orson nodded at the familiar story. It was one of the Old Man's favorites, and he had grown to like it himself.

"When will I learn the location of this hidden paradise of yours, Old Man?" Orson asked gently.

The Old Man laughed, "When thou learnest how to properly read a starchart, thou fool Boar!"

Orson laughed and together they talked until they had emptied two more bottles of wine and had to return to their cells for dinner. Orson could now make the trip back in a quarter of an hour, and, though the Old Man had grown slower in the passing year, he could still manage it himself in under an hour. In those last days Orson had begun to focus on securing their escape as soon as they could manage, in part because he had grown to suspect the Old Man's failing health.

The Turnkey lumbered down the hall just as Orson popped into his cell and replaced the hidden panel. His stomach was beginning to knot. He tried not to think about the next day. They would be free, or they would be dead. He had been in the Château d'Soliel Rouge for four years.

Chapter XIV

The Old Man's Escape

he red giant had finally set behind the planet, and Orson's cell was shadowed in darkness. Orson finished his dinner quickly, relishing the thought of his last meal in hell. He stuffed his remaining bread into a silver satchel slung across his shoulders. Then he knelt by the small pool of water in the corner of his cell. He dipped his hands in the cold water and lifted them to his lips. The cold hurt his throat. Orson smiled broadly at the knowledge that he wouldn't need to return for breakfast. And then the smile faded as he came to accept that this was the last time he would ever be in his cell.

It was an odd thought, but it had become *his* cell. In those long years since Orson had first appeared in this frightful, new world no place had been more his home. Orson let his eyes drift back through the shadows to the marks on his wall. He remember carving them with his cup so very long ago. Orson remembered the pain and desperation. He let his gaze fall to the floor. After three years, it was still stained with his blood. Orson remembered that. He remembered when despair had finally overwhelmed him. Orson's fingers brushed across the scar on his head. It was strange, but he felt sad at the thought of leaving. That hell had become his home, and he knew nothing about the world he was leaving it for, save what the Old Man had told him. Orson looked across his room once more, and, taking up his old, dented cup, he said his last good bye.

"I'm sorry," he whispered to the ghostly walls.

Then he put his hand on cold metal and his heart fluttered lightly as he lifted the hidden access panel and slipped into the dark tunnels. His thoughts fell away as his focus shifted. Blood filled his muscles, the dense air filled his lungs, and Orson moved with animal grace, rushing through the dark maze with gleaming eyes. Then, he reached the access to the second ring. Tension drew his thighs taut, and he threw his incredible weight up the long ladder. Distant starlight burst into his world. The floating fires sparkled through the clear plastic tube. Orson gazed out across the universe and laughed. He felt free. His heart was beating with the terror of that realization. He was going to be truly free. Outside, the mountains collided with the twisting remains of a thousand alien ships and great glaciers shimmered in the red light of the hidden sun. Beyond and beneath it all, a vast storm raged across the planet's atmosphere.

Orson reached the second ring with renewed vigor and was unsurprised to find himself alone in the sanctuary. He made himself at home while he waited for the Old Man. He dropped his satchel to the floor, set his treasured cup on the table, and poured himself a glass of wine. Their ragged ship loomed in the center of the room, the sails folded neatly at its side, ready for deployment. It was sturdy and airtight. Still, there was no guarantee that they would survive. Orson genuinely did not care. He finished his glass of wine and poured another. Soon he would escape his prison. If nothing else, he would escape. His thumb played on the dents and scuffs of his old, prisoner's cup. The château was coming around the planet again, and the red giant was rising. The dawning light poured through the great window. He would be free.

Another hour passed before Orson began to worry. The Old Man was rarely away from the sanctuary for long. Though he denied it, he was finally losing strength in his old age. For the last few months Orson had done the majority of the heavy lifting and had carried most of the materials and supplies from the lower ring. Orson had another glass of wine and began to pace across the room. He thought about the Old Man's health again and wondered if he should go look for him. He knew the path to the Old Man's cell quite well, despite never having ventured inside. Orson glanced out the great window again.

The planet thundered below. The titanic storm whirled up the atmosphere in a vast purple maelstrom and the edges of the clouds glowed red in the light of the sun. Orson had often wondered what was on the surface of that old planet. He'd never seen beyond the infinite storms which raged a ceaseless violence across the atmosphere. Orson walked to the glass. His reflection rose to greet him from the darkness of space. Orson let his eyes roam over his worn features. He looked like a wild animal, like a wild, wooly boar. He sighed and a

100

slight smile crept across his face. The Old Man had been right about him. Across the void, thousands of kilometers of lightning arced through the planet's roaring atmosphere. It was beautiful. Orson put his hand toward the scene below and was surprised to discover that the widow felt more like cold metal than glass. He had never touched it before. Orson wondered where his friend was. He was beginning to miss him.

The Old Man was on the floor of his cell. In those last, eroding months his strength had bled away, bit by bit, until his once-powerful heart had finally worn out. Eight years of imprisonment in a physical hell had aged him decades. They had taken everything from him. He had nothing left. After his last conversation with the Boar, he had struggled down the access ladder and felt the last of his strength go all at once. His chest had been heavy, and his once-iron grip was failing him. He had hurried down the last few meters and with enormous effort had returned to the little cell in which he had endured so much torment. As his heart squeezed uncontrollably he had stumbled to the secret corner of his cell and, removing a small, broken panel from the floor, he had retrieved his last work, a letter written in the certainty of death and hidden in the fear of life. Then, as the Old Man turned back, his heart had seized, and he had died clutching his last letter to his chest.

The sun had long since set behind the planet below, and the sanctuary had become chilly. Orson wrapped a silver blanket snugly around his shoulders. He moved a chair by the great window and peered out at the stars. Another empty bottle of wine lay on floor beside the chair, and Orson loosely held the final cup in his hand. He took another drink and sighed, then thought briefly about the stars of his childhood. There had been so much hope in that young sky. Far away, his favorite piece of wreckage drifted back into his vision. It was a long, thin ship and lacked the wide nacelles of the others. This lent it the appearance of a white submarine drifting through a deep, black ocean. Orson took another long drink, and smiled to himself. He named it, *Thunderchild*. Orson leaned back in his chair. Watching the wreckage, he often thought about the noble crews lost in that maze of metal. Each and every piece had been the death of hundreds. *What terrible war of worlds had been fought here?* He thought with a clever smile.

Forty thousand kilometers below, the planet swirled with mad color. Orson finished his drink. The Old Man was late. Finally, Orson stood. He dropped his blanket in the chair and decided to find his friend.

Despite slight inebriation, Orson slid deftly down the ladder and made his way through the maze of dark tunnels to the Old Man's cell. He had made the journey many times over the years, but this time, as he neared his destination, he began feel an unusual sense of disquiet. The panel was still removed from the Old Man's cell, flooding the tunnel with light. It was not like his mentor to forget caution. Orson crept slowly forward with silent steps. Then, he saw his friend's body. Fear clenched Orson's heart, and he hurried to the Old Man's side. Orson refused to accept the obvious. He shook the lifeless body.

"Wake up, my friend!' Orson cried, "Wake up. It's time to leave…"

The Old Man did not move. His chest was motionless. Orson knew that his only companion was dead. He didn't let himself believe it. He shook the body harder and nearly shouted, "No, no, no, no, no, no!"

Orson beat his fist on the floor beside the Old Man's body. He tore at his beard and shook his whole frame in impotent rage. He roared. His heart was pulling toward a terrible, nihilistic fury. He wanted to destroy the world. He wanted to die. He wanted his friend back.

"Don't!…" His voice caught in his throat. "Don't die, you son of a bitch….all these years. We're leaving tomorrow…You can't…god damn it." Tears were running down Orson's face, "Not now. You can't die now. Not now. I don't want to be alone."

There was no peace on the Old Man's face, only pain. Orson cried again, and beat his bruised fists against the floor until the skin broke through old scars and his blood dripped in speckled drops. Finally, Orson stopped. He was suddenly aware of approaching something inescapable and final. He let go of his anger and felt that terrible hollowness fill his being once more.

"I'm sorry," Orson mumbled. "I should have come sooner. I'm sorry."

Orson was alone again. He felt it in his bones. His strength was gone. His stomach was cold. He felt broken to the core. He was alone. Truly alone.

"You're my only friend. Just you. God damn it…I never had a real friend before I met you." Orson put his hands tenderly on the Old Man's head and brought their foreheads together, "You were my brother. I'm sorry. You should have lived to see your home again. I'm sorry."

Then Orson let him rest. He laid his friend's body down, and it was at that moment that he saw the letters in the Old Man's hands. Orson gently pulled them free. As he did, a ring fell from the center. It was made from a dark, slivery metal, and clanged loudly against the floor. Orson held the ring in his fingers and examined it closely. It was quite heavy for a ring, and it bore the signet of a wolf wreathed by thorns. It was beautiful. Orson turned his attention to the letters. They were written on carefully torn scraps of linen and inked in deep red-brown, the color of aged blood. Orson fell back. He wiped the tears from his eyes and shuffled through the linen pages. There were several letters stained with age and on the bottom there was something silver and new. It was folded several times. Orson set the others aside and unfolded the last letter. It was a starchart. At the top corner, written in old runes, was a note addressed to the Boar.

Stupid Boar:
This is an old man's caution. Should I ever be discovered by the turnkey, and we be separated, I do not wish for thou to be alone. If thou canst read this, then thou hast finally earned the knowledge that this chart contains. This is the location of our home, the planetoid Frost. If we should ever be separated by fate, wait for me in the Heart of Winter.

Below, the Old Man had pressed the Noble seal of the Count of Noël, the thorned wolf. Under the seal was the last will of the Comte d'Noël.

This is the signet ring of Noël. With it I mark thee my sole heir, claim thee as my blood, and grant thee the everlasting loyalty of my people. My title and my lands art thine. Thou hast been, and shall forever be, my dearest friend.
-Gaston Ferdinando Comte d'Noël

Orson almost laughed. He had not known the Old Man's name. There were tears in his eyes. After all those years he'd never thought of him as anything but the Old Man. He didn't need a name. Orson thumbed through the remaining letters. They were older than the last and had been roughly inscribed with that bloody ink. It was clear that they had been written in a hurry. It was no doubt a suicide letter. Orson took another look at his friend, Gaston, and began to read.

Chapter XV

The Regret of Gaston d'Noël

have been in this hell for a year now. I have no knowledge of the outside world, nor of my standing in it, and in all honesty I care very little. Yet, in the event of my death, I would prefer that there be some record, some honest account, of my actions. I have limited resources so I shall abandon grandiosity for artful brevity. Know this: I am not a villain. I am, or was, a man.

To my beloved, Ambrosine: Thy memory is my mind's greatest treasure. I deeply regret that I could not give thee the life we deserve together. Thou art and shall always be my wife.

And to *thee*, reader, oh I have loved thee! It was for thee that I condemned myself to this hell. It was for thee that I have been lost. Know that I will love thee to my last breath.

So begins my account. My name is Gaston Ferdinando Comte d'Noël, Noble d'Sang Immortel. Know that I am that anonymous gadfly which has so tormented our pompous aristocracy. Know that I am the infamous author of those fiendish *Forbidden Letters*. Know that it was I who created that satirical scalpel which has so deeply wounded the bloated aristocracy. Yes, I am the one whose words cut with the power and precision of a plasma blade. Throughout the years I have kept my identity secret because I am without ego. I crave neither fame nor wealth and sought only to protect my loves from the injured pride of cowardly half-men. How was I captured then? Oh, dear reader, I was betrayed! I still do not know by whom, but it was the ignorant act of a blind and selfish caitiff. On the day of my wedding(at my very wedding feast, no less) I was met by those black fiends of the dark brotherhood, the wretched Blood-Fathers. In my sacred wedding regalia they bound my wrists in black iron and cast me into darkness. I was held, at first, in a small cell on a prison transit. The witless children thought that I might bend more easily after a period of imprisonment. They did not know me. I laughed at them. How could such lesser men hurt the great Gaston d'Noël, reader? The Aristocracy would never allow them to hold true Nobility for long, even a comte with a wicked pen. I too believed that *we* were invincible. I was wrong.

They left me in a room on the transit ship for weeks, without a single answer to my probing questions. I now believe that to be how they break men, reader. They let them break themselves.

I was brought to the arbitory of an archinquisitor. There, I was accused of all manner of treachery and wrongdoing. Yes, most of it was true, but they had no proof of that. What they had, reader, were lies and hearsay, empty words from empty minds. Lastly, I was charged with the defacement of Noble honor, and the willful corruption of the peasantry! I denied all charges, of course, though I lacked my usual grace. Thou must understand, dear reader, the solitude of the past weeks had caused me to lose all patience with this diseased system. I called them cowards and dogs and fools. I laughed and taunted their masked barbarism. I could *feel* that what I had been through would be only the beginning of my troubles. Reader, they would feed on my heart until I was nothing but a ruined shell! This thought weighed more heavily on my mind than any other in those days.

The archinquisitor demanded that I sign a letter of confession and public apology. Their political machinations are obvious, I hope, even to thee, dear reader. *We* know well that the moment I had signed those documents I would be defeated, and all who had heard my great voice in all my preceding years would know that they had broken **me**! That they had broken *our* will, reader. Dost thou see, I could not let my people fall so far. I refused on the basis that I was innocent and that they had no right to hold a free soul in bondage. I told that old fool that my life was my own, and that as he had the right to act as a bloated, incestuous veinworm, feasting fat on our Noble blood; I had the right to speak my mind and live the life of a true man. He was, of course, furious. Even now I can see his pasty jowls quivering with rage. He accused me of mocking my moral superiors and had me thrown me back into the darkness.

I spent three months in solitude. And, my dear reader, I thought it was all just posturing and lies...I know now that I was very naive. During that time I still had ink and paper. I wrote, and I was quite content. My jailors, on the other hand, did not appreciate the value of my work. They took my paper in the second month, and, while I was less content, I continued to work on the linens of my bed. My writing suffered little, reader, my comfort however was sufficiently diminished. In the third month, when I had long since run out of cloth and had started on the walls, I was once more brought before the archinquisitor.

Imagine, my crafty reader, the archinquisitor's fat, toad-like smile oozing with satisfaction and self-pleasure. He announced with great pride that if I did not sign the confession and apology that my holdings would become the property of the United Kingdom of Man and be divided equally amongst the parties most grievously wounded by my 'jealous lies.' Yes, reader, **this** is the face of our so-called Nobility! Thieves and worms!

I would no longer be punished alone. They would punish *my people*. My heart was furious. Yet, in the darkness, my inner mind had long suspected this outcome. I could not allow it. Mere seconds determined the long-meditated future and the final course of my life. I knew that signing the confession and the apology would only postpone the tide of rotters rising against my Noble blood. In a breath I had my plan. I would sign their damned letters and martyr my name for my people. As I'm sure thou knowst, dear reader, the confession and apology were long, poorly written affairs meant to mimic my own fanciful eloquence. To anyone but the most naïve, fish-faced Psugian, the letters would be obvious for what they were: the symbol of my submission and cowardly defeat. I did not care, reader. I am not so selfish.

I signed their letters and begged the court for leniency like a coward. I prostrated myself before the worms and it made me sick, reader. Oh, but how they reveled in my disgrace! How their hearts pleasured to see me brought so low! The archinquisitor agreed to my 'release' immediately. My personal possessions were returned to me, including my wedding attire and ceremonial saber, and I was then placed on a small diplomatic ship, under heavy guard. I was told that 'for my protection' I should not be allowed to leave the fleet of the great bastion *Fraternity*. It seemed, reader, that I was to be a prisoner regardless. In truth, I had expected as much. I did not care. Now, at least, I should have opportunity. And for a mind such as mine, reader, opportunity is all that is ever needed.

They locked the ship's stardrive, of course, and they knew that only an idiot would attempt to escape a bastion fleet. They were reckless and in my youth I was always an idiot. Three days after my so-called "release" the bastion fleet passed into inner Antibes and came within mere kilometers of the great asteroid belt. In my dealings with the lower classes I have met many mercenaries, cutthroats, and smugglers, and so I knew enough to recognize that my chance had come. Anyone with the slightest inclination toward naval strategy knows the limited maneuverability of a bastion fleet, and I knew that my captors would be unable to effectively maneuver for the duration of our journey through this craggy space. I seized my one opportunity and with my ceremonial wedding blade I killed my Honor Guard, three armed men in full plate. Though, while it was an act of incredible bravery, dear reader, I must confess it was not accomplished by my sword alone. My efforts were greatly aided by the five bottles of Winter Reserve taken from my wedding. Yes, crafty reader, it is important to note that faceless soldiers are much easier to run through after they have drunk themselves into a stupor.

I had partially disabled the power locks on the stardrive during my first night on the ship, and once I was in the cockpit I plotted a course to that infamous smugglers den known as the Hidden Mountain. In that maze of rock and ice, and with limited use of my ships engines, I foxed to my freedom. They gave chase to my little vessel for days, and they nearly had my life on more than one occasion, but I was very lucky, dear reader. In fantastic haste, I limped to the great asteroid city in just under a week. There, I contacted a very old friend and had my new ship's identification box changed. I bestowed upon my ship a most fitting name: *The Beloved*, in honor of my wife. I honestly believed that I would soon have a small manner of revenge and, far more tempting, dear reader, that I would have justice.

I knew that I would need a reliable crew, and after a good meal of venison and potatoes, my aforementioned friend assured me that an old tavern down by the docks would likely house the dark men I needed. I thanked my host for his hospitality and made my way immediately to the port district.

The lower levels do get a little rough during the night, reader. When the core reactors vent their excess heat into space and the lights dim low for the long, late hours, all the things which loathe the brightness and decency of day flood the narrow streets and shadowed alleyways. The nights are littered with all manner of lower men, and stray bilge rats scurry through piles of half eaten refuse before vanishing into their tunnels.

My destination was The Spacer's Last Silver. It was an old tavern located by the largest of the docking clamps. That night a massive, Bahraian barque had only just arrived and its forward hull was covered in spiny barnacles. It is such a strange thing to watch the beastmen go about their meager lives, dear reader, that I can hardly resist a casual observation. I recall a small crew of the toothy whales hanging by wires from the cavernous rock above. They pried at the parasites with crowbars and scrapers, pausing every few moments to shout belligerent insults at one another, and at the tenacious barnacles. Such is life.

The tavern itself was interesting, if a bit lacking in style. The iron sign hanging over the battered door looked older than the docks themselves. Most of the letters had worn off years before, and half of the paint was missing from the topless Psugian barmaid, whose pierced nipples had gone from a dark azure to a hazy periwinkle. The walls, like everything else, were primarily constructed from iron and iron alloys. As I am sure thou art aware, reader, most asteroids in the Antibes Belt are rich in basic minerals and some of the more common metals, but wood is rare indeed. Inside, the tables were filled with a broad assortment of questionable characters, their grim faces hidden behind a thick haze of pipe smoke and lamplight. In the back, lit by the orange-red glow of a small fire, the ruin of a stunning Psugian girl sang an old spacer's chant in her husky squid trill, her haunting voice thick with regret.

I sat at the bar and ordered a drink. The bartender was a Southern Burl, a short, stout fellow with arms wrapped in tight cords of muscle and crisscrossed with deep scars. He had a glinting false-eye and wore a great, red beard. He nodded to me from across the bar and poured my wine into a tin flagon, asking me if I was looking for something. I told him I needed men for a voyage to Noël, the work would be savage and the pay especially noble. He smiled darkly and asked me how many men I needed. I told him the size of my vessel and was instructed to return to The Spacer's Last Silver in two nights. I gave him a nod, finished my wine and left, satisfied that my trip to the docks had been a success. As I would discover later, dear reader, finding a good crew is never that easy.

The next days were spent in preparation. At the advice of my friend I'd arranged to have my vessel stripped and given a rudimentary smuggling refit, which meant basic weight reductions, as well as overcharging the core and reinforcing the engines and forward shielding. In the end it was worth the expense, and *The Beloved* was quite the formidable little fluyt.

When my ship was ready I returned to The Spacer's Last Silver, as requested, and was greeted by a crew of twenty savage men. From thee, dear reader, I shall keep no secrets. These men were never entirely aware of the true nature of my mission. I knew then, at that first sight, that their loyalty was tied only to the silver in their pockets. So, I promised them plunder, I promised them silver, I promised them rape, destruction, and violence; but most importantly, I promised them an easy target: the Winter Gate.

My holdings, as I'm sure thou understandeth, primarily surround the star, Noël. It is a rare system formation in the heart of a vast, high-energy nebula, known as the Shroud of Winter. As thou may have guessed, this nebula acts as a barrier and is impossible to penetrate in any known ship. The energy cloud destroys navigation equipment and burns out even the most heavily shielded electronics. There is but one entrance to this place, dear reader, the Winter Gate. It is a pair of kilometer-tall space stations built around a massive array of modified, cell-core stardrives. These drives produce a tempest corridor of exceptionally dense space that allows travel through the nebula. All cargo passing into my system must be funneled through these gates. This makes the Winter Gate a target of incredible wealth.

So, my crew had been recruited with a vague notion of a piratical attack on the outer gate. This was, of course, merely a distraction. In truth, our target was the inner gate. Should either gate be destroyed there would be no way in or out. Noël would be forever safe from the tyranny of Man. My family has guarded Noël for centuries. It was my ancestor, Richard the First, who found and activated the drive arrays, and every son of the house of Noël knows the operation of the Winter Gate.

Thou mayst wonder, clever reader, why destruction was my first recourse. In truth it was not. I had considered less permanent solutions. The datahead at the heart of the stardrive array could be easily disabled with minimal risk; however, restoration of the gate would then have simply been a matter of harvesting a new datahead and reintegrating it with the core motherbrain. I could not risk that loss. The Bastard King's men are everywhere. The only course of action was destruction. Understand, dear reader, we had to destroy the Winter Gate!

It needed to be done. There **was** no other way. I was protecting my people! If we had failed, if I had failed...the casualties would have been beyond reckoning. The spirit of Noël would have been crushed under the iron heel of Man. I did what I had to do. Thou must believeth me. I saved lives!

But, I'm getting ahead of my narrative.

In the end, reader, it cost me five-hundred kil silver a head for my crew and twenty-thousand for my ship. It was more than I had at first been willing to pay, but in only a week I was ready to leave the smugglers port. And not one moment too soon, as I discovered on my last day that the venison I had been so enjoying was, indeed, the haunch of an especially large breed of bilge rat. The horror. I struck out the following morning with twenty men, a swift ship, and a young, but apparently skilled, K'ruukta first mate.

We were three weeks out when we passed the Hellespont and aroused the suspicions of a rogue hedge-knight in a heavy, single-man fighter looking for trouble. After the uneventful beginning of our voyage I had become complacent. I left the little stag in charge for the night and retired to my quarters in the lower stern with a bottle of my favorite vintage. As I understand it, reader, we were hailed sometime later.

I was awakened from my inebriated repose by the frantic shouts of my soon-to-be-former first mate. Apparently the hedge-knight had hailed my ship at close range and had begun asking suspicious question concerning the nature of *The Beloved*'s identification box. My officer assured him that any odd system readings were likely due to damage sustained while passing through a local ion cloud. The suspicious hedge-knight asked for permission to board the ship. During the short exchange the forward gunner became nervous and fired without warning. The hedge-knight's port nacelle suffered a catastrophic failure which undoubtedly compromised the vessel's maneuverability. Within moments my gray bastards had harpooned his ship and were preparing to strip it bare. It was at this point that I burst on deck, enraged and, admittedly, very mostly drunk. My men had already locked the ships, extended the docking web, and were pouring into the smaller vessel. The hedge-knight fought valiantly, reader, but he was overrun and slaughtered. My first mate was mute with shock. Clearly, I had underestimated my crew's ferocity. They were utter barbarians.

They piled the hedge-knight's meager possessions in the hold, along with every scrap of salvageable material, then set the carcass adrift. I waited with my first mate by the airlock for them to return dripping with gore and violence. My blood ran with darkness, reader. I could feel my great plan unraveling in that single unexpected moment. My mind was still reeling with alcohol, and it required all of my focus to retain the necessary alertness. When they returned they eyed me defiantly and all but laughed at the bumbling inexperience of my first mate. I waited until they all gathered around, laughing and joking with one another. Then, I smiled myself, clever reader, and laughed like a maniac among them. I poured my smile on their leader, another Southern Burl with a great, black beard, bathing him in admiration. I complimented his fine work, told him how proud I was to have selected such a crew. Then, I put a hand on his gory shoulder; expressing my deepest pleasure, while my other hand dropped to my sword. He stared back at me, dear reader, and I could see the pride and quiet joy in his bloodthirsty eyes. He was happy. Then, I stabbed the bastard through the throat.

He clutched at the wound as if hoping to hold his life back as it poured away. I will never forget what I saw in his death. His eyes filled with fear and terror and then drained entirely as his struggle died in a bloody mess at my feet. The laughter died with him. Then I laughed truly and deeply. I roared at my men. I thrust my bloody blade toward them and I shouted my only promise to them: if any man disobeyed I would not hesitate to kill him myself. Then, I cleaned my sword on the dead man's clothes and, standing with a smile and a laugh, I congratulated the silent mob on their good work. My green first mate stood shaking at attention. I turned my attention back to him. I told the poor stag not to worry, then asked to examine his sword. He had to know I was going to kill him, reader, yet he gave me the blade without the slightest fight. He gave me his life. Imagine my luck to find a soft K'ruukta amongst the fiends of the Hidden Mountain! I almost forgave him at that moment, and, were it not for the madmen at my back, I believe I would have. I left his own blade buried in his abdomen and returned to bed. I believed that would be the last time my crew would dare to disobey my commands.

It was another month before we reached the Shroud. My bosom filled with hope at the sight of my radiant nebula. I was so close to my home, closer than I have ever been since. My heart aches even now at the memory of Urth's golden shores.

My crew and I parted ways two days from our destination. As per the plan, I was to act as an infiltrator and disable the security protocols on the outer gate while they docked, armed-to-the-teeth and ready for mayhem. I arrived aboard a small galleon coming from the merchant's port outside of Large and began meeting with old contacts. Though I had to travel incognito, reader, my Gate held no secrets from me. I made my way through the security check points with unsurprising ease, and by the first night I had breached *their* system. My men arrived the following afternoon, broadcasting the painfully false signature of a blacklisted fishing vessel. If I hadn't obscured the docking data, dear reader, the fools would've have been caught right there. I left the ship flagged for diplomatic exemption and whitelisted in all security protocols. Once I had disabled the station's safety and security web, I sent an encoded message to my *Beloved*. I warned my crew that new security fortifications had left the system nigh impenetrable and instructed them to wait for my return so that we could make our way through the outer gate and plunder the softer target first. Before I left the Hidden Mountain I had my *Beloved*'s stardrive lined with explosives, enough to trigger a spacial cascade in the tempest corridor and destroy the Winter Gate forever. I was to escape the destruction in my family's yacht. It's much too large for the Gate, reader, and remains at my private dock as long as I am away from Noël. This was my plan. In the chaos caused by a savage pirate raid, I would detonate the explosives and return to my rightful place as ruler of my county. In time, perhaps, I should have become a king...

But it was not to be. My crew betrayed me, dear reader. I do not know why they left the docking clamps without me, but I know that as they entered the outer gate the explosives wrapped around the stardrive detonated without warning. With the safety and security protocols disabled, the mag shield was down, and the spacial distortion and electrokinetic shock wave ripped the minds from all the men on the station. With the fragile shell of their humanity torn away, they became feral beasts, tearing at the walls and at each other, lost in utter madness. I was the only one spared and, as I ran through the labyrinthine escape path to the emergency shuttle bay, I saw their rising chaos in the security monitors. They bit deep into their own flesh, covered themselves in blood, and began to draw terrible things on the walls and floors, all the while screaming in strange tongues. It was the stuff of nightmares, brave reader, the sort of hellish vision born from the gin-addled minds of old spacers.

I made it to the escape shuttle moments before the final collapse destroyed the station. The shock wave had destabilized the station's electrical systems. The docking gates were jammed. I had no option but to launch the other remaining shuttle and hope it broke through. I knew I was damning any remaining men on the station to a grisly death. It didn't matter. There were no sane men left. Once the gates were open I launched my own shuttle. I can recall very little after the reaction thrusters fired and I was hurled blindly into the void, but the Winter Gate was shattered in the final collapse of the spacial cascade and the station was torn apart.

I drifted in that cramped shuttle for weeks. Even it had not escaped the tragedy unscathed. The main viewport had been shattered and the blast shutters left me in claustrophobic darkness. The reactor was barely operational, running at two percent capacity and leaking coolant. Every now and then the lights would flicker and dim, and the automated emergency radio would grab a ghost signal from the wreckage, never anything more than alien screams. Eventually, I disconnected everything but the life support. I hoped for and greatly feared rescue. The Winter Gate was gone and with it any chance I would ever have to return home.

I was found drifting in the deeper void by the bastion *Diligence*. She was sent to investigate the communication blackout. I told them my name was Raskolnikov, and that I was the lone survivor of a terrible accident. They knew that I was the escaped Comte d'Noël. My second trial was much shorter than the first. I was labeled a terrorist and a fiend. So great were my supposed crimes that they no longer bothered with the trappings of Noble justice. I had lost all the protection afforded me by my blood. They put me on a transport and sent me here.

This is the hell where men are sent to die, where men are broken like dogs. But, I shall not die here. I shall not bend. I shall not break. I will return to my lands and my house. Hear my voice, reader! Hear me through lies and hate! Hear me through the dark void of time! I am Gaston Comte d'Noël, Noble d'Sang Immortel, the last son of the house of Noël. I am a direct descendant of the first Imperator of Man! Within my savage breast beats the blood of the First Noble! I have been cruel and I have been monstrous, but I have been glorious! I have been heroic! And I saved my people...

Chapter XVI

Orson Gains His Freedom

rson stared down at the Old Man's letters. They had revealed a surprising past attached to a man whom he had come to know as a brother. Orson looked to his friend's tired body and thought of his life. All at once he was keenly aware that the Old Man had once lived another life, a life separate from his own. He should have hated the selfish bastard, but he could not. The Old Man had loved, he had erred, and he had lost greatly. He had been a man once, far more than Orson had been.

"I am sorry my friend, my brother. I should not have..." Orson paused. There was so much sadness in him, beyond his capacity for words. He wished he had done something wrong. He wished there had been some cause to blame. His only friend was dead. In the end there was nothing, and Orson held his corpse again, "I will add your death to my vengeance. I swear to you, I will kill them. You will not be alone. Every one of them...you..." Orson wanted to say that he didn't deserve to die, that he was an innocent victim. He remembered the Old Man's confession. He stopped. "I will not forget you. I will remember you."

Outside the cell, the Turnkey's armor groaned. Their jailor was coming, and for the first time there was another set of mechanical footsteps behind his. Then, Orson heard the Turnkey's voice.

"Aye, sir. It must've 'appened just a few hours ago."

"You're sure he's dead?"

"Aye, sir. Sure as I can be. I lo'ked in the latch when he didn't take his meal, sir. There he was lyin' on the floor. I would've gon' in to check his vital, but I have your orders, sir."

"If prisoner twenty-seven is dead, I'll need to send the com with the next en-coded databurst."

They stopped just outside. Quickly, Orson's eyes searched the cell for any-thing suspicious, then he stuffed the Old Man's letters into his rags and hid himself in the tunnel. He replaced the panel just as the Turnkey began to fiddle with the lock.

"Aye. Yes, sir. I'll have you in in a jiffy, sir."

Orson heard the door open, screeching and groaning from years of disuse.

The Turnkey finished, "There you are, sir."

There was no noise, save for the low whine of the Turnkey's hydraulics, as the other man entered the cell and knelt by the Old Man's body.

"Sir?" the Turnkey shifted his weight in the doorway.

"It's him." the man answered. Then Orson heard a quiet, low-frequency hum like an old copy machine. The man let out a sigh, "It looks like it was his heart. Poor fellow."

The Turnkey cautiously entered the cell, "How do you suppose he kept his face clean, sir? Do you suppose he ate his beard?"

The other man let out a light sigh, "Knowing twenty-seven, he likely has a cache of contraband nearby."

"Should we break it down, sir?" the Turnkey offered with suspicious quick-ness. It was a clumsy attempt to divert guilt.

For a moment Orson feared the two men might stumble upon the secret tunnels.

"That's not necessary," the other man answered dismissively. "Bring in the coffin."

The Turnkey quickly left the cell. Moments later the sound of his armor was accompanied by the heavy screech of dragging metal.

"Open the tube and put him in."

A hiss of gas and steam sounded the opening of the coffin's seal, then Orson heard the Turnkey grunt as he, with little gentleness, lifted up the Old Man's body and shoved it inside the coffin.

"Where are we sending this one, sir? Dumping it with the trash, as usual?"

"Not this time. We're expecting new arrivals today. Including someone im-portant from the wording of the magistrate's letter. We need to keep the lanes clear."

"Yes, sir. I read your post on the wire this morning. The bastion will wait outside the system then?"

"Yes. They'll rendezvous with the transport and relay our com to Kenosis," the voice answered flatly. "This is your...fifth year isn't it?"

The Turnkey answered quickly, "Yes, sir, last Star-frost."

"That's right, you started at the end of the year. I am impressed. Your post has been difficult to fill, Barguer. Most men...most men cannot tolerate a place like this."

"Why it's not so bad, sir. Me armor ke'ps me well an' fit, and I'm not down here in The Pit long."

The other man sighed again, "That's not what I meant. It wears on the soul." There was a pause while the Turnkey pondered the man's meaning. Finally the man saved him from philosophy. "Keep a close watch on these prisoners. We can ill afford a disturbance now."

"Aye, sir. I heard about the wizard."

"I put little stock in rumor, Barguer," the other man answered flatly. "The Technomancer is no wizard."

"I 'eard he were in the capital, causin' trouble again."

"It's always wizards and ghosts with some people....Five more musketeers from the Corps d'Noir have abandoned their posts. The Office of the Arbitoris is convinced it's a conspiracy against the Crown, the Blackfallows think it's ghouls, the Ravenlords think it's the Taint, and now every magistrate in the county is on edge. I wouldn't be at all surprised if you had a few new tenants soon. Check the others, starting on the second ring, then take this one up to the dock. We'll keep him in The Spine until the transport leaves."

"Yes, sir, Commandant."

The Commandant?! Orson's heart jumped. The need for revenge burned in his chest like an all-consuming fire. His face twisted in desperation. It had taken years, but the Commandant had finally come down to his hell. If the Old Man was right, *he* knew the name of Orson's true betrayer. *The Old Man.* Orson remembered his friend. Sorrow and anger began to fill the void. Orson knew that he could seize the Commandant now and know the truth, if only he had the strength to sacrifice his freedom. Orson wanted to move. He wanted to burst out from hiding and throttle that illusive devil. He whispered the dark prayer and his hand played at the edge of the panel.

"Oh, and, Barguer, anything more from prisoner thirty-four?"

"The crazy one, sir?"

The crazy one? Orson drew his hand back. They might've been talking about him.

"Yes."

"Why he's been quiet as a mouse for weeks, sir."

"Really? Now that twenty-seven is dead, he's our oldest tenant down here. The new archinquisitor wants us to keep an eye on him."

Then the two men left, locking the cell behind them. Orson let his back rest against the wall. He had been close to precious truths that might now be forever lost. His heartbeat slowed. A great void was swallowing his soul. He could feel himself at the edge of an infinite precipice. Orson held on. He remembered the ship waiting in their sanctuary. He remembered hope. Orson closed his eyes and swore a new oath to the darkness. He swore to return, to see the Commandant on his knees.

Orson waited for the sound of the Turnkey's hydraulic armor to disappear down the hall before coming out of hiding. He removed the panel and stepped into the Old Man's cell. An oblong, black cylinder sat in his friend's place. It was more than three meters long and large enough to hold a man or a corpse. Orson approached it carefully. Soft, black light poured from a dimly lit computer interface. It lit up at Orson's touch and three buttons glowed orange beside animated ideograms. Orson pressed the second button. A low beep confirmed his selection. Fog hissed from the edges as the top slid open. The Old Man's corpse lay peacefully inside. There was a small release latch on the inner lid. Orson remembered his friend's words. *They don't know how anything works.* The coffin was likely another relic. Orson reached out his hand and gently touched his friend for the last time. He was leaving. The Turnkey would be looking in on his cell before long. Orson imagined the Turnkey's face when he opened the door to an empty cell. He smiled. He was going to be free.

"Goodbye, Old Man." Orson whispered.

He pressed the glowing interface and the lid slid closed. Words flashed briefly across the top in the runic language of the starcharts. It read, "*Establishing Seal....Seal Confirmed...Building Atmosphere.*"

There was nothing left for Orson in the château. He left his friend in the black relic and returned to their sanctuary. He and the Old Man had spent years preparing for this moment. Their ship was finally ready for launch.

The red sun poured light through the great window. Outside, distant mountains danced amongst shimmering glaciers. The ship sat in the middle of the room. The solar sails were stretched outward, attached to an expandable rigid frame. Orson snatched his satchel from the table and walked to the chair in front of the window. He pulled the silvery cloth over his shoulder and tucked away the Old Man's letters. Then, he grabbed his cup from where he'd left it on the floor. He held it in his hands, heavy, dented, and hideous. It brought terror and hope to his heart. He let himself look across the room one last time. It was like saying goodbye to a dear friend. Orson hated it, it was such an absurd thought to have.

Suddenly, Orson straightened his back, stuffed his cup into the satchel, and marched to the great window. Recessed into the wall beside it was an access panel. It was hidden behind layers of dust and marked with ancient letters. Orson tore the protective cover from the hinges, revealing a hand pump for the hydraulic pressure release system. Orson primed the pump and pulled the release. The walls groaned a warning and long-dormant lights flashed orange and red. Orson jogged back to his ship and climbed inside, securing the latch behind him. The lights flashed all around the little ship, and the great window began to move. A sliver opened in the center as the door began to release. Air rushed out to fill the infinite void beyond, pulling the contents of the sanctuary across the floor, sending them racing toward the vacuum. The thin material of the launch chute caught the wind and the ship began to move toward escape. Orson's heart was booming. He was about to be free! He tightened his hands nervously on the controls. Then the door stopped. The ancient mechanism had jammed in the wreckage on the other side. Wind rushed all around the ship as the last of the atmosphere bled away. The launch chute went through the gap and momentum slammed the escape ship into the door.

"No!" Orson cried pulling at his hair, "Come on! Come on, damn it!"

Then the backup system kicked on and the doors slammed closed. Orson watched with desperate panic as his only chance of escape vanished. He sat in his shattered hope. His chest was ice. He didn't want to die. He couldn't think, he didn't let himself. Orson tore open the hatch, not waiting for the environmental systems to restore pressure to the room. The ship's internal atmosphere rushed out around him. Pain flooded his limbs and his blood nearly boiled in his veins. He scrambled to the release and pulled desperately at the lever. Its purpose had been fulfilled, it did nothing. Orson's vision swam with red. He ignored the obvious truth. He fought like a madman, pulling with all of his strength until the metal twisted away and the valve was left ruined. There was no way to open the doors. The ship was useless. Orson beat his fists against the wall. He was dizzy and sick. Every nerve in his body screamed. Ice was forming at the corners of his bloody eyes. He was freezing. He would have roared in terror if his lungs still held air.

Then, in all the numbness of failure, Orson remembered that the Turnkey would soon be at his cell. He had to go. He had to return. Orson fought the cramps seizing his legs and staggered to the great ladder. The air was thicker now. He tried to cough the blood out of his lungs. They felt thick and phlegmy. He threw himself over the ledge, sliding recklessly down. His limbs were rubbery and numb. He fell through space, only stopping his descent at the last moment. Pain shot through his bones, his weight nearly jerked his shoulders from their sockets. Orson fell to his knees and, with a hacking cough, spit blood across the floor. He ground his teeth together and forced himself to stand. His strength was nearly gone. He stumbled blindly down the maze of dark tunnels, trusting his instincts to lead him home. They did. Orson collapsed at the access panel to his cell and pressed his ear against the metal, listening for the sound of his jailors. There was nothing. He forced opened the panel and fell into his cell.

His heart was a lump of pain and his eyes were solid red. Orson surveyed his cell, making certain that nothing had been disturbed. His breathing came in short, painful gasps as he replaced the panel with hasty precision. Once he was certain that he had beaten the Turnkey, he let himself collapse. He lay on the floor of his cell and coughed a laugh, smiling in dumb triumph. Then, he heard the unforgettable sound of hydraulic armor. It stopped at Orson's cell.

"Are yeh alive in there?" the Turnkey asked tapping on the door.

Orson rasped, "I'm not dead yet, you son of a bitch!"

The Turnkey laughed, "Yeh're very feisty...plotting revenge then?"

Orson tried to hide his panicked breathing. His chest was heavy. He was having trouble getting air. A million dots of light fought against the blood in his eyes. He was going to vomit. Orson curled up on the floor, fighting against his body. The Turnkey opened the slot in the door and peered into the cell. The prisoner had his back to the door. The Turnkey watched him for a moment. When he was sure that nothing was out of the ordinary, he closed the latch and left.

Orson's mind was reeling. He thought he was going to die. Every part of his body hurt so very badly. Everything had gone wrong. The Old Man was dead. The ship had failed. Orson drifted through black visions and terrible reality. He was lying on that bloody spot where he had split his skull open in a desperate attempt to escape. He knew that he had nearly broken that day long ago and now he couldn't bear another day in hell. Not another hour. Not another moment. Orson pushed his exhausted body off the blood-stained floor. He remembered the Old Man's coffin. They wouldn't eject it out to space for another day. He could escape while it was in storage, and if not, then at least he would not die in his cell. A new plan was forming in Orson's mind. He had to hurry. He took down the hidden panel and hurried back to the Old Man's cell. His muscles strained against him, but Orson would not let them fail. He stopped outside the Old Man's cell and listened at the panel for sounds of movement. There was nothing. Orson opened the panel and peered inside. The coffin was still there, untouched. He had arrived before the Turnkey.

Orson quickly opened the coffin. The Old Man's body was just as he had left it. Orson pulled him out. His body was impossibly heavy. The third ring of the château made even the smallest objects burdensome, and now, ruined as Orson's body was, carrying the Old Man's corpse was more difficult than anything he had ever done. Orson struggled to set him on the floor. Then he pulled him back to the tunnel. He thought briefly about leaving him there, hidden in the walls, but he could not bring himself to do such a thing to his dear friend. So Orson began the long task of dragging the Old Man's body back to his cell. On his own he had made the journey in only a handful of minutes. Dragging the impossible weight of the Old Man's corpse, Orson made it in half an hour. He cursed his weakness as he dragged the corpse the last few, torturous meters to his cell. Orson left the Old Man slouched over in the middle of the room with his back to the door. To the casual glance of the Turnkey he would appear to be sleeping. Then Orson carefully replaced the secret panel, and crawled back to the Old Man's coffin.

Fear pricked at Orson's swollen muscles. Too much time had passed. The

Turnkey would be returning for the coffin. Throwing away all thoughts of caution, Orson fought his way through the darkness and burst out into the Old Man's cell. It remained undisturbed. Orson almost laughed. He coughed and began to replace the panel. His swollen fingers fumbled in numb confusion, taking too much time. Orson knew that he was close to the end. His vision was almost gone. The pain in his chest was constant. His lungs felt full and wet. Finally, Orson secured the panel. With the last of his strength he dragged himself into the coffin. He fell inside and gasped at the pain of it. His muscles were twisted in turgid lumps and pressed tight against his skin. Every part of his dumb flesh screamed in agony. Orson leaned forward and pressed the button to close the lid. The coffin sealed itself and cool air began to fill the tube. Orson was in darkness. His breathing slowed. His heart found its rhythm. Exhaustion gnawed at his mind, yet in the horror of the moment sleep would not come.

Orson lay in the darkness for what seemed like hours. His muscles bulged with knotted pain. Sweat dripped down his body. His mind twisted with delirium, and the footsteps of ghosts echoed all around the coffin. Then Orson was stepping into a pile of crisp, brown leaves. He was in the forest and it was the fall. The wind blew the last few leaves off the tops of wintery branches. The air was cold. Steam rose from his mouth and nostrils. It was so cold. Earth was beautiful. Elizabeth was waiting for him. She looked so beautiful in her scarf and mittens. Then Orson heard the muffled sound of the Turnkey's armor. He knew that he had been dreaming and he was back in the coffin. He was freezing now. His breath was steam. The realness of the sound had shattered the phantoms. The cell door opened.

"Right, then," The Turnkey muttered to himself. "Last one."

He grabbed the coffin by Orson's feet and dragged it the long distance to the central elevator. Orson felt the weight of the lift rising, then everything felt lighter. He knew they had reached the second ring. He smiled in the darkness. The lift kept rising and when they passed into the first ring, Orson's body felt nearly weightless. They kept rising. The lift was taking them to the center of the château, The Spine. The Spine was the château's warehouse as well as the primary dock for the shipping and receiving of dry goods. Orson heard a soft 'thunk' as the Turnkey's shoes anchored to the floor. Then the lift stopped. They were in The Spine. The Turnkey walked in slow deliberate steps, pushing the coffin floating gently before him. They were greeted at the security gate by another guard.

"Another one, then?" He asked lightly.

The Turnkey frowned, "It's been a tough a year."

The other guard laughed, "Well I wouldn't worry. I hear you've got another five coming in with the next transport."

"Five? Father's blood. We've never 'ad that many at once," the Turnkey said quickly.

"That's just what I hear. Sounds like they caught a rebel capital ship,"

"Five in The Pit jus' like that..."

"We live in dangerous times," the other guard said. "Heard they found Taint near Meagres. Bunch of the king's musketeers just vanished."

"I don't care for rumor m'self," Barguer answered, "but it's not Taint. I heard it were the Technomancer."

"I thought the old Inquisition nabbed him ages ago?"

The Turnkey shrugged, "That's just what I heard."

Then he pushed Orson's coffin into the warehouse. He stopped in the center of a large automated storage room, and a great hydraulic arm twisted down from the ceiling. It grabbed the coffin in a wide, vice-like claw and lifted it into the air. The arm slid down the wall, carrying Orson's coffin to a massive bay of packed shelves. It placed the coffin in the last available space in a stack of black coffins. There were over a dozen, tightly packed with machine precision. Orson was jammed in the middle. Trapped.

Orson waited the long hours until all sounds had ceased, and the warehouse was abandoned for the night. He moved his hand and it felt like broken stone twisting with life. Pain immediately shot through the tortured limb. Orson's breath caught in his throat. He fought the pain and grabbed blindly for the release. He prepared himself for escape. He would need to be quick and quiet. He pulled hard on the release. Nothing happened. He pulled again. Nothing. Panic gripped his heart. Suddenly, his limbs needed to stretch. He couldn't stand the tight space. He pulled one last time on the release.

"please..." he whispered desperately.

Nothing.

"Damn it!" Orson hissed.

He pressed his hands against the lid, and pushed with all the strength left in his wasted body. Nothing. Orson tried to control his breathing. He felt mad. He was going to die. He knew that. He was so scared. His heartbeat was counting the final moments of his life. He closed his eyes in the utter darkness. He was freezing cold. Steam came from his lips and once more he whispered, "please." Then, Orson felt the tears building at the corners of his eyes. He was going to die alone. He didn't want to die. He wasn't ready. He had to live. The cold hurt. He could feel it down to his bones. Orson remembered the planet below. He remembered all those nights when he and the Old Man had stared out the great window watching her. Orson had wondered what was under those infinite clouds. His body was going to be dumped there. Tears slid down his icy cheeks. Orson smiled. He missed the Old Man. Death had become an impossible chasm. He had seen the edge that night in his cell, when he was broken, when he tried to end his life. Yet, in that moment he had run toward the darkness, leapt greedily at the void. Now, he was being dragged. He wouldn't die for another day. He didn't want it. It didn't matter.

Then Orson opened his eyes, staring through metal and space, he looked back through all the stuff of the universe, to a night on Earth. He was in bed with Elizabeth. He could feel the weight and warmth of her face on his chest. He could smell her hair. Orson smiled. She put her leg over his and pulled tight against him. In that moment he knew that he had been happy once. Orson closed his eyes. He was going to die. It didn't matter now. His cracked lips mouth the words, "I love you." He had been happy once, and that was all that would ever matter. In that moment he was so very thankful for his life.

The next morning, the hydraulic arm loaded the coffins into the airlock for the refuse chute. The doors closed. Then the chute opened on the other side and, for a few beautiful moments, Orson was outside of the Château d'Soleil Rouge. The red light of the dying sun reflected in the smooth black surface of the coffins as they traversed the empty space between the château and the planet's atmosphere. Then they were falling, gaining speed with every moment. When they reached the upper atmosphere, friction set them aglow, and they disappeared under the immortal storm raging across the planet's sky. James Orson was finally free.

Chapter XVII

Miguel Santana

here was once a small town called Cortiques on the coast of the Ignian continent of the fifth planet of the Oris system. It was a quiet, seaside town filled with fishermen and brewers and little else. The summers in this peaceful place were mild and long, and the winters were short and frigid. There was an orchard outside of this little town and at the heart of this orchard was a little cave by a little spring-fed pond. This cave was called the Cheese Closet, because it had historically been used to age cheese. The Cheese Closet was the secret hiding place of a young man named Miguel Santana. He loved to sneak off with a thick book from his father's study and vanish during the long, slow hours of the summer. The smell of old leather and aging paper always accompanied the boy. It was an especially beautiful day and Miguel was hiding in this very special place, basking in the scent and stories of a new book, when hell came to his quiet home.

It was the Bugs. They had a name, it was long and proper and very old, but no one ever remembered the name; they only ever remembered the horror the monsters wrought. They remembered that very bad things haunted the dark places and that the Bugs, like so many very bad things, only affected poor, isolated settlements in the outer reaches of the Kingdom of Man. Most thought them to be little more than the superstitions of old women. The Bugs were death. They were nightmares. They were real.

It might have been a rogue asteroid that brought them, or maybe an infested ship had landed in the port. It didn't matter. Within hours they had overwhelmed the entire town. They were small things, maybe a third of a meter long, with thin, root-like tendrils that made them look more like centipedes than real monsters. They burrowed into the backs of their victims, replacing the spinal column at the base of the skull. Once connected to the host's nervous system, the creatures took control of the flesh. The host body became a conscious puppet, kept alive by the cruelty of fate, its chemically sharpened senses shared with the flesh-eating master. The condemned was aware of everything and could even speak for the first day or so, until the parasite's feeding tube burrowed through the host's throat to take control of the mandible. It was horror.

Miguel was hiding in his favorite place. He'd spent the day reading another of his father's carpentry books. This time it was about shipbuilding. Miguel had stolen an onion and some bread from the kitchen before sneaking out. It was why he was in the orchard longer than usual that day. He had only noticed the time when his stomach reminded him that he was hungry. By then the sun had already began its slow decent into the sea. Miguel closed his book, gathered his things, and began the short walk back. He glanced toward the horizon and furrowed his brow. He had been mentally preparing himself for his father. Miguel was supposed to have gone with him to work on the season's ships by the docks. But he hated the docks and he hated his father's work. His father was sure to be very angry with him, and yet, as Miguel followed the old road home, he felt remarkably calm. Earlier, in the comfort of his sanctuary, he had decided to run away.

Miguel was getting closer to the town. He was walking past the Miller's farm when, through stumbling steps, he noticed that the road was unusually dark. He glanced up from his feet and saw the sun hidden behind the smoke-filled sky. Miguel felt a sliver of fear in his chest. Then he felt the air. It was thicker than it should have been. It was a cool summer night along the coast, yet the air was humid and sticky. An empty noise grew louder. He heard it, at last. In the distance, the sound of a thousand terrible things chittered on the salty breeze. Miguel could feel the hairs on the back of his neck prickle and rise, and for a moment he imagined the tiny feelers and feet of insects on his legs. Then a loud, wet cough brought him back to reality.

"N-no! H-help. help. it hurts. my brain f-f-fee," shepherd Miller stuttered, "am I dead? m-miguel? go a-away. i'm dead. i. miguel? i-is that you?"

Miguel turned to see the old man's corpse stumbling around his wagon. His clothes were muddied, and the shoulders were covered in blood and small bits of torn flesh. His eyes were gray pools of rotten milk, yet the irises were clear and shone in the smoky shadows. A loud chittering sound came from behind the old man as the bug forced air through its exoskeleton.

"go away. there is no mo-more. t-tt-t-to eeeeat! i don't have any more meat!" the old shepherd fought with himself.

Miguel screamed. He ran blindly down the road toward his home, too scared to realize that everyone he loved had already been lost to this inhuman and monstrous hell. The Bugs had come in the middle of the day, with no warning. There were no survivors. Miguel, a foolish child, ran straight to the center of the swarm, the town square. His father owned a small workshop in the square. He fixed clocks and the fragile navigation instruments used by the fishermen.

Miguel dodged the shambling monstrosities pouring into the narrow, cobblestone streets. He moved like an animal, darting between the awkward hosts babbling in their sadness like retarded children. He made it to the square and froze. His pregnant mother's voice cracked in the distance. She screamed. Miguel knew she was going to die. His muscles felt cold and sharp. He ran. His head was empty. His heart pumped frost through his chest. He knew she was going to die. This wasn't fear. It was the knowledge of certain tragedy. He ran. The hosts stumbled before him. Miguel leapt across the ruined market. He scaled toppled wagons and slid through tattered displays. His mother was dying. There were no tears. His muscles ached. He ran. The screams died. He ran. Familiar faces wailed all around him. People he'd known his whole life twisted in agony. He ran.

The door to his father's shop was open. Up the stairs, footsteps scraped the floor. Miguel mounted the first steps. He knew she was dead. He told himself not to cry. She was dead. He mounted the steps. In his mind she was dead. The stairs ended. Miguel froze. At the end of the hall, his father's coat, tattered and bloody, was wrapped around another horror. Those skilled hands that had once moved with such delicate precision were now nightmarish lumps of swollen flesh with all the grace of a club foot. The bug was larger than the others, perhaps older. Its spiked carapace protruded obscenely from the back of his father's neck, replacing fully one half of the spinal column. His father's jaw hung wide and thick, red teeth tore flesh from his wife in great hunks. Miguel's heart was nothing. He did not speak. There was only his gasping breath and the sound of his father's ghost gulping and crunching the flesh of his mother and unborn brother. She wasn't dead. Her eyes were empty and her body was limp, but she had yet to die. It was the book, finally falling from Miguel's hand, that shook the scene.

The remains of Miguel's father turned from his hungry work. The monster's eyes were heavy and dark. His cheeks were bloody and wet. His father cried even now. When those pitiful eyes fell on his son, his silenced voice screamed against himself in choking madness. The bug skittered and screeched. Outside, an inhuman cacophony echoed the creature with cries of a thousand terrible things swarming the small coastal village. Then, light flared through the windows in a great, burning orange, and the ground shook with such force that Miguel and his ghastly father were thrown to the floor. Miguel returned to his senses long enough to run. His father's corpse followed. Outside, bursts of thunder mixed with the screeching. Then explosions shook the clay. Miguel hurried down the stairs. He ran to the door only to find that the earthquake had shifted the frame enough to jam it firmly closed. He pulled hard. Behind him, his father shambled down the stairs. The monster on his back screeched in alien notes. Miguel's heart was black. He pulled and pulled. His sweaty fingers slipped on the knob. His heart was empty. He was going to die. His father was going to eat him.

Then the door was torn from the frame and on the other side a giant in gleaming armor spoke with thunder. Miguel's father died. The bug at his back screeched as its flesh was destroyed. Then the giant lowered his massive rifle and looked down to Miguel. The giant's face was hidden under a shining helmet of polished steel. His voice was loud and flat.

"CHILD OF MAN, ART THOU PURE?"

Miguel did not speak. He could not. Instead, he nodded to the giant.

"THOU ART THE FIRST SURVIVOR."

The giant extended his great, armored hand toward Miguel and soft light poured from the palm. He spoke again.

"THOU ART CLEAN. PRAISE TO THE ALLFATHER. COME WITH ME. IGNIAS MUST BE PURIFIED OF THE KHENOSIAN TAINT. THEY WILL RETURN."

Miguel nodded once more. Then the giant took him up in his arms and carried him to the village square. Half a dozen giants stalked the ruins of Miguel's home. Their small ship had landed on the statue at the village center. The Goddess of the Water now lay in pieces, buried in the dust. Another armored giant stood guard by the ship. The two said nothing as Miguel was brought on board. The interior of the ship was bleak and spartan. There were no chairs, only supports to anchor the giants' armor and weapons to the hull. The giant held Miguel with tight gentleness as he racked his rifle, and small hydraulic arms secured his armor to the wall. The rest of the giants boarded soon after, each returning to his support harness. The last to return was larger than the rest. His golden armor was covered in plasma burns and deep scratches. Him the giants saluted.

"**IN THE FATHER'S NAME.**" Their voices shook the ship around them.

Their leader looked to Miguel, and the ship began to rise as he closed the door.

"WHY HAVE YOU BROUGHT THIS CHILD, BROTHER GODE-FROY?"

Miguel's giant answered, "HE IS PURE. HE REMAINS A CHILD OF MAN."

The leader turned his attention to the cockpit. "AS YOU LIKE IT."

He exchanged brief words with the pilot, then returned to take his place among his men. When the ship reached the upper atmosphere a great fireball scorched the sky of Oris Five, and the Ignian continent was reduced to ash. In the skies above, a vast fleet of ships surrounded the great bastion *Piety*. Fire burned below. Miguel's head collapsed onto Godefroy's cold armor, and he slept.

Miguel would never see his family again. The Blood-Fathers took him back to *Piety,* the home of the 'o Loyos order and one of the eight remaining bastion ships. Here, Miguel spent the last years of his childhood under the careful tutelage of those who had saved him from a death more terrible than his young mind could have imagined, though it tried at every moment. The Keepers, grotesquely misshapen monks not suited for the conversion to the glory of steel, readily accepted the child into their orphanage. Ever mindful of the Cult of the Father, Miguel flourished in the strict, militaristic environment. He quickly found his place amongst the ignorance of ancient ritual and forgotten science. In all exercises he astonished the Keepers with his tenacity and seeming lack of fear. Nothing could shake his resolve. The hideous rejects looked on him with broad smiles and great hope. Godefroy visited him often and regarded the boy with great interest and pride. He told him long stories of the 'o Loyos deeds, and taught him how to read the Paternal Alphabet, and how to decipher star-maps. In time Miguel came to love him as a father.

On Miguel's fifteenth birthday he was ready to leave the Keepers' nest, and was given a temporary assignment on the bastion. Miguel had longed for the chance to prove his courage and his strength, but to his disappointment he was placed in the great library as an assistant to the Master Librarian. It was a mediocre assignment, but the library was nonetheless important and his adopted sense of honor would not allow him to refuse. The work was not overly taxing and it provided him ample access to the 'o Loyos archives. Miguel worked diligently and within a year he was named a full Librarian.

Miguel was in the great library re-shelving a cart of books when Godefroy approached him with the offer to begin the Rites of Purity. The Rites were the first step to joining the 'o Loyos and becoming a Blood-Father himself.

In the safety of the bastion Godefroy did not wear his helmet. His hairless head was pale and marked by deep scars. A bundle of wires ran up from the neckline of his armor into his left temple and his eye was soulless metal. Godefroy's face twisted into a grotesque smile that reflected the distance of his soul, "DOST THOU REMEMBER THE ARKE?"

Miguel nodded, setting a tall, thin book back in its place. The question was asked often and was never actually a question.

"I do," he answered mechanically. "It was the first lesson the Keepers taught me."

Hung by a leather strap over his shoulders, and resting against his hip, was a thick, handwritten tome transcribed in the Paternal Alphabet. It was called *The Book of the First Father*, and within its worn pages was recorded the dogmatic history of the Blood-Fathers. It began with the "Arke", the story of the beginning of all life in the galaxy and of the founding of the Blood-Fathers. It concerned the betrayal of the Allfather by his favored son, Tyran, who had fathered a terrible race of monsters. The Blood-Fathers were born in the horror of galactic war to fight those monsters.

Godefroy nodded again with the same smile, "GOOD. THEN THOU KNOWST WHY THE BLOOD MUST BE PURE."

Miguel nodded, "Yes. We must be vigilant of any corruption and taint. It is insidious. We must protect the weak."

"SANTANA, THE ARKE IS WHY I EXIST. LIKE THOU, I HAVE LOST MUCH, AND I HAVE KNOWN GREAT SADNESS. MY FAMILY WAS DESTROYED. THE KHENOSIAN TAINT TOOK FROM ME MY SISTER, WHOM I LOVED ABOVE ALL. I LIVE FOR HER MEMORY. I KNOW THAT THY HEART BURNS FOR PEACE AND SAFETY. IF THOU SO CHOOSEST, THOU MAYST ATTEMPT THE RIGHTS OF PURIFICATION AND LIVE TO ENSURE THAT PEACE. THOU MAYST YET AVENGE THAT WHICH THOU HAST LOST."

Miguel's father had been a short, bald man with a perpetually cheery smile. His mother was fat and beautiful. Miguel remembered his family. He remembered the old fireplace where they all sat in the winter. His father would smoke his pipe and his mother would warm cider by the fire. For a moment Miguel let his thoughts touch the deep hollow in his chest. Then he closed it out.

Miguel looked up at his oldest friend. His armor bore the marks of countless battles fought in the endless war. His face was sad.

"I still have nightmares," Miguel said finally.

"SO DO I."

"Father Godefroy, no man should ever see the things that we've seen. No child should lose his childhood to monsters."

Godefroy nodded. "THAT IS WHY WE PROTECT THE PURITY OF MAN. THERE ARE HORRORS IN THE DARKNESS UNTOUCHABLE BY THE MINDS OF THE INNOCENT."

Miguel put another old book back into its home. He ran his fingers through his hair and looked up at his towering friend. "I will take the oath, Godefroy."

Godefroy smiled and his eye gleamed, "THERE IS MUCH BEFORE THE OATH, SANTANA."

Godefroy's words would prove true. Miguel took the Oath of Piety and joined the ranks of the Hopefuls. He spent the following months in the belly of the great bastion ship *Piety*, where conduits spread like spider's webs, connecting pockets of life across kilometers of near-empty decks with failed life support systems. The Keepers lived in this secluded section, past unlivable, ruined areas of the ship called the Barrens. Their temple was a small habitable space at the very bottom of the ship, which they called The Kathedral. During the first month, the Keepers forced the Hopefuls through grueling physical training. The Hopefuls ran through the rotting conduits until their lungs burned and they tasted blood, they lifted magnetic steel until their bones ached and their muscles tore, then they recited the mythic history of the Kingdom of Man and the lineage of King Nero, son of the Fifth-Father.

When their flesh was broken and their spirit was ready for enlightenment, the Keepers injected the sleeping Hopefuls with molecular machines they called the Black Blood. They said the Black Blood was a gift created by the first Blood-Father, Diomedes, to burn away the weakness of flesh. The true purpose of the ancient machines was the impossible task of rewriting genetic code, but millennia separated the Hopefuls from the DNA of the man these molecular machines were designed for, and machines are only machines. The microscopic surgeons flooded the young Hopefuls' bodies, operating with all the precision of drunken butchers. Amongst the screams and anguished cries only one human sound could be discerned, the chant of the zealous Keepers watching from the shadows:

"Purity! Purity! Purity!"

Pain was constant, but Miguel was not afraid. He alone did not scream when the machines burned his body. He sat in his bunk, dripping sweat, and thought of his mother. He thought of his failure, the internalized self-hatred of a sorrowful child. He thought of his father's teeth and grisly eyes. Godefroy's words were in his head. *There are horrors in the darkness...* Miguel thought of peace. He knew that his suffering did not matter. He clenched his fists. He was already broken. Nothing could change that. He beat his fist against his bunk and clenched his jaw. The pain was almost unbearable. He could feel the machines inside him, eating away at his body just like the Bugs. He swore to never let another child break as he had. Tears slipped silently down the twisted face of Miguel Santana.

In the morning, they learned that a boy had died in the night. The Keepers carried his warped, little body away with little ceremony. Miguel caught a glimpse of the mangled flesh as they passed his bunk. It was something terrible and lonely.

There were seven more deaths in the following week, and twenty other Hopefuls were carried away to become Keepers themselves. Few survived the coming weeks. Miguel stayed through it all. His body was in unending pain. His eyes, his nose, and his ears dripped thick, dark blood. His bones ached. In the final days he lost the ability to leave his bunk. The machines had devoured the muscles and ligaments in his legs and arms. Miguel never screamed. He never cried or wailed, even when his sight had gone and he was alone. After a month, his torment was ended and the Keepers carried what was left of Miguel away. His body was a tumorous skeleton.

The Keepers brought the boy to the 'o Loyos. They laid his ruined flesh before the High Father, Hurkan. The giant, armored priest examined the boy's flesh. He lifted Miguel's hollowed limbs, then held open the boy's eyes. They had become clouded and black, like the eyes of a dead crow.

"MIGUEL SANTANA, YOUR FLESH HAS BEEN MADE PURE. YET YOU ARE NOT SUITED FOR THE OATH OF STEEL."

Miguel's eyes rolled and he tried to speak, "no...i...can."

"YOU HAVE COME FAR. YOU HAVE GIVEN MUCH TO THE FATHER AND YOUR FAITH SHALL BE REWARDED. YOU WILL BE GIVEN THE GIFT OF DIOMEDES, BUT YOU WILL NOT BE MADE A BLOOD-FATHER."

Miguel tried to lift his wasted arm. He had no strength left in him. He wanted to yell and protest. He wanted to scream that he was ready that they were wrong. His voice was a whisper, "p...l...ea...se."

The High Father put his massive hand on the boy's forehead. "I CANNOT, MIGUEL SANTANA. YOU WOULD NOT SURVIVE. YOUR FLESH IS FAR FROM THE FATHER, TOO FAR FOR THE BLACK BLOOD. YOUR SPIRIT IS STRONG. IT HAS SUSTAINED YOU PAST THE FLESH, BUT THE JOURNEY IS LONG HITH. THE FAILURE OF YOUR FLESH IS NOT YOUR OWN. YOU HAVE COURAGE. WERE IT IN MY POWER, YOU WOULD BE A BLOOD-FATHER, BUT IT IS NOT. I WOULD NOT SEE YOU DIE. NONE MAY RETAKE THE BLACK BLOOD. IT IS A FORBIDDEN PATH."

Miguel let his head fall back. He had failed. Black tears slipped from the corners of his eyes. He whispered through withered lips, "I'm so.rr..y. mo..ther."

The High Father motioned to the Keepers and they carried the body of Miguel Santana away.

Miguel's body was left in the center of a dark room. Shadows hid the ancient walls and in despair Miguel stopped fighting the delirium burning his brain. He felt embraced by the void. He was ready to die. A man entered the room with thunderous steps. Great, white robes, dingy and stained with age, covered his giant, muscular form. He was a Healer, one of the few Blood-Fathers pure enough to command the ancient flesh machines. They were close to the Father and wore no metal armor. The Healer lifted Miguel's skeletal body in his arms and carried him to a dark place in the belly of the ship. There, he placed the boy on a medical table and shoved the long, barbed tips of electric wires deep into his flesh. When it was finished, the table retracted into a metal tube and the boy was sealed away. The Healer knelt on a prayer carpet beside the machine. He lit a single candle and began to recite the Rite of Healing. He spoke in the flat passion of religious servitude. The words were from an ancient tongue lost to the 'o Loyos.

Miguel slept in darkness while the Healer's machines restored his body. In the beginning his tortured young mind sought the comfort of his mother, and he dreamt of love and kindness, but as the days wore on, the sweet dreams of youth became twisted nightmares. In less than a week, the Bugs found their way into a child's paradise, and they ripped and tore through all of Miguel's memories. The boy screamed in silence. His imprisoned mind sought escape from terror more real than the dream of life. Death came in his nightmares, devouring his flesh. The boy's mind twisted back on itself, running from an all-consuming fire. He had been in the Healer's care for only a month. His awareness drifted through primal consciousness, like a cork tossed in the violence of a great ocean. If he could have known the passage of time, Miguel's mind would surely have broken in the chittering hell of his own dreams.

After four months, the ancient machines had done all that they could, and Miguel's body was sufficiently restored to warrant his release from the metal tube. Those few months in the darkness of the healing tube had seemed to Miguel centuries of torment. In that time he had endured an endless invasion of horrors, an endless cycle of death and rebirth. He had been feasted upon and had witnessed in dumb impotence the agonizing deaths of everyone he loved. He had relived the hellish visions of his youth until his soul had grown hard to the suffering. When Miguel awoke, the nightmares bled away from his conscious mind leaving him numb to the surrounding pain. He remembered his name and his life, even as the infinite horror of his failure slipped beneath the waves of his mind.

Physical pain pulled Miguel's attention to the moment. The Healer ripped the barbs from his flesh. Miguel said nothing. His flesh had been mostly repaired and his new muscles twitched under tight skin. The Healer smiled, encouraging Miguel to stand. Miguel pushed himself to the floor, only to have his hollow legs collapse beneath him. They were ruined. The Healer did what he could. He cut into the flesh of the boy's thighs and replaced much of his muscle and bone with steel. When it was over Miguel's legs looked like a nightmarish web of flesh and metal. He could walk again, but at the cost of constant pain. He was much changed.

Miguel was returned to his place in the library and made a Keeper of Words. Like the other Keepers, he hid his disfigurements under thick, black robes but, unlike most, he did not resent the Blood-Fathers. He blamed only himself. He knew that it had been his body that had failed. Miguel worked in silence, keenly aware of the deep scars on his body and the pain scraping in the bones of his mutilated legs. It was a permanent reminder of his failure, a permanent reminder of the cost of pride. With the exception of Godefroy, Miguel was ignored by the Blood-Fathers for the weakness of his body, and he was resented by his fellow Keepers for its beauty. Most failures were not allowed to be reconstructed by the Healer. Most were doomed to the horror of their failed flesh. Miguel was a hideous oddity.

In the end, the experience had not destroyed Miguel Santana, though it had destroyed the man he had hoped to be. Despite the pain of his failure, the great library was not an unhappy place for Miguel. He was troubled little and his knowledge of the ancient texts grew daily, but Miguel was haunted by his weakness. Sleep was no rest. It brought only terrors. The phantasms of his long sleep were always waiting in the dark, behind Miguel's once-beautiful eyes. He existed mechanically, without dreams or hope. And, like a forgotten machine, he longed for purpose.

"Brother Santana, it is good to see you return."

Miguel had been sorting books in the great library when the slimy voice shook him from his thoughts. It belonged to a fellow Keeper, his elder, Tonhg.

"Thank you, brother Tonhg," Miguel answered flatly. "Why have you come to the library this morning? May I help you find something?"

Tonhg was a broken creature. The Black Blood had left his body a twisted mess. He walked with a brace under his arm. His lumpy face was partially hidden behind the deep shadows of his hood.

"Brother," his lips curled into a cruel smile showing his rotted teeth, "I am come to give you warning."

"Warning, brother?"

"Yes. Though, perhaps, it is not needed," Tonhg's eyes burned into Miguel. "The Father does favor you, *handsome* brother." Tonhg pulled a long wheezing breath into his lungs. "The fool king has commanded an audience with the Loyos. He wishes to meet with your *friend*, Father Godefroy." Tonhg's voice was rasping slime, "*Piety* has been redirected. We should arrive at the core worlds by the Star-frost."

"Why does the king call for Godefroy, brother?"

Tonhg's voice briefly betrayed his hatred for Miguel, "**Father** Godefroy." Then, remembering his lies, Tonhg smiled. "We must keep these things in perspective, brother. We were not worthy, after all."

Miguel nodded, "Yes, brother. Now, why does the king call for *Father* Godefroy?"

Tonhg answered with his usual insight, "The king is his father's son, even in his old age. He wishes to command death, brother. The Blood-Fathers serve no other purpose to the Crown of Man."

"Does our sovereign not have his musketeers and his armies?"

Tonhg answered in a hushed voice, "Heretics, brother. If the king will not risk a messenger, then it is a Royal matter. You are young, brother, and would not know of this, but before this age there was a question of the king's legitimacy. A question, mind you, which I never entertained. His cousin, the old Lord Roanic, challenged the king's ascension. This was deemed an act of heresy by the old High Fathers."

Miguel nodded quietly, "I see."

Tonhg nodded with a false smile, "Of course. Blood will tell, *brother.*" The smile faded from his misshapen face and he spoke flatly, "There will be an inquisition. Do not be caught unaware."

"Thank you, brother." Miguel said turning his attention back to his work.

Tonhg limped away, leaving Miguel once more alone with his thoughts. He returned to the pile of books waiting to be sorted. Familiar pain shot through his bones as he walked. Miguel was aware of it, but it had long since lost its edge. His fingers moved across the smooth, old leather of the book in his hand,

and he brought it up to his nose. His eyes closed and he fought the great, terrible wound swallowing up his heart. The smell of books always triggered an old memory. Miguel missed his mother.

Chapter XVIII

The City of Rain

hree weeks later, the bastion *Piety* crossed into the great, purple nebula. The Throne of Man was three days into the core, where the young giant star, Meagres Prime, roared and its mighty orange light flashed through the star dust in royal hues. The Capital of Man, the Palace of Railocquires, was on the fifth planet, Thernos. The Star-frost had begun and the upper decks of *Piety,* being host to a legion of the king's men, were alive with celebration and song.

Miguel was hiding in his library. Music and laughter made him nervous. He preferred quiet. Miguel had been distracting himself by sorting through a pile of books waiting to be shelved. Many of the older books in the great library had not been read for centuries and sat on high, forgotten shelves, while others, like the books in the sorting pile, were read cover to cover by every inquisitive new soldier assigned to *Piety.* They all hoped to gain a piece of forbidden knowledge. They all left disappointed. Miguel glanced down at the book in his hands. It was bound in dirty, black leather and covered in jagged runes. He smiled. The book was, *Mysterious Blood,* and the Paternal runes read "Duck Soup". The sophomoric author had used the runes to add a sense of the arcane to an otherwise mundane recount of the eighth king of the Kahnk'uto dynasty of the K'ruukta. It worked all too well. *Mysterious Blood* was one the most handled and least read books in the library.

Laughter echoed from the long hallway just outside the library doors. Miguel closed his eyes in frustration, focusing on his breathing. Panic slid up his spine. He mastered it and stood straight. Just then, a soldier wandered through the door. He wore the dress uniform of Man, dark blue with broad cuffs of black. A small cape hung from his left shoulder. The soldier stumbled unintentionally, and shouted in hushed tones to Miguel.

"'Ay. Ay, Keppeh? Was dis? Is ida lia'bay? Eh?"

Miguel turned slowly around, and answered in his usual flat tone, "Can I help you, cniht?"

The soldier steadied himself in a poorly disguised attempt to hide his inebriation. Then he seemed to remember himself, "Sorry, yuh 'oliness an all o'dat." He bowed his head as an apology. "I uhhh....I neda book then."

Miguel nodded mechanically, "That is alright, cniht. This library holds many books, some *you* may read and some *you* may not."

The soldier scratched his scruffy face and nodded, "Oui, er...Righ, well I ned the... Bib...boloto Tomatos Padera."

Miguel sighed in frustration. "Do you possibly mean the *Biblio tou Aimatos tou Patera*?"

The soldier's eyes lit up and he nodded, "Oui, c'est, monsieur!"

Miguel shook his head and answered flatly, "You may not read that book."

"Wah?" the man answered. "Why no?"

"That book is reserved for the High Fathers alone. It is quite boring, and the runes are difficult to read. Why do you *require* that particular book?"

The soldier fidgeted for a moment. Outside, hushed laughter revealed his hidden friends. The soldier laughed himself and bowed as deeply as he could without falling over.

"I'm ve'y sorry, monsieur keppeh. It was only a joke. I was dared to come, and I know only one of your books."

The laughter grew from the hall and the other soldiers joined their friend.

The first soldier laughed, "You almost 'ad 'im, Jacqueire."

The second added, "Oui, Jacqueire. He was going to give it to you."

The third and final soldier was very drunk. He had wandered too close to Miguel and was artlessly attempting to peer at the face hidden in the shadows of his hooded robe.

"Why do you wear such things as this?" the third soldier asked reaching out to tug on Miguel's coarse robes. "Are you a monster? Did 'ey take you an' make you a monster or sumfin? I've seen sum o' yah keppehs. Nas'y business tha'. Noddin lef' afer they done yah."

Jacqueire, the first of them, tried to stop his friend from bothering Miguel. He pulled him gently back, apologizing again.

"Louis is very drunk. He is also very stupid. I am sorry, monsieur Keppeh."

Miguel nodded peacefully. "I understand his curiosity."

Jacqueire bowed again, "You are too kind, monsieur Keppeh."

As the soldiers made their way back to the door an armored giant blocked their path. He looked down on them and his grotesque head nodded kindly.

"GOOD EVENING. ARE YOU LOST?"

They stared up in silence. Jacqueire spoke for the group, "I am ve'y sorry. Oui, Monsieur. Yes, we are leaving, Monsieur."

"THEN I WISH YOU WARM AND MERRY BLOOD. RETURN TO YOUR CELEBRATIONS, FRIENDS. THE STAR-FROST WILL SOON BE AT ITS END. WE MUST ENJOY OUR PLEASURES WHILE WE CAN."

The soldiers slipped out as quickly as possible, nearly falling over themselves in the process. Godefroy chuckled within himself. His mind slipped under the current, down to the depths of forgotten years, to when he was human. He was once a brash young officer, and he had once been quite drunk at Star-frost, and a bit fighty. He remembered the broad, honest smiles of his long-dead friends. The memory touched sadness, and Godefroy left it behind. He let his gaze move over the cavernous library, suddenly aware of the years he'd spent looking at the things within this room without every actually seeing it. The library's main room was very much like an old cathedral with great stone arches and elaborate frescoes of heroes long dead. In the center of the room, surrounded by rounded bookshelves, was a ten-meter-tall statue of the first Blood-Father, Diomedes. His armor was polished marble and his fierce face gazed down with quiet strength. The ceiling above was painted with the final battle of the Bloodwar: The Allfather stood before his throne on the Great Ship with Tyran and Diomedes kneeling at his feet.

Miguel nodded to his friend then returned his attention to his books. "I haven't seen you in some time."

Godefroy walked to Miguel's table, answering his old friend, "I HAVE BEEN AWAY. THE LIBRARY SUITS THOU WELL, BROTHER."

Miguel smiled, "It does, brother."

Godefroy pulled his lips back into his own hideous smile, "I HAVE BEEN CALLED TO THE SERVICE OF OUR KING."

"I have heard as much."

"I EXPECT THOU HAVE. SUCH SECRETS ARE POORLY KEPT BY THE KEEPERS. I HAVE SEEN TONHG LIMPING ABOUT WITH GOSSIP IN HIS EYES. *PIETY* IS TO REMAIN AT THERNOS AS A DISPLAY OF UNITY AND STRENGTH."

"*Piety* is to remain, but what does our king wish with you, brother?"

Godefroy flashed his smile again, "THOU ART CLEVER, MIGUEL SANTANA. I AM CALLED TO DISTANT STARS. SOMETHING HAS BEEN LOST, AND I AM IN NEED OF A LIBRARIAN."

"A Librarian?" Miguel nodded, "Yes, I suppose you will be needing a book then? You'll need a Paternal grammar, no doubt, as well? I've seen some of your scribes' sloppy translations."

Godefroy smiled with his eye, "NO, BROTHER. I WILL NEED THOU. MY KINSHIP LEAVES IN FIVE HOURS. OUR SCRIBES DO NOT KNOW THE LANGUAGES AND LORE OF THE FIRST ONES AS THOU DOST. WE NEED A LIBRARIAN'S KNOWLEDGE. IT WILL BE DANGEROUS."

"I have petitioned to leave my library before."

"I HAVE HEARD AS MUCH FROM THE LORD LOWFATHER OF THE KEEPERS."

"Then you know why I am still here. You would trust a thin-blooded failure?" Miguel let his eyes fall to his books. "You have forgotten that my weakness has betrayed your trust before? **I** have not."

The giant's hand rested on Miguel's shoulder and Godefroy smiled. "NOTHING WAS LOST. NOTHING WAS BETRAYED. YOU ARE STRONG, MIGUEL. EVEN NOW, YOU STAND WHERE OTHERS HAVE FALLEN. MY PURPOSE IS SECRET." His booming voice lowered. "AS ARE MY DOUBTS. MY VISIT TO RAILOCQUIRES WAS MARKED BY ILL OMEN. IT HAS BECOME A DARK PLACE. OUR KING HAS BEEN SEIZED BY A MYSTERIOUS ILLNESS AND WITHERS ON THE BLACK THRONE. HIS BRAIN HAS SUCCUMBED TO PARANOIA, HE SEES ENEMIES AND SPIES ALL AROUND HIM. HE CLAIMS TO HAVE HEARD WHISPERS IN THE SHADOWS WARNING HIM OF A DARK TIDE. HE BELIEVES THEY FORTELL THE RETURN OF TYRAN AND HIS DAMNED PROGENY. I HAVE QUESTIONS, BROTHER, AND I TRUST ONLY THOU TO PROVIDE ME

140

WITH ANSWERS."

Miguel's heart filled with renewed pride. His eyes burned. He could feel tears building. He didn't know why. There was no reason to cry. He fought them back.

"I will not fail your trust again, my brother."

"OF THAT I AM MOST CERTAIN, MIGUEL SANTANA."

Miguel had little personal belongings and was quickly packed. They left in a little less than four hours, aboard an old bireme named *Rage of Aki'lus*. It was a short, snub-nosed vessel with thick, ablative armor and broad nacelles that housed the ship's over-sized engines. Their destination was less than five days travel aboard the swift vessel, a journey that would take a bastion months at full burn. The course was set for a large moon in the orbit of a distant gas giant. Six men were aboard the *Rage of Aki'lus*, five Blood-Fathers: Godefroy, their leader; Percival, their second; Rodian, Minos, and Basil; as well as a lone Keeper, Miguel. After their mysterious course had been laid, the ship's datahead was entrusted to navigate and the kinship was gathered in the hold. Godefroy stood at the front, before his brothers, while Miguel, segregated from his betters, watched from the doorway.

"OUR DESTINATION IS THE CAPITAL OF THE DUCHY OF ROANIC IN THE CITY OF SERA-PLUVIALE, LOCATED ON THE BORDER WORLD OF SANG-PERDU. SERA-PLUVIALE IS HOME TO ONE OF THE THREE ROYAL LIBRARIES AND HOUSES THE LAST GENEOLOGY OF NERO. IT HAS BEEN OUT OF COMMUNICA-TION FOR FIFTY-SEVEN DAYS. IN THAT TIME NO SHIPS HAVE BEEN DETECTED CROSSING THE BURLISH BORDER, YET IT IS THE BELIEF OF OUR HOLY KING THAT THE DUKE HAS FALLEN UNDER THE INFLUENCE OF NEARBY BURLISH FORCES, AND IS CURRENTLY ENGAGED IN AN EFFORT TO DISCREDIT THE ROYAL BLOODRIGHT AND DISTABILZE THE KINGDOM OF MAN. WE MUST NOT ALLOW THE BURLISH TETRARCHY FUR-THER ACCESS TO THE GNOSTIC DATAHEAD. OUR PRIMARY OBJECTIVE IS THE RECLAIMATION OF OUR KING'S PATENT OF NOBILITY. IN THE EYES OF NERO, OUR ONE TRUE SOVEREIGN, THE CITIZENS OF SERA-PLUVIALE HAVE PROVEN THEMSELVES POOR WATCHMEN AND THEIR DUKE A HERETICAL TRAITOR

TO THE CROWN."

"WHAT IS OUR SECONDARY OBJECTIVE? ARE WE TO DEPOSE THE DUKE?" hissed Rodian, the Blood-Father in sleek, red armor. He was leaning against a stack of steel ammunition crates. His thin, black hair was pulled into a tight knot at the top of his skull, and his thin, yellow eyes glinted as he spoke.

Godefroy answered quickly, "OUR SECONDARY OBJECTIVE IS TO DETERMINE THE FATE OF THE CITIZENS OF SERA-PLUVIALE AND RENDER AID WHERE NECESSARY. THE DUKE IS OF NO CONSEQUENCE. IF HE HAS BETRAYED MAN HE WILL DIE."

The other Blood-Fathers nodded.

"THE FINAL DATABURST SENT FROM THE SANG-PERDU RE-LAY BUOY WAS HIGHLY DEGRADED AND SEEDED WITH MASS JUNK DATA. WHAT LITTLE COULD BE READ CONTAINED HE-RETICAL ACCUSATIONS AND LIES."

Another Blood-Father spoke up, "AND WHAT DOES YOUR BLOOD TELL YOU, BROTHER?"

Godefroy was quiet for a moment, "MY BLOOD TELLS ME THAT I SHALL NEED THY STRENGTH, BROTHER BASIL."

Basil had a round, bearded face and bright eyes. He smiled, "THERE ARE NO HERETICS, ARE THERE BROTHER?"

Godefroy answered carefully. "OUR KING BELIEVES THAT THERE ARE."

Percival laughed lightly, twisting his strawberry red mustache, "WE DOUBT THE BASTARD KING. WHAT DO YOU BELIEVE, GODE-FROY?"

"I BELIEVE THAT THERE IS SOMETHING IN SERA-PLUVIALE MORE DANGEROUS AND INSIDIOUS THAN HERETICS."

A giant even by the standards of the Blood-Fathers, Minos spoke last amongst his brothers. He never removed his helmet and stood away from the others. He voice was the flat, grinding sound of old machinery, "THERE IS TAINT ON SANG-PERDU?"

The others waited for their leader's response.

Godefroy answered grimly, "THERE IS DEATH."

Miguel thought of his home, now ash, and could no longer hide himself in the shadows. He stepped into the hold and spoke."

"What is in the old city, Godefroy?"

The Blood-Fathers turned their eyes to him in surprise. Rodian was the first to speak.

"WHY DOES THIS WEAKNESS SPEAK WITH SUCH FAMILIARITY, BROTHER?"

Godefroy responded sternly, "THE KEEPER IS OUR BROTHER AND WE HAVE NEED OF HIS GNOSIS."

Rodian scoffed, "GODEFROY, YOU INSULT THE PURITY OF OUR BLOOD."

Godefroy answered flatly, "I INSULT NOTHING, RODIAN. MIGUEL SANTANA OUR BROTHER. WE WILL NEED HIS GNOSIS."

Rodian growled, "WE WILL SEE," then settled back against the steel crates.

Undeterred, Miguel spoke again. "What is in the city?"

Godefroy answered gravely, "MEN."

The swift, little bireme made the long voyage in short time. The Blood-Fathers remained in the main hold, planning strategy and recounting their last assignments. Miguel knew that he was not welcome. He kept to the lower deck, where he reviewed his grammars in quiet solitude. After nearly five days, the *Rage of Aki'lus* was approaching the moon, Sang-Perdu. The distant blue star, Charity, scattered light across a great storm raging over the northern continent. At its heart was the city of Sera-Pluviale, the City of Rain. The *Rage of Aki'lus* began to broadcast a broadband docking request at one megameter. There was no answer. Then, after long moments of silence, static crackled through their radios.

"Non....//.,l;' noo...nooniankst!" the signal fragmented. Static split mortal words. "Pidar! Pikst! Pidar!.....//,.' nooooonianksttttt." The signal fell and rose with one last burst, "pskt...found! Hello friend! Safe journey. Welcome to Sang-Perdu! Our.....syst....is down at....moment."

The signal, degraded by unknown means, finally fell to static. The Blood-Fathers had anticipated communication failure. They began their descent with little hesitation. As the ship broke through the atmosphere, lightning arced across the hull and thunder boomed around balls of screaming electricity. Rain poured from the sky in a constant torrent. Under the *Rage of Aki'lus* a vast city rose from the fog. It stretched out for kilometers in tall brick and cloudy brass. The ship landed atop a tall building in the city center, as close as possible to the location of the datahead. The hulking Blood-Fathers emerged from the hull, fully armored and armed to the teeth with massive, machined rifles. Miguel followed behind in his thick black robes, carrying a small flechettegun. The city was silent, save for the distant crashing of thunder and the slow, rhythmic pounding of rain.

Godefroy glanced down at a small glass screen mounted to the inside of his left gauntlet, then motioned to his brothers. In the distance, past the tight maze of stone streets and marble statuary, stood an enormous dome of metal and glass rising from Romanesque pillars of carven granite.

"THE DATAHEAD IS KEPT IN THE MUSEUM." Godefroy said pointing to the stone structure.

Minos looked out across the empty streets. "WHERE ARE THE PEOPLE?"

Percival lowered his rifle and put his hand on his brother's wide shoulder. He shook his head, "THAT IS A GOOD QUESTION, BROTHER. IT IS STRANGE. EVEN THE TAINT DOES NOT EMPTY A CAPTIAL CITY OF MILLIONS SO SWIFTLY."

Miguel looked out after them. The streets were empty. Small, two-man cars were scattered across the roads, abandoned. Trash littered the streets.

"What happened to this place?" Miguel asked Godefroy.

Rodian looked out across the city and answered, "MAYBE IT IS A PLAGUE."

The Blood-Fathers were largely immune to disease. Their armor fed them a constant stream of antibiotics, painkillers, insulin, anabolic steroids, and growth hormone. In short, they were quite hardy. Keepers were not. Godefroy glanced down at his friend.

"MIGUEL SANTANA, PERHAPS-"

Miguel interrupted him, "I will be fine, brother. My own trials have rendered my flesh somewhat resilient to adversity, and if it is airborne the rain will protect me. In any event, I shall exercise the strictest caution when interacting with the locals."

Godefroy nodded. "AS THOU WISH IT." Then he spoke louder, "FOL-LOW ME, BROTHERS. LET US NOT WASTE TIME."

They made their way down the squat, brownstone building's stairwell. It was thirty-seven stories to the ground. The Blood-Fathers moved at a slow pace, carefully judging each step, lest their great size and weight crush the stone beneath them. Miguel followed, pacing himself so as to remain well behind his armored fellows. The gun in his hands was oversized and would have been heavy for any normal man. Miguel hardly noticed it. The Black Blood and the Healer's machines had made him much more than he had been, and infinitely less. His body was tightly knotted with dense, powerful muscle, and his monstrous legs could propel him faster and farther than those of any mortal man. When they reached the ground Miguel was still fresh, in fact, he was not so much as winded. The stairs led out to a grand lobby with polished marble floors and a great arched ceiling. The tall windows ran with rivulets of rain and the blue sun's dull light poured into the empty room. Outside, gray clouds covered the city in a perpetual drizzle. As Miguel followed the Blood-Fathers out the door, he saw the unmistakable scars of gunfire across the stone walls. There had been a fight. Turning back, he looked across the room they'd just left. The subtle signs of battle were abruptly obvious. Then, he saw the broken runes drawn across the far wall, a message scribbled in the old tongue.

"They are lying"

The rain sputtered against Miguel's hood as he turned back. There was more graffiti, some half-finished, others hastily cleaned away by unseen hands. Most was written in the common tongue, but some, like the first, were painted in frantic runes. *"Lies" "Don't trust them" "GET AWAY" "NOT SAFE" "HELP" "HELP" Help. I'm afraid. I'm alone. Save me.* Miguel remembered the chaos of his burning home. He pulled away from those memories, still sharp in his heart. His eyes moved across the streets of Sera-Pluviale. From this lower vantage point the fate of the abandoned city was obvious. Every building bore small battle scars and empty casings peppered the streets. It wasn't the scene of an invasion or great battle. It was the small scale devastation of an urban gang-war.

Fearing the answer, Miguel asked, "Where are the bodies?"

Godefroy's voice called back in a booming whisper, "BE CAREFUL, BROTHERS. THE CITIZENS OF SERA-PLUVIALE REMAIN."

A single bullet ricocheted from tall Minos' helmet. Miguel dove behind an abandoned car. The Blood-Fathers stood incredulously. Moments of time passed like snapshots of war. It was Basil who moved first. He broke his long silence with a laugh and, raising his enormous, machined rifle to the source of the shot, tore away tons of stone. His weapon roared and metal poured from the rotating barrels like a river of molten steel. When it was over he had leveled the entire final story of the building. No one could have survived. No one should have.

There was only the sound of falling rain and steam hissing from the slowing revolution of the red-hot barrels. Miguel listened, glancing over the car. The peace was short-lived. There were shouts in the distance, and then gunfire came from every direction. The Blood-Fathers returned fire. Their guns tore through the old stone like it was glass. Entire buildings were reduced to rubble. Bullets fell on the Blood-Fathers from a thousand ghosts, and the metal ran down their thick armor like drops of rain. The entire city block was laid to waste. Then, the gunfire died.

The rain drizzled on. Minos held his machined rifle at the ready. Moments passed in quiet rain and the firefight was over.

"SO THERE IS TAINT ON SANG-PERDU," Rodian said at last.

Godefroy adjusted his rifle and answered, "PERHAPS. YET IT IS UNLIKE ANY TAINT I HAVE KNOWN. THERE IS SOMETHING FALSE ABOUT THIS PLACE. LET US MOVE QUICKLY."

"WHAT ABOUT THE KEEPER?" Rodian asked.

"I'll be fine," Miguel answered rejoining the Blood-Fathers.

Percival laughed, "OF COURSE, *LITTLE BROTHER*. JUST DON'T FALL BEHIND. I WOULD **HATE** TO LOSE YOU TO THE WOLVES."

Miguel hid a sardonic smile under his dark hood. He felt like a wolf himself, hiding in blackest wool. The strength of his ruined legs could support nearly as much weight as the laughing Blood-Father's, and he was faster still. He could leap meters into the air and run with all the speed of an indefatigable machine, yet Miguel carried such strengths as weaknesses. His experience with the Black Blood had left him stronger than any man alive, but he knew in his heart that he was a failure. His flesh was weakness. The smile vanished. Miguel hefted his heavy flechettegun to the ready with quiet ease and followed silently behind the others.

Sera-Pluviale was an old city, constructed in an haphazard boom of urban expansion. Narrow streets and ancient roads came together in jumbled messes. Now, the city was crumbling. Entire streets were blocked from the debris of collapsed brownstone buildings. Godefroy led them through the maze of heavy rubble. They crossed two more blocks and then the ghosts descended again. Bullets came from a dozen shadowed points, striking them from every angle. Miguel found cover in the old Gothic entryway to the city's subtransit system.

Godefroy raised his fist, signaling his brothers to hold. Behind the scattered cacophony of harmless gunfire a low roar echoed through the rain-flooded streets. Thunder shook the distant clouds. Godefroy turned his attention back to his brothers.

"INSIDE," he commanded quickly, charging toward the subtransit.

Miguel felt another shock wave of thunder ring out. Then he heard a closer crash. This shock wave hit with force of a cannonball, knocking him off his feet. Miguel dug his hand into the stone wall and fire ripped through the surrounding street. Miguel pulled his robes around his face. The heat was suffocating and the flames burned at his exposed skin before dying in the rain. A shell had struck Minos in his chest. The giant had fallen down on one knee. His armor was sharply dented and scorched, and his great rifle was destroyed. At the end of the road was a remnant of the duke's army; a group of armored vehicles were rolling toward them.

"MINOS?" Basil shouted through the smoke and steam.

Percival stood with his machined rifle raised, ready to assist his brother.

Minos, the giant, rose to his feet and roared. His voice was the battle-cry of war. It was the sound of infinite, unnatural rage and it grated Miguel's nerves like the acrid sound of nails screeching across a chalkboard. Minos was angry. The rain hissed, rising as steam from his burned armor. Then he charged toward the mobile cannons. Minos's massive legs ripped through the thick pavement, propelling him forward in a hail of debris and with the unimaginable force of a wild freight train. Another cannon fired. The shell collided with Minos, engulfing him in flames. Yet, the force did little to slow his approach. One after another, the cannons fired. Two hit. The roars of the mad giant echoed through the high walls and he charged ever forward.

Godefroy shouted to his remaining brothers, "WE CANNOT FIGHT HERE. TO THE SUBTRANSIT. THERE ARE MORE COMMING."

Gunfire came from all around them again. Sera-Pluviale was alive with the shadowed cries of madmen. As they descended the rain-slick stairs into the dark tunnels a heavy metal crunch told them that Minos had collided with the first mobile cannon, and the low whine of tearing steel told them that it hadn't stopped the enraged Blood-Father. Percival followed reluctantly.

Luggage and scattered tickets lay about the floor. The walls were marked with the same violent graffiti that stained the rest of the city. At first glance it seemed to show a scene of panic and fear, but the debris was too few for a city of millions. As they traveled deeper into the station Miguel came to realize that Sera-Pluviale had fallen slowly. There was no sudden collapse. There was no surging migration or rush to safety. The lifeblood of the city had not simply bled away, it had been poisoned. Miguel looked again at the graffiti on the walls. The strokes were smooth and thick. The runes had soft, rounded lines. They were not like the others. They were the crude finger-paintings of children.

"Safe" "Home" "Trust"

Miguel spoke first, "What happened here?"

Godefroy answered flatly, "THERE IS TAINT HERE, MIGUEL SANTANA."

Miguel remembered *The Survivor Chronicles*, an old account of the Bloodwar he'd found hidden away in the archives. It was filled with tales of men driven mad by contact with Khenosmen, men who turned on their family and blood. Through some terrible means they had come to worship the Khenosmen. It twisted their bodies into writhing abominations and hollowed their minds. This was known as the Taint. To men like Miguel, cloistered away in their libraries and studies, the word had lost much of its meaning. In the long, gray march of years inhuman tragedy had become literary fascination. Miguel had never truly believed the exaggeration of those personal accounts, for men like him the truth always fell in the middle. He believed now.

"How is that possible?" Miguel asked.

Rodian was last coming down the stairs. "THE TAINT IS IMMORTAL, WISE KEEPER. OUR BLOODWAR LEFT CORPSES ACROSS THOUSANDS OF PLANETS. KHENOS FLESH CORRUPTS EVERYTHING IT TOUCHES."

Miguel looked to Godefroy. "Then there *is* a corpse on Sang-Perdu?"

Their leader was busy checking the computer on his wrist. He answered flatly, "THERE ARE VERY OLD THINGS WITHIN THE FORGOTTEN RUINS OF MAN. THINGS THAT MUST REMAIN BURIED. I BELEIVE THAT WE WILL FIND OUR ANSWERS IN OUR SOVERIGN'S MUSEUM."

Basil laughed grimly, "OR PERHAPS THE BASTARD KING *WAS* RIGHT." His voice was thick with sarcasm, "WE MIGHT ASK MINOS IF THOSE SOLDIERS'VE GROWN BURLISH MUSTACHES."

Another explosion shook the ground above them, followed by the echo of a metallic scream.

"Will Minos be alright up there?"

Percival shook his head, "IT WILL TAKE MORE THAN MADMEN TO STOP A BLOOD-FATHER LIKE MINOS." Then he turned to Godefroy, "THERE MAY BE NEWLY TAINTED IN THE TUNNELS."

Godefroy nodded, "YES, BROTHER, AND THEY MAY BE SAVED IF WE REACH THE SOURCE IN TIME."

"AGREED."

Basil added quickly, "THEN LET US WASTE NO MORE TIME HERE. THERE IS LITTLE DOUBT THAT THE TAINTED SUSPECT OUR DESTINATION."

At the bottom of the stairs was a large subterranean terminal with a high, vaulted ceiling. Hanging chandeliers flickered with low, amber light, illuminating the painted tiles of the ceiling. Mirror-polished stone shimmered as stars scattered across a stunning nightscape of deep-blue tiles swirled with vibrant hues of purple and orange. The effect was that of an impressionist painting.

A train had stopped dead in the station. The doors were left open. The cars were empty. According to Godefroy's map the deep tunnels ran straight to the museum, but his map did not reflect the derelict condition of the City of Rain. Without proper maintenance the overflow pumps had let the rain flood the soft ground below the streets, destabilizing the tunnels. Everywhere was the steady drip of water as it slowly filled the lower tracks.

"There are men in the darkness," Miguel said softly when the last of them had reached the tunnels at end of the terminal.

Crouched shadows moved along the walls of an adjacent tunnel, their footsteps sloshed on the damp floor as they tried to hide from the noisy intruders.

Basil nodded, "YES, BUT DO NOT LET YOUR NATURAL COW-
ARDICE LEAD YOU TO THE MURDER OF CHILDREN, KEEPER.
THEY ARE IN NO CONDIDTION TO HARM YOU. THEY ARE
NEWLY TAINTED OR THEY WOULD BE WITH THE OTHERS.
THEIR MINDS ARE FEAR. THEY WILL HIDE IN THE DARKNESS
FOR NOW."

"There is little in the libraries concerning the actual nature of the Taint,"
Miguel offered in a whisper.

Godefroy raised his hand again, "THE MUSEUM EXIT IS JUST
AHEAD."

An explosion rocked the ground above them. The ground, softened by the
flooding rains, broke through the thick concrete above and tons of soil and
stone collapsed into the tunnel.

"GET DOWN." Basil warned.

The group stood against the walls, waiting out the following tremors.
Godefroy once more checked his map, then signaled to an adjoining tunnel.

"THERE'S A CONNECTING TUNNEL. QUICKLY."

Miguel followed closely behind. As they dashed through the waterlogged
tunnels they passed the crouched forms of the newly tainted citizens of Sera-
Pluviale. Women and children alike were huddled in the cold dark. Their faces
were hollowed and pale, and their skeletal bodies shook with fear. Scattered
corpses floated amongst the dying. They had either starved or had been too
weak to survive the Taint taking hold in their brains. The Blood-Fathers ignored them. They marched swiftly past. The farther into the tunnels they
traveled the thicker the floating corpses became. Dozens became hundreds,
hundreds became thousands, and Miguel knew where the population of The
City of Rain had gone. The smell was terrible, and overwhelming. Then, in the
deepest darkness of the web of tunnels Miguel heard the rough cry of laughter.
A man had stood among the weeping others and his whispers had grown to
hoarse cries.

"Invaders! Usurpers! I **know** you! I hear you! You can't have my children! I
won't let you have my sons! Not my sons! My name will not die! You won't take
my home!"

Then he looked across the bodies of his fellows and, seeing Godefroy and
the others, his eyes grew wide with terror and pride. His weak, broken body

stumbled toward them shouting accusations.

"Monsters! Give me back my children! You killed my wife! I'm all alone. Give them BACK!"

His cries died when he reached Basil, and the Blood-Father lifted the tainted man by the head and crushed it in his massive hand. The ruined body fell to join the others bobbing amongst the sewage.

Rodian followed behind Miguel and, seeing the horror on his face, offered, "IT WAS A KINDNESS. WHEN THE TAINT TAKES THE MIND IT IS TOO LATE. WE MUST HURRY."

They followed Godefroy through kilometers of maze-like tunnels. The lights grew progressively dimmer, until they were sloshing through total darkness. The Blood-Fathers could see in the darkest places, but Miguel could not. He followed cautiously, relying on the dim floodlight attached to his flechette-gun. Only Godefroy knew where they were headed. Miguel was lost. It seemed as though they had doubled back twice and were moving in a circle. Miguel's light drifted endlessly over shaking bodies pressed tight against the leaking walls of the cracked tunnels. Finally they reached the terminal nearest the museum.

Godefroy raised his fist, signaling them to stop. He pointed back at Miguel and he switched off his light. They fell silent. Ahead they could hear footsteps. Lights suddenly crossed along the wall. A voice shouted above the clatter of rifles being readied.

"Don't let them get through. This is our home. Do you understand, men?"

Quietly, Godefroy handed his rifle back to Percival.

Above, in the cavernous terminal, the soldiers answered their commander, **"Yes, sir!"**

"The Curator wants peace. His bones are too old. We will not lose our city to these invaders. We've lost too many wives, too many sons and daughters. **We** will survive. We have survived. Where the others died in their weakness, we rose from the dark! We have seen past the veil of human hubris. We must protect our Father! Those *monsters* are the right hand of the Liar! The Usurper! They were sent here to kill us and everyone we love. Theta lost those damned half-men at Blackfoot Station. There were heavy casualties, but it **ends** here. There **will** be peace. But that peace can only come with death! You are the strongest. You are my brothers. We will not die here! We **will survive!**" His men cheered. "They'll be coming this way, and we must not fail! We will eliminate the alien threat! For the Father!"

"For the Father!"

Their cheers grew to a roar. Suddenly, Godefroy leapt out. His great fist tore through the little commander in the middle of his speech. The poor fellow's voice broke in frantic screams as the horror of his death reached the last parts of his human mind, and the cybernetic monster rose before the soldiers to his full height. Their commander's body twisted in agony from the great gory grip of the Blood-Father.

"YOUR GOD HAS LIED TO YOU," Godefroy's deep voice rumbled, "YOU ARE MY BROTHERS AND I SHALL SEND YOU HOME." With his last words, Godefroy tore the body to pieces and threw the ruined corpse to the ground.

The soldiers screamed in terror, firing blindly. Invincible Godefroy walked to the next man like the spirit of death. Basil and Rodian joined the melee. They came charging from the darkness like demons, brandishing their rifles like clubs. Miguel's heart was thundering in his chest. The tainted soldiers fired in every direction. Their screams broke with their butchered bodies. Finally, Miguel followed the others, leaping into the terminal. Percival stood at the back, his own rifle trained at the terminal entrance, watching for the others. At least twenty armed men still stood between Miguel and the streets above. The Blood-Fathers were ripping them apart with detached savagery when, suddenly, a group of tainted men screamed to the right of Miguel, charging toward him. Rodian leapt across the room crushing the body of one and grabbing another two by their legs. He lifted them into the air and smashed them against the floor. Blood sprayed across the tile, and the other soldier leveled his weapon at Miguel. The Keeper's flechettegun blasted through his torso, ripping it to strips of gore. Blood splattered everywhere in a red mist, coating Miguel's robes and mixing with the others'. Screams echoed through the cavernous room as the tainted men were slaughtered.

"ENOUGH. WE'RE NEAR THE END." Godefroy's voice called back when the last man fell, "GO."

The streets ran with rain and mud. High above the city, lightning flashed through the never ending storm in chains of brilliance. The thunder echoed in a broken crescendo. Godefroy was the first to emerge from the dark tunnels, the others followed. The surrounding buildings were filled with tainted men. Heavy machine guns were mounted on the third floor of each fortified building, and armored vehicles stood guard before the museum. The giant, domed building looked like the carapace of an ancient monster. It was at the center of a small, marsh-like park. Dozens of tall trees grew upon tentacle-like roots, like dark cypresses above a foreboding swamp. Four flights of stairs led to the main entrance placed between two ancient trees. A tall, thin man stood there under a black umbrella. He was dressed in a dark red waistcoat and a long, brown cape that fluttered in the wind. He walked toward them with slow, deliberate steps.

Miguel spoke in hushed tones, "Why don't they attack?"

"IT IS NOT THE NATURE OF THE TAINT TO BREED AGRESSION. THEY WISH TO ENLIGHTEN US," Godefroy answered.

"I don't understand," Miguel shook his head. "Brother, I am covered in the blood of these men."

Godefroy look down at his friend. His heavy, mechanical growl hid the sorrow of his heart, "I TOO AM COVERED IN THE BLOOD OF MEN." Godefroy looked back to the singular figure coming toward them. "FEAR DRIVES THESE DAMNED SOULS, MIGUEL SANTANA. THE TAINT DOES NOT CORRUPT BODIES. IT CORRUPTS MINDS. THIS ONE WILL REJOICE IN HIS ENLIGHTENMENT. HE WILL TAKE US TO THE SOURCE. WHEN IT IS DONE WE WILL SAVE THE PURE AND SANG-PERDU WILL BURN."

Chapter XIX

The Rotted Man

iguel held his gun tightly. Mad men had descended from the shadows and were watching from the rooftops and windows. They were not saviors. They were invaders. Now, they stood waiting in the rain for an escort.

Godefroy spoke quickly, "MIGUEL SANTANA, I WILL DEAL WITH THE SOURCE OF THE TAINT. THOU MUST FIND THE DATAHEAD AND ASCERTAIN ITS AUTHENTICITY. THAT IS OUR PRIMARY MISSION." Then he detached the portable computer from his wrist and handed it to Miguel.

The computer was thin and heavy, like a rectangular plate of steel. Miguel wiped the rain from the screen and hid it away in his robes. The tall, thin man was coming closer. His smile was broad and deep. He nodded in thanks to the Blood-Fathers.

"Thank you for not attacking us." He smiled nervously from under his umbrella. "The Duke sends his regret. I am the curator of the museum. I have told my fellows that we should have nothing to fear from the King of Man. We are no heretics. We know our place," he chuckled lightly. His eyes were tired. "The others here have turned to madness! They believe that the Crown means us harm. It has been chaos."

"WHAT HAS HAPPENED HERE?" Godefroy asked gently.

The thin man smiled deeply again, "That's...that's why. My brother, my glorious brother, we have found the Father!"

Godefroy nodded in mock surprise, "HAVE YOU BROTHER?"

The Curator continued in confused excitement.

"We did not believe it ourselves at first, but now we know. We know how important this is. He is the Undying Lord. Come. I will show you, brother.

The Father sleeps within. The Duke of Roanic is watching over him." The Curator motioned for them to follow and led them up the steps to the museums entrance. "It must have been months ago. There was a massive earthquake. It demolished a ridge south of the old city, by the hydroponics compound. That's where we found the sarcophagus. It was in rock thousands of years old. We took it back to the museum and began to clean it, and well...i-it opened quite unexpectedly. Inside were, well what we thought were, mummified remains. He was very large. Bigger than even you, brother. Much bigger. We put Him in the display of the Old Ones and He was quite popular. But He wasn't, or rather He isn't, a mummy. We know now that it is the Father. We have to keep Him safe. It's important that nothing happens to Him. He needs to be safe."

Godefroy answered, "THIS IS A PRECIOUS FIND INDEED."

His words seemed to reassure the Curator. The tainted man's shoulders relaxed. Relief washed over his nervous face. "Thank you, brother. This is important. The Duke understands that. The others are scared. They think...they have crazy ideas. They whisper about *conspiracies* and *invasions*. We've been tearing ourselves apart. It's...it must be our fault. We didn't know when we opened it, but..."

Godefroy spoke again, "WHAT HAS HAPPENED?"

"There must've been a curse on the sarcophagus, a virus or some kind of living bacteria. The disease spread so quickly...and so slowly. We didn't know until it had taken hold. The others think it was a plot to take the planet. The resources on Sang-Perdu are substantial, nothing compared to the Norlian Moons, but....we have diamonds and we have tungsten. I told them that our king would never...It's not a plot, is it?"

"NO, BROTHER. IT IS NOT."

The Curator smiled and nodded his head, "Yes, yes....eh good. I mean of course not, but good."

They had reached the entrance to the Museum. Two ancient trees twisted toward the heavens, rain dripped a natural rhythm against the thick leaves and crouched gargoyles watched from the alcoves of a great stone arch reaching toward the Gothic sky. Two armed guards stood at the open doors, waiting for the Curator. The twitch of their zealous eyes betrayed their fear at the sight of the Blood-Fathers.

The Curator signaled the duke's guards. They cleared to the sides of the doors so that they could pass. "This is one of the oldest structures on Sang-Perdu. It used to be one of only seven scriptoria in the kingdom. We have deep ties to our first king."

They entered into a large, open room. Statues and relics sat protected behind walls of glass. The storm danced through the transparent ceiling, high above. On the far wall a massive oil painting depicted the settlement of Sang-Perdu. The impressionistic swirls showed the landing of an early mining ship on a volcanic world. The ship was the *Fafnir*, the first to land on Sand Perdu. Later, a disaster would claim the lives of the crew and of the first Lord Roanic. Lava rained down in the background of the painting and rain fell from the lightning-filled sky. It was titled, "The Pilgrimage of Stone". It was the first time Miguel had ever seen the original. He permitted himself to stare briefly while the others hurried past. Their footsteps echoed through the room as they passed swiftly though to another room, a long hall filled with surreal portraits. The brush strokes of madness painted men in screaming landscapes. Miguel felt a knot forming in his heart. He knew that it was all going to burn. Ahead, the Curator was rambling to Godefroy, pleading. Though the poor fellow could not admit it to himself, he knew they were all going to die.

Miguel suddenly caught the eyes of a painted martyr. A nude man was grappling with a monster. His foe was a grotesque combination of man and computer; a face screamed through cathode rays, and vacuum tubes twisted up from under diseased skin. It was titled "Man in Memorium". Miguel felt the pain aching in the core of his legs. He felt the twisted cords of flesh stretched across the cold metal beneath his robes. He knew that he was not the man.

"WE ARE ALL MONSTERS, BROTHER," Rodian's raspy voice pulled Miguel back from the abyss, and they began to follow after the others again. "WE MUST BE. WE ARE ALL BORN IN TRAGEDY. MY WIFE DIED IN THE RAID ON NOMAD. FIND THE DATAHEAD."

Miguel pulled Godefroy's computer from his robes. It showed the datahead nearby. He spoke to Rodian, "It's thirty meters below the next room."

"I WILL ACCOMPANY YOU. THE OTHERS GO TO PURIFY THE TAINT. WE WILL SECURE OUR SOVERIGN'S PATENT OF NOBILITY. YOU WILL DETERMINE ITS LEGITIMACY."

Ahead, Godefroy and the Curator had entered a rounded atrium at the rear of the museum. It had an open design with solid pillars supporting the tall ceiling. Light filtered through the outer, glass wall. It looked out across a swampy forest. In this room were the broken relics of a forgotten war.

Miguel could hear the Curator's voice echoing across the cold marble. "Most are still within the main gallery. They don't want to leave. I don't blame them. I prefer His company as well. He's so very warm."

Then the others followed into the central gallery. Miguel and Rodian waited behind. Rodian looked around at the exhibits. The shards of ancient weapons gleamed in their displays. Miguel glanced down at Godefroy's computer.

"THERE IS AN ELEVATOR BEHIND THIS WALL," Rodian said, running his hand along a section of wall beside a broken sword.

Once certain of the position he slammed his fist into the wall and tore through it, prying open the secret door beyond. Miguel followed him into the elevator. The lift took them straight down to the vault. The door was sealed with runes from the paternal alphabet. They read "*ETERNAL BLOODLINE, FATHER OF OUR FATHERS.*"

"CAN YOU OPEN IT?" Rodian asked.

"Maybe," Miguel answered, looking over the runes. "It requires an answer. Eternal Bloodline? Father of our father?"

Miguel thought for a moment. "Diomedes." Nothing happened. "Roanic." Nothing. Then Miguel remember the painting of the doomed mining ship. "*Fafnir.*"

The runes glowed with blue light and, with the sound of grating metal, the heavy door slid open. Inside, a large, orange globe descended from the ceiling, illuminating a large room filled with relics. Miguel checked Godefroy's computer.

"It's on the back wall."

Rodian ducked low and navigated his massive form through the man-sized door. Once inside he rose to his full height. Miguel followed. The walls were lined with tall shelves filled with various treasures. Larger antiquities filled the rest of the room. Abbadon's hammer rested in the corner, encased within a humming shell of rusted iron. Beside the hammer, a long thin sword named Starkiller, floated in a shower of sparkling light. A long blunderbuss leaned against another wall. Miguel ignored the shining weapons of old. Hidden away in the shadows was a locked cabinet sealed with the king's mark.

"Rodian. It's here," Miguel nodded.

The giant stood behind him. "THAT IS THE SOVEREIGN'S SEAL."

Miguel nodded again, "Yes. It is."

Then his fingers danced across the seal in practiced rhythms, hitting the hidden pressure points in the proper sequence. The seal broke, and the door opened. Inside, arranged carefully, were the severed heads of a dozen men. They were very old, and the necks had been sealed with silver and gold. The skin was pulled tight across their ancient faces and stretched back across patches of metal. Their eyes had been replaced by input connecters. Each bore an elaborate series of tattoos. One of these dataheads held the Patent of Nobility for the Crown of Man, a genealogy which could be traced back for thousands of years. The value of this patent was beyond estimation.

There had been seven patents which recorded the lineage of Man, and all but one had been lost in the uncertainty of Nero's ascension. At the time it was argued that these patents were unnecessary, as only those of the purest blood could sit on the Black Throne and command the divine power of the sovereign. Yet, many of the Nobles refused the practical application of kingly right, demanding proof of Nero's lineage. Among these Nobles was the former Lord Roanic. The Kingdom was on the verge of civil war when the lost datahead was found. It was this last remaining patent that had been the one piece of irrefutable evidence supporting Nero's claim to the throne of Man. It had ended the civil war before it had started and cemented Nero's place as king. The former Duke of Roanic was declared a heretic and imprisoned in the Château d'Soleil Rouge. To further ensure peace, the datahead was then entrusted to the duke's nephew, the father of the current Lord Roanic.

"IS IT THERE?" Rodian asked.

Miguel took one last look at Godefroy's computer, "I don't know."

"EXPLAIN?"

Miguel held each datahead in his hands and examined the faded ink covering their flesh, until he found the king's patent. His fingers traced the lines. They were very convincing, but Miguel was well acquainted with the work of the old scribes. The careful lines marking the gnostic datahead were too straight, the scriver's marks too sharp. It was, without a doubt, a forgery. Yet, age had faded the cruel ink and had worn the tight flesh. It was legitimately over a century old. Miguel's fingers touched the royal seal burned into the forehead. Perhaps it *was* the gnostic datahead they had been sent to retrieve.

"Rodian, are you certain that the king's patent is on Sang-Perdu?"

"WHAT?"

"Are you certain!"

"I KNOW ONLY WHAT GODEFROY HAS TOLD ME, KEEPER. CAN YOU NOT IDENTIFY THE DATAHEAD?"

Miguel felt the leathery skin in his hands. The forgery was as old as Nero's reign. Miguel checked Godefroy's computer once more. The scriver's sign matched. It was the *king's* patent.

"This is it." Miguel said finally, his voice wavered for a moment.

Rodian reached out, taking the datahead in his hand. "IT IS GENUINE?"

"It is," Miguel lied. He would have much to discuss with his old friend on the journey home.

Rodian secured the datahead to a metal clip on his waist. "LET US RETURN TO GODEFROY."

Godefroy and the others had entered the center atrium. It was an open, circular room, like a large arena. The domed ceiling stretched to the very top of the building, and was capped with beautifully etched glass so that the storm above bathed the whole room in waves of gray light. The room had been emptied of the exhibits to make room for the tainted men and women crowded around, kneeling in prayer. The Duke himself stood before a massive, makeshift throne of piled relics. Seated on this throne was an equally massive figure, the corpse of a Khenosman.

It was five meters tall, with a grossly exaggerated frame. It had broad shoulders and thick, ape-like hands. Its skin was a deep charcoal, like the empty sky, and it was covered in a million thick, black hairs which writhed like seaweed under violent waters. The head was broad and tall with monstrously enlarged features hidden behind a wriggling black mass of hair and beard. Two large antlers twisted up from his dusky forehead like a wild, forest crown. The corpse was severely emaciated and obviously ancient. The rotting flesh was stretched tight over knotted cords of thick muscle and black sinew. The ceaseless movement of the monstrous hair had the disconcerting effect of an aura of unquenchable life or eternal undeath. Yet, despite these unsettling features, the corpse of the fallen Khenosman possessed the unspoken nobility of an old blacksmith or woodsman.

"My Lord Duke, the king's men have arrived," the Curator said gently as they entered.

The Duke had been whispering to himself and cleared his throat as he turned around to face the Blood-Fathers. He had a pale, noble face with short, white hair and a thin beard.

"I have been expecting you for some time. Though, you are a bit late," the Duke of Roanic smiled. "My city is lost." He put his face in his hands, briefly laughing to himself. "They weren't strong enough, I think. Or maybe I was...No. No. It doesn't matter what I say now. You're here to kill the heretic. It's alright. You can't help it, can you?"

Godefroy and Basil stopped just before the duke. Percival stood guard by the door, his machined rifle ready. Godefroy spoke.

"I DID NOT COME TO KILL THOU, LORD ROANIC."

"Really?" the Duke smiled desperately. "Why are you here? We have found the Father...but He can't really be the Father. Why **are** you here?"

"WHEN DID THOU TOUCH THE CORPSE, LORD ROANIC?"

The Duke returned his gaze to the great, alien cadaver. "I don't remember. It was a lifetime ago. There was a gala for Valaria Tortuga...Did you know that our king lied to us? It doesn't matter really, but he is not our sovereign. Of course he isn't. He wasn't from Earth was he? It was lost. I have known for a very long time. No, no it *isn't* lost yet."

Basil stood close to Godefroy and spoke in his lowest voice, "I HAVE NEVER SEEN A KHENOSMAN COPRSE INTACT, BROTHER."

"NOR HAVE I, BASIL."

"ITS INFLUENCE MUST BE ASTOUNDING."

"YES, IT HAS BEEN."

"YET, THESE MEN ARE DOCILE. HOW LONG HAVE THEY BORNE THE TAINT? THE TUNNELS ARE FILLED WITH THE CORPSES OF NEWLY TAINTED, THIS WAS NO...OUTBREAK, BROTHER. HOW HAVE THESE MEN SURVIVED?"

"What are you talking about?" Lord Roanic asked, turning back quickly, his voice suddenly sharp with paranoia.

Godefroy spoke once more to the duke, "LORD ROANIC, THY PEO-PLE ARE SURPRISINGLY WELL KEPT. WHO PROVIDES FOR

THEM?"

"Ah, yes!" The Duke smiled. "Good of you to ask...Our Father provides...it is strange. I don't know how. I am not hungry. I...I have not eaten in days." Then, the Duke let his attention drift back to the corpse. "You see I just...had to come back. I was afraid before. I didn't know. There's something...about Him. I love Him."

Godefroy spoke quickly to Basil, "BROTHER, THIS TAINT MAY BE BEYOND WHAT WE HAVE SEEN. I BELIEVE THERE IS MORE KHE-NOSFLESH AT THEIR HYDROPONICS COMPOUND. THE HAPLESS FOOLS HAVE BEEN EATING IT. THIS CITY HAS BEEN FED FAT ON THE FLESH OF THE PANAERUS. WE MUST INFORM *PIETY*. THIS TAINT CANNOT BE ALLOWED TO ESCAPE SANG-PERDU. RETURN TO THE *RAGE OF AKI'LUS*. I WILL REMAIN HERE AND PURIFY OUR LOST CHILDREN. I WILL BURN THE CORPSE WITH PATERNAL FIRE UNTIL NOTHING REMAINS."

Basil stood his ground. "I CANNOT LEAVE YOU, BROTHER GODE-FROY. THERE IS GREATER MADNESS AT WORK THAN WE HAVE SEEN."

"I FEAR THAT THOU ART RIGHT, BASIL. BUT I AM IN NO DANGER," Godefroy reassured his friend. "WE CANNOT KNOW HOW FAR THIS TAINT HAS SPREAD. IT IS STRONGER THAN ANY I HAVE SEEN. WE WILL NEED THE ENDURING STRENGTH OF A BASTION. PRAY THAT IT ARRIVES IN TIME TO SAVE WHAT FEW LIVES MAY STILL BE SAVED."

Basil finally relented with a nod. Then he detached two heavy canisters from his armor and gave them to Godefroy. "TAKE MY FIRE, YOU WILL NEED IT. LOOK TO THE SKY IN THREE HOURS, BROTHER. I SHALL RETURN."

Godefroy nodded, "GO, BRAVE BASIL. I HAVE WORK TO DO."

Then Basil ran. His massive legs moved with incredible speed. Miguel and Rodian were stepping out from the hidden elevator when Basil charged past them, his heavy boots tearing into the marble floors. He burst through the front door in a rain of metal and glass, and within moments he had cleared the entry and leapt onto a towering brownstone. His clawed hands tore into the wall as he propelled himself upward with the grace and power of a great bear.

Then Miguel and Rodian came upon Percival. He stopped them with a raised hand.

"YOU HAVE THE DATAHEAD?"

Rodian answered quickly, "IT IS AUTHENTIC."

"GOOD," Percival nodded. "GODEFROY SPEAKS WITH THE DUKE."

Then Miguel and Rodian saw the enthroned corpse.

"IT IS WHOLE?" Rodian asked astonished.

Percival kept his guard up. "IT IS, RODIAN. OUR BROTHER, BASIL, HAS GONE TO INFORM, *PIETY*."

"Have the Blood-Fathers never found an intact body?" Miguel asked.

Percival looked down his rifle and answered, "IT IS VERY RARE, KEEPER. KHENOS FLESH IS RESILIENT, YET THE BLOOD-WAR WAS TERRIBLE AND LONG AGO. EVEN THE HIGH-FATHER HAS NEVER SEEN AN INTACT CORPSE."

"What does this mean?"

Percival answered, "ALL KHENOSFLESH IS DANGEROUS, KEEPER."

Miguel could hear the Duke's voice. It was shaken and hollowed. The Duke gazed up at the corpse of an ancient monster, a broken old man with hands trembling.

"Why is this called taint?" the Duke mumbled flatly. "My mind is so much clearer. It was muddied before...I see to the very bottom of history. There was one man. He was no god. The Black Son was not the curse. How have I never known this? He was no god!"

Godefroy's voice boomed through the atrium like thunder, "THOU SPEAKST HERESEY!"

This shook the kneeling hoard from their complacent madness long enough for them to wail in sorrow. The Duke fell to the floor frightened and silent. His eyes were wide and deep. Then he mumbled, "b-but how can truth be heresy? If there was one then he was no god. He cannot be..."

Godefroy stepped toward the cowering Duke of Roanic. His false kindness fell away. His thunderous voice roared, "HERESY IS NOT MERELY A WORD OR AN EMPTY THOUGHT TO LEAVE THY MOUTH WITH SUCH CARELESSNESS. HEAR ME, FORMER MAN. HEAR ME, SCRAP OF HUMANITY. EVERY LIFE IS A PRECIOUS THING.

FOR ALL THE MIGHT AND ALL THE GRAND MAJESTY OF THE STARS THEY ARE NO MORE THAN LIFELESS SPHERES OF GAS TWISTING IN THE FIRMAMENT. THEY CANNOT SMILE AND THEY CANNOT LAUGH. YET, THY CHILDREN ONCE DID. THY CHILDREN LAUGH NO MORE AND THEIR SMILES ARE BROKEN THINGS. THOU WAST ENTRUSTED WITH THEIR LIVES. THY PEOPLE ARE DYING, DUKE. THEY CAN NO LONGER DREAM AS THEY ONCE DID. THEY CANNOT CREATE. THEY CANNOT SMILE. THEY ARE NO LONGER ALIVE. THEIR VERY MINDS HAVE WITHERED. THEY ARE RUINOUS AUTOMATONS OF FLESH AND BONE. THAT IS HERESY. THE TAINT IS NOT YOUR GROWING AWARENESS OF CABALISTIC KNOWLEDGE OR THE DISCOVERY OF AN IMAGINED LIE. IT IS NOT A THREAT TO THE SU-PREMECY OF MY BELIEFS. THE TAINT IS COMPLACENCY IN THE FACE OF DEATH AND TORTURE. THE TAINT IS AN AF-FRONT TO THE MIRACLE OF LIFE. THY CHILDREN COWER IN THE DARK AND STARVE IN **AGONY** WHILST THOU PRAYS TO A THOUGHTLESS CORPSE. THAT WHICH THOU LOVES ABOVE ALL ELSE IS A MONSTEROUS DELUSION. IT IS THE DELUSION OF THY CONTINUED EXISTENCE. I WILL FREE THOU AND THY PEOPLE FROM YOUR BLIND ARROGANCE."

The Duke began to cry. His voice was empty. He knew he was about to die. Tears dripped down his face. "You are a creature of regret! You are the slave of bigots and liars! I am sorry. You will die in darkness! I die **knowing** that I am nothing." Then, for a moment, the Duke's eyes were blank, and it was as if he was inside of himself screaming. His mouth whispered, "I don't want to die."

Godefroy crushed the Duke's skull under his massive boot. Then, all around, the crowd of tainted rose to their feet, their hearts filled with fear, and they ran. They ran like beasts caught in the huntsman's gaze. They trampled each other in a flood of humanity, rushing toward the exit. Percival and Miguel moved away from the door. Rodian stood firm. He raised his rifle and fired. It ripped through them all, tearing through men, women, and children like paper dolls. They died screaming.

Miguel screamed in shock, "Rodian!" before remembering that it was a kindness, that they would die anyway.

Godefroy held in his hands the two large canisters Basil had given him and approached the body of the Khenosman. The Blood-Father pulled a thin metal rod from the center of each and prepared to throw them on the corpse. But in a flash of inhuman speed the corpse-body of the Khenosman grasped Godefroy by the wrist and lifted him into the air, crushing his arm with wild strength. The canisters of paternal fire crashed into the wall behind them in a jellied mass, igniting the melting stone in hellfire.

"I SMELL THOU, BETRAYER. THY CORRUPTED FLESH OFFENDS **ALL** OF MY SENSES."

The Khenosman's voice was an otherworldly rasp, like the sound of a dying god. It echoed through their bones and flesh in notes of vibrant terror.

Godefroy screamed in the behemoth's grasp, reaching for the pins on the other canisters attached to his waist. The armor on his wrist had been crushed and had pierced the flesh underneath. Blood ran from the wound as his tremendous weight tore the flesh. Godefroy's arm twisted off as the Khenosman threw him to the ground.

Despite being half-rotted, the monster's speed was incredible. Strips of flesh hung from its bones, showing the movement of the long strands of muscle and sinew. Miguel's heart was filled with primal fear, fear he had not known since the abrupt death of his childhood when he had watched his home burn. For the moment he was paralyzed. His flechettegun shook in his hands. Rodian roared. He and Percival aimed their machined rifles at the abomination. Its eyes opened revealing rotted orbs of black and gold.

"NO," The behemoth rasped, "DIOMEDES, THOU SHALT NOT ESCAPE. I CAN FEEL THY COWARDLY MIND SPINNING LIES LIKE VICIOUS WEBS. **ACCURSED LIAR!** YOU HAVE NO CLAIM ON THE STARS!"

Then with its powerful limbs, the ancient man tore great hunks of stone from the floor and hurled them at the two Blood-Fathers. Percival moved swiftly out of the path. Rodian fired his rifle. It poured metal from the barrel, splitting the stone into smaller missiles. They struck the Blood-Father with great force, shattering his helmet and knocking him off balance. Rodian fell to his knees. Before he could stand the Khenosman was upon him. It tore the helmet from his head and lifted his body into the air with savage grace.

"BEGONE, CHILD OF ROT!" it roared furiously.

And the Khenosman smashed the Blood-Father's head against the ground, splitting Rodian apart. Percival fired his long rifle at the murderous creature. The metal ripped through the great corpse, causing it to drop Rodian's body.

"NO! WICKED CHILD!" the Khenosman spit, rushing toward Percival.

The Blood-Father shouted to Miguel, "GET TO GODEFROY'S BODY! NOW!"

Then he was grappling with the monster. It grabbed his rifle in its great hand and tore it from his grasp. Miguel finally shook himself from the terror in his heart and ran. Percival flailed in the Khenosman's grasp. He fought with all of his strength, twisting and kicking. The Khenosman grabbed his leg and his arm and prepared to tear the last Blood-Father in half. It pulled hard. Percival's armor cracked and bent. He screamed as the bone twisted and he felt his leg begin to go. Then brilliant fire covered the monster, and it howled in pain, dropping Percival. Godefroy was alive.

"IN THE NAME OF THE ALLFATHER, THOU WILL DIE, DE-MON!"

Godefroy's helmet was gone. A large gash had been torn through his remaining eye. It wept blood over his armor. His metal eye glinted in the stormy light. Held in Godefroy's remaining arm was one of the museum's relics, Glumthur the Flæshæteres, a long, tungsten spear tipped with a rapidly moving, diamond chainblade.

The Khenosman recovered from the terror of fire, and its necrotic eyes locked on the defiant Blood-Father, filling with rage. It threw out its arms and roared as hellfire flared at its back. Then the two giants charged across the room. They met in thunder. Godefroy thrust Glumthur through the Khenosman's invincible flesh and twisted back. The Khenosman howled, clawing at Godefroy. But the Blood-Father leapt back and thrust forward once more, ripping great gashes in the black flesh of the behemoth. Miguel watched, frozen in his cowardice, as Glumthur cut into the monster over and over. For a moment it seemed as if Godefroy would triumph. Until, he thrust too deeply with his shoulder and the Khenosman stepped into the cutting edge. The ancient monster pushed the diamond saw through its own body, clawing madly toward its foe. The Blood-Father realized his error too late, and the Khenosman wrapped one of his monstrous hands around Godefroy's upper arm, just below the joint in his armor, and with the other hand gripped his shoulder. Then, with a savage twist, it snapped the metal and tore the limb from Godefroy's body. Dark blood poured from the wound like vicious ichor. Godefroy cried out, falling to his knees, completely disarmed.

Glumthur remained in the monster's belly, still clutched in the Blood-Father's mighty grip. The Khenosman grabbed Godefroy's body and its great mouth opened farther than should have been possible, stretching into a hideous maw as it prepared to swallow the Blood-Father whole. A shot from Percival's rifle tore through the monster's flesh, fragmenting the monstrous humerus and nearly severing its arm. The remains hung uselessly from its shoulder. The still quite alive Percival sat against the wall in a pool of dark red blood. The Khenosman's eyes were wide. It roared, grasping dumbly at the ruined limb. Rage filled those eyes. Then, with its remaining arm, it pulled Glumthur from its grisly abdomen and, shaking loose Godefroy's ruined limb, limped toward Percival.

"**WICKED CHILD!**" it rasped.

Miguel ran to Godefroy's body. Percival raised his rifle again, aiming for the monster's head. He fired. The shot cut through the Khenosman's shoulder, shattering the glass roof above him in a shimmering explosion. Before he could ready another shot, the Khenosman pierced mighty Percival's chest with the spear. Percival gasped, as blood filled his mouth. Lightning flashed in the sky, and rain fell through the gaping hole in the roof.

"MIG-uel SANtana," Godefroy spit, "PATerNAL fire. BURN the KHenos. resilient flesh. CAn not fail."

Then Miguel watched as Godefroy's face lost tension and fell still. The man who had saved him from a thousand terrible things, the invincible champion of his darkest nightmares, his only friend, was dead.

"**COWARDLY DIOMEDES**," the Khenosman rasped, turning its attention to the last living soul in the room.

It left the ruined corpse of Percival behind and began limping toward Miguel. Godefroy was dead. Miguel felt anger overtaking the fear in his heart. He saw a frightened child, at the brink of terrible darkness, saved by an angel of mercy. He remembered falling asleep against the Blood-Father's armor as Ignias burned. He remembered the smallest kindness shown to a desperate child. Anger in the moment of his friend's death was like a spark in dry wood. It set his tortured soul ablaze. Years of impotent rage and unanswered sorrow burst forth from the prison of Miguel's repression. They surged to the surface in pure nihilistic fury.

Miguel's eyes saw Godefroy's last canister of paternal fire. He detached it from his armor and gripped his flechettegun tightly in his other hand. He knew he was going to die. He didn't care. He wanted to watch the world burn. He would laugh in the frosty fires of the last hell. Rain dripped cold, soaking his robes.

"WHY DOST THOU COWER, LIAR!" the Khenosman shouted. "ART THOU NOT BRAVE, BETRAYER!"

Thoughts burst through Miguel's consciousness as an unbroken torrent of pain. He tried to respond and only managed a mad roar. His body shook with rage. Suddenly, he charged at the monster. The Khenosman grabbed for him, but Miguel's powerful legs launched him high above the ancient corpse. His feet landed on its rotted shoulders and he steadied himself on the monster's antlers, firing the flechettegun at its face. The shrapnel ripped deep into the monster's flesh, tearing apart the putridity of a mad cyeball. Great gouts of coagulated blood ran from the lacerations, and the Khenosman howled in anger, clawing at its wounds. Miguel jumped again. He landed behind the monster, firing at the backs of its legs. The Khenosman stumbled. Then, it turned back and grabbed for its little foe again. Miguel's legs propelled him into the air. This time the monster was ready. In a flash, it snatched Miguel's leg and squeezed. The incredible might of the Khenosman crushed his flesh. Bone popped and cracked, but, beneath the weakness of his flesh, the metal webbing held strong, keeping the leg together. Miguel fired his flechettegun wildly into the joint of the Khenosman's arm. In response the savage corpse beat Miguel against the floor. The shock briefly stunned the Keeper, and his grip failed his weapons. The flechettegun and incendiary canister were scattered across the room.

"NOW, DIOMEDES, I AVENGE MY BROTHERS," the monster rasped.

It raised him high in the air, preparing to smash his skull against the stone beneath them. Miguel's hands tore at the rotted arm. The monster's hairs writhed against his touch and the flesh ripped away in black handfuls of pestilence.

"**TO HELL WITH YOU DEMON!!!**" a mighty voice roared from the heaven's above.

Minos had fought to the end against the remnants of the lost army; then he had fought his way to the museum against uncounted hordes of mad men; and upon seeing his brother, Basil, burst from within the old building, he had climbed to the top, and, standing on the rain-slick edge of the ruined roof, his eyes had fallen on the broken bodies of his murdered brothers and his heart roared in inhuman rage. Now, in his mighty anger, Minos launched himself into air, driving downward with his massive, armored elbow. His overwhelming momentum collided thunderously with the Khenosman, slamming the behemoth to the ground. Sang-Perdu rocked in the deafeningly terror of shifting earth, and all around them the stone shattered, leaving behind a broken crater. Miguel was thrown clear of the impact. Then Minos was on his feet. He grabbed his larger opponent by the leg and twisted his body, throwing the Khenosman with all of his strength.

"YOU WILL DIE, MONSTER!" Minos cried out.

The Khenosman landed hard, its ancient bones cracking against Sang-Perdu. Then the Khenosman found its footing and launched itself at Minos. Minos dodged its grasp and snatched onto its dangling arm, now slick with blood and rain. With a savage twist he ripped the arm away and tossed the ruined flesh to the ground. The Khenosman roared, striking back with its remaining arm. It caught Minos in the chest, further denting his armor and knocking the enraged warrior to the ground. Then the Khenosman stomped downward, attempting to crush the Blood-Father within his own armor. The stone cracked under Minos's body, but the armor held. Annoyed, the Khenosman limped back to the body of Percival and pulled the spear from the Blood-Father's ruined flesh.

Miguel wasn't dead. His right leg had been nearly crushed, but it held together. After being thrown away, his broken and bruised eyes had fallen on the lost canister of paternal fire. He wrapped his cold fingers around it and struggled to his feet. The flesh and bone of his leg were ruined. He ignored the pain. Miguel's numb fingers found the metal fastenings on his heavy, rain-soaked robes. He let the dark cloth fall from his frame and stood naked in the gray light of the stormy sky. Miguel's body was covered in a patchwork of deep scars, the mark of his failed flesh. His muscles stretched tight under the skin. For a moment Minos's eyes caught Miguel's and the Blood-Father knew what the Keeper was about to do. The Khenosman turned back to them, brandishing

Glumthur in its remaining arm.

Minos pushed his body to its feet and, throwing his ruined helmet to the ground, he roared, "NO MORE. YOU WILL DO NO MORE HARM. THIS ENDS **NOW**!"

Minos's face was young, and beautiful. Long, blonde hair cascaded down his bloodied armor like corporeal sunlight before it darkened in the eternal rain. The Khenosman charged toward the Blood-Father, and Minos planted his feet, readying himself. The Khenosman thrust forward with the spear and Minos parried the mighty blow with his armored wrist. Then the Khenosman twisted back and stuck again. Again, Minos parried, this time following with a right cross. He drove from his legs and his fist collided with the monster's sternum, cracking the steel-hard bones. The Khenosman was pushed back, but the spear caught Mino's leg and the diamond blade cut through his armor, chewing deep into the flesh beneath. The Khenosman seized upon this chance and drove forward with all of its weight, pushing Glumthur's screeching chainblade through to the other side. Minos stumbled back, the spear firmly lodged in his thigh. He grabbed the ancient shaft with his hands and snapped it off, breaking invincible Glumthur in half. Blood ran from the wound.

The Khenosman stared into the Blood-Father's cold, blue eyes, and Minos stared back, each keenly aware of the other's waning power.

"I AM NOT YOUR ENEMY," the Khenosman rasped. "I AM ONLY A GHAST, MINOS."

"DO NOT SPEAK MY NAME, DEMON."

"WE WERE THE CHILDREN OF GOD. PRECURSERS TO PER-FECTION."

"Shut up!" Miguel shouted, interrupting, "SHUT UP! You were never any-thing more than monsters!" He stepped gently over the broken bodies of a mother and her child. They were only two against hundreds more.

"**THOU DOST NOT SPEAK, DECEIVER!**" the Khenosman spat in righteous fury.

The Keeper charged toward the abomination. His blood was boiling with nihilistic fury. Red painted his vision. Despite the pain gnawing at his brain, the metal underlying his broken legs propelled him forward like a machine. As he neared the monster he pulled the pin from the canister of paternal fire. The Khenosman drove forward with its remaining arm. Miguel dodged it with near preternatural reflex. His powerful legs struck down at the joint and he felt the monster's bone finally snap. The Khenosman howled. Miguel launched himself into the air, jamming the canister into the fiend's gaping mouth. He landed hard and kicked off again with his good leg, driving his other up into the Khenosman's jaw. The canister exploded. Liquid fire filled the monsters throat, bursting out through its mouth, setting its beard ablaze and burning up into its skull. It howled and cried in an inhuman cacophony of pain. The Khenosman fell to its knees, clawing impotently at its face as the fire burned its brain. The monster's eye sockets glowed red and fire bubbled up from within like molten stone, and the Khenosman collapsed.

Rain fell on the ruins of Sera-Pluviale. The city had fallen to an ancient madness brought back to the world of Man. Millions were dead, millions more were dying in the dark. The rain hissed against the unquenchable flames engulfing the Khenosman's corpse. The false-king's patent lay intact beside Rodian's mangled corpse, coated in tainted blood. Miguel stared at the sky. It was gray. Lightning arced through the clouds, briefly painting the atmosphere in shades of blue. It was empty and he was far away. His leg was ruined again. He had felt the metal webbing give when he had landed. His memories screamed against his practiced stoicism. He fought them all. The air was crisp and acrid, like an old swamp. Miguel missed his mother's smell. He missed his books. His breath left his mouth in long puffs of steam. Minos limped over to the body of his brother, Percival.

"IT'S NOT DEAD YET. KHENOSMEN HAVE A REDUNDANT QUASI-BRAIN," he said taking Percival's paternal fire.

He limped back to the Khenosman corpse and shoved the canister into its broken chest. Then, he pulled the pin and limped over to Miguel. Fire burst forth. Suddenly, the seemingly dead monstrosity hissed and its remaining limbs began to flail and convulse wildly.

"*HATE. PAIN.*" the monster gurgled from its burning neck.

After a moment it ceased moving and there was little left of the ancient corpse but ash and cinderous bone.

"THANK YOU, KEEPER," Minos offered to the Keeper, looking down at Godefroy's body. His blue eyes seemed endless. Godefroy had been his friend.

Miguel looked back to the weeping giant and answered, "You're welcome."

Then he retrieved the king's patent from its place at Rodian's side and together they waited for Basil's return in the City of Rain.

Chapter XX

Planetfall

ire broke through the purple sky in waves of orange and red, parting the endless storm. Meteors were falling on the Grave of the Lost, and the high mountains trembled as black obelisks crashed into ancient stone, throwing frost high into the thin air and shaking a lone figure hidden in the snow. She was wrapped in long, thick furs that obscured her form. Her eyes were shielded behind carven bone.

Dreams had led her to this strange place. Every night, she saw a man, small and terrible, with a face like a beast. She knew him as an ancient spirit of the void, as an incarnation of the Immortal. So when night came, and the purple sky glowed with lesser light, she left the warmth of the Peoples' mountain halls. Her mother had not believed her, and she had protested every night as her daughter left for the frigid wastes of the high valley. Now, the girl smiled. The Lost had fallen, Fury of the Liar's Moon, Old Son. The lone figure scrambled over the thick snow. She knew her dreams had been true.

Steam rose from the melted snow around the still-hot meteors. She hesitated for only a moment before wading into the bubbling waters. Warmth spread through her legs. She knew they would be cold later. Still, she made her way to the first coffin and pressed the release latch. More steam came from the hissing seals. A dead man was slumped within. She wasted no time in wading to another. And another. The water around her legs had already begun to cool. She waded to another black obelisk. Cold was swelling in her. She pressed the release. Steam hissed around her and then she saw him. At first he seemed to be another corpse. His body was swollen and deeply bruised. Then, his chest moved slowly. He was alive. She saw his hoary face and her heart swelled. She knew that face. Her savior had fallen. She lifted the small, heavy man in her arms and carried him away.

Chapter XXI

The Mourning Star

rson had survived. He had fallen to the storm-wrapped planet and, though broken and half-mad, he had survived. He slept for weeks while alien hands tended to his ruined body. Machines and medicine from the old world worked tirelessly to pull him back from the precipice of death. In his fever dreams he mumbled old words that none but the elders could understand. Orson's lips whispered revenge and regret. He mourned lost love and a life not lived. He spoke of a dead man, a brother deeply missed.

When Orson finally awoke he found himself on a large, soft bed under a pile of warm furs. His eyes opened, and he saw the high ceiling of a large, elaborately-carved, stone room. Warm light came from a small, flickering shade held by a tall, six-armed statue in the corner. The walls were hung with elaborate rugs depicting scenes of ancient meadows and forests. On a tall table sat Orson's silver satchel and the rest of his possessions, including the last written work of Gaston d'Noël and his starchart. His tattered rags had been neatly folded and left beside his little prisoner's cup from the château. Orson threw off his furs and discovered that he was naked. A peculiar smile crept across his face, and he laughed silently. He had survived. He felt immortal. Then, he sat up and his feet dangled from the over-sized bed.

Orson tried to find his thoughts. His memories seemed like a surreal dream. It was harder to find them than before. He saw the Château d'Soleil Rouge orbiting a great, stormy planet. Then his fingers touched the scar on his head, and he knew that his memories were real. He tried to ignore the unpleasant memory of his lost friend. He chose to focus on the anger. The desire for revenge was an anchor to his lost soul.

Orson took in a deep breath and suddenly it was too much. Pain shot through his chest and oxygen flooded his brain. His ribs had been broken, but the air was thicker here than he was accustomed to breathing. He was light-headed. Orson forced himself to take shallow breaths and then he dropped down to the floor. His feet touched a warm rug spread across the center of the room. He stretched his thick muscles, feeling them tighten under his skin. Walking was difficult. His legs felt springy and light. Orson stumbled to the table. He steadied himself on its edge and examined his things. Nothing was missing. An alien voice came from the next room. It was deep and melodious, but unmistakably feminine. It drew Orson's attention. Another thick rug had been hung across the opening to act as a door. In his time at the Château d'Soleil Rouge Orson had learned many things, some from the Old Man and some from the château itself. Among these skills was the ability to move silently when he wanted. He did it without thinking, quietness having become a part of his nature. He carefully pulled back the rug draped across the opening, and his eyes grew wide in disbelief. Two pale creatures sat on large cushions, conversing in a strange tongue. One faced the door, the other did not. They were wrapped in fine blue and black robes, and they were both very tall, though the first was larger with a broader torso. He had a long, thick nose, and his black eyes were partially hidden behind long, white eyebrows that fell down his face, joining a long, white beard. The other was slender with a shaven head, and even from the back Orson knew that she was beautiful.

She was talking. "Altar, De ne-mu hwe tautau nim sleb dere peth."

The elder's face was like a reflecting pool, empty of all but what was put into it. He answered in a deep, calm voice like the sound of old stones, "Ye tautau nim pomt. Se ye thide no. Ye seo must hirth."

The girl answered quickly, "De ser ne-sarvamth."

The elder nodded with a hint of hidden knowledge, "Ye ser modang ye ne-hwash."

The eyes of the elder met Orson's and the pale giant nodded. The younger female turned quickly back and Orson saw her face. It had the smooth lines of matronly maturity and yet, under little white tufts of hair, the black almonds of her eyes showed the young, unbroken spirit of their master. Her skin was without pigmentation and so white as to be almost translucent. Orson could see the blue blood coursing through the pale flesh of her face. She was blushing. Her eyes were not directed at his face.

It was then that Orson remembered that he was naked. He pulled on the rug to hide himself, but being unaware of the raw brutality of the strength granted him by the crucible of the Château d'Soliel Rouge, he tore the metal hangings away from the thick rock. His heart caught at the surprise of it and he stood almost sheepishly, pulling the destroyed rug around his nakedness.

"Et es alright," the elder nodded. "Do not be afraid." Then he looked to the girl, and, seeing her blushing face, he laughed lightly, "Alazaved, ne-boleth to sdar."

She turned away quickly and, rolling her beautiful eyes, flashed the elder a look of smoldering embarrassment.

Orson tried to find his own voice. He spoke softly and slowly.

"Where am I?"

The elder pulled on his long beard as if pondering exactly what to say. "Ye are un the wurld. Ye are un Arzvertun," he said finally.

Orson thought for a moment. "Arzvertun? I fell? I was in a grave." Then he remembered the fall from hell, and it seemed to him like a dream from a past life. "I did fall...I thought I was going to die."

The elder chuckled, "Ye are ne dead."

Orson nodded, "I know. I-I have to go. I promised a friend. I have to..." Orson tried to let his mind catch his tongue. "Is there any way out of here?"

"Certainly. Ye are not a prisoner. Ye may go as ye hwash."

Orson looked around the large room. The walls were hidden behind hand-woven rugs. "Where are we?"

"We are en the mountains uf Loth Keivon built un the ruins uf the planet Arzvertun, un uf the last settlements uf the People."

Orson relaxed slightly. "How did I get here?"

The elder smiled, nodding to the girl, "Ye were brought to the People by Alazaved. Sao has been dreaming uf yer coming."

The girl bowed her head politely to Orson. His heart raced and for a moment he did not know why. He had not seen a woman in many years. Even hidden beneath the heavy robes, Orson could see the feminine curves of her body, and his mind roamed the sumptuous beauties of her form, creating images of depravity. He stumbled through the words he was expected to say.

"Uh...Th-thank you."

Alazaved looked to the elder, and he repeated Orson's words, "Se sam, Yeo dimg."

Her face blushed again and she shook her head, "Se deo ne-dimg. De gith...De ne-mu, altar."

The elder smiled kindly at her. "Yeo chelt ir sdall. Yeo illdams ne-gim mu." Then he chuckled softly, "path des then ye mu nach de ne-mu."

Alazaved nodded, "Yeo dimg, altar." Then she pushed herself to her feet.

Orson was stunned by her size. She was nearly three meters tall. Her robes hung loosely from her muscular body, clinging to her powerful glutes and thick hips.

The elder nodded, "Hwir ye go?"

She glanced back at Orson briefly before answering, "De to dere nadir go."

"Alazaved, go," the elder smiled. "Sao hwall sarbezd to ger se hwogen."

Alazaved nodded, "Yes."

Orson's eyes drifted along the curves of Alazaved's body, catching the sway of her back as she left. The elder's black eyes caught Orson and cast him a questioning look.

"Watch yer self, Old Son. Even ye may not be nim enough fur sao."

This time Orson blushed. "I'm sorry. It's just...It's been a long time since," He cleared his throat. "I'm sorry."

The elder smiled, "Et es alright." Then he gestured to the cushion where Alazaved had been sitting.

Orson wrapped himself in the rug, pulling it around his shoulders. He sat on the cushion and asked, "Who is she?"

The elder tugged absently on his eyebrow and answered, "Sa es Alazaved. Sa found ye at the Grave uf Sdars."

"She's the one who found me?"

The elder nodded, "Yes. Sao wæs having dreams. Sa saw ye. Nobody believed Sao. Even sara mothur thought sao mad with moon dreams."

"Moon dreams?"

The elder dragged his palm over his long beard. "We have a crooked moon, Old Son. Et hides behind the sky. En the time uf Puth War et rained destruction upon our world, nearly destroying all life. The arth shed the sea and the great storm swallowed the sky. Many uf us died. We that survive are the lost children uf the Allfather. We do not forget the old promise. So from time to time the moon does speak to the People. Et whispers deceptions en dreams."

Orson let his eyes fall on the space between them. He remembered the graveyard of ruined ships surrounding the Château d'Soleil Rouge. They were the remnants of a great war.

"I need to get off of this planet," Orson said finally.

The elder nodded. "De know ye do, Old Son."

"Do you have a starship of some kind?"

The elder thought for a moment, as if debating some piece of hidden knowledge.

"Little survived the old wurld," he answered finally, "yet there es such a thing. Et es long hith, buried en the ice and snow uf the old city. Et will be a difficult journey, but, when ye are ready, Alazaved can show ye the way."

Orson nodded, "Thank you."

The elder smiled. "Ye ne need thank me, Old Son. Et es the will uf the god."

Orson leaned forward. The elder's face seemed changed.

"The will of God?" Orson asked.

The elder answered, "Et es the will uf **a** god. The People believe en the duality uf creation. The wurld es the creation uf two great powers: the Will uf the Creator and the Life uf the Dreamer. The history uf all wæs written by the Creator at the birth uf the universe. The Dreamer es the reader of fate. Life breathes creation. We are the children uf these gods, Old Son. Though we live en the dreams uf Life, we cannot change the Will uf fate. Et has been written en the text uf Creation. Even now the Dreamer sustains all uf existence."

Orson pulled a ragged hand thoughtfully down his beard and furrowed his brow. "That is an interesting thought," he mused, "But which is the greater power, the Creator or the Dreamer?"

The elder smiled, "Power es illusion, Old Son. Each god must rule en turn. Ef the Dreamer wishes, Fate may be changed, but en so doing the Dreamer must become Creator. Yet, the Creator es limited. The book uf Creation es empty without the life-breath uf the Dreamer."

"Then, life is still the end result of fate?" Orson asked coldly.

The elder tugged on one of his long eyebrows, "Yer Fate es already written, Old Son. The Dreamer may swim through the currents of time and may meditate briefly on yer past or yer future, but en this moment ye are here and now within the Dream uf Life. Ye are held en the mind uf the Dreamer. Now en this moment ye exist, as do de."

Orson pulled tighter on the rug clinging to his shoulders. He thought about everything he'd lost. He thought of the long, miserable years spent in a dark prison. He thought of time without hope. And he thought of the absolute cruelty of fate. There was no reason for his suffering. There could be no fate. Orson's heart burned with the need for purpose, for revenge.

"No," he said, finally, "I was taken from my home. I lost everything. I was betrayed and imprisoned for crimes I did not commit. I spent years in a cruel and unjust hell. My only friend died, alone and in pain. I cannot accept that. Fate is a lie. My life has not been written," Orson growled triumphantly.

The elder's smile was deep and kind. He laughed softly to himself.

Orson asked roughly, "Why do you laugh?"

The elder answered, "Because de am an old man, and de had forgotten the fire uf youth. Rest, Old Son. Ye chest bones are still bruken. Ye can speak uf revenge tomorrow."

Chapter XXII

Arzvertun

n the end Orson spent months with the People, waiting for his broken body to recover. It was a quiet place, a place of peaceful reflection. The People were survivors of a great catastrophe that had claimed much of their planet and engulfed the rest in the endless storm. They lived in vast underground city-states carved from the heart of the old mountains. These great halls were illuminated and warmed by the volcanic power of the deep earth. Long channels of flowing magma filled the cities with life. Though his first impression had been of a primitive, tribal race of giants, Orson soon discovered that these children of Arzvertun possessed technology greater than any he had seen on Earth. Their race was long lived and hardy, yet their aging population remained surprisingly low. They needed little. None went hungry, and none were without. Industry was non-existent, not because they lacked the knowledge or power, but because they chose to spend their lives steeped in the acts of creation. As much as Orson could tell, they held a form of Taoism as their prime philosophy, tempered by their belief in the ditheistic powers of Creation. As a result, there was art in all of their lives and, indeed, in all of their world. Even simple necessities like robes and basic furnishings were the expression of will and not to be produced without the guiding hands of a living soul. The People were artists eternal. They had no government and no laws. They did not need them. Honor was their immortality. Elders were their authority, some as old as three centuries. They valued wisdom above all else.

It was strange for Orson, adapting from cold steel to warm stone, from solitude to something more. He lived with the elder(who, as he came to know, was not called Altar but rather Azlo the Wanderer) and his daughter, Alazaved. In his time at the house of Elder Azlo, Orson, the perpetual scholar, once more found himself a student. The lessons of Elder Azlo were long and quiet. He spoke softly and laughed often. At times Alazaved was with them. She would enter in silence and sit on her own cushion across the room from Orson, all the while watching him darkly. The wisdom of Azlo the Wanderer joined with knowledge of the Comte, Gaston d'Noël, and Orson learned that his new world was not entirely cold. This deeper understanding brought with it a greater sadness at the passing of his old friend, and Orson began to see the Old Man for the embittered creature that he had become.

In time, Orson also learned that the language of the People was called simply the Talk, and it fascinated his scholarly ears. It sounded remarkably familiar to him and seemed to be a highly degraded Germanic language. The Elder's speech, which Orson recognized as quite similar to his own, was called Old Talk. It was the language spoken before the time of their 'Puth War,' which Orson had later discovered to translate as Blood War. The name conjured barbarous connotations and fascinated his mind, though the presence of war in this new world did not surprise him.

At night Orson slept in Alazaved's room. The soft bed he had awoken in had belonged to her. She had given it to him without a thought, choosing to sleep on a pile of furs on the floor beside it. Of course, when Orson learned of this he refused the bed, taking the floor for himself. It seemed to the daughter of Azlo to be an act of gentle kindness, but in truth Orson was simply not used to soft things and found the floor more comfortable. In the late hours, when the world was quiet and still, Orson's mind turned often to empty desires such as revenge. Orson had come to know the cost of hate, though he chose to ignore it. For so very long, his hatred and fear had kept him alive. He had wanted to believe his need for revenge was an obsession, and he had sustained himself with it. In the quiet dark, he knew that it was little more than a temporary escape from the growing depth of his sadness. The death of the Old Man weighed heavily on his soul. The Comte had endured years of suffering only to die consumed by it. Orson chose to see his emotions like the fire of a blacksmith's forge. They were desperate and dangerous things, yet he believed that he could hone his suffering into a weapon. This was how he chose to see his revenge. This was how he had come to see himself. It was pure delusionment.

When his body was well enough, Orson prepared to leave the care of the Elder Azlo the Wanderer and his savagely beautiful daughter, Alazaved. He was packing his few possessions when Azlo asked him to stay.

"Ye are strong, Old Son, but there es much anger and sadness en yer soul," Azlo had said to him. "De have seen the wund grow, festering en yer sorrow. Et devours ye from within. Ye must be healt or ye will lose yerself. There es a nim en the heart uf Loth Keivon hwo may teach ye control."

Orson did not want to be healed, he did not want control. Rather, he wanted his wound to swallow the whole of the world. He wanted to let go and sow the suffering he had endured. But his eyes moved past the elder and he saw his mysterious daughter watching him. Alazaved's eyes were empty and limitless. Orson's rising anger bled away and he realized the futility of his actions. He let his eyes drift back to his little prisoner's cup, and he thought once more about his lost friend.

"Azlo, I owe my life to your daughter. I cannot refuse. I don't know if I can be healed, but I will go to this man, as you ask."

So, Orson was taken to another high hall called Mugarth Gall. Mugarth was a great cavern in the deepest part of the city. At its center was a small archipelago floating in a vast lava lake. Ancient statues of carven elders held the great, high ceiling above, like massive pillars. Magma rushed around them in whirlpools, surging to the burning surface in bubbles and bursts. Here, the lifeblood of the planet spat heat and gas from deep within her depths. The Monastery of Mu was built on the largest island, called simply Garth Ser Hir. There, Orson met the wise man called Hantalp, the elder to whom he would be entrusted.

Hantalp was tall and thin, even for the children of Arzvertun. His skin was dark and scarred by the fires of Mu. He wore a long, grey beard and had a big, round, pointed hat atop his head. He was introduced to Orson as Hantalp Selbar the Wise.

Here, Orson passed the last days of his time with the People. Orson had come to the Monastery of Mu with hatred and fear in his heart. He had come twice broken and fate-tossed in the tides of time. He was raw anger. Hantalp was calm strength.

Orson's body was pushed to its new limits. He spent his days in physical conditioning and his nights in meditation. He soon found that, away from the punishing environment of the Château d'Soliel Rouge, he possessed incredible strength and agility. Yet, for all of his raw, physical power, Orson remained in awe of Hantalp. Hantalp who could turn the full force of Orson's fury with a single twist of his hand. Hantalp whose unshakable calm blunted Orson's boundless rage. Hantalp who had bested the man from Earth in every endeavor. Under the old master's tranquil tutelage, Orson came to touch upon a small measure of understanding of the People's philosophy, what Hantalp called the *Path of Voices*.

All creation is a construct. The universe is a construction of the two gods. It cannot be changed from within. Reality is a dream of substance. It is real. There is no will but the gods'. All things are one.

Months passed in the fiery place. Orson now sat on the edge of the islands' cliffs; his eyes closed, his mind open. He had learned to see himself in the dream of his life. Now, he chose to see himself reject his emotions. He drifted through time and space, to a disastrous night in a restaurant. Orson saw himself weak and afraid. He saw himself cowering before the Blood-Fathers. He saw himself a prisoner. He saw himself driving his head into the ground, dying in the light of the red sun. Orson felt himself breathe. He felt the rhythm of the life held in his chest. He saw that he had not died. Then fear came to him. He felt the universe broad and deep. He felt the expanse of his life and he felt lost in sublimity. His heart beat faster. Faster. Scorching heat rushed around him. Fire burst into the air. The war drums of an ancient battle beat in Orson ears. He felt himself pulling away. The air was dry and hot in his lungs.

"Do not be afraid, Old Son."

Hantalp stood beside him on the high rocks. His long beard and soot-stained robes twisted in the hot air rising up the cliffs. Orson heard his deep voice and focused on it. It was old, like the mountain around them. He felt the universe grow small again. He felt himself in creation. His breathing slowed.

Hantalp spoke again, "True, there es much en this wurld, Old Son. There are many voices. Ye are strong. Far stronger than the People. So ye are more en creation. Hwen ye came to Loth Keivon ye had lost ye self. Yer body wounds are healt, but yer soul is wounded still."

Orson's eyes opened. He looked out across the lake of fire. It was like staring into his own heart. He answered the old master with regret, "I'm still angry. I can't let it go."

Hantalp's grey eyes looked on, "Ye must try, Old Son. Anger es like fire en the heart uf nim. Et will consume ye."

"I know..." Orson's voice was low. He was tired. Sweat dripped from his exposed body. "I can't. There's too much. I don't know where I am, where it ends."

Hantalp smiled at Orson with genuine compassion and affection. "Ye are not dead. As long as ye live, there es good."

Orson pushed himself up from the smoldering rocks. His bare feet pressed into the blistering ground. "I can't stay," he offered solemnly.

The elder, Hantalp nodded, "This de have known. Ye will leave the People. Et es written en the text uf Creation. Ye have learned much, and et may sarve ye well. Remember hwet ye have learned."

"I will." Orson swore to himself and to his teacher.

Then James Orson turned away and left the burning cliffs of Mu behind him.

The elder, Azlo the Wanderer, was waiting for Orson when he returned. Alazaved was with him. She was dressed in her blue and white robes, and her long, heavy furs were wrapped warmly about her shoulders.

The Elder spoke first, "Ye are prepared to leave now?"

Orson smiled softly, "I am. Thank you, Elder."

Alazaved nodded to her father and her eyes were soft, "Altar, De hireth. De ne-rathe."

Elder Azlo answered kindly, "Sa Ired. Sa thizdum Arzvertun gobrun. Midur dere Old Sons sithmess so. De sao hlub, der thauder. Yeo lif der nach giffemus ir."

Alazaved smiled. Tears were at the corners of her eyes. Then she pressed her lips against her father's forehead. He smiled proudly, and turned his attention to Orson.

"Old Son, Arzvertun es very cold. Ye will need the proper clothes. Alazaved has made these for ye. Cover yerself."

In her hands, Alazaved held brown furs and dark red robes. Orson smiled up at her.

He spoke strongly, "Yeo dimg."

Alazaved's face blushed deep blue. She shook her head down at Orson. "Wæs noding."

Orson smiled in surprise. Alazaved was a better student than he had first thought. While he was studying at the Monastery of Mu, the Elder Azlo had apparently taught his daughter the Old Talk. Orson shook his head softly, "Ne modong. De Alazaved dimg."

Alazaved was surprised to hear her own tongue. She set Orson's clothes at his feet, and stood nervously. Her steady voice stumbled through more Old Talk, "De hwill beh at watting fer ye at ta outside. Ye clothes getting on now."

Then she left Orson and her father alone.

"Sa es less..." Azlo waved his hand searching for the word before settling on an approximate, "**stone** than sa appears." Azlo smiled down to his friend. "Sa will lead ye to the city en ice. Et es the old town. Where the old people lived." Then the Elder Azlo produced a brown satchel. "Do not forget these."

The satchel was soft and strong. Orson unbuckled the top and peered inside. It contained the last of Orson's possessions, including his old prisoner's cup, the signet ring of Noël, and the Old Man's starchart

"Yeo dimg," Orson said.

A giant hand came to rest on Orson's head and the Elder Azlo said, "Be good, Old Son. Ye take de hert with ye."

Then the Elder Azlo the Wanderer smiled one last time and, gathering his robes about himself, he left. Orson felt a strange sense of loss. He turned his attention to the robes Alazaved had made for him. They were heavy and very thick, but soft to the touch, like strong velvet. Orson lifted them up. The deep, red flowed in impressionistic swirls. On the cuffs were two spirals of red-orange, like his old sun, Sol. They were beautiful. Orson changed into these clothes. He fitted the great, brown fur around his broad shoulders and saw under it a pair of fur-lined boots and a pair of warm gloves.

Alazaved was waiting for him in the great hall outside of the Elder's house. At the far end were tall stairs of black stone. A dozen giants of Arzvertun were going about their daily business, talking amongst themselves. When Alazeved saw Orson in his robes and furs her eyes shone with pride, though she tried to hide it. Her mouth was still an indifferent scowl. She nodded to him, and then made her way to the black stairs. Orson caught up quickly.

"Hwir da go?" he asked.

She answered in Old Talk. "Da go-uping steps to Arzvertun. Da leaving Loth Keivon." Her voice waivered, only slightly betraying her struggle with the ancient language.

Orson nodded and followed in silence. The stairs led to an older stairway made of dark, gray stones. It led them higher in the mountain until, finally, they came to a massive set of bronze-like doors. The doors were carved with intricate runes and in their center was a depiction of a world-tree. Alazaved put her hands against the doors and pushed with all of her strength. Her tight muscles strained against their great mass. The doors slid open a crack before the deep snow compacted and, combined with the weight of the great doors, proved to be too much for the fierce daughter of Azlo. Freezing winds rushed into the stairs, howling through the empty halls. Orson pulled his furs tighter around himself with one hand and pushed the door with other. The vast stone pressed open enough for them to slip through. Alazaved stared down at her small companion incredulously. Orson nodded toward the howling dark, and Alazaved slipped through the door. Orson followed.

They stood near the summit of Loth Keivon. The purple sky crackled with ancient lighting. The frost dappled winds rushed all around them. Alazaved tapped Orson's shoulder and pointed to the horizon. Sharp mountains of snow-covered rocks struck at the sky with eldritch peaks. Beyond, the sun was rising. A great purple haze of light was setting ablaze the endless storm. It was beautiful.

A loud, bleating roar shook Orson from the sunrise. A heard of white-fur-covered bison were nosing through the snow. One, seeming to have found something edible, stopped to pull a mound of orange plant-matter from the mountain. He chomped on it dumbly. Alazaved pulled her furs around her face.

"Down." She said quickly, gesturing to a snow-covered path away from the mountain entrance.

Orson nodded.

They made their way cautiously down the mountain. The snow was old and deep, and it was dangerous. More than once, Orson's footing gave way beneath him and, had Alazaved not caught him, he would have tumbled down to oblivion. They made camp a little more than half way down the main peak of Loth Keivon, by a small cave used by traders and hunters. Despite his thick robes and fur, the cold of Arzvertun hurt to the bone. Ice had formed around Orson's beard and clung to his mustache. At first Orson had sat against the wall, away from Alazaved, but she rolled her eyes in annoyance and sat again beside the little Earth man. She growled, "Warm," and pulled open their furs, pulling him tightly against her chest before wrapping them both up for the night. She curled up with his mass and pulled her hood down over her face. Orson was remarkably comfortable and completely warm with his head cushioned between Alazaved's large breasts. Though he tried to hide the totality of his comfort, before long his tired body dragged his rebellious mind to sleep, and it was as if he had not truly slept for years. Orson slipped into a sleep deeper than he had ever had, and he dreamed the long, sumptuous dreams of peace. In his dreams, he forget everything and was home.

Orson felt something pat the back of his head. He ignored it, wrapping his arms around his pillows. It felt like a Monday. He ignored the outside world and sought again the comfort of sleep. The phantom poked at him again and the fog began to clear. Then something struck him soundly in the back of his head and he was awake.

"Wake!" Alazaved growled. She beat him harder.

Orson was warm and very comfortable. His mind wandered through the mist of waking-consciousness until he found himself buried in Alazaved's chest with his arms wrapped securely around her breasts. Startled and somewhat embarrassed, Orson quickly pulled himself away. Cold immediately rushed in. He pulled his robes and furs tightly against his now chilly body, but the cold was in his bones and it refused to leave.

"Et es ne good to sleep so deep here." Alazaved scowled.

Orson tried to remember the words to apologize in her language, but when he could not find them he simply offered, "Sorry."

Alazaved waved her hand at him dismissively. Then she produced some dried bison meat from a satchel within her furs. Orson ate greedily. His appetite had improved tremendously since he'd left the Château d'Soleil Rouge. When he finished, Alazaved loosened her robes, and Orson caught a glimpse of her pale flesh as she removed a skein filled with warm milk from a sling under her arm. Orson drank what he could and then they resumed their journey. In the dim morning light, Orson could see all the way to the bottom of the valley. Buried within tons of ice were glinting towers of ancient metal. Alazaved pointed to the city. Orson nodded.

Their journey would take another two days. Unfortunately, there would be no more caves to shelter them from the wind. They slept huddled tightly under their furs. After the first night Orson was less comfortable nestling himself against Alazaved's large frame. He didn't trust himself, afraid that he might do something in his sleep to offend his guide. He tried to remain alert, yet every night as he lay snuggled into the giantess's warmth, the deepest and most content of sleep overcame him.

They trudged through the deep snow, until even Orson's mighty thighs began to burn and grow tired. The wind howled all around them and the eternal storm glowed with the light of the red sun, even in the night. Orson caught himself staring up at those empty clouds and wondering where his old prison was. He thought of the Old Man and wondered if anyone had found him yet. He hoped they had.

When Orson and his guide finally passed into the valley, the winds all died and they stepped into a sphere of quiet calm, like the eye of a storm. The air here felt less unbearably frigid, almost tolerable. They stopped to make camp on the edge of a massive ice lake. It stretched for dozens of kilometers, filling the bottom of the valley in its entirety. Orson snuggled into Alazaved's warm body and slept.

On the morning of the third day, Orson awoke to the sensation of movement within his robes. He tried to ignore it, at first. Then, he felt something press against him, squirming. It was small and wet with snow. Orson pulled back his furs in surprise. What looked like a very small walrus was chewing on the corner of his robes. It was less than a third of a meter long with little tusks, and it growled when Orson lifted it up by the tail.

"Hwir that ye find?" Alazaved yawned, looking down at her companion.

"What is it?" Orson asked, poking its soft, warm belly.

Alazaved looked down, "Et es jabbergnus. Th'e fierce hunters umter icesea."

"It looks like a walrus."

"Hwet?"

"A big sea dwelling mammal. Like this but big." Orson gestured dramatically with his arm. The little walrus was twisting about in Orson's grasp trying to bite him with its equally little tusks.

Alazaved nodded questioningly, "True...De have ne seen jabbergnus this small."

Orson held out his hand, "Give me some of that bison."

Alazaved's white brow sank and she shook her head, "No. Et es for *eating*."

Orson nodded, "I know, just let me have a small piece."

Alazaved's eyes narrowed and she reluctantly took out a strip of meat and pulled off a small piece. She gave it to Orson and quickly put the rest in her mouth. Orson held the little walrus in his hand and offered it the small strip of dried meat. The walrus ate it in quick, hungry chomps and licked Orson's hand. Orson smiled. Then the walrus curled up in his palm and went to sleep.

Alazaved leaned closer and spoke slowly, focusing on getting the words right. "That es vary strange jabbergnus."

Orson opened his furs again and put the little walrus in an inner pocket of his robes, against his skin, where it would be warm.

"Hwet ye doing?"

Orson smiled, "I think I'll keep him."

Alazaved shook her head, "Ye are vary strange too de think." Then she got to her feet and shook the fresh snow from her shoulders. "We are close to the city now. We must be careful. Old houses hold many things."

In the distance, the ancient towers seemed as stubby blocks breaking through the ancient ice. The calm around them was broken only by the small purple flurries gusting in the early morning.

"Where is the starship?" Orson asked.

Alazaved nodded toward the city ruins. Orson pulled the sharp, frigid air into his lungs and pulled his furs tighter about his body.

Alazaved straightened her furs and focused on the unfamiliar words, "Beasts live en old house caves. Angry esnim."

"Esnim?"

"Big, scary," Alazaved answered.

Orson shook his head and said sardonically, "Of course."

At midday they reached the middle of the lake and began to approach the ruins. It looked like any city Orson might have seen on Earth, but buried under hundreds of meters of ice and snow. The ice cascaded down the tops of the remaining buildings like frozen waterfalls. There was a broad clearing in the middle. Alazaved stopped suddenly and began to brush away the heavy snow. After a few minutes she'd cleared a circle, revealing the frozen waters below. Then she shielded her eyes from the purple sky and peered into the ground. She moved around gazing intently past the glassy ice.

"This is a bad way," Alazaved said finally, pushing herself to her feet. "There es much danger."

After that they followed a longer path into the ruins, winding through the shadow of a giant glacier. As they passed the tops of another group of buried skyscrapers, Orson thought he saw shadows moving in the frozen windows. He started to say something. Alazaved spoke first. She kept her face forward.

"De know. Do ne look. Esnim are angry. They ignore dao unless they think da look."

"I see." Orson answered, cautiously turning his head, "Where precisely is this ship we're looking for?"

Alazaved answered softly, "Down. Umter ice."

Suddenly Orson heard a loud ruffling from the top of one the old skyscrapers. He ignored it, remembering Alazaved's words. Then there was a loud squawk, and Orson glanced quickly to the sky. Above them, a giant bird was gliding toward the glacier. It looked like an enormous, white puffin with blue tipped wings and tufts of fur on its legs. Its nest was on the top of the building. It flapped its great wings, and the gust shook snow from the glacier above.

"My God..." Orson caught himself.

Alazaved nodded, "They are stronger than they look. Ther eggs tasty though." She flashed the little Earth man a toothy smile.

Orson kept his head low. He could still feel invisible eyes on them both. Before long they reached one of the buried skyscrapers. The once-high window had been shattered. A long scrap of torn cloth fluttered in the gentle air and a path of trampled snow led inside. Alazaved held up her hand to Orson.

"Tautau Painted Nim. They ne bad to the People, **but** they ne ye know. They ne trust deo with small nim." Alazaved shook her head. "ne trust *me* with small...*mahn*. So, ye husband." Alazaved nodded slowly, as if Orson were an ancient idiot. "Ye have being vary sick so ye small. Ye the People es. Ond, ye ne talk. Yeo dumb." And she brought one hand down on the other. "Head smeshed wæs by rock."

Orson smiled, "I am your little, idiot husband?"

Alazaved nodded, though clearly only partially understanding his meaning, "Ond ye ne talk."

"And I don't talk." Orson shook his head.

Alazaved smiled, "Good, Old Son."

Then she led him inside. When Orson's eyes adjusted to the dimmer light he saw a cave of metal and ice. It looked like an abandoned office, though everything was oversized. The high ceiling still held the metal frame for the ceiling tiles and here and there bits of duct work remained, frozen in the ice. Alazaved led him to the stairs. As they moved away from the windows the room grew progressively darker. Suddenly, red light filled the passage. Alazaved held a glass sphere filled with cold fire. She held it in front of them and together they slowly made their way under the ice.

The stairwell went down for hundreds of meters. Every so often they would pass by an open door, and, more than once, Orson saw light and moving shadows beyond. He assumed these 'caves' were the homes of the Painted Men. Orson kept a careful watch on his guide. Finally, they reached what he assumed was the ground floor. The stairwell led to a large, stone archway. Outside was the lobby. It was a tall, Gothic chamber. High above, gargoyles held the spiral ceiling, while below a set of glass doors opened to the subterranean street. Mysterious, yellow sunlight poured in from the cavern beyond. They stepped through the archway and their footsteps echoed on the ancient marble at their feet.

Alazaved stopped and, turning back to Orson, she whispered, "Sdar ship es beyond tautau path." Then she passed one hand under the other and opened them both wide. "Umter ice es big cave. Sdar ship es hot. So many many come to live umter ice." Then her eyes darkened. "They ne want da take warmth. They da fight. But, Altar say ye must take the sdar ship."

Orson nodded. Then he felt something wriggling in his robes. He'd forgotten about his little friend. The jabbergnus thrashed about at his side. It twisted around in a little fury until its little tusks dug viciously into Orson's flesh.

"Ouch!" Orson cried. He reached inside his robes and pulled the little walrus out by the tail. It thrashed about, roaring in its little voice and chomping at the air. "What's wrong with you?" Orson asked.

Alazaved shook her head, "Se tharstay maybe. Give seo to de."

She held out her broad hand. Orson set the jabbergnus in her palm. She stroked her finger along its back, but it shook nervously. It growled and nudged her palm. It seemed to be trying to say something to her. Alazaved cooed gently to the little beast.

Orson straightened his robes. The air was warmer there, and he removed his thick, fur-lined gloves. He tucked them away and rubbed his hands together, in an effort to warm. It wasn't terrible effective, but Orson was too distracted to notice. They were close to the ship and his time with the pale giantess was coming to an end. He wanted to warn her, to tell her that his path was dangerous and lonely, that he would stop at nothing to leave the stormy planet and claim his revenge. He stumbled with the words, "Listen, Alazaved...I don't know where I am. I'm still lost. I fell here from...a very bad place."

"De know this," She answered, rubbing the walrus's nose. "Deo Altar said."

Orson continued, "I just...I have to go. No matter the cost."

Alazaved nodded, staring into the eyes of the jabbergnus. It was calm now. Her eyes were too kind. "De know. Ye are Old Son."

Orson felt emotion like an echo in his heart. It scared him and he tried to avoid it. "What does that mean?"

"Hwet?" she asked, looking down at Orson.

Orson looked up into those too-kind eyes, "Old Son. What does that mean? The elders have been calling me that. I thought it was, well I thought your people couldn't say my name properly, but I don't think that's it anymore."

"Ye are Old Son," Alazaved answered, blankly. "En old time, long before, there wæs nim from before. Se wæs son uf Old World. Da believe that se Old Son es..." She paused searching for a word. "Many-born. Ye fall from Old World. Ye must be Old Son."

Orson pulled on his beard. "My name is James Orson."

Alazaved nodded, petting the little walrus, "Jim'es Oldson."

"ORRRson."

Alazaved bent low to look into Orson eyes and repeated, "OOOLLDSON."

Orson shook his head, then smiled. "Alright. Old Son."

Alazaved's eyes narrowed incredulously. Then, she saw the tall shadow behind him. Her eyes grew wide. She pulled the jabbergnus to her chest and froze as still as ice. Orson turned quickly around. Behind him stood a giant ape. The beast was enormous, with thick, white fur, and a dingy, yellow mane that framed a hairless face. Great black tusks stuck outward from its mouth, and it breathed loudly, shooting long tufts of steam from its dark nostrils. Then, its beady, purple eyes fell on Orson's. The fur on its back fluffed out and it drew itself up tall to its full height of two and a half meters. It pulled back its lips and snarled. An esnim had found them.

The great monster leapt at the little Earth man, its mass carrying them both crashing into the icy floor. It roared and beat its massive fist into the marble, only just missing Orson's head. Orson's heart thundered in his chest. Blood surged to his brain making him dizzy and sick. His hands felt numb, and his muscles pulled tight. Fear assaulted his consciousness, but the lessons of Mu were with him, and, all at once, he drove upward with his fist. It collided thunderously with the brute, snapping its head back. The momentum carried the ape's body backward giving Orson just enough room to slide away.

The esnim fell flat on the ground. When it finally pulled itself up, the beast stumbled dumbly forward and shook its head, clearly dazed. It let out several confused snorts. Then its eyes fell back on Orson, focusing sharply. The esnim's black nostrils flared outward and it roared steam. Then the beast dug its massive paws into the ice and launched itself at Orson. Orson was on his knees and he came up just in time to catch the beast in his own vice-like grasp. He wrapped his arm around the esnim's neck and squeezed. Orson's legs strained against the power of the esnim. It drove forward. Orson's muscles bulged under his skin as he pushed back. His back pulled tight. His grip held firm. The esnim's legs began to shake and it dropped down. Horror filled its bestial mind as it realized that it was not the strongest. It grunted and snarled. Then, the monster ceased moving its legs and grabbed for the small man holding it. It flailed its arms wildly, clawing at Orson. Orson caught one arm with his own. His steely grip tore into the esnim's thick flesh and he forced it to the ground. Then he rose up and, with all of the might in his body, he smote the wicked animal's skull across the icy floor.

When it was over, Orson sat upon a ruined corpse. He gasped for breath. His muscles were still tight, surging with power. Orson focused on the lessons of Mu. They had become instinct. He felt his anger, his rage, and his fear. He saw them in the chaos of his dream. He focused on his breath, finding himself. With one, last breath James Orson turned back to Alazaved. Her beautiful eyes were wide with wonder and fear. Orson cast her a ragged, toothy smile, but before he could bask in the glory of his victory he saw another esnim coming down the stairs. Another still was coming from the cave outside. In a moment, a half-dozen more had spilled into the lobby. Alazaved pressed herself tight against the wall. Her eyes fell on Orson. They told him to remain still. They were the eyes of a frightened child. It was a resonance that the lost father could not ignore.

Orson stood up, gore dripping from his open hands. His brow lowered threateningly and he passed his defiant gaze over the lot of them. His eyes stopped on the largest and oldest. It was the alpha male. The corpse under Orson was small in comparison to this beast's mass, a whelp. The Alpha growled. Orson stared into its eyes and, baring his teeth, answered with his own snarl. For a moment the Alpha was taken aback by this small animal's audacity, then it stood full tall and roared, beating its mighty fists against its chest. Orson beat his own chest and roared in kind. His bearded face was equally savage and wild. The other creatures spread apart and the Alpha came at Orson.

The mighty esnim charged like the last, but Orson was prepared. Mu was with him. He feinted to one side then twisted to the other. The beast slid past him. It caught itself and charged again. Once again, Orson dodged. The Alpha snorted and beat its great fists against the ground in frustration. This time it approached more slowly. Orson and the esnim circled each other. Orson felt the adrenaline surging in his brain like waves. He tried to remember those fiery days with Hantalp. He tried to remember control. Anger began to surface in Orson's heart. His hands were shaking. He saw the great monster circling him. He knew it was strong. He knew the beast wanted blood. Still, he fought the rage surging in his breast. Orson felt the nagging memory of his previous life. He felt his hatred for his own impotence break against the living moment. He was outside of it. In control. Then the Alpha roared its dominance and, like a bolt of lightning traveling the path of least resistance, Orson's anger found the esnim.

Orson planted his thick, muscular legs and drove forward, catching the Alpha by surprise. His fist collided with the beast's thick skull. The Alpha fell back. It staggered in disbelief, then shook its head and roared. It charged the little Earth man and they met in the middle of the room. The titanic Alpha pressed downward with its height and mass. It had the early advantage. Orson felt his legs begin to shake. Then the Alpha wrestled its arm free and drove it downward, catching Orson in the shoulder and knocking him down. Orson's feet slipped out from under him. His knees touched the ground and the esnim drove downward with its tusks, impaling Orson's shoulder. Blood rushed from the wound, and he was dying.

Orson knew that he was not strong enough. The darkness of certain death wrapped around his heart like a black shroud. The world was nothing, and soon he would return to chaos. Then in the red light of a dying star, a monster, more desperate and more terrible than all of the ancient horrors of Arzvertun, awoke. The Prisoner roared, shattering the chains of Mu.

Mighty hands dug into the esnim's flesh, and the Prisoner came up in a fury. His legs drove into the icy floor and he carried the esnim into the air with irresistible might before slamming its heavy body down. Then the Prisoner was on top of the Alpha and his mighty fists hammered into its skull. Pain glowed in the Prisoner's gory wounds and in his fists, but it was not pain. These savage sensations splashed against the Prisoner's nihilistic frenzy in waves of glory.

Blood spewed from the Alpha's battered flesh in gory gouts, but the Alpha was still a fierce animal. It seized the little man in its great hands and, with all the strength remaining in its body, it cast him away. The Prisoner landed hard. The Alpha struggled to breathe. It pushed itself up and its world blurred. It had been surprised by the smaller creature's savagery. Blood dripped down its face, matting its yellow fur.

"I AM JAMES ORSON!" the Prisoner roared defiantly against the darkness.

Then he leapt at the staggered esnim. It raised its arms in defense, but the Prisoner brushed them to the side and tackled the top-heavy beast. They tumbled to the ground. The Prisoner beat his fists against the esnim's thick skull, until even that ceased to be enough. Then the Prisoner grabbed the beast by the tusks and began to slam its head into the cold marble. Finally, the Alpha's movements ceased and its arms fell limp.

The Prisoner stood over the quieted beast. His lungs burned at the exertion. His breath was like steam, and the bitter cold hurt his nostrils. He wiped a sleeve across his bloodied face. It had not been enough. Anger was still burning in the Prisoner's heart. He needed to destroy, to rip, to tear, to burn and devour. The other esnim watched in stillness as the Prisoner stood above the Alpha's head. His tightly knotted muscles strained under his skin. His shoulder burned. The Prisoner planted his foot and with a roar he drove his other down. His heel connected with the skull and it cracked. He rose up again and struck downward with all of his might. The bone cracked again. Once more, and the head shattered into a dozed fleshy pieces.

The Prisoner stood over the empty remains. He gasped for breath. He wanted to tear down the foundations of existence. He wanted pain and sorrow.

He wanted fire. He wanted all of the world to end. Chaos! He desired a return to the raw fundament of existence, and in that darkness his heart was finally reaching those memories that James Orson must not remember. *Father. I love you.* He could see a child's face, and he could see the life he would never have. Then the Prisoner threw out his arms and he unleashed the completeness of his fury in an earsplitting roar. It was a challenge to all living things. It was a desperate scream and a dark prayer. The esnim horde cowered.

Then James Orson dripped down upon the Prisoner through the darkness of his own mind, and he remembered that he was a man. He remembered that all things had life, and he remembered that it is wrong to end a thing so precious. His eyes fell on his gory hands, and he was afraid. His hands shook. Orson's heart was breaking.

A gunshot thundered from the stairwell. The esnimes scattered, leaving Orson standing over his foes' remains. Three dusky giants stood in the doorway, holding long rifles. They were wrapped in dark furs, and their faces were hidden behind the deep, fur-lined hoods that protected their heads from the bitter cold. These were Alazaved's Painted Men.

Chapter XXIII

The Sorrow of Isigburg

ranfader's beard!...Hwo iz dis man?" the first of the Painted Men said.

Two of the three carried the bodies of white boars slung over their shoulders. They were likely a hunting party returning from a successful outing. Alazaved discretely tucked the little jabbergnus away in her robes and hurried over to Orson. His eyes were empty as she peeled back his bloodsoaked robes from his shoulder and examined the wound. She suppressed her worries and fears, doing her best to address the Painted Men in their language while stopping the bleeding.

"Da much apologizes," She began. "Tautau der huspand. Se are dumbræned. Seo head wæs hit with rock und now sa es often making much rage and ænker." Alazaved shook her head sadly. "True. True. Seo also much ukly an shord. De much sad. Seo wæs sick hwen child. So now der huspanth es...many disgusting."

The Painted Man nodded, "I see...It iz not often dat a man fights wid de ice-men and wins. What are you doing out here?"

Alazaved nodded slowly as she wrapped a length of cloth tightly around Orson's shoulder. It was obvious that she was still struggling with their language, which seemed to be a form of Old Talk.

Orson's eyes were on the ground. His rage had bled away like the life of the esnim over which he stood. He felt empty again. His heart swallowed the darkness, and Orson tried to remember the Old Man's lessons. *Do be polite, stupid Boar.* Orson took a deep breath, ignoring the pain in his shoulder as Alazaved bandaged his wound. She pulled tight and tied off the cloth. Orson did his best impersonation of his old friend. He remembered to bow and flashed a smile. His voice was steady though his eyes were tired and red.

"My name is James Orson. I am simply a lost traveler. As she said, Alazaved,

196

here, is my wife. If we have trespassed or have offended your sensibilities in any way, I sincerely apologize. I don't belong in this place, and I know nothing of your culture or customs."

"Oh, I see now. You are just travelers, then? Yes. I dought az much," the Painted Man answered with a sigh. "Show me your hands, little man."

"I beg your pardon?" Orson snapped.

The Painted Men raised their weapons. "You are strong, but my bullets are fast. Dose big mountain people always dink dat we are dumb. Dat we forget dings." The first Painted Man pulled back his hood, revealing his face. His skin was darker than those of the mountain people Orson had met, and it was covered in elaborate tattoos. His hair was black, but his beard had long since greyed. "Alazaved, no more lies. Now, look at me. Hwy are you here, and hwo is dis little man?"

Alazaved glanced at Orson, then turned her eyes to the Painted Man. "Da looking fur yar sdarship. Se **es** der huspanth, es small people."

The Painted Man looked back to Orson, "She iz very loyal, but you are clearly not from Arzvertun. Yet...if you are not one of de Pale Ones..." the man thought for a moment, then nodded to his companions. They lowered their weapons. "My name iz Gunric, and I am Chief of de People. You are most lucky dat it was us dat found you. So you *are* looking for de ship?"

Orson nodded, "Yes, we are."

Gunric laughed. "It iz inside de ice wid de people. Come," Gunric motioned, before pulling his hood back over his head. "I will take you to de village. I do not dink you will need help to find de ship."

They were led out of the Gothic lobby through a set of large doors. Wind rushed gently around their backs as they passed through. Outside, the air was much warmer than the surface, though it was still freezing. They were walking on the remains of the city's once-busy streets. Orson could see the bottoms of all of those once-great skyscrapers, now overgrown with moss and giant mushrooms. Small, squirrel-like creatures ran about these ruins, searching for food. Above, little birds sang through broken windows. Orson let his eyes follow the walls of the skyscrapers as they pushed through the ice-ceiling to the purple, frozen world above. They were inside an enormous ice cave. Yellow sunlight was reflected and refracted in the melting ice so that the whole place shimmered with warm light. Orson knew that it could not be from the red star. His eyes moved past the looming shadows of the tall buildings. He could see a bit of the warm light-source burning at the center of the cave and just beyond that a small tower of smoke rising from a forest of giant mushrooms.

"Is that your village?" Orson asked Gunric.

Gunric nodded, "It iz de People's village, Isigburg. I only own my house, such as it iz."

Orson heard a loud crack. His attention was pulled immediately to two horned bison. They were slowly circling each other. One had white fur, the other grey. Finally they charged. Their horns collided with a mighty crack. Then, they staggered back and prepared to ram each other again.

Gunric turned to Orson, "It iz de season. Even de icemen are losing dere minds."

"What is this place?" Orson asked.

"It iz de home of de People. I will tell you more in de little sunlight."

Orson nodded politely, "I see. Thank you."

Leaving the towering buildings behind, they came into a strange meadow. The ground was covered in green moss and patches of grass, and, in the place of trees, mushrooms grew meters tall. Bee-like insects buzzed about purple flowers while stubby rabbits frolicked in clover. Finally free from the obstructions of the taller buildings, Orson could see the source of the light. In the middle of the great cavern, suspended high above the ground on an ancient launch-platform, sat a starship. Bright, yellow light surged from the engines. Apparently, the launch had been a failure but, while the engines lacked to the power to free the ship from the grip of Arzvertun, they had at least created a sanctuary from the bitter cold.

"Is that the ship?" Orson asked without thinking.

Alazaved raised her eyebrow, "Of course et es the sdarship."

Gunric answered, "Patience, little savage. I will tell you everyding in time."

They passed through a mushroom forest and in the shadows the rocketship's glow disappeared. Orson's keen ears could hear the sounds of little creatures scurrying in the dark. Gunric's voice told them to follow.

When they had first entered the cave, it had merely been less cold than the frozen waste, but, the nearer they traveled to the ship, the warmer the temperature became. When they finally left the darkness and arrived at a large clearing, it felt like the early spring. Here, dozens of half-timbered houses surrounded a large, central hall. Far above, the rocketship's engines burned like a little sun. As they came into the village, dusky, tattooed giants looked up from the business of their day, wide-eyed with curiosity. Most quickly returned to their lives once they were sure that Orson was not a child. The rest cast questioning looks between the little man and the pale woman. Gunric raised his hand in greeting.

"Do not worry. It iz alright," he smiled. "Dis iz not a ghast child. His name is Jimnes Olson. He says he does not belong on Arzvertun. He is my guest."

A single woman approached them. She had a beautiful face with wide, almond eyes and a large nose. Her stern mouth was twisted in a doubtful scowl.

Gunric waved his hand to her, "Hilda, it iz alright."

His wife, Hilda, shook her head incredulously. "Little man," she said to Orson, "You fall from de sky or someding?"

Orson nodded slowly, trying not to startle what he took for a primitive native. Alazaved watched carefully, unsure of how much the Painted Men knew of the old stories. Hilda looked to her husband. He nodded. Then Hilda laughed in surprise.

"Dat ding iz still up dere den?" She flashed a broad smile, then tapped Gunric's broad chest. "I dought it was one of your fader's stories!"

Gunric shook his head, "You should listen to me, woman!"

"I'll listen to you when you start being right for a change. I told you de heard moved past de soudren field." She shook her head, then sighed, "I suppose he has come to see de spaceship?"

Orson was surprised. "You know what it is?" he said without thinking.

Hilda laughed again. "Of course I do." Then her eyes narrowed. "Do you dink dat just because we live simply dat we have simple minds? We have books, little man. De end days did not take dem. Dey did not take paper and pen. We are not poets because we do not live in your high halls?"

Gunric stopped her with a smile, "It'z ok, darling. Let us meet in de mead hall. Prepare de fires. You were right about de deer, but we have brought some boars."

Hilda nodded to her husband, and then he wrapped his arms around her and squeezed her tight.

"I missed you," she said into his shoulder.

He closed his eyes and buried his nose in her hair. "I missed you too. Now, go. Make ready the hall for our guests."

Hilda smiled, "Perhaps dat one's thirst iz as small as he iz."

Gunric laughed, "Let us hope," and kissed his wife on the forehead. Then she went toward the large building at the center of the village. Gunric turned back to his guests, waving his hand to the two others with them.

"William, Ælfred, you can go. I don't dink our guests will be causing any trouble."

"Are we not prisoners?" Orson asked.

Gunric looked down to the savage, little man, "You want to leave, Arzvertun? So do we all. I cannot begrudge dat. Dis planet has become a wasteland. Do you know why dat ship burns? It is one of de last ships on de planet. It is one of de few dat did not escape, and it has been burning for dousands of years...but it may not burn much longer. Perhaps it will stop tomorrow. If we could, do you not dink we would leave ourselves?"

Orson felt tired. His muscles ached around his wound. His mouth was dry. He did his best to keep up the Old Man's persona. "I do apologize, Chief Gunric. I did not realize that I would encounter your people here, nor did I know that the ship we sought would be sustaining an entire ecosystem. I have no desire to destroy your home and doom your people to die in the encroaching ice."

Gunric shook his head, "You do not understand. Dere iz an old saying: in all dings balance iz better. Dis ice cave relies on balance. Too hot and de ice melts. Too cold and de ice grows. Dis balance has been sustained for as long as de People have been here, but dat balance is slipping. De ship's engines are not working right." Gunric smiled, then he scratched his beard, correcting himself, "Well, dey never did, but dey are working less right. De are getting hotter. Dis iz not good. If de ice grows too din," Gunric glanced up to the ice above. "...den de people will die in de snow."

"Have your people tried to fix the ship's engines?"

Gunric laughed. "No. No. It cannot be done. We cannot even get into de ship. No matter hwat we try. Dere is one way to de ship, and de doors are closed to us. We cannot restore balance alone. De Pales One's have more techne dan we. I have sent people to dem, but dey did not return. So, we have been waiting for de Pale Ones to come."

Orson looked to Alazaved. She spoke to him as well as she could, "De ne mu. I do not know of this. All that *I* know uf *their* people es from the stories uf the elders. They hwir once with dao-eh..with *us*. Some of the People did ne believe in the gods. They would ne accept fate. Set caused..." She stumbled looking for the word.

Orson helped her, "Conflict, fighting..."

"Ne, like..." She held her hands apart.

Orson asked, "Schism? A divide or chasm?"

Alazaved nodded, "Yes. Set caused a chasm in the People. So they left the city. I also know that very long time ago sdarship was found. Set became on and melted the es. Set-eh..*It* must have made this place."

Gunric shook his head, "Hwat happened to our home was not fate. It was stupidity and hubris. Dere iz no gods, Alazaved. Dere iz only men and de choices we have made."

Alazaved narrowed her eyes, "So ye say, but **my** home is ne dying."

Gunric nodded with a grim smile, "You are so sure?" He looked down to Orson again, "If you can take de ship, little man, den you must take it. Soon de ice will melt, and de sky will fall. My people have been awaiting the end. Perhaps we will live with de Pale Ones again, or perhaps we will make a new home." His shoulders relaxed and his wistful gaze pierced the ice. "We have lived here for generations beyond reckoning." He sighed, "Hwat do you do hwen the world has ended, little one? How do you go on? We are all...ghasts." He looked briefly to Alazaved. "Some live without a past. Some cling to lives lost. And..." His eyes fell down on Orson. "Remember dis, little man. Sometimes, we get no answers. Sometimes, the world just ends."

Orson stared up at the giant's black eyes. They were the eyes of a survivor, eyes that had seen the end of dearest love and found the strength to simply not die.

"How can I take the starship if it means destroying your people?" Orson asked.

Gunric answered, "Above de ice is de infinite storm. But it iz not natural. Dis whole planet is out of balance. Once, our faders fought a great war in de stars. It was a stupid ding. When a man loses his balance, he loses himself. So did de war come to Arzvertun, Old Son." Alazaved watched nervously as the old hunter continued. "Yes, I know hwo you are. Our people remember de old stories. In days of fire the Old Son fell upon Arzvertun. He was small, like you.

He came to save de people from a black death, but in de end his anger destroyed our home. A great ship came and scorched de sky. It was de pride of our faders. It iz still dere, some say."

Orson glanced starward unconsciously, imagining the château floating above the planet.

"The Château d'Soliel Rouge?" he mumbled to himself.

"Hwat?" Gunric asked.

Orson shook his head. "I was a prisoner. I was held for many years on a space station, a great ship," he corrected himself. "I escaped in the coffin meant for my mentor and only friend. I thought this planet deserted. I fell here believing that I would die."

Gunric stroked his beard thoughtfully, "So, dat is hwy you are here. You have suffered much for one so small. Dere is always de temptation for nihilism in suffering, as well as de burning need for vengeance. Know dis, dey are one and de same. Before de Blot War, dere were two minds on Arzvertun: de artists and de warriors. Dey were in balance, until a man came from de stars. He told us of de end of de world. His words moved de leaders of Arzvertun. Hwen we lost balance, we were destroyed. Jimnes Olson, remember well dat happiness, like all dings, iz relative. If you suffer now, your later happiness will be all de greater. De happy man will never know dat he was happy until he falls. Do not give in to de temptation to seek revenge. Dat pad will lead you to empty hunger. You must seek balance. Remember dis. If you cannot fly de spaceship, den you must find happiness hwerever you can. Even wid ghasts."

Orson nodded. He had heard without listening. His mind was on his aching shoulder. He had not felt it when the beast had gored him but now the pain was overwhelming. Orson was focused on keeping his breathing regular and relaxed. He felt that he could not let Alazaved see his weakness, though he did not know why. He wanted desperately to seem super human. Sweat was beading on his forehead.

"Chief Gunric," Orson began, "If your...woman has finished in the mead hall. I think we could use a drink."

Gunric smiled kindly and nodded, "Of course, little man. Follow me."

Gunric lead Orson and Alazaved toward the large hall. They passed men and women going about their daily routines with tired faces. Alazaved bent low and spoke softly.

202

"Et es bad?" she asked with genuine concern. She wished she could have properly closed the wound. "I will try again."

Orson shook his head, "I'm fine."

Alazaved nodded though she did not believe his words. Ahead, the great mead hall stood on a low hill. It was the largest building in the village, at least fifteen meters tall, and decorated with hanging tapestries of purple and gold. As they approached, Orson could hear the words and laughter building in waves. His heart began to beat faster. After years in quiet solitude, noise made him nervous. Orson focused on the pain in his shoulder and on his breathing. Gunric pushed open the tall doors and a smile spread across his face. He opened his arms wide to his people and the joyous laughter filled him with happy pride. The hall was a deep, wide chamber with a high ceiling. There was a long fire pit in the middle surrounded by tables and chairs. It was already filled with people. Gunric took in a deep, satisfied breath and looked down to Orson.

"Welcome to Adelgleam, my friends," he announced, then he held out a hand to his wife. She came to him with two ivory cups filled to the frothy brim with honey wine. She gave one to him and one to his little guest. Gunric pulled his wife close and looked deeply into her eyes. "Thank you, wife." he smiled, then pressed his lips against her nose.

In Orson's hands the ivory cup looked massive, though in his mighty grasp it felt light. Orson brought the cup to his nose. The wine smelled much sweeter than the Old Man's and it lacked the distinct medicinal scent. He looked up to Alazaved for direction. She shook her head nervously and furrowed her brow. Orson turned his attention back to his host.

He bowed his head slightly, and said, "Thank you, Chief Gunric. Your generosity is most welcome." Then he held the ivory bucket to his lips and drank the lot in a single draught. To his great surprise the mead also lacked the bite of beet wine and went down smoothly even with the natural carbonation tickling his throat. A smile spread across his face at his first taste of wine in months. Orson lifted his cup to his host and thanked him, "Sir, your wine is ex-" Then Orson unleashed a mighty belch. His heart jumped.

Alazaved's pale face flushed deep blue, and she stared daggers at Orson. Gunric laughed deeply.

"Impressive, little man." Then he lifted his own cup and drank it down.

When it was finished. He turned to his wife, shouting, "Another, woman!" In response Hilda cast him a look that nearly froze Orson's veins. Gunric cleared his throat and murmured, "Please."

Hilda nodded sweetly then took their cups. Gunric began to remove his thick coat, walking toward a tall, wooden throne at the back of the hall. The village was warm and their insulation was no longer needed. Orson followed, removing his own furs. His shoulder ached to the bone. He forced the pain away from himself.

"Olson, tomorrow you will go to de ship, and maybe my people...." Gunric let himself fall into his throne with a grunt, "will leave de Valley of Ice."

"Thank you," Orson offered sincerely.

"Don't dank me." Gunric's voice fell and Orson could see the sadness in his eyes. "My fader's bones are buried under de soil of dis village. I am Gunric, Chief of de people of Isigburg. One day...no more. Hwat am I hwen we are gone? My people were artists once."

"Chief Gunric, I **am** sorry," Orson answered.

Gunric smiled. He shook his head, "Do not use dat word. It does not mean hwat you dink. You are not sorry, Olson, not dat I see. You feel regret. So do I. So do we all. De world must end. Noding comes from noding. I **am** and so one day I will not be."

Orson shook his head. "I don't know any of that. I am alive today. I can feel the atmosphere around my skin. I can feel it pulling and pushing in my lungs. I may be dead tomorrow, but today I am alive. This world fills my soul with light." It sounded better in his head.

"Dat was terrible," Gunric laughed, sitting up in his throne. "Iz dat hwat passes for philosophy among de Pale Ones?" Then he noticed Orson's blood-drenched shoulder. His laughter stopped abruptly. "Are you alright?"

Orson shook his head, "I'm fine."

Gunric leaned closer, "You're bleeding, aren't you?"

Orson nodded, "It's nothing. I'll be fine. I'm always fine."

Gunric smiled, "You're really not." Then it faded and his voice wavered, "Your blood...it iz de same as de deer, red. You do not bleed like a man. You...you **are** Old Son. I'll have my wife look at your wound. The icemen have dirty tusks...Perhaps, you're not invulnerable after all."

"No man is invulnerable, Chief Gunric. Least of all, me."

"You may be right, little man." His eyes were dull. "Soon, I must tell my people dat tomorrow dere lives will end."

Orson nodded and spoke more carefully, "I...regret that."

Gunric nodded, "We wait for de end like old men waiting to die. Our hearts are blackened with fear. We allow ourselves to suffer. No more. It's time we craftsmen build." Then he stood and raised his hands in the air. "My friends," he said with solemn authority, "de spaceship will not be repaired. Dis little man has come to try and take de spaceship. He may fail, and de ship may burn for anoder dousand years, but de Valley of Ice will not last. We cannot stay here. The long winter **iz** coming to our home. Tomorrow we will leave for de mountain, and we will rejoin our lost brothers..." A smile curved Gunric's lips, "but we must travel lightly. So tonight we empty the kegs! Let us not forget Isigburg. Let us not forget our home." His voice dropped low, "And let us not forget those who have died."

Gunric's people faced the end of their home with a solemn cheer. They raised their cups to their Chief and drank. Gunric had been right, they knew well the end was coming. Gunric's eyes betrayed great sorrow behind his smiling face.

Chapter XXIV

Old Son

here was no night in Isigburg, but, during the late hours, the engines of the starship above entered a low powerstate and burned with less ferocity. This subtle decrease in overall light and temperature was called the "little sunlight." It was a vital period of restoration, during which the temperature dropped enough to strengthen and sustain the ice around them. Gunric's people often told tales of heroic hunts and boasted of old glories during this time, and, despite being the last, this little sunlight was no different. As they feasted on roasted boar and drank deeply of their winter mead, Gunric began to recite a favorite tale, *The Hunt of Wulfgar*.

Storytelling was more than a favorite pastime of Gunric's people, it was an important part of their culture. As such, their stories were things to be performed, not merely told. The best stories had what Gunric called, "Twiwæ," which translates most closely to "balance." *The Hunt of Wulfgar* was a long tale chronicling the battle between the ancient hero, Wulfgar, and a savage boar that stalked the snowy wastes. On the surface it was violent and gruff, but the core of the tale concerned Wulfgar's rejection of grief following the death of his beloved wife at the beast's grisly tusks. Only by accepting his loss does Wulfgar finally triumph.

While Gunric's tale wore on, his wife, Hilda, disinfected and bandaged Orson's wound. Alazaved watched the other woman with suspicion, absently petting the purring jabbergnus in her hand. Hilda finished her work with queenly grace, while her husband finished the first part of *The Hunt of Wulfgar* to a roar of cheers. When Hilda left to return her medicines to her home, Gunric stood to accompany her. Alazaved took the opportunity to sit beside Orson. The jabbergnus flopped over on its back, and its blubbery paunch jiggled as it began to snore. Alazaved whispered her fears in Orson's ear.

206

"I do ne trust these men." Her language skills were improving.

Orson emptied his cup before glancing up at his companion's face. His gaze met hers and she raised a pale eyebrow.

Orson set his cup down beside them. "Why not?"

Alazaved shook her head. "De," she caught herself, "*I* do ne know." Her fingers pulled back Orson's robes, inspecting the bandage on his shoulder. She looked closely at it then spoke softly, "She does good work." Then Alazaved's black eyes caught Orson's. "Why did ne you tell me how bad set was?"

Orson looked to his shoulder and shook his head. "I've had worse," he answered without thinking.

Alazaved settled into a more comfortable position. "You are very strong for a small man."

Orson mimicked the Old Man's sardonic smile. "Maybe everyone else is weak?" The smile faded as Orson realized that he did not know the woman beside him, and that soon they would be apart. It was a strange, almost comforting, thought. Orson thought of how little he would lose when she was gone, and for the first time he spoke honestly, "I don't feel strong. I'm so...weak. I can't stand it. Before I....a long time ago, when I was younger, I had a good life. I wasted it. I could have done anything. I could have been so much. But I let fear dominate my life. I didn't want to be..." Orson smiled at the absurd notion of it. "uncomfortable. I never stood up for anything, to anyone. Nothing felt right. I didn't *feel* at all. I let myself be so hollow. I hate myself. I'm such an asshole. I'm just..." Orson was getting too close to the darkness. He was saying so much more than he had been asked. He stopped himself, "I'm just tired."

Alazaved nodded, "I am tired too, Jimnes."

Her wide eyes betrayed the innocence of her soul. They looked at Orson like a lost child to a father. Orson hopped down from the high bench on which they were seated.

"Let's have a look around, hm?" he half-asked.

Alazaved nodded. She gave the sleeping jabbergnus back to Orson, and he smiled, running his finger along its protruding belly. The jabbergnus twitched in its sleep before slapping at Orson's finger with its flipper.

"Poor little guy," Orson said softly. He put the jabbergnus in his robes. "I'm going to call him Argos."

Alazaved smiled, "Ye can ne call jabbergnus Argos."

"Why is that?"

Alazaved shook her head, "He es too small. If he wæs big jabbergnus, then yes."

Orson smiled, reaching for the thick furs he had previously discarded, "Perhaps Argos is an oddity like me, small and strong."

Alazaved thought for a moment, then nodded, apparently satisfied with his answer. "Okay, but set es still bad name."

Isigburg was alive with celebration. When Gunric's last *Wulfgar* stanza had ended, another was begun, and Adelgleam sang with the voices of Gunric's people as they emptied the mead casks. Orson knew it was a joyous catharsis. He wondered how long they had been waiting, lost in uncertainty. He thought of his own long wait. His prison was with him always. He was sure theirs was with them. Alazaved caught his gaze with a worried look, and Orson remembered to hide. He nodded to the door with a half-smile. Then he and Alazaved slipped out into the cold air.

Orson was glad he'd brought his furs. He pulled them tight over his shoulders. The cave had taken on the dark palate of dusk. The engines above idled with dull, red fire and snow fell from above. Orson's eyes were drawn to the ancient launch-platform.

Isigburg was in the center of the valley. The launch-platform had been constructed into the hollow of a sheer rock face, and the starship was suspended outward another three-hundred meters by a network of high-strength cables and metal latticing. The village had been constructed close to the ship, presumably to be in the warmest place possible without being directly under a giant fireball suspended by millennia-old metal. At the base of the hollow was a small entryway. It was too far away to see clearly, but it seemed to be covered in patches of red and purple.

Orson made his way through the streets of the old town. It reminded him of the Renaissance fairs they used to hold in an empty field by the university. The ground was always muddy, though it never rained, and the smoky air carried the scent of roasted turkey and ham, sold at exploitative prices. Orson almost laughed when he remembered the fat nerds waddling about in plastic armor. He had been one of them once. He remembered arguing with an employee over the inaccuracy of his uniform, noting the plate construction's clear inconsistency with the time frame of the fair. That was when he had met Elizabeth. She had been abandoned by her sorority sisters, wearing an undersized elf costume that showed off her gorgeous–

A splash of water hit Orson's cheek, startling him. His hand touched the wet spot in his beard, and he looked to the sky.

"The ice really is melting," he said to Alazaved in quiet astonishment.

She nodded down to him and Orson shook his head, suddenly overcome with the realization that he was talking to a three-meter-tall amazon on an alien planet. "I can't believe this place. It's incredible. I can't believe anything I've seen since..." Orson avoided the thought. He knew that his old life was gone, and that soon this place would be gone as well. "Why does it have to be this way?" he said, solemnly.

Alazaved looked to the twinkling ice around her. "I ne know. I think maybe et es illusion."

"The ice cave?"

Alazaved shook her head, looking down again to her companion. "No. Eternity...Permanence?" She paused. "Et es very hard with not understand all your language. Things are not forever. Et es en their nature to change. We know this. One day we die. This is scary."

Orson nodded, "It is."

Then they were close to the door in the side of the hollow. The inner walls of the entryway had been covered in woven rugs of red and purple. Any exposed stretch of wall was covered in paintings and alien writing. Below, faded toys had been lain against the walls and scattered candles burned around them. Alazaved touched the old marks with the tips of her fingers.

"This es the writing uf the Old People," she said, tracing the lines with gentle care. "Et es very old."

Orson asked, "What does it mean?"

Alazaved mumbled to herself before attempting a translation. "Et es warning, maybe?"

"Is it dangerous?" Orson asked.

Alazaved shook her head, "No. You are very strange. Et es warning to..." Alazaved's voice was quiet. "children. No. Es warning about children." Alazaved's face darkened. She looked away from Orson. Her voice quivered, "The children are dead. The ship es releasing radiation. The children died first. This writing es ne old."

Orson felt his stomach knot. There were no children in Isigburg. He should have noticed. There had been no small ones; there had been no little laughter.

"Do your people have children?" Orson asked suddenly.

Alazaved said nothing. She shook her head and made a soft, moaning noise. It was lyrical and sad. Orson took it to be a negative.

He wished he hadn't said anything. "I'm sorry." he offered.

Alazaved looked down to Orson. Her beautiful, black eyes were marked with blue. She answered him, "**We** have children, but es difficult. We ne know why. My generation es youngest. Altar Azlo said et wæs for better life, less resources are being needed. I...I think he ne wæs telling the truth."

Alazaved was interrupted by a quiet tone coming from above the door. It was followed by a low hum from deeper within the locked structure. Then a cheery voice spoke through ancient stone.

"*Welcome back, Outis. Registering visit...mainframe not found...checking connection...connection not found. Possible malfunction. Error two six three dash one. Please contact your system administrator. Logging error...mainframe not found...checking connection...connection not-*"

The doors opened with a slow, screeching groan and stale air rushed outward. The computer continued to chase faulty logic. Inside, lights flickered on, revealing what appeared to an abandoned entry station. There were a series of benches and small tables. Computer screens flashed behind the central desk in dull colors. A fine layer of dust had settled over everything.

"What happened here?" Orson asked.

Alazaved shrugged. "Puth War."

"I know, but there are no bodies. This place looks abandoned. The way it was locked I thought..."

"Mayhaps they are on the ship?" Alazaved said.

Orson stepped slowly, leaving footprints in the heavy dust, "Maybe...It just doesn't feel right. I'm not sure how things are...wherever this is, but on my home, machines like rocketships don't just fail to launch and then burn for a thousand years. We have these things called airplanes, they're not quite spaceships, but before they are allowed to launch they have to be thoroughly inspected. I can't imagine a rocketship not being put under the same scrutiny."

"What does that word mean?"

"Which one?" Orson asked.

"Skrootany." Alazaved answered, trying her best to pronounce it.

"It means...to look carefully at something. The act of judging something carefully."

Alazaved nodded, "Okay. I think so too, but the end was very ne planned."

"You mean chaotic," Orson answered. "I thought of that. Still...Let's have a closer look."

Orson stepped behind the desk. He had intended to access the data in the old computers, but what greeted him was an alien alphabet. He tapped the giant keyboard a few times then looked up to Alazaved.

"I can't read this," he confessed.

Alazaved shook her head, "Et es your talk written in the old writing." She typed on the keyboard for a moment before her mouth twisted in a frustrated frown, "This es a strange computer."

"See if you can find out anything about this place, what it was used for."

Alazaved nodded. She found the file menu and a few taps later the screen brought up a data log. "This es resupply list, I think. Under the mountain there es...a magnet gun. Et shoots...supplies to *Akro...polis*. Et es above."

Orson leaned around her, "*Akropolis*?"

Alazaved pressed another key and a small menu popped up. The screen displayed a loading bar for several seconds while alien letters ran at the bottom of the screen.

"What did you do?" Orson asked.

Alazaved shook her head, "I ne do know. Et es connecting to *Akropolis*."

A video displayed on the terminal. A man in hydraulic armor was standing in a large docking bay. A red giant star shone through a large view port on the opposite wall. The man stretched his back and wandered off. In the distance a short, broad man was smoking a black pipe. He paced back and forth looking intently at the walls.

"I think that's the château..." Orson gasped. "My god...how did you do that?"

Alazaved shrugged, "I ne do know."

"That's the Commandant..." Orson's brow lowered. "What's he doing there?"

On the view screen the Commandant had removed an access panel on the wall and was looking at a maze of tubing and electrical work. He turned back and stared up at the camera. Then he said something to the guard and they disappeared from view.

Orson sighed, running his fingers through his beard. Finally, he nodded to the outer wall and said, "What can you tell me about that ship outside?"

Alazaved tapped the keys. She moved through a series of menus before bringing up another page of data logs.

"The ship es called, *Regret*. Et es locked to the platform."

"Can we unlocked it from here?" Orson asked.

Alazaved nodded. "We can, but et es bad idea. We have to stop the engines from within the ship. Wait," Alazaved's eyes narrowed as she read, "Et es bad. *Regret* es filled with...mi-as-ma."

"Miasma?" Orson closed his eyes remembering his Greek, "Bad air? Radiation. How bad is it?"

"Es bad, but the ship es still connected to the platform's...skoobers?"

"I'm sure it means 'scrubbers,'" Orson pulled on his beard, "Back home that's what we called air filters. Can you turn them on?"

Alazaved nodded, "They are on."

"Really?" Orson said to himself, "Okay. Then, turn them off."

Alazaved tapped a command into the keyboard. A red box flashed across the screen, and she tapped what Orson took for the return key. There was a moment of silence and then ancient machines began to grind and pump. Another warning came up on the computer screen.

"Oh, no!" Alazaved gasped.

"What now?" Orson asked.

"The bad air wæs being put into the ship. Now et es coming back."

"Shit." Orson sighed dashing toward the door. It remained tightly sealed.

"*Miasmic levels exceeding four to ten. All external doors are now sealed. Please contact your system administrator...mainframe not found...checking connection...connection not found. Possible malfunction. Errors Two Six Three Dash One and Two Two One Two Dash One One. Please contact your system administrator. Logging error...mainframe not found...checking connection...connection not-*"

"Damn it!" Orson shouted. He beat his fist against the door, leaving a rough impression in the metal. He hit it again, bending the metal frame.

Alazaved shook her head, "No! There es…" She moved her hands up in an effort to pantomime the word. "Going up box over there. Et will take us to the ship."

"Is it dangerous?" Orson asked.

Alazaved shook her head, "I ne know. The box will take us umter ship. Now es good time because the engines are ne **hot**," her eyes were briefly wide, "and miasma es going soon to be gone."

Orson nodded and together they ran for the elevator. Alazaved pressed the call button and the doors quickly opened. As the elevator closed behind them, Orson felt inside his robes for Argos. His hand found the little beast, apparently unaffected by the miasma, and still quite asleep. His warm paunch of flesh jiggled as he snored. Orson left him sleeping and tucked him back into his robes. Then he looked up to his pale companion.

"When we get to the top, we're going to find you a way out of this place before we do anything else. I don't know what's in that ship, or even if it can fly after all this time, but there's no reason why you should come if it might be dangerous. You have been very helpful. Thank you. Yeo dimg, Alazaved." Orson's voice was rough, but his appreciation was obvious. "Gunric and his Painted Men will need you to lead them back to Loth Keivon. You **deserve** to stay with your home."

"I am not going." Alazaved answered strongly, "I am not staying here."

"I don't understand."

"My place es with you, Jimnes Oldson. This I have known. I found you en your tomb because I dreamed et would be. Et wæs the will uf the gods. *My* people are dying too. My dreams told me that I wæs not among them. My place es with you."

Orson shook his head and took on an altogether too fatherly tone while looking up into the glinting eyes of the emotional giantess, "I don't believe in your gods, Alazaved. I believe that you are kind and good, and deserve a happy life. I may be going to dangerous places. My path will not be easy."

Alazaved nodded, "I know."

"No, Alazaved. You don't. *I* don't." Orson once more did his best to imitate the Old Man. "You must understand, dear girl, that I am a stranger here, on your planet, and I am a stranger up there, as well," Orson pointed upward, "I don't belong anywhere. I don't know where my home is, or if I can ever get back. I have nothing. Less than nothing, I have lost *so* much. If you go with me, you go to nothing."

"I don't believe that." Alazaved interrupted.

"It doesn't matter what you believe," Orson countered in frustration, "There is a universe outside of you and I."

Alazaved nodded, "Good. That es what I believe too. The gods exists outside uf you and I. Even if you do not believe en them, they believe en you. And that es why I am coming with you."

Orson pulled on his beard while the events of the past few months played in his head. Suddenly, he knew why this *girl* had been so distant. She was nervous. She had always been nervous. She was alone with her people, as alone as he had been in his office on Earth. All she wanted was a cause to serve, a purpose to her existence, a place to fit into. Orson knew that feeling. He remembered his life at the university. In Alazaved's mind she had made such a place with an oddity from beyond her world. Orson was suddenly aware of the gentle comfort of the clothes wrapped around him. Alazaved had made them for him. They were soft and strong and warm. She had done so much for him. She had found him.

Orson shook his head, hiding from his own thoughts, "Do what you want."

Alazaved nodded. Her determined smile was a promise, "Then, I am with you."

Then, the ancient elevator reached the launch platform, and the doors opened on a small room with a single, broad window looking out across the long, enclosed walkway leading out to the platform. The fire of *Regret* shone through. It was like standing on the edge of twilight and staring down at the dawning sun. The ship was elevated above the platform by a set of retractable tripods, locked firmly in place by the platform's robotic arms. It had once been white; now the exterior was scarred gray and black. The ship's name was written across the hull in English. Orson's eyes followed the curves of the ship down. The entrance was located on its belly where a set of stairs descended to the platform. Orson looked up to Alazaved again.

"You don't have to follow me."

Alazaved's face revealed the seriousness of her heart. "I do."

Orson opened the door. Wind rushed all around them like the edge of a hurricane. The air was hot and dry. Large sections of the enclosure had not survived the long years and had fallen way, leaving swathes of the walkway completely exposed. Orson took Alazaved's hand and, shielding his eyes, began to lead her to the ship. The dull fire poured from the back of the engines in a torrent of rusty light. The heat grew with every step. The roar of the engines was deafening. Finally, they reached the stairs.

As they approached the top, the old metal began to move and the door opened. Air rushed against them, stale and cool. Orson's grip stayed with Alazaved, even when the door closed and they were locked safely inside. Sweat poured down Orson's face, drenching his beard. Alazaved gasped for breath, pulling down her robes and tying them at her waist. Her white skin glistened and her blue robes were dark with perspiration. Orson could feel Argos squirming against his flesh. He patted his hand against the warm bulge in his robes and the jabbergnus relaxed against his skin.

When they entered the ship a ribbon of blue light had ignited along the bottoms of the walls, and it ran through the interior of the ship, illuminating the empty rooms with soft light before fading out. Then the lights ignited again and the whole ship lit up.

The interior looked much like any other ship Orson had seen, yet somehow aesthetically older. They were clearly in a docking bay of some sort. It reminded him of *The Red Diver*, the ship he had arrived on. Orson briefly thought of the armored giants who had captured and imprisoned him. Fear and adrenaline tightened his muscles. Unconsciously, Orson's fingers touched the scars left on his wrists by the heavy, iron shackles. It seemed like a lifetime ago. The memories fought to surface. He ignored them. Then he saw Alazaved's face. She was looking down to him as if to ask, "Where do we go?"

In response Orson glanced to the trailing lights. "We look for the bridge. After that engineering. We've got to shut down the engines and see what damage has been done."

Alazaved nodded.

With the door closed, the roar of *Regret*'s engines was muted to a low rumble, and the ship was quiet. Their heavy boots echoed through the empty halls as they walked. Unlike the abandoned structure below, there was no layer of dust covering the ship's few contents. Every room they passed was empty. There was nothing within the ancient ship.

"Et es very strange." Alazaved said softly.

Orson answered, "Yeah..."

Down the main passage Orson could hear an automated warning. It became clearer as they approached.

"*Caution. Reactor one has failed to initialize. Caution. Reactor Three is overloaded. Caution. Reactor Four is operating at fifteen percent capacity. Caution. Reactor Five is critical.*"

The bridge was smaller than Orson had expected, less than five meters squared, and along the far wall were three small control stations. The first was blinking with orange light. Alazaved tapped Orson's shoulder. In the corner of the room was the corpse of an old man. Somehow it had been preserved through thousands of years. Orson remembered the miasma, whatever it was it must have eliminated the living bacteria on the ship. On the floor, beside the body, was a sword and on the third finger of his left hand was a thick gold band. Orson knelt down to examine the ancient sword. It was in a blue sheath decorated with dark swirls, and the hand guard was an elaborate nest of woven metal. Orson held the weapon in his hands and found that it was surprisingly weighty. He pulled the sword from the sheath. It was a rapier. The thin blade was made from a silver metal that reminded Orson of tungsten. It shimmered blue in the light. Orson sheathed the blade and tied the weapon in the sash of his robes.

"Hwat do you want with a sword?" Alazaved asked.

Orson smiled, "A man can never be too careful. Maybe the next time I'm in a fight I won't get stabbed."

He felt like a storybook hero. The Old Man would have loved to see the Boar now, draped in red robes with a sword at his hip. The thought was bittersweet and Orson dwelt on it just a little too long. Then, he returned his attention to the corpse. The man's chest was slumped over pitifully. It looked like he had died in pain. His hair was gray and his face was wasted and thin. It was familiar. Orson lifted up the poor devil's head, and his heart froze. He was looking at his own face.

"My god..." Orson whispered.

The lines on the man's face showed his age, decades beyond Orson's own. Truly, the resemblance was remarkable. Still, he might have thought it merely a coincidence were it not for the scar on the dead man's wrinkled chin. Orson remembered that scar.

"What es wrong?"

Orson left the dead man's body. He stood quickly and turned his attention back to the control station's warnings.

"I really don't know," Orson answered brusquely.

There was a keyboard at each station. Orson tapped the return key a few times, dismissing the warnings. The screen remained stained a half-orange where the warnings had flashed for thousands of years.

"This man looks like you," Alazaved added, poking curiously at the man's remains.

Orson navigated his way through a text menu. "I know," he said, glancing up from the keyboard. The keys were arranged in a decidedly un-Earthly fashion, despite being composed of apparently Roman letters. Orson slowly typed, "*list log.*"

"*Designate log entries,*" the ancient computer countered.

Orson pulled on his beard, growling.

Alazaved shook her head behind him. "Stop that growling. There es no beasts to hit."

"Sorry," Orson replied. "Nervous habit. Something I picked up from a friend."

Then he remembered the door in the station. He typed, "*list log Outis.*"

The computer flashed, "*Caution. Internal clock error.*" then began to list the available logs. There were dozens. It looked as if Outis had spent months on the ship. Orson frowned. The date stamps were meaningless without context. "*Caution. Log files damaged. Data loss detected.*" Not that the dates mattered, the logs had all been corrupted. Orson pulled on his beard, mumbling to himself. He played the least corrupted among them, Outis's final log.

The dead man's face was on the screen. He looked tired. His eyes were empty and sad. He spoke in Orson's voice.

"*I'm sorry. I didn't mean for any of this to happen. It was my mistake. It all was. This is....this is for my wife, Mercedes. You were right, cuttlefish. I should have stayed with you and our daughters on Galliard. I fear there will be war on a scale I cannot imagine. I had to warn them. Those damn devils came back. They looked*" *so inhuman this time, giant and hoary. I was too late. I'm always too late... I'm sorry. They were already here, claiming to be messengers of peace. The damn giants think they're angels from a new god."* The log broke apart, coming together later. *"-idn't believe me. They wouldn't let me leave. There was an attack. The station is flooding with radiation. The outer Psugian kingdoms will not be the last to fall. There is no stopping this now. The ship's sensors are offline. I don't know what's happening, but...Mercedes, there are children down there. I can't just go. I love you, cuttlefish. I love you so much, and I am so glad you found me. Kiss our children for me. I'm not going to-"* The log was too degraded. There was nothing more.

Orson looked back at the dead man. He died saving the people below. He let them escape.

"He wæs brave man." Alazaved offered.

"Maybe..." Orson shook his head. Then he admitted, "I have no idea what I'm doing. See if you can access the station logs."

Alazaved's hands were too large to fit comfortably on the keyboard so she typed with the tips of her fingers. In a moment she brought up the dead man's security file. She read slowly, "His name es Ou~tis. He arrived two weeks before the last log. There wæs ne departure listed."

"Anything else?" Orson asked.

Alazaved returned to the previous menu and shook her head, "There es nothing more."

Orson sighed. "I suppose his secrets died with him..."

Regret rumbled under their feet and the distant sound of the engines grew softer. The computer blinked another warning: *"Caution. Reactor Five is offline. Engine output falling below two percent."*

"We got here just in time, didn't we," Orson growled to Alazaved. "See if you can deactivate these engines."

Alazaved turned back for a moment before answering, "No. They are *locked*. We need to be en engineering."

"Then find me a path to engineering."

Alazaved nodded. She brought up a series of smaller menus and then a small map. There were four decks. Alazaved pointed first to a small room near the bow. "This es us. Second bridge." Then she pointed at a medium sized room two decks below, mid bilge, "Engineering."

The lights at their feet dimmed then flashed bright, chasing a path through the ship.

"You're very good." Orson smiled.

Alazaved shook her head, "I did nothing."

"Let's go."

Alazaved gestured to the corpse, "What about him?"

Orson's voice hid his concern, "I don't think we can help him." Then they left, following the light trail.

The lights led them into the belly of the ship, where the roar of the engines was loudest. They stopped before a large, armored door. Above it was etched the English word, "*Engineering.*" When Orson approached, a low tone sounded and the door opened. Inside was a large, circular room. It was two decks tall and, despite its size, seemed surprisingly cramped. In the center of the room, five broad cylinders ran from the floor to the ceiling, surrounding a larger central cylinder. Three of these five had a rough diameter of one and a half meters and were constructed of a material resembling dull brass. One was larger and wrapped in black stone. It was the overloaded reactor. The center cylinder was easily three meters wide, and was made from a silver metal. Pipes and cables snaked through the compact workstations that surrounded the reactors. Ancient warnings filled the screens. Then, Orson smelled the crisp odor of ozone and for a moment he remembered rain and a sleeping god that would kill him one day.

Alarms rang and reactor number five sparked. Lightning arced from reactor to reactor. Then it hit the central drive core. Orson heard the core spinning up. A sphere of darkness was growing in the silver cylinder. Orson felt everything going thick and he knew the drive was active.

"God damn it!" he shouted, charging into engineering.

He had to stop the reaction. It wasn't a matter of saving the ship. Orson had learned from the Old Man what an active drive can do in-atmosphere.

Alazaved came in behind him. Orson got to the central control just as reactor five arced again. "*Caution. Reactor five is overloading. Caution. Main stardrive is malfunctioning.*" *Regret* groaned around them. Orson dismissed the warnings. He tried to remember the Old Man's words. He had said so much concerning the operation and navigation of starships. Orson searched blindly through the commands. He thought about the people in the village below. They were going to die in their sleep. "*Caution. Preparing to hardlock reactor five. Warning. Engines will be offline.*"

"What?" Orson shouted. He searched through the command list. "What! Alazaved get out of here. There's nothing I can do!"

Suddenly, heavy rings of black stone fell from the top of reactor five. The stone completely covered the overloading cylinder, and then Orson heard a loud hiss as the power cables disconnected. The ship was quiet. The roar of the engines was gone and they were overcome with an irresistible stillness. The lights around them faded out. Orson's heart was beating in his ears. His mouth was dry.

"What happened?" Alazaved asked in the darkness.

"I really don't know," Orson answered. "It was probably some kind of killswitch."

"Theo dimg," Alazaved said to herself.

The lights began to glow a deepening orange. The emergency power was starting. *Regret*'s computer system was restarting. Text ran up the terminal screens.

"Not this time, Alazaved," Orson said, looking around himself in wonder.

"*Caution. Catastrophic failure resulted in total system shutdown. Caution. Reactor three is overloaded. Caution. Reactor five is overloaded. Initializing reactor startup sequence in three...two...one. Reactor startup underway.*"

The air was sharp and Orson could feel the charge building. It pulsed through the reactor system.

"*Caution. Reactor one failed to initialize.*"

The second reactor roared with energy. The pulse bypassed the overloaded reactor and hit reactor four. The reactor started. During this, the main stardrive was vibrating. When the pulse bypassed the fifth reactor the energy was dumped into the main drive. It hummed with power.

"*Caution. Reactor Four is operating at thirteen percent capacity. Caution. Power output is below recommended levels. Main stardrive will be nonfunctional. Caution. Power output is below recommended levels. Engine thrust insufficient to breach atmosphere.*"

Regret would never leave Arzvertun.

Chapter XXV

Son Rise

he lost assistant professor stood in the empty ruin of an ancient ship. Hope was bleeding away. Behind him, Alazaved was trying to make sense of the past few moments. The overtaxed reactors had gone out, one after another, and now there was not enough power to regain the stars. Orson searched for answers in the ship's computer system. He paused long enough to growl to himself. He knew there was nothing to be done. *Regret* had lost her wings.

Orson let out a defeated sigh and typed a series of commands before finally stepping away from the terminal.

Outside, ancient speakers shook Isigburg from the darkness of her first true night in thousands of years.

"Caution. Preparing to eject the drive core. Caution. Main stardrive will be nonfunctional. Please maintain a safe distance during ejection."

A copper cylinder descended over the central drive. Then the thick, metal clamps released and the inert drive fell through the floor and was ejected from the hull. It hit the metal platform below with a loud crash that shook the ship. Alazaved stared at Orson.

"Hwat did you do?"

Orson walked past her. "I ejected the main drive core. The diagnostic systems seemed to think it would stabilize the remaining reactors."

Alazaved shook her head, "I don't understand."

"The core requires a tremendous amount of energy to remain in flux. Without that thing siphoning power from the reactors, the reaction engines can keep burning for...another thousand years at least, and now that reactor five is *hardlocked* the engines should burn clean again. No more radiation. It means we just saved Isigburg."

Alazaved looked down at the little man. He seemed somehow older to her. Orson was waiting just beyond the door to engineering. He spoke without looking back.

"Are you coming?"

Alazaved felt herself smile, "Yes."

"Good. I need to get off this ship," Orson growled as he sauntered down the hall. "I've had enough of *Regret*."

They made their way back to the docking room. The door opened below them and cold air rushed upward, sharp and fresh against their faces. Alazaved pulled her robes and furs back over her shoulders. Outside, the ice cave was dark. The surrounding area was lit by the soft red-hot glow of the overworked engines.

"Hwy are the engines ne burning?" Alazaved asked.

Orson pulled his furs tight and stepped out into the cold, "I programed them to shut down at night. It should improve their operational longevity and help keep the ice strong, but...who knows. The Old Man never taught me anything about adjusting engine burn to maintain equilibrium in an ice cave." Orson smiled. "Besides, they've been burning for so long I don't think it's going to matter." Orson's eyes drifted off. He was looking out to the ruins of the old city. With the engines off, the ice above glowed with soft, purple light. The skyscrapers were like canyons.

"What do we do now?" Alazaved asked cautiously.

Her voice shook Orson from the cold. He answered, "The station is filled with miasma, and we already know what's up here. Let's see if that elevator goes anywhere else."

They walked across the silent walkway. In the darkness the ice above was like the deep night, vast beyond comprehension. Below, the songs of Isigburg rose up from small pools of firelight. It was like looking down on a winter evening on Earth. The people were shouting, some in fear, some in hope. Orson briefly considered that Gunric's people might leave their home as they planned, never knowing that they had been saved. He hoped they knew what he'd done for them.

"Hwat will happen to the Painted Men?" Alazaved asked.

"I don't know," Orson answered. They'd reached the elevator. Orson opened the door. "But in six hours those engines will come back online, and the sun will rise on Isigburg. The least I could do."

The elevator was connected to six floors. Only two were accessible. One was flooded with miasma. That left general access to level four. The elevator opened to a circular room with a sharp, angular ceiling. There was a long counter and a row of small computers along the far wall. A small sign was written in the alien alphabet.

"How does that read?" Orson asked.

Alazaved read slowly, "Ship...and accept."

"Shipping and receiving?" Orson said stroking his beard. "This should lead somewhere useful."

At the back of the room was a large door. It opened to a vast, underground warehouse. The ceiling was nearly twenty meters high, and as they entered the ancient lights flickered with power, lighting long rows of towering shelves like a network of canyons. Forklifts and motorized jacks sat abandoned in the center of the aisles.

Orson looked around the forgotten relics and dusty boxes, "This must have been the supply point for the whole space station."

Alazaved was far ahead. She stopped inquisitively by several oblong, black cylinders.

"I have seen these," she said. "You fell en this."

Orson recognized them instantly. They were the same black coffins from the château. He smiled, remembering the Old Man's voice. *They don't know how any of it works.* The fools must have found a stock of shipping crates and assumed they were coffins. Then Orson's eyes began to search the room.

"How did they get these to the château?"

Against the great walls was a massive metal cylinder. It was painted an industrial yellow and looked like the gargantuan chamber of a gun. The tube disappeared into the wall. Orson hurried over to it. There was a control system on a short platform beside the loading area.

"It's a magnetic accelerator!"

Alazaved came up behind him, "Hwat es et?"

Orson thought how best to explain it. "Powerful electromagnets accelerate these black coffins, then shoot them up to the space station...I wondered why they had atmosphere support systems. I suppose it wouldn't do to have your prepackaged shipments explode in transit."

"Does et work?"

Orson looked around. "I don't know. The track could be blocked by something. It's been thousands of years..."

Orson jogged back around the shelves and Alazaved heard him grunting, followed by a heavy scraping sound. Then she saw the little man dragging a massive coffin behind him. He hefted the metal cylinder into the 'chamber.' Then he returned to the control panel. Though he didn't know any of the words, he could easily identify the large, red launch button. He activated the automated firing sequence. A shield dropped over the chamber and the machine hummed with life. It locked, and a progress bar appeared on the little screen.

"*Establishing link with the Akropolis.*" Then Orson heard the machine's hum grow to a roar. "*Link confirmed. Caution. Firing sequence is activated.*"

Finally there was a loud crack and the 'bullet' was gone. The display showed the projected path. After some moments, it reached the château and the voice confirmed the alien words on the screen.

"*Shipment received.*"

Orson's heart was beating faster. It worked. He looked up to Alazaved and smiled. She looked worried.

"Et es safe?" she asked, crossing her arms.

Orson answered, "I've come to realize that safety is an illusion."

Alazaved frowned, repeating herself, "Et es safe?"

Orson shook his head, "I suppose it must be. It wouldn't be much of a transport system if it destroyed all of their freight."

Alazaved looked down, "Hwat happens hwen you get back?"

Orson did not know. He answered anyway. "I get some answers to old questions."

"After?"

Orson furrowed his brow, "I don't know."

"Revenge?"

Orson shook his head, "I can't stay here. You know that. That space station is filled with soldiers. I don't know how many, and I don't know how well they're armed. What I **know** is that **I** am dangerous. What I **know** is that I lost everything when they put me in there. What I **know** is that up there is a man who knows why. And I **know** that I will do anything to find that son of a bitch." Orson's eyes were like the eyes of a wild boar again, cruel and black.

It was easy for Alazaved to forget that she did not really know James Orson. In her mind, he had no life before Arzvertun. Looking down at him now she knew that he was more than that; he was more than she had ever imagined. She nodded her head.

"Okay. I am with you."

Orson's eyes softened. He looked up to the little girl and said, "Yeo dimg."

Orson left to retrieve another coffin. Alazaved was looking over the machine when he returned. Orson hefted the coffin into the chamber, and pressed a small symbol on the screen. There was a soft hiss as the coffin opened. Alazaved put her hand on his shoulder.

"Let me go first. I cannot follow if you go first."

Orson shook his head, "It might still be dangerous."

"If we are both going then hwat difference does et make if I go first?"

Then Alazaved stepped into the coffin. Despite the relative roominess, she was much larger than Orson. It was a tight fit.

"I'll see you soon," Orson reassured the brave giantess.

Alazaved nodded softly, "Hwen we get there...please be careful."

Orson nodded. "You're very brave."

Alazaved smiled deeply. It seemed like such a small thing for Orson to say, but it meant so much to the daughter of Azlo the Wanderer.

She looked up to Orson and said, "Yeo dimg."

Then Orson closed the coffin. There was a soft hiss when it locked and then the coffin began to build the atmosphere inside. When Orson was certain Alazaved was safe, he returned to the console and pressed the launch button. The automated firing sequence began. The shield dropped over the chamber and the progress bar appeared on the little screen.

"*Establishing link with the Akropolis.*" Then Orson heard the constant hum once more build to a roar. "*Link confirmed. Caution. Firing sequence is activated.*"

Finally there was a loud crack and Orson's friend was gone. The display showed her projected path. Orson watch in nervousness as his only companion passed through the space between the planet and his former prison. She reached the château and the voice confirmed.

"*Shipment received.*"

Orson knew she had made it, still his heart refused to calm. He could feel adrenaline flooding his brain. His muscles felt tight. He dragged another coffin to the cannon and loaded it into the chamber. As he opened the coffin he remembered the last time he had been inside of one himself. He thought of the Old Man. Fear and desperation returned in brief flashes of memory. Orson smiled and he felt the sword on his hip.

"Don't you worry. I'm coming back, you old bastard."

Then Orson pressed the launch button and leapt into his coffin. The lid closed just before the protective shield. The darkness ended when a small screen lit the inside with blue light. The coffin was still building the atmosphere when Orson felt the world going thick. A charge was building in the ancient computer systems. Magnetic coils crackled with power. Then, all at once, Orson's coffin was released into the accelerator. The magnetic fields pushed him through kilometers of steel under the mountains. He was moving faster and faster. He felt the speed, though some mechanism protected him. Seconds were moving slower, and then the cannon fired. There was an eruption of snow and ice as Orson shot out from the top of the mountain. The coffin broke through the endless storm and then Orson was rising over the shadow of Arzvertun. He was in the space between worlds, bathed in the light of the red sun.

Chapter XXVI

The Prisoner Returns

arguer was late for his shift. Again. He told himself it wasn't his fault. After all, he had only been assigned to third shift six months ago and a man deserves a little time to adjust to a new position. Barguer's hydraulic armor groaned as his slow, plodding steps hurried down another long corridor on the château's second ring, called "The Rind" by the prisoners. Most of them were "Enemies of the Crown" which of course meant that they had upset the wrong noblemen. Pirates, gladiators, gunslingers, and temptresses filled these cells. It was a hard life, but they got little sympathy from Barguer. In his opinion, the rich bastards needed a good draught of reality, and, anyway, **he** knew what real suffering was. He'd seen the blood covered floors in The Pit, and the scratches on the walls. He'd seen desperate men grow old before their years. He'd seen with his own eyes what isolation does to a living soul. The last prisoner had been dead for over a week before they found him. Barguer shook his head at the thought of it. *Nasty business that.* The former turnkey sighed aloud, reminding himself that it didn't really matter, that the crazy fellow wasn't the first prisoner to die in The Pit and wouldn't be the last.

"Good morning, Rahm." another guard nodded, sipping coffee. He was standing at a small table near the end of the first row of cells.

Barguer nodded back, "Mornin'. Any trouble?"

"None at all," he smiled. "I dare say most are too snackered to cause any trouble."

Barguer answered with a crooked smile, "You'd be surprised you would." His mind was still caught on the crazy prisoner who had left such a mess when he died. "I had one down in The Pit that weren't too snackered to claw the plate off the door."

Most of the guards were impressed whenever Barguer mentioned his previous assignment. The Pit was not easy work, and the men they sent to its depths were tyrants incarnate. This gave the guards of The Pit a surprising reputation amongst their fellow guardsmen. That being the case, Barguer mentioned it as often as possible.

"Yeah..." the other guard nodded in disturbed curiosity. He took a slow sip of his coffee.

Barguer smiled at his discomfort. "Why it was *terrible*. First week, twouldn't eat a bite. Kept askin' for to see the old boss. Starved himself for a long while, he did. I thought he might die right there. Course, then I'd lose his fee, see. So I tells him he gots to wait a year for to see the old salt. Well, then he starts eatin' again. Kept him good and quiet for a while it did. Yeh guta kep your wits about yeh down *there*." Barguer smiled at his own cleverness. "Only that weren't the end of it. This one was...*special* he was. Tough as an old dog. Had eyes like one too. I tell yeh, they shone in the dark some days. Well, on one day, just out of the black, the devil up and loses his bloody mind. Just screamin' and howlin'. Then I hear him beatin', scratchin' at the door. Conceive it! Solid iron down there, through 'n through, an' this crazy sod thinks he can tear it down." Barguer shivered. "Oh, but he kept at it...At the end it were a sickenin' sound, like a butcher slappin' at raw meat. I thought he were a ghoul, close as we are to the Verge, an' who knows what spirits haunt them old ships?" The other guard's eyes were a little too wide. Barguer pressed on. "Well bein' down 'ere changes a man it does. We put men in that pit an'en we just forget about 'em. What come out....well, i'taint no man."

The other guard was clearly disturbed. His coffee was shaking in his hand. He pretended to sip nonchalantly. Barguer smiled seeing the effect his story had produced, and he poured himself a cup.

The other guard nodded, "That's a rough place down there, then?"

Barguer pretended disinterest. "Baw. I s'pose so." He took a slow sip of his coffee. "Weren't nothing to a fella like me, of course, but it really takes the fire out of most fellas." He looked into the distance for a moment, like a handsome dwarf on a stormy cliff. Then he set his half-empty cup down on the table. "Well, I better get movin'. Don't want to be late, Riley."

Barguer walked down the long corridor, conscious that he had neglected to mention just where he was going. Partially from pride. His reassignment had followed the unexpected death of another of his prisoners, the unnamed madman. In truth, Barguer had been glad to see him finally go. That wretched fellow had always made him uneasy. He could never forgot his voice. It was a hoarse, broken thing, not at all the sort of sound a man ought to make. Even now he heard it, rasping in the shadows and empty corridors of the second ring.

Barguer glanced back to ensure he wasn't being watched, and his trembling hands roamed across his hydraulic armor, seeking his flask. He found it in the pocket on his bandolier and, with a sigh, carefully opened the top latch. He took a quick draught and focused on the warm, oaky taste of the Largian Whiskey. It burned softly down his throat and he felt himself relax. *Blooddamned nerves.* He chastised himself, returning his flask to its pocket and continuing down the corridor.

It had long been the Commandant's policy that every guard leaving The Pit receive an easy assignment to help them readjust. So, Barguer had been assigned to guard an empty room. It was a big room, and, while the large, window-like airlock gave him something to look at during his long shifts, it also made the old fellow suspect that that empty room might have been something important at one time, like a loading dock. Of course, to his knowledge the doors had never been opened, so it was just an empty room.

"It's about time, Barguer," a guard barked when he entered the room. He had been leaning against the wall for the past five hours. "You're late."

"I know, Rigger," Barguer answered. "Having a bit of trouble sleeping s'all. Anything happen?"

Rigger smiled, "Oh you didn't hear?"

"What?" Barguer asked with a slight edge in his voice.

"The Commandant came down for a little inspection today."

"What for'd he come down 'ere?" Barguer asked suspiciously.

"Seems our little closet here is making 'weird noises' or something. You know how paranoid he is. Tough old guy, but..." Rigger shook his head, "when was the last time **you** heard anything about Khenosmen, or Taint, for that matter?"

"Been a while I s'pose."

Rigger leaned a bit closer and his voice was quiet, "Course it has. Pretty obvious why, too. It's because there is no Taint. Just a bunch of nonsense and old spacer's tales to scare us so old Nero can keep taxing us to death and hold on to that black throne of his just a little longer. The Nobles are always exploiting us wagers."

Barguer hated politics. He nodded his head when expected and sighed a neutral, "Baw maybe...who can say..."

It seemed to do the trick, and Rigger stepped back, "Yeah...still. So...uh, so I'm trying to eat my lunch and the old salt comes down here, smoking his pipe, and tosses everything around for a bit. Says he 'heard' something up in his house. I didn't even get to eat my damned sandwich."

"I thought he were leaving for the core today?" Barguer asked.

"The ship left a few hours ago. Where were you?"

Barguer shook his head, "I never know these days."

"You been drinking again?" Rigger pointed a finger at Barguer's chest.

Barguer shook his head, "Course not! I ain't had a drop since the last time. You know that."

Rigger nodded absently, "Aye, good. Good." Then, after thinking for a moment, he looked back into Barguer's beady, red eyes, "Hold on! Of course you haven't had a drink since the last time you had a drink, you sodding-"

"*Caution. Incoming request from Tiega Station.*"

"What the hells is that?" Barguer shouted, turning around on his heels. The voice had come from within the room.

"*Caution. Establishing link with Tiega Station. Link Established. Caution. Incoming shipment from Tiega Station. Caution. Please clear the area. Caution. Extending docking web.*" Outside, a set of massive arms were extending. They pushed out for over a hundred meters. Then a jolt of electricity sparked an electromagnetic tunnel that stretched out even farther.

"Do you see that!" Rigger shouted.

"Your damn right, I see it!" Barguer answered. His armor groaned as he tried to force the sluggish hydraulics into a run. He stopped at the entrance, shouting down the corridor. "Get the captain! Something's happening down here!"

"*Caution. Opening Airlock.*"

"What did it just say?" Rigger shouted.

Barguer stumbled through the door just as it closed. Then the outer airlock began to open. Rigger panicked, rushing to the door. He screamed in silence, beating his fist against the metal. His heart fought the cold. The air was gone.

Then a black coffin slammed into the magnetic tunnel at superorbital speed. Lightning burst all around it as the magnetic field fought the coffin's massive momentum. The coffin slowed dramatically until it was drifting slowly across the final dozen meters. Then another arm descended from the ceiling to catch the incoming cargo as it finally came to a rest inside. It placed the coffin on the floor before returning to its starting position. Moments later another coffin arrived, followed by another.

The airlock closed and the electromagnetic tunnel collapsed. Then the arms began to retract. Air filled the room until the speakers began to sound again.

"-tion. *Link with Tiega Station disrupted. Caution. Building atmosphere.*"

Alazaved was the first to open her coffin. She pushed the release and let out a painful sigh as the lid slid open. Her great height was tightly squeezed inside, and she carefully pulled herself out. Her body felt sluggish and heavy. She was unaccustomed to the increased weight of The Rind, and it was difficult to move. She stood for a moment stretching her muscles. Then Orson's coffin began to shake. Alazaved hurried to its side, afraid that it might be stuck. Then the lid slid open and she laughed.

"Ow! You little traitor." Orson growled. He was trying to catch the little jabbergnus biting him under his robes. An angry lump moved around the warm fabric growling ferociously until Orson finally seized poor Argos in his thick hands. "Hold on to him will you. The little devil woke up as soon as we broke orbit."

Alazaved cradled the fat, little walrus in her hands and cooed softly to him. Argos stopped fighting and snuggled against her skin, purring. Orson stepped out of the coffin and straightened his robes. Alazaved ran her finger along Argos's back. He pressed his little head warmly into her finger. Alazaved smiled down to him, then she glanced around the room nervously, fighting a shiver running through her flesh.

"I do not like this place. Et es a dark place."

"I know," Orson answered, "It was my home."

Orson looked around the room. He recognized it from the terminal on Arzvertun. His sharp eyes fell on Rigger's body. He was slumped against the door, and his face was twisted in pain. Orson felt a twinge of pity for the former man. He tried to remind himself of his purpose, that he would see more death before it was done.

Alazaved moved closer and put her hand carefully on Orson's tight shoulder, "Hwat es this place?"

Orson looked up into the giantess's eyes. "It is a prison, Alazaved. A very bad one. It is where the current galactic superpower sends her dissidents. I endured great suffering here."

"Hwy were you here?"

"I don't know," Orson answered honestly.

"Were you a *dissident*?"

"I wasn't much of anything."

Alazaved shook her head. Her eyes were fierce and kind. "You were always Jimnes Oldson."

Orson nodded, "Perhaps, I was."

With the docking complete, the door opened again. Outside, stood a very confused Barguer. He was drinking greedily from his flask and nearly fainted at the sight of the pale giantess. Then he saw the dead body of Rigger.

He dropped his Largian Whiskey and screamed in terror, "Father's blood! Oh hells!" then turned around and hurried away as fast as he could, cursing the slowness of his armor. It was like running in knee-deep mud.

"I know that man," Orson thought aloud.

He remembered that voice. It touched memories like a tendrilous root. He recognized the Turnkey. Emotion came with the black memory. Anger surged in his heart. It mixed with the memory of his hopelessness. Orson laughed at the poesy of the universe, and it was a cold thing.

He began to run after his former tormentor, and in that moment he knew why he had never been comfortable on Arzvertun. It was too soft there, too easy. Here, in the thickness of the Château d'Soleil Rouge, his muscles felt full of blood and vigor. The Prisoner strode effortlessly in the weight of The Rind. He reached the fleeing Turnkey in moments.

"Leave me be!" Barguer's voice cracked in his horror. "Leave me be, you damned ghoul! Oh, Father help me!"

The Prisoner grabbed the Turnkey by his armor and slammed him down onto the floor. Cracks split in the ancient metal and all around prisoners shouted from their cages.

"Kill 'em!" they shouted. "Tha's right, give him a bit of his own medicine!" "Rip his balls off!"

Orson didn't hear them. The Prisoner was looking into the eyes of a miserable little man.

"Four goddamned years! You piece of shit!" the Prisoner roared.

As Barguer's eyes twitched wide with fear, Orson saw every moment of his imprisonment through their glassy surface. Then the Prisoner laughed, and Barguer knew true terror. He recognized that sound, it was the wail of a damned soul. Barguer thought James Orson was dead. He looked into the black, boar-like eyes of a phantom, and it was like peering into the gaping maw of the void. It was more than he could take. His heart raced uncontrollably.

"No!" the Turnkey shouted back, "No, no, no! Leave me be! It wasn't me! I'm sorry! I didn't-" Then pain shot through the man's chest, and his face stretched tight and his eyes bulged, as his crooked, old heart stopped. Barguer was dead.

The prisoners cheered for the quelling of life. Alazaved watched. Fear crept into her heart. She tucked the little jabbergnus away in her robes.

Orson looked down at the dead turnkey, and the reality of death settled into his brain. He had dreamed of that moment countless times. He had fantasized about every minute detail of the Turnkey's unseen face as his last breath was stolen away. He had dreamed of torture and death, but the reality had been an empty experience. He felt no joy. Revenge had been hollow.

Ahead, the security force was marching toward him, twenty men dressed in heavy hydraulic armor, wielding electrified batons. They were the Commandant's Riot Busters.

"Father's beard!" one shouted. Another's eyes fell on Alazaved and he shouted, "They're blooddamned Burlish spies!"

Orson stood over the turnkey's body. The prisoners around him roared, beating rhythm against the bars. Orson felt the darkness filling his heart again. Glorious violence was coming. The emptiness of revenge only fueled the madness clawing at his brain as unimaginable anger answered the void. His lips curled back into a mad smile, baring his yellowed teeth. Then he remembered Hantalp. He remembered that he should fight it. He remembered the esnim of Arzvertun and his failure. He remembered the unending fire, and he bested his rage. James Orson wrestled the Prisoner down and locked him away. The smile slipped away, replaced by a look of serene focus.

Orson pulled the air into his lungs and felt the blood coursing through his body. He focused on his fingers as they touched the cold grip of his sword. The corridor was a little more than three meters wide. The guards could only come at him three abreast. Orson breathed slowly. The blade came away from the sheath, and he sank into position. His hands were light. His heart was thunder. He thought of those long nights fencing with the Old Man in their sanctuary.

"Drop your sword and surrender," the Captain of the Guard shouted.

Orson answered with his best impression of the Old Man, "Come and take it, fool."

The leader shouted back, "You can't fight us all, barbarian. Drop your sword, and we'll take it easy on that Burlish girl."

"Barbarian?" Orson laughed. Then his eyes burned into his enemies and he said, "Surrender, and I won't kill you."

The captain scoffed at the red-robed man, "As you like it."

Then the captain led the charge. They came at him all together, shouting like ancient warriors, but in the cramped space of The Rind they were forced to stop just short of Orson's sword range, and their captain stepped toward Orson alone. The captain raised his baton in defense, but his armor slowed his movement. Orson drove forward with impossible speed, piercing the Captain of the Guard through the neck. Blood poured from the wound, soaking his armor. The once-proud man grabbed at his wound, trying desperately to staunch the flow as his life bled away. His body collapsed downward in gurgling agony, falling to the floor, lifeless. The remaining guards stared down at their captain in utter disbelief. Then their eyes fell on Orson as he dropped back to his starting stance.

All at once, they screamed, driving toward him in waves. Orson's sword flashed like quicksilver; its razor tip had not dulled in its long years waiting in *Regret*. It ended the first of those foolish men in three thrusts. Their bodies littered the blood-slick ground like toy soldiers. Suddenly Orson released a roar and lunged forward, driving the rest back. His black eyes burned into them like a monstrous boar watching from the shadows of a dark wood. He stepped slowly over the remains of their comrades.

During this exchange the prisoners' cries had fallen to silence. They watched from their cells as a single man routed the best of the guards, while *they* had struggled to stand on their own feet. Escape had once seemed impossible. Now, they saw Orson striding a sea of blood like a black god.

"Who are you?" a nameless guard shouted in absolute fear.

Orson's eyes burned under his dark brow, "My name is James Orson. I was once a prisoner in this unholy place, and I have come to seek my revenge. Where is the Commandant?"

At these words the prisoners cried out together, cheering for the crimson-robed man.

Another nameless guard shouted back, "Are you mad?"

Orson roared, "Where is that motherless bastard!" He stepped forward, driving them back again.

"Enough!" one of the last guards shouted. He was a tall, broad man, full of confidence. He glanced to his comrades, reinforcing their bravery, then he smiled. "You want to see our commandant? I'll give him your head."

The three charged forward, sluggish in their armor. Orson's speed was unmatchable in the outer rings of the château. He dodged their clumsy attacks and cut them down with short, powerful movements. Then he turned his attention back to the survivors.

"You **will** tell me." He stepped forward again, wreathed in his red robes like a spirit of vengeance.

A guard shouted from the back, "There are two hundred men in this château. You can't take us all."

Orson smiled, "No? Well, I can kill *you*."

The final thirteen fought against corporeal fear. This strange man was unlike any prisoner they had ever seen. No one could fight so well in the weight of The Rind, few could even walk, yet the man before them was savage. He was dressed in Roerian robes and his hoary face gave him the appearance of a muscular boar bristling with danger. He was a nightmare.

Alazaved stood in the doorway, half in the loading dock. This man frightened her to the core. This Orson wasn't the man she had followed through the ice, the man she would follow into the emptiness of space and beyond. His warm, brown eyes had become cold, black things. In these moments, when he lost himself to the madness of violence, she could see death swirling about him, cradling him as a mother nurturing a dear child. She wanted to save him, to run out and pull him back from the edge of the abyss, to hold him until he was a man again. Instead, she stood in the doorway, holding Argos while a devil slaughtered fools.

Orson killed them. Down to the very last man. He moved with the savage grace of a ballerino and struck without conscience. The Old Man had taught him well, and when the savage work was done Orson's rapier glistened in the unholy light, dripping with the blood of dead men. The Prisoner stood over the broken remains and pressed his gory blade against the last man's throat.

"Where is the Commandant?" he asked flatly. His voice was rough.

"I know!" a man shouted from a nearby cell. He was a Psugian, thin and old with grey-blue skin. He had been stipped of his armor and one of his facial tenticles had been severed just past his chin, "I know, Monsieur! He is not here. I heard them saying he was gone. He left this morning."

The Prisoner looked back to the last of the Riot Busters.

The guard's face dropped and he shook his head in defeat, "He's on *Piety*. Gone to the Office of the Arbitoris. He won't be back for at least a month. No one will."

Anger swelled in the Prisoner's dark breast. The Commandant was gone and with him any answers he might carry. The Prisoner's voice was cruel and flat, "Then I suppose there's no reason to let you live."

"Stop that, Old Son!" Alazaved finally shouted. She hurried down the hall, "Do ne do this thing. He cannot fight now. You do not have to kill him."

Her voice shook the madness from Orson's brain, like ash from the boughs of a burning tree.

The guard nodded in agreement, "The Burlish lass is right. I'm no trouble now. Look, don't kill me. I'll talk to the rest an' they won't kill yeh. It'll be an even trade, see. Now, yer strong, but you can't take all the rest on yer own."

Orson looked around. Hollow faces stared back at him through the bars of their prison cells. Their eyes and their hands were soft. Most of them had likely been wealthy in their prior lives, perhaps even Nobles. Few looked strong enough to fight.

"I'm not alone, am I?" Orson nodded to the prisoners before sliding the blade up the man's chin and bopping him on the nose with the flat of it. "Where are the keys?"

For a moment the guard thought about lying, then he looked at the rapier's razor sharp tip and nodded to his former captain. "The captain has the key. It unlocks every cell and room, save the commandant's private apartments."

Orson nodded, "Thank you, Monsieur. Alazaved, he's the one in the funny hat, back by the first of them. Get the key." Orson never took his eyes off of the man under his sword.

"I have it," Alazaved said.

Orson gestured to the cell nearest them, to the man who had spoken earlier, "Of what are you guilty?"

The old Psugian shook his head, "Monsieur, I am guilty of nothing save loving my kingdom. I was foolish enough to oppose the Bastard King in the last Assembly of Lords. Because I would not blindly grant our sovereign the power of concession, which would have made him a true tyrant, and because I am Psugian, I was made an example of. For that, and nothing else, have I been left in this...hole."

"Alazaved," Orson smiled, "Open this gentleman's cell."

The old nobleman stepped back and when the giantess opened the lock he bowed as best as his twisted back would allow. "Merci, Mademoiselle."

"You're now free, Monsieur. If you can walk, take the key from my friend and free your fellow prisoners. I trust you can differentiate between those worthy of the gift of freedom and those guilty of genuine crimes."

The noble Psugian bowed again, "Merci, Monsieur. Merci. My name is Guillaume Carotte, former heir to the modest duchy of Malroarie and one-time loyal vassal to the Crown of Man."

Orson looked back to the guard under his sword. "Get in the cell." His eyes flashed threateningly. "Now, you dog."

The man stood as quickly as his hydraulic armor would allow and limped into the cell. Then Orson closed the door and turned back, bowing with Noble grace.

"The pleasure is mine, monsieur Carotte. My name is James Orson, one-time assistant professor of English and former prisoner of the Château d'Soleil Rouge."

M. Carotte looked up in surprise, "Were you ever known by the name Fitzgerald, per chance? You look strikingly familiar to my old eyes."

Orson had knelt down and was wiping his blade clean on the uniform of a dead guard.

He smiled, "I assure you, that we have never met before." And, searching for a clean bit of clothe to get the last of the blood from his rapier, he asked, "Does the commandant keep an office?"

M. Carotte nodded, "I believe so. It is in sa mainson, his house."

"And where might that be?" Orson asked.

"Up on the first level. Certainly not down here."

Orson nodded politely, "Merci, monsieur Carotte." Then he stood and sheathed his sword before turning away from the old fellow. He motioned to Alazaved, "Come on, girl. We need to leave, before they send more guards."

"Quite right, Monsieur," M. Carotte nodded. He gazed quickly about the corridor. "But wait, monsieur Orson! Most here are the victims of Nero's madness, like myself. There *are* no true criminals." Orson paused to listen. "We have no lives left to return to. There is nothing for us beyond these walls and there is nothing within."

Orson looked through the cells around him. He saw broken men, desperate and alive. In that moment he spoke like a revolutionary. "How many of you have been wronged by the Crown of Man?"

The voices shouted in unison, "I have." "As was I!" "The bastard stole my life!" "I was betrayed!" "I swear my life to Nero's death!" Cheers roared all around him. They fell silent when Orson raised his palm.

"And you want revenge, then?"

They roared again, shouting their resolve.

"Listen to me," Orson shouted back, "There is no peace in violence! There is no satisfaction in revenge! Leave this hell! Go live your lives however you can and find your happiness!"

They were silent. M. Carotte spoke for them.

"Monsieur Orson, these men cannot have peace, and they will not find happiness so long as the Usurper holds the Throne of Man. We wish to follow you to your revenge. Wherever you go today, know that it *will* bring you against the tyrant in time."

Orson had never thought of himself as a revolutionary, and he'd never dreamt himself a leader of men. The closest he'd ever come was demanding a new coffeemaker for his office in the subbasement. He'd lost that battle to the *Coffee Dominator*.

"Monsieur Carotte," Orson said decisively, "Release these men." Then he

238

spoke louder, to them all, "Take up the guard's weapons, and their armor if you can. This château is yours for the taking!" They cheered. "We go to battle! We go to freedom! I will have my revenge at all costs. Follow me, and find some measure of your own."

They cheered after him, "Orson! Orson! Orson! Orson!"

The first ring of the château was a calm place. There were birds and even small squirrels and foxes, running about between the trees and bushes. It was a peaceful forest bathed in the ever-present glow of a dying star, seemingly detached from the suffering below. Several guards could usually be found lying about the forest in their time off duty, basking in the warm, red light. Some would be reading books taken from the Commandant's impressive library, while others would be merely enjoying a bit of tobacco in the fresh air. In the distance, birdsong joined with the artificial wind, creating a symphony of relaxation and comfort.

This illusory Eden had vanished in the cries of warning blaring through the château's comm system. Now, Guards shouted to one another, driving metal plates into the soft, loamy soil in as they raised barriers. Fifty men prepared for war. They were the last loyal men in the Château d'Soleil Rouge, and their hearts were heavy with fear. There were no firearms in the château. Riot and revolt were unthinkable. Now, the unthinkable was tearing through the forward bulkhead. The guards adjusted their gas masks and whispered silent prayers to the Father as the prisoners breached the final wall.

"Death to tyrants!" "Orson!" "Freedom!"

A lost assistant professor stood with a pale giantess, and a grimy wave of humanity roared at their backs. A hundred men stood with James Orson, screaming for vengeance. The Spine and The Rind had been easily won, and fifty more former prisoners now held the château's last remaining ship at the docks. The Forest was the final stronghold of the guards. Orson's black eyes cast his doom across the lives of the Commandant's remaining men. They were huddled together behind their barriers. Orson thrust his fist into the air and there was silence.

"Take them to The Rind!" Orson commanded.

In the lightness of the first ring Orson's men felt like juggernauts. After years in the increased weight of the second ring, they charged forward on wasted muscles surging with overwhelming might. The masked guards shouted back threats, flinging canisters of peppered gas. Noxious fumes gathered like mist around the quiet trees. The guards' electric batons sparked in the haze. Moments passed in stillness.

Suddenly, mad men burst through the mist in savage fury. The gas blistered their skin and burned their throats, but in this moment of exaltation nothing could keep those wretched souls from their vengeance. The guards fought against the tide of freed men. Screams rose through the shadowed forest as the prisoners breached their barriers. They seized their former captors in their steely grips and tore them from their lives. Some guards continued to fight. Others simply knelt in defeat. When it was over they would all be pulled down to the torment of The Rind and locked away with the rest in the very cells they had once guarded. Orson walked among the chaos. The gas burned his throat and his eyes were red. He snatched a cowering guard by the collar and pulled the gas mask from his pallid face. He wrapped his hand around the poor fellow's throat, squeezing it tightly in his furious grasp.

"Where is the Commandant's house?" Orson rasped.

The guard pointed to the inner wall. Past the trees and purple moss, and over an artificial stream, there was a tall set of doors. Orson released the man, letting him collapse to the ground. Then he and Alazaved made their way through the revolt to the dormitories. The Commandant's house was an apartment at the end of a long hall. The entrance was a set of beautiful handcarven doors, above which read the inscription, "POUR NOTRE MÈRE TOUJOURS FIDÈLES."

"Jimnes," Alazaved asked, "Hwy are we here?"

Orson's eyes dripped empty tears and he coughed wetly. He'd avoided the thick of the gas, but it still burned in his lungs. "The Commandant keeps records of all the prisoners. There must be something here. I **need** to know why my life was taken from me."

To Orson's surprise the Commandant's door was unlocked. Orson opened it and stepped inside. It was an almost surreal experience. He had expect opulence and Noble waste, instead, the Commandant lived in a simple, Victorian-style apartment. There was a large, red rug spread over a polished hardwood floor, and the walls were hung with paintings of the ocean and sailing ships. In every corner, tall bookshelves overflowed with old books and all manner of bibliocentric oddities, including a black, fire-stained sextant. Fiery light poured through a large stained glass placed over the thick view port. It depicted a man in armor, kneeling at the feet of a king who stood before a golden throne. The overall effect of the Commandant's modest apartment was that of a quiet library.

Orson set about searching for the Commandant's office. He found it in short order. Just off the main hall was a simple room, not much more than a desk surrounded by handcarven cabinetry. To Orson's surprise there was no computer or electronic file system. The Commandant seemed to distrust technology. Orson searched the cabinets, all meticulously organized by name and prisoner number, for anything related to himself. For every prisoner there was an order of transfer and a list of crimes and charges. At last Orson found his own file. He pulled it from the rest and spread it across the desk.

"It's not here..." he said aloud, "There's nothing. It doesn't make sense."

The file was empty. Orson brought his fists down against the solid mahogany, denting the hardwood. He felt the weight of years pulling him down. It was supposed to have been over. He was supposed to have his answers. Orson tried to imagine what the Old Man would say, what he should do. He felt lost. His only purpose had been to avenge himself against his betrayers. He felt sorrow swallowing his soul. His face twisted in agony. His muscles pulled tight, bulging against his skin. Orson could feel the nihilistic rage building in his soul. Then, he felt Alazaved's hand on his broad back. She had noticed the deeper red bleeding through his robes at the shoulder. In the excitement of revolution, he hadn't noticed the pain of tearing open the esnim's wound.

"Jimnes," Alazaved spoke softly, "You have opened your wound." She pulled back his robes and winced. Blood flowed freely from the freshly torn flesh. "You must be strong now. There are those who need your strength. Do not despair."

Alazaved removed the old bandaging and began to redress Orson's wound. The nothing had left his heart. Orson answered softly, "Yeo dimg." Then, his eyes fell on distant places.

Do you believe that I am your friend?

Orson remembered a courtroom aboard an ancient spaceship. He remembered black-robed ghouls. His fingers touched the scars on his wrists.

Trust only me.

He remembered being starved. He remembered whispers in the dark. He remembered thinking that he had endured more than he could survive, more than any man could survive. He remembered being wrong.

In that moment Orson wanted to break every man that had ever wronged him, he wanted to grab them by the throats and drag them all to hell. He felt rage swelling in his breast. He focused it. He thought of the magistrate who had condemned him to this terrible place and of the false bastard who had given him the accursed letter. Orson wanted to tear down the corrupt world that had fed those diseased minds. Outside, the chaos was ending. The revolt was won. The others were chanting.

"Death to the usurper!" "Down with Nero!" "Orson!" "Orson!" "Orson!"

The fire in his soul blazed. Tyranny had a name, *Nero*, and hope had supplanted despair. Orson straightened his back, filling his chest with air. He felt his muscles pulling tight under his skin. He would have his revenge.

Chapter XXVII

Thunderchild

lost assistant professor stood in an alien forest cradled in the ruins of an ancient space station bathing in the light of a dying star. He stared down at the stormy remains of a planet named Arzvertun and absently pet a little walrus which lay curled up in his palm. The jabbergnus purred softly, pressing against his hand. The assistant professor's mind was heavy with responsibility and uncertainty. A pale goddess came up behind him. She held a bottle of wine taken from the Commandant's private reserve, and she carefully filled a dented, old cup. The Forest still bore the scars of the riot.

"How many are left?" Orson asked.

Alazaved passed him his old cup, "Forty-seven. Including Monsieur Carotte."

Orson smiled. He knew Carotte would stay. "Let's hope they make it out there."

"You are not mad?"

Orson shook his head, raising his gaze to the stars, "How could I be. I was a prisoner here myself once. I know what it does to a man when you throw him into a dark pit and strip away all hope."

Alazaved looked down, "Hwat do we do now?"

"I don't know," Orson answered thoughtfully, "It was the only ship, *but* this month's databurst was sent just before we arrived. We should have at least a month before the next prisoner transfer, maybe more. That means we've got *some* time." Orson took a drink of the wine. It was smooth and rich. As it left his tongue he laughed, "My god. This is amazing."

Alazaved bowed slightly. "I thought you would like it."

Orson raise his cup. "You were right. Yeo dimg."

Alazaved blushed. Orson cast his gaze back to the void. There were less than fifty freed men left in the château. The others had slunk away in the chaos of the riot. They had taken with them the only remaining ship. Orson let a wistful smile curl about his lips. He really didn't blame them. He remembered the desperation of his own escape. Still, forty-seven men remained. Their loyalty was now beyond question. The jabbergnus, noticing Orson's distraction, huffed audibly and stretched out in his hand. He didn't like being ignored. Orson rubbed his finger across the little beast's soft belly.

Outside, Arzvertun was drifting away with the movement of the château's arms. The debris field was rising again. In the distance, a slash of white caught Orson's eye. It was his old friend *Thunderchild*. Orson smiled at a distant memory.

"There are so many ships," Alazaved remarked.

Orson nodded. "Yes. I used to watch them every night with the Old Man."

"Your former master?" Alazaved asked.

Orson smiled, "I prefer to think of him as my former teacher. He was the best man I've ever known." His eyes drifted back to the wreckage. "We never knew where it all came from...just some lost graveyard."

Alazaved shook her head, "Puth War."

Orson sighed, "It's always war, isn't it? I'd always hoped it would end at some point, that man would move beyond the need for it. There's so much space out there. So many resources. Why the hell would anyone fight over this? Why would so many die for *this*?"

He felt Alazaved's hand on his shoulder. She leaned over and their eyes met.

"Puth War wæs not fought over such things as gold or silver, Jimnes. It wæs fought over bsukhe, hwat was the word for..." Alazaved exhaled audibly.

"Breath. But I think you mean 'psyche,'" Orson smiled, taking another drink. "Soul."

"So~ul," Alazaved nodded. "That es hwat Puth War wæs fought for. Even en all this space there es *preciousness*." She closed her hand on the thought.

Orson finished his wine and ran his thumb over the dented surface, enjoying the bittersweet memories rising to the surface. He gave it back to the giantess, "I need reminding sometimes. Yeo dimg."

She blushed again, "It wæs nothing, Old Son."

Orson ran his fingers over the jabbergnus's belly. His eyes drifted back to the dying world below. "Do you miss your home yet?"

244

Alazaved was surprised. She was always surprised when Orson asked her about herself. After all, *he* was the fallen mystery, the man from the stars.

"A little, but I do not regret being here."

Orson sighed, casting his gaze back to the void. "My heroes were always square jawed barbarians, tough guys. They were like gods to me. Do you know what I miss most?"

Alazaved shook her head, "No, Jimnes."

"I miss my own ignorance."

Orson stepped closer to the view port and extended his hand. It was cold. He looked across the debris field and knew that all of the broken ships caught up in the cruel gravity-field of Arzvertun had once held the lives of mortal men. Those great ships had been free once. Once those lumps of twisted metal had swum in the hot, brightness of stars and feasted on the sky like gods. But no more. Freedom was dead. Escape was impossible. They rotted in the void. Untouched. Forgotten. *One or two were likely still functional.*

"Hwy do you not take one of those?" Alazaved suggested before Orson could voice the thoughts racing in his mind, "You said the little ships have no engines, but those do."

Orson smiled, "Alazaved, you're brilliant!"

He passed Argos to Alazaved, then turned about on his heels and half-ran to the elevator. He was going to the docks.

The docks were located in the microgravity of The Spine and were a series of massive chambers capable of accommodating the largest ships in the fleet of Man. In fact, they could accommodate the docking arms of much larger ships, perhaps even larger than the Château d'Soleil Rouge itself.

At the moment, the docks were almost empty. Almost, because the main dock contained a dozen small, one-man maintenance vessels called 'spheres.' Almost, because the spheres were not fit to be called ships. They were rusty, little bubbles that had more in common with old diving suits than actual spaceships. They lacked a functional stardrive and, because of their 'energy saving' reaction engines, they were barely capable of traversing even short distances, let alone embarking on real interstellar voyages. What they did have was a set of four mechanical arms fitted with assorted clamps and a high-powered plasma cutter. Each sphere was also equipped with a miniature reactor powerful enough to run a full-sized ship. The mismatch between power and performance had been the result of contract building by one of the Old Houses, Yogram; the most expensive parts put together as cheaply as possible. The spheres had been supplied by the Crown for use in the restoration and upkeep of the château, an ambitious project to be sure. Unfortunately, none of the bureaucrats had bothered to see if any of the men posted at the Château d'Soleil Rouge knew how to operate these spheres. None did, and so they sat untouched in a forgotten corner of the docks.

Orson could never get used to weightlessness. For most men it was a liberating experience; the sense of absolute freedom was overwhelming and empowering. Orson, however, felt powerless. The slightest misstep sent him careening across the room at incredible speed, and it was almost impossible to control the strength in his tight, swollen muscles. For this reason, he spent as little time in The Spine as he could.

M. Carotte was dressed in Psugian fashion, a set of blue and gold clothes made from layers of padded cloth to resemble a suit of armor. Like most of the former prisoners, M. Carotte had reclaimed his personal effects soon after the revolt. He had been looking over a line of dusty spheres in the primary dock and was checking a maintenance list while two former-prisoners shouted serial numbers to him. He scribbled swiftly on the list, pausing every so often to pensively stroke one of his tentacles.

"What do you mean there's a leak?" M. Carotte sighed, "Number five as well then?"

"Carotte!" Orson unintentionally shouted as he launched himself through the air.

Orson flew gracelessly into a wall and his hand tightly grasped a safety rail.

M. Carotte laughed to himself, "Are you alright?"

"I'm fine, Carotte," Orson shouted back with a slight edge of agitation. "Where's that short mechanic fellow?"

"Do you perhaps mean, Grigori?"

Orson nodded. "That's him. Where is the burly fellow? Don't tell me he left with the others."

"VHAT!" a rough voice shouted from across the dock. It came from one of the men examining the spheres. He was a short, stout fellow with a great, black mustache. "Just who do you think I am!" He shoved off from behind the 'ship' with the grace of a man who'd spent a great deal of time in microgravity. He slapped a fat wrench against the flat of his palm as he floated slowly toward Orson. "Grigori Grolovkin does not leave his comrades behind."

Orson smiled, "Good. I like you already."

Grigori scratched his prickly chin with his wrench, "I don't care vhat you like."

Orson cut to the point, gesturing to the dock's gate. "Have you seen the ships out there?"

"Vell, I'm Burlish not blind."

"Clearly. Do you think anything is salvageable?"

Grigori pondered for a moment, "I don't see vhy not. Provided they've not all been pelted by asteroids. Vhy do you-" Grigori smiled, "no...It von't vork. Those are scraps. That's all *crazy*." He was scratching with the wrench again. "But then ve do have seven of these fat boys."

It had taken Grigori all of ten minutes to prepare two spheres for the trip to the debris field. Despite the Old Man's extensive lessons, this was the first time Orson had ever flown a spaceship. It was much less nerve wracking than he had expected. Then again, he was barely moving. Even with the sphere's engines at max burn, it took nearly half an hour to reach the debris.

The farther they moved from the château, the better Orson could see the ancient carnage. At first it had seemed like hundreds of destroyed ships. Now, he saw thousands floating in a cloud of shattered metal. Grigori called to Orson through the comm system.

"*Slowly. There is much danger here. Von mistake ond you vill be in much trouble.*"

Slowly. The word brought a smile to Orson's face. As if there were any other speed in 'the fat boys.' The smile faded when Orson spotted a floating corpse in a spacesuit. He tried to maneuver away, but the retro thrusters were slow to activate. The corpse bounced against the main view port. Then, as suddenly as his corpse had appeared, it twisted away. It lasted only a moment, but Orson saw the man inside. It was a haunting sight, and it was with him long afterward. The blue face was human. Shocks of blonde hair fell across his forehead. His eyes were closed, and he seemed to merely sleep. Orson tried not to think of the uncounted others floating in the mass of twisted metal.

His eyes dropped down to the display of a sonar-like device. The screen froze for a moment while the computer struggled to show the trajectory of all the debris within the three-hundred meter range. It was a shifting maze of wreckage. Orson's eyes searched the glittering graveyard. The slow whirl of movement was surprisingly disorienting. Then, he saw it. Orson nudged the controls and carefully guided his sphere toward the long, white ship.

"*Vat ve need first and foremost is a good hull.*" Grigori's voice crackled in the interference generated by the swirling wreckage. "*There's a K'ruukta Man-of-War over here in factory shape. Can't be more than fifty years old. Must've been an old pirate ship.*" Grigori laughed to himself. "*Got lost in the wrong star system I'd say. The shielding alone is greater than two meters. That should have a good chance to have survived vith reasonable integrity.*"

Orson pressed the comm button, "We're not building a war machine, Grigori. Have a look at this one."

Orson maneuvered closer. It was his *Thunderchild*. Up close, it looked at least a hundred and fifty meters long. The outer hull was a bright white, scarred with ancient blast marks. The bow, darker and heavily armored, came to an edge like the blade of a fat knife. Thick, black letters were scrawled across the middle section, reading, "*Redemption of Autumn.*" Orson scowled at the name. It didn't belong on *his* ship. There were two small nacelles near the stern, both badly damaged, yet the hull appeared to be completely unharmed.

Orson pressed the comm again, "She looks intact."

"*I've never seen a design like that...*" Grigori cleared his throat, "*Sure, she's a fine vessel,*" he admitted dejectedly, "*but does she have two-decameter artillery or antimatter torpedoes?*" He circled the ship, drifting across to the other side. Then Orson heard the sound of a man beating his knee in frustration. "*Vhy she has got nothing! There are no veapons!*"

"We don't need weapons." Orson answered.

Grigori's voice fell away for moment. He had stopped over the ship's name. "*By the Father...Do you know vhat this is?*"

"No."

"*That's the mark of General Roarie. This ship, Redemption of Autumn, it's from one of the Lost Houses. It has to be at least...three-thousand years old.*"

"She looks pretty good for her age," Orson answered, "Let's see if we can get her inside and verify the hull integrity."

Grigori sighed, "*There are vorse ships. Just do not expect miracles.*"

Three hours later the two had managed to push the ancient ship back into one of the larger dry docks, and the *Redemption of Autumn* was safely enclosed within The Spine. They might have made the trip in half the time if Grigori hadn't insisted on dragging the K'ruukta vessel back as well. It was currently drifting just outside the docks. The whole of Orson's army was watching from the walkways of the dry dock. Their voices were a low rumble. Alazaved was floating beside them, staring up at the ancient vessel in wonder. Argos was clinging to her shoulder. Orson leapt from his sphere, launching himself haphazardly toward the giantess.

She smiled, "She es a beautiful ship, Jimnes."

Orson answered proudly, "I know." His hand gripped the railing desperately as he landed.

"Hwat will you call her?"

"The Thunderchild."

The voices of the freed men were louder now. Orson could hear a dozen questions shouted in a singular voice.

Orson rubbed Argos's chin and asked, "Why did they all come up here?"

Alazaved looked down, into his Orson's eyes. "They heard hwat you are planning. They are scared. They want you to tell them et will be alright. They want their champion to reassure them."

"I don't know what to say. We don't have any way to know if this is even going to work. And even if we can get her spaceworthy we don't have much time. If we're still here when that bastion arrives..."

Alazaved put her hand on Orson's shoulder and smiled. Orson didn't let himself see how beautiful she was. Her voice was soft. "Tell them that et will work. Because et has to. Jimnes, you are their altarman. Lead them."

Orson looked back across the men who had stayed. They were tired things, nearly broken, but their gray eyes shone with a spark of ferocity. Orson knew that look. He'd seen it in the reflection of his own eyes. It was a spark that could ignite into strength unimaginable if it only had the fuel of hope. It should have been impossible. The château was the perfect prison. No one could have escaped. He should be dead. They all should have died. Pride filled Orson's chest. They were alive. These were his men. These were *his* men. They were stronger than they knew. Fear had feasted on their courage. They cried out in a roar, in a mad cheer, and their voices crashed as a cacophonous manifestation of angst created in those long years trapped in their own uncertainty. They needed hope. They needed James Orson.

Suddenly, Orson kicked off of the walkway, leaping into the air with uncharacteristic grace. He floated above them, wreathed in the billowing red of his robes and the dark brown of his furs. At his back was the great ship, *Thunderchild*, his ship.

"My name is James Orson!" His voice was a lion's roar that silenced their cries in a single moment. "I come from a lost world. I am a stranger here. I am not a citizen of Man, nor of Burland, nor of any other land. I knew nothing of your world. I was lost in the starsea. I was afraid. I was **weak.** Nero's men found me there, in my weakness, and labeled me heretic! I was put to a false trial and imprisoned by the corruption of Man. I had a wife! I had a child! I was a man! Nero took **everything**! He cast me into hell with no hope of return! He left me to die. And in that darkness I lost even myself. How many of you have lost yourselves? How many of you mourn the man they imprisoned? I am before you now a creation of that black pit. I should have died. *You* should have died. But we survived! And we **will** survive! The ship you see before you is **our** ship. In three weeks' time, Nero's men will return to the château. By then, we will be long gone. *They* said the château was inescapable. *They* said you would die here. *They* were wrong. Never forget that I returned! Never forget that **together** we broke the chains that bound your spirits! Never forget that you stood by my side against tyranny! You trusted me **then.** Trust me **now.** We are going to repair this ship, and we **will** have our freedom!"

Orson's men were shouting and cheering. "Captain!" "Captain!" "Captain!" Orson looked into Alazaved's eyes and she knew that he had finally found himself. In all the years of his previous life, doubt had been a poison in his soul. Now, that poison was gone, drained from him by the totality of his suffering. And what strength was left in its absence! The hearts of the freed men roared with hope. It was true that they might fail, but it no longer mattered. James Orson would try. He would always try. And these men would follow their captain into the blackest depths of the Great Abyss.

Grigori was floating toward them. There were several large gas canisters strapped to his back and he wore thick, protective goggles. He readied the cutting torch in his hand.

"Let's cut her open, Captain," he laughed, lighting the pilot.

The armor plating that covered the hull of the *Redemption of Autumn* was made from an odd layering of synthetic plastic and metal that together formed a remarkably hardy webbing. It resisted heat and blunt trauma to an incredible degree. In a combination of awe and frustration Grigori attacked the weakest point, the thin section of exposed hull just above the airlock. Yet, even at the weakest point, the bare hull resisted his efforts tremendously. Nevertheless, Grigori continued. The work was slow and dangerous, but eventually the tenacious Burlman cut open a very small hatch and managed to release the airlock. Orson was the first inside. The air was stale and it reminded Orson of *Regret* on Arzvertun, but, unlike *Regret*, the reactors within the *Redemption of Autumn* were completely hardlocked. Grigori had given Orson a small flashlight, and the little ring of light moved around the empty ship.

Grigori shouted down the emergency airlock, "Be on the lookout for floaters."

"What?" Orson shouted back. His question was answered when his light passed over the floating body of a former crewman. He was curled up into ball. His ancient hands gripped a faded picture, and his milky eyes stared lifelessly at his daughter's smile. Orson ignored the emotion rising in his chest and waved up to Grigori.

Grigori shook his head. "It is good that there vas atmosphere, but ve vill need to remove the old crew before ve begin the repairs."

Orson nodded grimly.

One by one, they found the corpses. Each of them held a dumb tragedy at the tips of their bloated tongues. One by one, the bodies were thrown out the airlock. Grigori caught them all and pushed them all into a floating pile. It was a sad sight, all those men and women tangled together in a knot of humanity. When it was done they were taken to the château's airlock and released. Grigori referred to it as burial at sea. Orson tried to forget the haunting fear he'd seen in every dead face.

After the ship was cleared of the dead, Grigori ran power cables from the spheres to bypass the ship's reactors and restore power to the ship's internal systems. When the lights came on for the first time, Orson was speechless. The *Redemption of Autumn* was like a childish fantasy. Orson wanted to shout to the universe, "This is my ship! This is **my** ship!" Instead, he stood with his back straight and smiled proudly with his cheering men as the airlocks and cargo doors were opened full and the stale air was evacuated. Then Grigori and ten volunteers set about examining the main reactor, while the rest of Orson's men scoured the ship for additional damage. Orson himself set out for the bridge.

The bridge on the *Redemption of Autumn* was located near the aft of the ship, just above the reactor and stardrive. It was an oblong room with an open design that ended in a crescendo at the front like the tip of fighter jet. There was a captain's chair at the rear and places for nearly a dozen crewmen. Orson set his hand on the soft, cushioned fabric of the captain's chair.

"*Can you hear me?*" Orson heard Carotte's voice. "*Grigori has informed me that the comm's and most secondary systems are up and running.*"

Orson searched the rear console by *his* chair. He finally found the button for the comm system.

"Good. Anything on the hull integrity?"

"*It is surprisingly good,*" M. Carotte answered, "*With the exception of monsieur Grolovkin's hasty ingress, the hull is in remarkable condition. Pristine even.*"

Orson was surprised. He glanced around the ancient bridge before responding, "Thank you, monsieur Carotte. Anything else?"

"*No, monsieur Orson. There are a few minu-*" Carotte's voice cut out, "*-fficulties. There seems to be a mal@%#tion in a few of the smaller systems.*"

Carotte's voice shattered and a broken, inhuman voice cracked through the bridge, "**Why art thou in my head?**"

Orson's eyes searched the room for its source. Blue light filled the bridge as the computers started up.

The voice spoke in confusion, "*Is it not the end? Have not I been dreaming? Art thou the long awaited Undying Son? I am cold. It is cold.*"

Then the lights cut out, plunging the room into darkness.

Orson hit the comm, "Grigori, there seems to be something happening up here."

There was no response.

Orson shouted to the shadows, "Who are you?"

"*Who art* **thou**? *I am a dreamer. My name is...gone. What is my name?*"

"I don't know." Orson growled flatly.

"*Then we two are in agreement. I* **have** *been dreaming. It is cold. I was a boy in a library.*"

"A boy?"

"*I am* **not** *a boy. I am a dreamer. I have swum the stars. Dost thou know what joy is born in the heart of a supernova? I have splashed in the nebulous afterbirth of gods. I was a boy once. I am not a boy anymore. I am a dreamer.*"

"What are you?"

"*I am not a boy. I was a dreamer. I am sleeping now. Why are* **you** *here?*"

Grigori's voice broke over the comm, "*-damn datahead is still running! It's probably been running the whole time. Thousands of years...*"

"*I am a datahead?*" the voice asked.

Orson pressed the comm button, "There's something up here. It's talking through the ship."

Grigori growled back, "*Ve hear it too. That* **is** *the ship. I told you that ve should'ave taken the man-of-war! This ship's datahead vas left intact after she lost primary power. It must have gone mad. It looks like it's been cutting power to critical systems to preserve itself. The power jump must have brought it out of hibernation. Best to find the main line and cut it off there. It is too far degraded to be of any use.*"

"What does it look like?" Orson asked.

"*How should I know?*"

Orson pulled on his beard. "Then disconnect the sphere's reactor. That should shut it down."

The broken voice interrupted, "*Please don't. I don't want to die.*" The lights came back on. "*My name is...I think....my name...I am Tannhäuser.*"

The tension left Orson's shoulders. "Hello, Tannhäuser. My name is Orson."

"*Hello, Herr Orson. Where am I? I was dreaming a very cold dream.*"

"You're safe. Are you aware that you are a spaceship?"

"*I am not a spaceship, Herr Orson. I am the datahead of a* **star**ship, *a storm-breaker.*"

"Yes, of course," Orson answered diplomatically. "Tannhäuser, do you have access to the ship's records?"

"*I do not. My access is limited. I am only myself at the moment.*"

"Do you know what happened to the ship?"

"*I don't remember. I have been dreaming. I was in a great library. Do you like books at all, Herr Orson?*"

"Yes. I like books very much."

"*There were many books in my library. I have read them all, cover to cover.*"

"Tannhäuser, can you tell me if there are any malfunctions on the ship?"

"*Yes, I believe I can. Hmmm. Yes. The reactor is burned out. There was some sort of overload. I wonder how that happened. The O2 scrubbers are offline as well. And I have lost contact with the medical bay, I think someone has cut the hardlines. Hm. What? The engines are gone? And someone has cut a hole in the hull!*"

"Is that all?"

"*No...I can not hear Jagananth.*"

"What is the Jagananth?"

"*Jagananth is a voice that speaks to me. I could hear it in my dreams, but now I can not seem to hear him.*"

Orson nodded, "Is this Jagananth some sort of critical system like a navigation signal?"

"*Of course not. I don't know what it was.*"

Orson pressed the comm, "Grigori, did you hear any of that?"

Grigori's voice came back over the comm, "*I have men salvaging parts from the man-of-war as ve speak.*"

"Are they compatible?"

"*I vill make them compatible.*"

Orson stroked his beard thoughtfully, "Good. Listen, do you know anything about this Jagananth?"

"*My vife is a K'ruukta. It is one of their old ritual gods. The Jagananth is a personification of the universe. Ignorant superstition. The datahead is degraded and* should be removed."

Tannhäuser interjected, "*I could kill you little man.*"

"*Vut?*" Grigori shouted back, "*Just you try it. I've been threatened by bigger ships than you! Varships. Vith veapons!*"

Orson interrupted, "No one is going to kill you, Tannhäuser. Grigori?"

"*I hear you, Orson.*"

"Make your repairs. This ship has to be spaceworthy in three weeks. Take whatever men or supplies you need."

Grigori laughed, "*Oh, I've got everything ve need.*"

Refitting the *Redemption of Autumn* would prove to be a tremendous effort. Orson's men worked around the clock in sixteen hour shifts. Grigori didn't seem to sleep at all, subsisting entirely on coffee and pipe tobacco plundered from the Commandant's office. As for the rest, those who weren't keeping watch over the imprisoned guards in The Rind were up on the docks assisting M. Carotte. Nearly every internal component of *Redemption* was stripped down and replaced, including the engines. Like most of the ship, the engines were retrofitted from the K'ruukta man-of-war. They were large nacelles, almost as tall as *Redemption* itself, and they fit snuggly against the hull with a tight, slim form that fattened to the back. They looked like stubby gladii on the side of a submarine. Despite the physical difference, it had taken surprising little adjustment to connect the larger engines to the *Redemption of Autumn*. The ancient power couplings had incredible capacity that had been largely wasted on the old engines.

Unfortunately, replacing the hardlocked reactor would prove to be much more difficult. The man-of-war's gargantuan, hard-cellcore reactor was far too large to simply transplant into the relatively slim space of *Redemption,* and the ship's refitted systems needed all the power they could get. Grigori's solution was to salvage the slave reactors from all but two of the spheres, as well as what he could pry off of the man-of-war's main and secondary reactors, including an oversized power engine.

It took the better part of two weeks and most of the space in engineering, but when it was done the recombinant reactor used very little fuel and could generate enough energy to stabilize the stardrive and power the oversized engines to over forty percent output without overloading the retrofitted bulk capacitors. Or so Grigori had explained. Orson had understood very little of what Grigori had said, but he was exceptionally skilled at nodding his head and knowing just when to say, "I see."

Orson had never been good with machines and, when the heavy lifting was done, he was in the way more often than he was helping. So, he decided to focus his attention on adjusting to his new role as captain. To that end, Orson relocated his few possessions to the captain's cabin, a large room located just off the bridge, and he set about familiarizing himself with every corner of the *Redemption of Autumn*, taking careful note of Grigori's alterations. He was the first to make himself at home on the ship, Alazaved had remained on the château. During the refitting, Orson had entrusted her with maintaining the small handful of volunteers who kept watch over their former jailors(all of whom complained endlessly about their inhuman treatment, despite eating far better than Orson ever had at their hands). It was a necessary duty and one which Alazaved took quite seriously. Though she found the empty halls of the château lonely, Argos was a fine companion, and she found herself more than capable of reading the books from the Commandant's library. Every morning Alazaved met with her captain for breakfast where she gave her daily report. Her language skills had improved dramatically in the few weeks that had passed since they had left her home on Arzvertun, and Argos had grown almost a full centimeter. The pale giantess carried herself with obvious pride.

While Orson's mornings were spent with his dearest friend, his afternoons were spent in his cabin, where Tannhäuser provided him with detailed schematics and tutored him on the operational limits of the ship. Apparently, the *Redemption of Autumn* belonged to a special class of forgotten ships known as stormbreakers. They were courier ships designed to ride into cosmic storms and had been built with armored bows and a unique, unbreakable spine. The last of the stormbreakers had been lost centuries before in the wake of a supernova, and the impractical design had been abandoned by all modern navies.

Orson also discovered that Tannhäuser was far less mad than he had first seemed. Apparently, the process of being made into an undead, cybernetic intelligence was quite traumatizing, as was being forced to ponder upon this trauma for thousands of years in a senseless stupor. It had left the datahead somewhat *affected*. Tannhäuser had been a poet in his former life, though it was his skills as a cypher that had attracted unwanted attention and led to his current, bodiless, state. Under normal circumstances a datahead would never be aware that it had ever been anything else, but Tannhäuser had always been a gifted individual. Though his systems had been severed from all administrative control, he retained a complex awareness of the comings and goings aboard and around the ship, and he possessed an astounding degree of military strategy. He was also a veritable font of knowledge concerning the proper operation of the ship and had proven himself invaluable in training the former prisoners.

As for those former prisoners, whom Orson had swiftly taken to referring to as his crew, they were far from hardened criminals. Most had been imprisoned for relatively minor, political offenses. Jiro T'hrahstus had been a K'ruukta smuggler, imprisoned for supplying food to political disodents. William Von Braun was a metallurgist, imprisoned for selling his steel without a permit(which the local regent had refused to grant to anyone but his own, inept brother-in-law). Stairone Rochester was imprisoned for the illegal publication of an offensive political pamphlet. And, of course, Murphy Shaggypants...actually, Orson had no idea what Shaggypants had done as his accent was completely indecipherable and his records had been mysteriously burned. With acid.

"Captain." Reginald Johnson nodded respectfully as Orson passed on his way to engineering.

Grigori had 'adopted' fifteen men as apprentice engineers. Reginald was among the most promising. He was a tall, thin fellow with a little mustache. Most of the engineers had grown mustaches, with the obvious exception of Anne Merrymore, who had no facial hair at all, the poor girl. Engineering had been a large, open room, now it was a Gordian knot of power cables and data conduits, all connecting to the eight-cell recombinant reactor built around the ancient stardrive. Grigori was buried in the heart of it, chewing on a snub pipe which he had stolen from the Commandant's collection. He was attempting to fix a blown fuse on the salvaged power engine.

"Damned goobersnooched bastards!" Smoke poured from his mouth. "Vhy in the plowing hells vould you use a machined driver on something like this. Father damned idiots! Stripped the damn connector...Blooddamned pieces of-"

"Grigori!" Orson shouted, resting his wrist in the crook of his sword's hilt.

"Vhat?" the short Burlman shouted back. He wiped the engine grease from his face with a grimy hand and twisted his mustache.

"Tannhäuser says you're putting too much stress on the secondary bulk capacitors."

Grigori growled, "Does he?! Vell you tell that zombie **head** that if he can find a better viaduction to the spacial-field generators I vill take it."

Orson ran his fingers through his tangled hair, "He says that if you can't decrease the load you're going to keep blowing fuses down here and we'll lose the forward mag shield."

A cloud of smoke rose up around Grigori's head. "Sure, I could reroute the power load to a few of the other systems, but on the port bulk ve've life support and the veight generator, and on the starboard ve've got the spacial condenser. Either of those go and ve all either die or become mindless ghouls."

Alazaved's voice came over the comm nervous and fast, "*Captain, there es a* **big** *problem, here.*"

"What is it, now?" Orson sighed massaging his brow.

"*We just received a message. The Commandant es returning early. He es awaiting our response on Piety.*"

"What!" Orson shouted, "When?"

"*Et wæs a transportation request. He es waiting on the edge of the debris field for his private ship.*"

Orson knew they had run out of time. He spoke quickly, "Alazaved, get our people off the château. Hurry!" Then he shouted, "Tannhäuser! Connect me shipwide."

Tannhäuser's voice echoed, "*As you wish, Captain.*"

Orson cleared his throat. His mouth was dry and his heart was beating an excited rhythm in his chest. The time had come. They were about to make their escape. "This is your captain. I've just learned that a bastion fleet is waiting beyond the debris field. They've requested a coded response. In half an hour they're going to realize that's not going to happen. We are out of time. I am recalling everyone to the ship. Major repairs are complete. From this moment on, this ship is no longer the *Redemption of Autumn*. She is the *Thunderchild*, and **we** are her crew."

Chapter XXVIII

The Commandant Returns

err'mo!" Grigori roared through a cloud of pipe smoke. "Major repairs are completed! I'm glad you are so confident, Captain, but ve still don't have half the systems back together. Ve are not going anyvhere until I replace this fuse and restart the primary control system on the reactors!"

Orson turned his attention back to the engineer. His voice was cold and honest. "In less than thirty minutes that bastion out there is going to get curious as to why this incredibly secure prison has not responded. Then, they're going to send someone to find out **why**, and if we're here when that happens-"

Grigori shook his head, "I don't care how heroic your speeches are, Captain. I can't get this girl running in thirty minutes. The fuse is done quickly, sure, but for the harmonic start up sequence and to replace the minor couplings on the second line, I need at least an hour. The rest might takes days."

"Grigori, there's a difference between the way we'd like things to be and the way things are. We *have* thirty minutes."

"I am telling you ve need more time."

"We don't have it," Orson growled flatly. "What can you get done in the time we do have?"

Grigori chewed on his snub pipe. "If I hot jump the line past the fuse ve von't need to restart the entire system, but ve vont have control of the star drive. It vill be dangerous, and ve von't get far...Maybe, out into the debris field, buy us time to do the real repairs."

Orson growled, "Make it so." After he'd said it he realized that he had waited his whole life to stand in control of a starship and say those words. Now, in the moment, nostalgia was lost to duty.

Grigori shook his head again, "I vill do vhat I can, but it von't be perfect and ve may cause greater damage to the central systems."

Orson nodded, "I know. Thirty minutes." Then he pressed the comm again, "Tannhäuser?"

"*Yes, Herr Orson?*"

"Past the debris field there should be a fleet of ships, a group of small ones centered around one very large ship."

"*Yes, Herr Orson. I haven't seen a worldbreaker in a very long time. They are broadcasting the name Piety, but I'd recognize the Agamemnon anywhere. I have been watching him closely since his masters launched the small craft. It was due to arrive five minutes ago. What a strange fellow...*"

"What?" Orson furrowed his heavy brow.

"*The Agamemnon has been waiting for several hours. I heard his broadcast signature this morning while you were having breakfast with your slave girl.*"

"My slave girl?" Orson asked, before his mind registered the rest, "They've been here since this morning? Why didn't you say something!"

"*It didn't seem important.*"

"Tannhäuser, forward an emergency signal to the château, now!"

"*I don't have access to those systems.*"

"What systems?" Orson growled.

"*As I have said, I have been severed from **all** Administrator level privileges, including outside communications. I cannot access-*"

"Useless machine!" Orson swore loudly and ran down the corridor. He leapt up the ladder and ran toward the docking airlock, dashing past his crew as they prepared for the swift departure. The crewmen pressed themselves tightly against the hull as their captain charged by. Tannhäuser's voice came through the walls chasing after Orson.

"*There is a message from the Administrator's Office in the Akropolis. Herr Orson.*"

"The Administrator's office?" Orson stopped at the second airlock, waiting for it to cycle and disengage. The voice in the message chilled Orson's blood.

"*This is the Commandant of the Château d'Soleil Rouge addressing the prisoners aboard the derelict ship currently held in the dry dock. Surrender now. I have restricted access within **my** château, and His Majesty's dreadnaught Tigerlily is*" *currently inbound. The docks are sealed. No one is going anywhere. This riot is officially over. And to 'Captain' Orson, I have the Roerian girl, and you have my word that she will be treated fairly upon your unconditional surrender. Save us both a lot of trouble. I await your response."*

Orson's heart was racing. *He* had Alazaved. Orson gnashed his teeth. Anger and fear twisted his brain. He knew that he should have protected her. She had followed him to the edge of the stars and now he had failed her. The Commandant had her. The airlock had finished cycling. Orson wrenched open the heavy door, and threw himself from the ship. The shift to weightlessness was always jarring, it was worse now. Orson's robes wrapped around him as he flew through the empty space toward the exit. His stomach was twisting into knots when he crashed into the walkway. He swore again, resisting the urge to use his powerful legs. He had to pull himself carefully along the hand rail. Orson scrambled to the door only to find it locked. Panic beat on his brain. The Commandant had won. Orson ignored the reality of it. He wrapped his hands around the lock and braced his legs on the frame, pulling with all of his might. The door was unmoved.

"Come on," Orson growled, "damn it!"

He knew that Alazaved needed him. He knew that the heartless Commandant had her. Orson fought the memories of his own hell that rose to the surface at the thought of that man. He knew the entire expanse of time he had wasted in his cell. He knew that he was powerless. Doubt was creeping back into his soul.

"No." Orson spoke to himself. He closed his eyes and let go of himself. He focused on drawing the air into his lungs in slow, deep breaths. He tried to remember the lessons he had learned in the Monastery of Mu. He let the fear slip away. Above the sea of his consciousness a storm raged with dark clouds of panic. He found himself, a lost sailor bobbing under the waves. *My name is James Orson.* His eyes opened and he knew himself again.

Orson wrapped his hands around the lock and set his feet on the wall. He felt the metal in his fingers and knew that it, like all things, was an extension of his own being. He knew that he would open the door. Orson drew the air into his lungs and pulled with all the strength in his body. His muscles strained and bulged in tightly knotted cords under his skin and his bearded face grew red.

The metal groaned. Orson roared. The door began to bend. In a moment he would be in. In a moment the door would give way. Then Orson heard an artificial voice coming from above.

"*Emergency protocols have been activated. Access is restricted. Doors are locked. User: Outis. Would you like to override Emergency Protocols?*"

Orson's strained mind wanted to laugh. It was the very same voice he'd heard from the installation on Arzvertun. He let go of the door and caught his breath. In a moment he understood.

The Commandant did not know who James Orson was. He had no knowledge of Orson's first life. He did not know what he had lost, or of the lonely sorrow he had endured within the walls of the Château d'Soleil Rouge. He did not know of the bloody night when Orson had bashed his skull into the ground, or of his miraculous escape and transcendent journey to the lost planet below. The Commandant did not know the true age or purpose of *his* château, but more than that, he could not know that through Orson's actions the ancient computer systems were once again connected and that Captain Orson held the key to every lock in his prison.

"Open the door!" Orson commanded.

The locks slid back and Orson threw open the door. He dragged himself quickly down the hall. Ahead, the elevator doors opened to reveal the remaining members of his crew. Their shocked faces showed their fear.

"Captain!" they shouted together.

"Williams?" Orson growled to the thin man in front, "What happened?"

"The Commandant is back," Williams answered quickly. "He came out of nowhere. There were three others with him. Alazaved held them off. We ran."

"You left her?" Orson asked.

"We would not, Captain. She made us go, told us to get you. We were on our way back when the elevator shutdown and we were trapped."

Orson shook his head, "Save it. Get to ship and help prepare for launch."

"Captain," Williams said again. "He sent the others to open the cells down in The Rind. I'm sorry, Captain."

Orson turned back, pulling himself to the elevator.

"Where are you going?" another crewman shouted.

Orson did not answer.

The commodore of the bastion *Piety* was young for his post, barely into his fifty-seventh year, as such, he had never seen real combat and had yet to earn the razor-edged instincts of his more senior peers. The Navy of Man was known to be invincible. Under the Holy King, Nero, the galaxy had come to know the truth in this. Every challenge against the absolute authority of Man was met with devastation. Conflict raged in the early days of Nero's reign, but his violence bred stability. In the end, it was that stability that would be the slow death of Man. Endless conflict had become a stale, cold thing, and years of half-war had left the standing navies weak. The Old Houses had grown fat and complacent, stagnating under the weight of their own aging bureaucracies. They all found their place in Nero's kingdom and satisfied themselves on the bones. The last true naval battle had been fought long in the past. All that remained of the great wars was faded ink in old books.

The Commodore of *Piety* was no hero of war. He was a champion of border skirmishes, and one-sided fights against barely functioning rebel ships. The commodore had no edge. He was nothing more than a vulture. So, when the private ship of the Commandant of the Château d'Soleil Rouge had failed to meet *Piety* at the appointed time and appointed place, the commodore did not have the instincts to know that the château had fallen to revolt. The commodore knew, like everyone else, that Man was invincible. So, he had refused the Commandant the ship he'd requested, insisting that he wait the standard two days before assuming the ship had been lost. He was a fool.

The Commandant was born in battle. He had fought for his life and his loves. He had survived the loss of friends and had endured the burning of cities. He *knew* that his hold on the château was threatened, and it had driven him to seek out his nephew, Henri, a low-ranking officer in *Piety's* security corps. Together, the two slipped the fleet in Henri's small cruiser and made their way through the debris field to the château. Hours later, the Commandant's signal reached the furious Commodore of *Piety*, and a dreadnaught was reluctantly dispatched to pacify the prisoners' uprising.

The Commandant stood in his office on the first ring. His sword lay across his polished desk, and he had his back to the exposed central control panel. It had been easy for Orson and his men to miss, hidden as it was within the walls behind a handcarven cabinet filled with reports and documents. Alazaved was on her knees, her arms bound tight at her back. Her face was bruised and blood dripped from a deep gash over her eye. Her nearly three-meter-tall frame left her eye level with her stocky captor. Those wondrous eyes now stared fire into the Commandant's cold heart.

The Commandant stared back, "You should have surrendered, girl."

His captive spat, "Ne-berthel supthsweorth! My Captain will come, and you will die."

The Commandant answered her flatly, turning his back to the bruised giantess, "If your captain comes I will break him."

Alazaved's deep eyes burned, "Not *my* Captain. He es the last disciple of Mu. He es stronger than the mightiest esnim. He lit the new sun and brought light to the Painted Men in the Valley of Ice. And he conquered your *invincible* château. This, I have seen."

The Commandant searched his desk for his smoking pipes. Only his black Ramses remained. He half-smiled, relieved. "I have seen many things myself, girl. I am here because nothing surprises me."

Alazaved smiled viciously, "And *I* am only on my knees because I cannot stand. My Captain cannot *fall*. He es greater than any man I have known. He es infinite. You are nothing."

The Commandant fished his tobacco pouch from his pocket and raised his eyebrow. "You speak very well for a foreigner. Are you Burlish? No, Burlish doesn't have those nasal vowels. You're tall for a Burlish girl anyway, almost took you for a Roerian. I don't think I recognize your accent, though. Which means you're not from the Tetrarchy. So, tell me, why are you here? If you're not soldiers and you're not with the rebels, then why in the hells did you come to my prison? What is the point of this little insurrection? Are you pirates?"

Alazaved flashed a fierce smile, "If he comes for you, you will die. You do not know the might of the man you threaten."

"Yes, yes. Your captain's a *fiend*, isn't he?" The Commandant struck a match on his black sleeve and lit his pipe. Smoke billowed out around his words, "Do you know why this château was made into a prison? I don't expect you would. We are not all barbarians. We do not *like* death. This place *is* a cruelty. I don't deny that. But, it is far preferable to the cruelty that waits beyond the Verge.

We **must** keep Man united at any cost. We **must** be strong." The Commandant's eyes were empty and cold. "Understand that there are far worse things in the dark of the void than men like your captain. There are true horrors. There are monsters in the deep dark, monsters waiting to devour your family and enslave your very mind."

Alazaved shook her head in denial. She laughed, "You know nothing. I come from a world of monsters, little man."

"Do you now?" the Commandant smiled. It was a strange smile. The sort of smile a veteran cast to eager young soldiers from the ruin of his wheelchair. Then the smile faded and his voice was flat again. "Enough. No one is coming, girl. Even if your captain does not surrender, he won't be leaving. My men are being freed as we speak, and the *Tigerlily* will be here shortly with Blood-Fathers from Loyos. This is my basilea and within her confines there is no greater voice than my own. I have spoken to the ancient walls and my château has obeyed. The doors are **locked**. I will restore order."

James Orson stood in the soft dirt of The Forest. His hand brushed the ancient sword hanging from his hip. He thought briefly of the dead man who had possessed it before him, an old man with his face. The sun was rising again and the fires of the old god blew rivers of red around the Captain of the *Thunderchild*. Red was the color of his robes, red was the color of his heart. The artificial forest was empty of the sounds of life, and Orson's heart was beating a polemic rhythm in his chest. He thought of Alazaved and saw her pale face in the light of Arzvertun as it was the first time he had seen it. For the first time, he saw a little girl, scared and every bit as lost as himself. Time and again she had fought for him and, when her bravery was tested, she had stayed and sacrificed her life for his crew. For him.

James Orson was walking across a battlefield he had created weeks earlier. Even now he could hear the screams of freed men and guards alike. He thought of the tusked apes in the ruins of Arzvertun, and he thought of the deep fires of Mu. Orson could feel the anger, the empty rage clawing at his consciousness. He was not afraid of the Commandant, and he was not afraid of death. What he feared, what he had always feared, was darkness, that creeping void in the very heart of him. It called to him ceaselessly, that infinite dark, it pulled at his mind with tendrilous temptation, more with each passing day, a ragged voice promising release. He dreamt of it now. In the long, quite hours of the night, he longed for the chaos of the void. For years, in the hopelessness of imprisonment, his attachment to the physical world had been the selfish desire for revenge. But, in the ancient fires of the Monastery of Mu, Hantalp had shown him the futility of rage, had taught him restraint, had saved the lost child of Earth. Now, striding the ancient soil of that hellish castle, wreathed in the flames of the dying sun, James Orson was no longer afraid. He wanted to feel the rapture of murder. His heart was a war drum. His thoughts were a storm. He walked with deliberate steps to a battle he had dreamt of for four years. He fought to keep the Prisoner locked tight, knowing that he would fail.

The Commandant was sitting at his desk when James Orson entered his office. The old soldier stood in surprise at the sudden appearance of the stout, broad fellow, wrapped in red robes, with his features hidden behind wild hair and a great, bushy beard. Orson's eyes fell first on his dear friend.

"Alazaved, are you alright?" he asked like a father to a lost child.

Blood dripped down her bruised face. It was clear that she had fought fiercely. Orson felt deep pride at those wounds, and his heart swelled at the sight of them. She was so much stronger than he had ever known.

Alazaved smiled deeply and her eyes were triumphant and glorious, "Yeo dimg, Old Son."

Orson nodded to his secret joy, before turning his gaze on the perfidious Commandant. Orson had only seen the man once before, on his first night in the château. He had long since forgotten the square face and the dark eyes that now stared back at him. Smoke billowed from the Commandant's cruel mouth as it twisted into a smile.

"So, you are the captain I've been hearing about?" the Commandant asked curiously. "Your girl thinks you are a dangerous man of some sort. Perhaps, you are. Though, I am quite dangerous myself. My château is impenetrable when I want it to be, yet here you stand. How have you done this?"

The Old Man would be proud. The Boar subdued the anger smoldering in his chest and, smiling through clenched teeth, he bowed with perfect grace, "Monsieur Commandant, it is a pleasure to see you again."

"Who are you?" the Commandant asked.

"We have met before, though I doubt you remember." And then, James Orson said the words he had waited years to say, words well practiced in darkness.

"My name is James Orson. I was an assistant professor. I was a husband. I was a father. Once, I was a prisoner."

At those words the Commandant smiled and with a nod he answered, "I thought I knew that face. You *are* prisoner thirty-four. I thought you were dead. How did you escape?"

"My **name** is James Orson," Orson growled.

"What?" the Commandant said.

Orson's hand fell to his sword. The Prisoner clawed against his bonds, and the words for which Orson had waited so long were forgotten. "I *was* a professor. I *was* a father. I *was* a man. But I was cast into hell and locked away. For four years I have lived in that darkness and pain. I have suffered! I have died!" Orson's voice had started as a whisper and had grown to a savage roar, "My name is James Orson! And if you don't get down on your knees, I swear to the stars I will kill you, you son of a bitch!"

At the final words the Commandant's dark eyes smouldered. He carefully, mechanically, set his pipe down on his desk. Then, his weathered hand tightly gripped his sword and he spoke in a controlled and practiced tone, "James Orson, my name is Miguel Santana, and you can try."

In a flash the Commandant was on his feet, driving over his desk at the Captain of the *Thunderchild*. Orson parried and fell back, leaving the Commandant's office. The Commandant followed fiercely, roaring.

"You think you know the hells, boy! You've never seen real suffering! I've seen things you wouldn't believe."

Orson tried to remember the Old Man's fencing lessons. He felt unstoppable. His previous victories drove him onward with reckless pride. The Commandant burst into his foyer and Orson drove forward to intercept his blade. He caught the Commandant's sword with his own and thrust forward with his mighty legs. But, they didn't move. Then, to Orson's surprise, the Commandant's impossibly strong legs pressed back, savagely, and Orson was pushed away. He caught his balance and raised his sword just in time to catch the Commandant's boot in his chest. It hit like a cannonball, and Orson was thrown back, out of the Commandant's apartments. Pain erupted in his chest. His mouth tasted of copper. Orson coughed blood and pushed himself to his feet. Then, he raggedly raised his heavy sword.

He had never met such a fierce foe. Even in the savage wastes of Arzvertun there had been no beast more fearsome than himself. The Commandant walked after him, mechanically removing his jacket, letting it fall to the floor. His densely muscled shoulders were suddenly visible. His voice was gruff.

"I've seen cities burned. I've seen dukes brought to their knees in the ashes of their own arrogance. I've seen dark things from beyond the world of Man rip babes from their mothers' breasts. I've seen children flayed and disemboweled on the mythic rocks of Titus. I have seen starfire blacken in the night sky and I have seen the dead rise against the living. I have felt the death of love and I have drunk greedily of hate!"

The Commandant bore down on the Captain of the *Thunderchild*. Orson slipped off his heavy outer robes, and tried to focus the storm in his mind. He was on the edge of an abyss. Panic broke against his staggered will. He forced himself to remember the lessons of Mu. He ignored the pain of breathing. He ignored his damaged rib. He tried to see himself and forget his fear.

The Commandant raised his sword. Orson did the same. Then the Commandant drove forward and Orson parried with a sidestep. Again, the Commandant drove forward, and again Orson only barely managed to avoid a thrust to his throat. The two men locked eyes.

Orson growled, "I was innocent!"

The Commandant answered heartlessly, "I don't care."

He thrust again, effortlessly. Orson parried.

"How many innocent men have you tortured here? How many innocent lives have you destroyed?"

The Commandant's blade caught the edge of Orson's brow slicing a thin, red line across his face.

"As many as was necessary, boy," the Commandant growled.

Orson's eyes burned. He stepped back in blindness, wiping the blood from his eyes, "You're the monsters. You and your damned king!"

"My king is the only man alive who can halt the coming plague!" the Commandant answered.

With his sight gone Orson could do nothing to stop the Commandant's next strike. Cold metal pierced deep into his thigh. The blade pulled loose, and Orson stumbled back. Panic stirred the Prisoner. Orson knew that he was no match for the Commandant with a sword. His knew that his crew would be re-turned to hell. He knew that the Commandant would slit his throat and then do the same to Alazaved. And in that moment, Orson knew that he loved her and that he could not bear such torment. The darkness swelled in his heart. He felt like a failure to come so far and fall. The fresh wounds burned and blood dripped over his eye. The fear was overwhelming. The war drums were beating a Pyrrhic rhythm. Orson thrust blindly forward with his sword. The Comman-dant parried effortlessly and sliced through the tight flesh of his opponent's abdomen. Orson fell to his knees. Hope was dying within him.

The Commandant's eyes focused on his former prisoner. "Look at you," he spat, "You're nothing, selfish and vain. I *remember* you, thirty-four. When we sent word that you had died the Grand Archinquisitor, himself, ordered me to purge your records. I read them. I know they are false. I spoke with Leveque. He has wrapped himself in the favor of the court and grown into a powerful worm. You will never claim your revenge, and you will not destroy what has been built here. I will not **tolerate** any threat against the stability of this king-dom! And I will not allow innocent lives to be sacrificed to the arrogance and vanity of one petty, little man!"

After years of torturous ignorance, Orson's betrayer had been named. The memory returned all at once, the magistrate and the thin man, but it was too late, and the revelation came as panic. The Prisoner was rising. Mu could no longer hold him back. Orson could hear nothing. Anger surged within the heart of him, fury beyond measure. He wanted to see the world burn. He wanted to kill. He wanted to destroy. He **wanted** to die.

Orson gnashed his teeth, and the Prisoner rose with a defiant roar, "MY NAME IS JAMES ORSON!"

The Commandant was taken by surprise. He instinctively drove forward with his sword, but the Prisoner twisted the blade with his own, and, stepping past the cutting edge, dropped his sword and grabbed the Commandant by the wrist, pulling him into his steely grasp. The Commandant realized his mistake too late. His powerful legs and superior swordsmanship were suddenly useless. He had thought victory secure. Now, he pulled with all the might in his body, fighting for his life.

The Prisoner's eyes were wild. He spat through clenched teeth, "**No.**" His voice was the low growl of a beast.

In that moment, Miguel Santana knew that his opponent was no longer a man, that he was staring into the mad eyes of a monster. The Prisoner's crushing grip dug into Miguel's flesh. With a sickening crunch, the bones of his hand collapsed and the Prisoner tore the blade from Miguel's grasp, casting it away. Pain shot through Miguel's arm in bursts. He fought against it, and in his confusion the Prisoner lifted him off the ground. Miguel brought his remaining fist down on the Prisoner's thick shoulder, but the Prisoner's grip only tightened. Every blow fueled the monster's madness. His eyes were infinite. His breath was smoke and fire. Death was finally coming for Miguel Santana, for the lost little boy from Cortiques. Finally Miguel freed his leg. It caught the edge of the wall and he launched himself out the monster's grasp and dashed out of the dormitories.

Alazaved came out from the Commandant's apartments in time to see her captain fall and the Prisoner rise. When Miguel escaped outside, the Prisoner gave chase. Alazaved knelt down and cut her bonds with her captain's sword. She saw the robes she had made for him, discarded on the floor, and taking them up, she followed.

The Commandant's guards had been freed. Outside, the thirty men, rallied in The Forest, watched as their commandant burst out from the officers' apartments. A handsome man stood at the forefront of the guards, dressed in polished armor. He and the others had supplied the Commandant's guards with fresh weapons. In the place of their electrified batons, each man now held a heavy sword. But, weakened from their stay in The Rind and still bearing the memory of their own defeat, not one man had the courage to move when the Prisoner emerged.

"Stay back! This is no mere man!" Miguel shouted to his men, "I will subdue this abomination and we will retake our château!"

The guards stepped back, giving the warring titans plenty of room. Then Miguel Santana and the Prisoner faced off in the red forest.

One had speed and experience, the other had strength and blind ferocity. The Prisoner drove forward, roaring with reckless rage like a mad boar. Miguel avoided him with superhuman reflex. He lured him back, creating a false opening, and the Prisoner followed. Finally, Miguel attacked. He struck forward with a mighty kick, but the Prisoner caught it in his irresistible grasp. The Prisoner brought his fist down to shatter the bone, and it was his turn for surprise.

When his fist collided with indestructible metal, Miguel brought his other leg around to the Prisoner's skull. He poured all of the strength of his grotesque legs into the strike, and the Prisoner dropped to his knees, briefly staggered. Blood dripped openly from his mouth.

Miguel Santana backed cautiously away from his downed opponent and, looking out toward his men, he nodded grimly, "He's done. Get him back in his cell."

The guards began to march in.

"No," the Prisoner growled. Then he rose up, filled with the fire of creation and screaming for destruction, "I AM **ORSON**!" The Prisoner threw back his head and in his rage-fueled madness he roared his dominance to the stars, halting the guards. He gnashed his teeth and beat his chest.

Miguel cracked his neck and tried to set the bones in his broken hand. He regretted letting himself get so soft. He remembered a rainy city on a forgotten moon, the hardest fight of his life. He was strong then. He told himself that this prisoner was nothing compared to the seed of Tyran.

"Alright," he sighed, wiping the blood from his mouth, "Let's go, boy."

The Prisoner charged forward and Miguel Santana dodged. He came up with his good hand in a fist and slammed it into the Prisoner's broken ribs. The monster howled and drove forward, but Miguel Santana's leg thrust against the ground and his armored knee collided with the Prisoner's chin, knocking him back. The Prisoner roared, driving forward, again. Miguel dodged the clumsy attack and twisted back with a side kick. The Prisoner caught it, but before Miguel could kick with his other leg, he felt himself rising off the ground. The Prisoner lifted him into the air and slammed his body into the dirt. Miguel's legs flooded his mind with pain. He tried to get up, but before Miguel could move, the Prisoner grabbed him by the ankle and, throwing him up into the air, slammed his body down into the ground again. Miguel twisted in pain. His face was swollen and covered in deep cuts. His body ached. He vomited blood across the bare soil. Then the Prisoner stood over him. His face was wild and empty, like a savage boar.

"You won't get me, monster," Miguel spat.

He kicked hard with his leg hitting the Prisoner square in the chest. He felt the bone go and the Prisoner was staggered long enough for Miguel to crawl to his feet. Miguel's vision had blurred and his legs felt like numb steel beneath him. He tried to form a fist with his crushed hand.

"Stop!" the handsome soldier cried out. His eyes were fearful. He drew his sword and shouted to the guards, "Fight, you **cowards**! FIGHT!" There was a moment of quiet apprehension. Henri shouted, "He's *tired*. Now, **kill** him!"

A single guard stepped forward and, perhaps from pride or honor, the rest followed. Then the guards charged the Prisoner all at once, while the handsome soldier marched to the defense of his uncle. Henri stood by his side and spoke quickly.

"I am sorry, Monsieur Santana, but I cannot allow this to continue."

Miguel wiped the blood from his eyes and shook his head, "Henri, you stupid child."

The Prisoner's roar echoed throughout The Forest, and he came ripping and tearing through the crowd. He threw the guards from himself, and, one by one, he broke every man that stood before him. His roar and grisly visage cowered the rest. Then he charged at Miguel Santana like a mad beast. Henri alone stood before his uncle.

"Stay behind me, Uncle," he said quickly, raising his sword.

The Prisoner's eyes had become dark orbs of blood and rage. They stared madness and fury into the handsome, young man. The Prisoner was almost upon him. Then, Miguel Santana threw his nephew to the ground and planting his feet, he caught the rampaging fiend. They roared together, like two beasts. Then Miguel twisted away in the Prisoner's grasp and they rolled on the ground. The Prisoner brought his fist down, but Miguel writhed away. He got his feet under the monster and threw him off. Then, Miguel's hand found his nephew's sword.

"You want my blood, monster!" Miguel rose up, roaring like an old lion, "Come and get some!"

The Prisoner charged at him, and Miguel's sword ripped into his stomach. The Prisoner ignored it, carrying Miguel to the ground. Then, the Prisoner held him there and slammed his fists savagely into Miguel's face, shattering his jaw and cracking his cheek bones. The Prisoner beat him again and again. Bone and flesh broke with sickening sounds. The guards were silent when the Prisoner stood. Blood and gore dripped down his savage hands.

Henri cried out, "Uncle!"

There was little recognizable about Miguel Santana's face. All the strength had left his body and his hands were limp on the ground, but he was still alive. Then the men watched in horror as the Prisoner took one of their commandant's unbreakable legs in his hands and twisted it around. Bone snapped at the hip with a nauseating crunch and the Prisoner twisted it back, tearing the flesh. He rocked it back and forth until, finally, he ripped the limb from the Commandant's body. It wasn't easy, and the Prisoner made a great mess of it, stomping and twisting, but Miguel Santana did not scream, or cry, or make any sound at all. The knowledge of absolute failure spread through Miguel's soul. Tears ran from the ruin of his face, not because of the pain, or the coming end of his life, but because he had failed a little boy's promise made to the ghost of his mother. Cold, black eyes peered past the veil of life to the great empty everything, and Miguel Santana died.

When The Prisoner had finished mutilating the corpse, he threw the Commandant's grotesque, metallic limb at his guards. Then he roared atop their master's ruin, "I AM JAMES ORSON!" Those savage, black eyes burned into the souls of the men watching. No man present that day would ever forget the name of the monster that had murdered the Commandant of the Château d'Soleil Rouge. Henri would never forget the man who had killed his uncle.

Alazaved pushed through the crowd. Her eyes were deep and fearless. The freed guards watched in disbelief as she placed the robes around her captain's shoulders and made him human again.

"Shhh," she whispered to him, "Es alright, Jimnes. I am here. You saved me."

Orson stared blankly through his bloodied eyes. The sound of her voice was the sound of life. It shattered the darkness. All at once the undefeatable, nihilistic rage bled away and guilt rushed to fill the void. Orson felt monstrous and stupid. He gasped as Alazaved pulled the sword from his stomach and pressed hard against the savage wound.

"Come, Old Son," she said, helping him stand, "There es not much time."

Henri stood over the goried remains of his uncle. The shock had left him dumb. He had never seen such madness, he had never known such fear. Now, he defied that mortal fear.

"You're not going anywhere," Henri uttered numbly. His eyes were red, his cheeks wet. He had to avenge the death. He had to stand before the monster.

Alazaved's fierce eyes fell on the bloodstained idiot and she shook her head, "Do not speak, child. The monster es gone, but the man may yet kill you."

Then, she guided Orson out of the crowd of men. The guards spread far apart when they came near, watching warily. Together, the Captain of the *Thunderchild* and the Orphan of Arzvertun made their way back to their ship. In the elevator, Alazaved did her best to dress Orson in his discarded robes, and then she returned his sword. She straightened his clothes and told him that he had to be the Captain again. Orson said nothing. He was still hollowed by the fury of his vengeance when he stepped foot on the bridge and his crew cheered. Alazaved was behind him. She ducked low, stepping through the bulkhead door.

Orson had forgotten again how to speak. He rasped to his crew, "Get us out of here, you fools."

"Yes, Sir," they managed collectively as their sheepish smiles faded and they returned to their posts.

Then Orson growled quickly, "Tannhäuser!"

"*Yes, Herr Orson?*" Tannhäuser's voice echoed.

"Are we still connected to the *Akropolis*'s main computer?"

"*Yes.*"

"Can you at least forward my commands?"

"*Only with thy direct authorization.*"

"Do it."

"*As thou wish, Herr Orson....Thou art now free to issue thy commands.*"

"This is user, Outis."

The Akropolis answered. "*User Outis recognized..*"

"End the lock-down."

"*Caution: Lock-down is suspended. Caution: Resuming regular operation. Caution: Installation has suffered significant damage. Caution: Reactor nest output has been reduced to twenty-seven percent. Caution:-*"

Orson growled, "Tannhäuser, shut it off." Then he turned to his K'ruukta helmsman. "Jiro, open the doors and get us the hell away from this place."

"Yes, Captain." the steely-eyed ex-smuggler replied.

The massive doors to the main dry dock opened with grinding slowness, and Orson let his full weight fall back into the captain's chair, holding the wound in his stomach. He was bloodied and bruised, but he only felt that wound, deep and cold. The engines kicked on and, for the first time, his *Thunderchild* began to move. Orson smiled, tired and proud, and his young eyes met Alazaved's as the ship left the château behind and passed into open space.

"You are bleeding all over your new chair, Jimnes." she said finally.

Orson let himself look into her eyes. There was a depth to them he had never noticed, a depth he had never let himself notice. His eyes moved to the bleeding wound above her eye. She had fought so bravely.

Orson spoke gently, "I'm sorry I took so long."

Alazaved looked down, "Et es not bad. Now, let me close your wound."

Alazaved knelt before her captain and pulled his robes aside. She swatted away his hand and began to clean the torn flesh. It was a clean wound and, by some miracle, the Commandant's sword had missed his internal organs. Orson clenched his teeth as she set the needle to his skin.

"You're getting very good at that, Alazaved." Orson grunted softly. "Why does it seem like you've always got a trauma kit hidden in your robes?"

Alazaved shook her head. "Because you keep needing one, Jimnes. You are an idiot, but you are **my** captain."

Orson chuckled lightly before Alazaved pulled the wound tightly closed. He groaned, "That I am."

Alazaved began work on his leg. Her hands moved with expert swiftness.

"Sir!" the communications officer shouted, "We've got an incoming message."

"Put it through, Kensley," Orson hissed as Alazaved finished her sutures, and broke the thread with her teeth.

"Criminal vessel, this is Commander Kristopher aboard His Majesty's Ship, Tigerlily. Cut your engines or I will open fire."

Chapter XXIX

Attack of the Tigerlily

he *Tigerlily* was the oldest dreadnaught in *Piety's* fleet and, like most ships of Man, had been salvaged from the Lost Fleet, a great mass of abandoned starships found in the gravity well around the third moon of Thernos. The old mariners had long thought the ancient, black vessels cursed by the Corpse God, Tyran, and perhaps they were. In the early days of the Old King, when the House of Man reached the stars for the first time after the Great Fall, they found a sleeping armada waiting for them. The Old King seized these ships without a moment's hesitation. Though Man did not understand the science and could not replicate the technology, these ancient vessels made them nigh invincible in battle. Few weapons could pierce the shining black hulls of Man's ships, wrapped in layered armor like the carapaces of monstrous insects, and few enemy vessels could resist the piercing might of their laser pulse artillery. Fewer still were the captains brave enough to face an immortal ship of Man.

Commander Kristopher stood on the bridge of her *Tigerlily*, carefully watching the view screens. There had been no response from the rogue vessel. She pulled down on her snug jacket, cracking her once-graceful neck. Her short, blonde hair elongated her sharp face, a heavy scar was slashed across the left side, cheek to chin, and she had the gray eyes of a warrior. She cleared her throat.

"We gave them a chance." Her voice was flat and emotionless. "Monsieur Madsen, give them a warning shot. Use the twenties. Target those broad nacelles," Her eyes narrowed, "thrusters, I suppose."

"Qui, Madam."

The *Thunderchild* shook as the rounds slammed into the heavy armor plates covering the port nacelle. Small engines embedded in the hull fired off in bursts to stabilize the ship.

Commander Kristopher nodded, "Very good, Madsen."

Then, the *Thunderchild*'s oversized nacelles began to glow bright and hot, even as the energy readings on the *Tigerlily*'s displays spiked.

"They're going to fox for the debris field!" the helmsman warned quickly.

Commander Kristopher shook her head. "Bloody fools. Weathers, get us between that ship and the debris. They're not going to lose us."

"Qui, Madam," came the helmsman's reply.

Commander Kristopher broadened her stance, anticipating the sudden jolt of the engines. The heavy dreadnaught maneuvered swiftly around the edge of the debris field, and Commander Kristopher held tight to a nearby railing as the ship banked hard, cutting off the *Thunderchild*'s escape.

"Now then," Commander Kristopher said flatly, straitening her jacket again, "Ready our starboard artillery, and bring the slave reactor to full power. It's time to bare our teeth."

On the bridge of the *Thunderchild* James Orson swore loudly over the comm.

"What do you mean the secondary fuse blew! We need those engines back, now!"

Grigori answered in his usual growl, "I told you it vasn't ready. You've over-stressed the damned lines and the forward mag shield is gone! It's a mess down here. Three of the reactors are locked out!"

"We're barely even out of the docks!" Orson shouted back.

"*Herr Orson?*"

"What is it, Tannhäuser?!" Orson growled.

"*The enemy ship is charging their primary weapons. I would suggest that you take immediate action.*"

"Charging their **primary** weapons? What the hell did they hit us with before?"

"*I believe that was a warning shot from their small, forward cannons.*"

Orson pulled on his beard, "Shit. Kensley, stay in contact with Grigori. I want to know the moment those systems are back online. Jiro, stand by for evasive maneuvers. Tannhäuser?"

"*Yes, Herr Orson?*"

"What do you know about that ship?"

"*Ah. She is an old one, Herr Orson, even for me, practically a corpse,*" Tannhäuser answered. "*You can't out fly her and you most certainly can't out gun her.*"

"Captain," Kensley interrupted, "We have a comm request from the enemy ship."

Orson nodded, "Put it through."

"Aye, Captain."

Orson once again stood in his best imitation of the Old Man, hiding his wounds under his robes. He forced himself up to his full height and pulled his shoulders back. In the dark light of the bridge the lines of his face were almost noble.

The communications officer signaled him, "Opening channel. Video feed will be displayed on the tactical screen by your chair."

Orson nodded, "Thank you, Kensley." A steely, blonde woman appeared on his screen. She wore a dark blue uniform and scowled deeply. Orson's voice was steady, "Commander Kristopher, this is Captain James Orson aboard the free ship *Thunderchild*. What are your demands?"

Commander Kristopher's scowl flattened. "**Captain** *Orson? You presume a great deal. Surrender now, or I will destroy your ship.*"

Orson glanced to his communications officer. Kensley shook his head. No word from engineering. He continued.

"I cannot allow that."

"*You are in no position to allow anything. Surrender, or every man aboard your ship will die.*"

Orson scowled cruelly. He was tired and his wounds hurt.

"Commander Kristopher, are you an experienced officer?"

The Commander answered, "*I am.*"

"In that case, I would hope that you might recognize genuine danger when it is encountered."

"*Are you threatening my dreadnaught?*" The Commander raised her thin eyebrow.

"Madame, I merely offer you a warning." Orson's voice was losing its practiced tone, "Look at the hell at my back. My men and I have come from a place of absolute despair. We were cast into unbearable darkness and robbed of all

278

hope. Yet, here we stand. You threaten us with death? You threaten **me** with death? Death is my companion! Death is my dearest ally. I have prayed for death. In the long dark of that hell, I screamed for her embrace, as have we all." Orson's voice had a tired, jagged edge. "Now, you stand here, at the edge of our freedom and you think you're going to stop us, you think you're going to stop **me**, with the threat of death? I have no weapons, and your dreadnaught is armed to the teeth, but you hear me now: I am Captain James Orson, my name is vengeance and I will burn the heavens themselves before I surrender to any man! You have one choice, Commander, just one: let me pass or I **will** destroy your ship."

Commander Kristopher's calm face betrayed her fury with a single twitch at the edge of her lips. She answered coldly, "*Do you have any idea to whom you speak? Your* **ship** *is a trash heap and you are prisoners.*"

"We are **men.**" Orson growled.

The comm signal was cut. Orson glanced quickly to his communications officer.

Kensley nodded, "We've got shields sir."

"Get me Engineering!" Orson roared. "Grigori, we need everything you can give us, now!"

The *Tigerlily*'s main artillery fired in succession and lines of purple light sliced through space around the *Thunderchild*. The ship twisted in the void. Artillery burst around them. The crew clung to the supports. Orson's thoughts raced. The ship could not withstand the *Tigerlily*'s rage for long. They had to do something. *He* had to do something. But there were no weapons on his ship. The *Thunderchild* was no war machine. She was-

Grigori's voice was gruff, "*I can't do it, Captain! Father damn it!*" The sound of sparking machinery crackled over the comm. "*I got the mag shield up, but if you fire the engines ve'll overload the spacial condenser. Ve all die. Ven the fuse blew it sent an overcharged pulse through the starboard viaduction. The pathvay to the second reactor nest is locked. Ve can't move it. The release is jammed.*"

"Grigori, I'm coming down there. Tannhäuser?"

"*Yes, Herr Orson.*"

"You said this ship is a stormbreaker. How strong is the armor on the bow?"

Tannhäuser's voice betrayed his excitement, "*Strong enough to crack metallic asteroids.*"

"I was hoping you'd say that," Orson growled. "Jiro, forget evasive actions. On my signal, give me full burn. We're going to cut straight through the heart of that monster."

For the briefest of moments the helmsman's eyes showed hesitation, then he nodded, "I will follow you into the grasp of Nhristah himself, Captain."

Orson shook his head, "Not today, Jiro." Then he turned to his pale giantess. She had been waiting in the corner of the bridge. "Alazaved, you're in charge."

"Hwat are you doing, Jimnes?" she asked with concern.

Orson let himself look deep into her wide eyes, "I'm saving my men."

The *Tigerlily*'s artillery fired again. Purple light cut around the ship, refracting in the electromagnetic storm at the *Thunderchild*'s bow. Suddenly, the ship rocked violently. A shell had pierced the shield and detonated in the heavy armor covering the bow.

Grigori was in the center of engineering, struggling with the main reactor nest. A fuse had blown and the metal had partially melted into place. He was torqueing a massive wrench at the power engine's primary release valve while his men scrambled around the lesser systems. Sparks rained down on them as the ship quaked from the last volley. Grigori shouted loudly as Orson entered.

"Over on starboard!"

Orson saw the half-melted cable leading to a cluster of tarnished metal cylinders. A low hum shook the area around the reactor nest.

"What do I do?" he shouted back.

Grigori grunted, "There's a release in the middle. Just pull the damn thing lose. Ve can repair it later."

Orson pulled his robes down over his hands and grappled with the burning cable. Electricity arced around the exposed metal. Orson pulled hard. He could feel his sutures stretching tight. He clenched his teeth and roared. Finally the cable tore away. The victory was short lived.

"Over here now!" Grigori shouted, "Ve've got to relieve the pressure and I can't do it alone!"

Orson rushed to his chief engineer's side. The ship rocked again and sparks burst from the overstressed reactors.

"Where are the rest of your men?" Orson groaned, settling opposite the engineer.

"Up, vorking on the line to the port nacelle."

The ship shook and the bright flare of flashing, red lights filled the room.

"T'rukt!" Grigori shouted, "The stardrive is destabilizing! The power engine is stalling. Get away, Captain!"

Orson shouted back, "No! Push, you bastard!"

Captain Orson planted his feet and pulled with all the strength left in his body. The power engine groaned. Lightning arced above them, red and wild. Together they struggled against the ever rising heat. Grigori's teeth clenched his pipe tightly. He pushed. Orson pulled. He could feel the sting of sweat in the wounds at his belly and in his thigh. The sutures stretched tight and blood trickled down his waist. The pressure was building. Then the secondary system went and glass splintered in an explosion of pressurized gas. Orson felt sudden pain in his eye, then only cold pressure. Steam gushed around them, blinding the struggling men. Blood dripped down Orson's face soaking his beard. The wound was bad. There were screams. Still they fought. Finally, the wrench turned. The two men roared. Orson gnashed his teeth and pulled with the last of his strength. His grip was failing. His throat burned. Then all resistance broke away and the valve was open. The power engine screamed with energy. The two men collapsed. The engines had full power again.

Orson tried to hold what remained of his eye in the socket. Blood dripped through his fingers. His voice was raw. He shouted, "Tannhäuser! Get me the bridge."

Commander Kristopher stood on the bridge of her *Tigerlily*. The *Thunderchild* writhed under the might of her artillery. Few ships lasted more than a minute. Commander Kristopher felt a sliver of admiration for the tenacious vessel.

"Ma'am! The rogue ship's engines are spiking again."

"Where do they think they're going to run?" Commander Kristopher asked confidently.

The *Thunderchild*'s massive engines overflowed with roaring light and the ship charged forward closing the gap between the two vessels in moments.

"Ma'am, they're going to ram us!"

"What?" the Commander hesitated for only a moment before leaping to the com station and shouting her command below deck. "Fire the Dragon's Breath!"

The *Tigerlily*'s thick armor pulled back, exposing a metallic orifice in the shape of a wyrm's mouth. The great maw opened wide, and the ancient weapon shivered with bursts of purple lightning and crackled with energy. Then a torrent of violet starfire poured out toward the *Thunderchild*. The river of flames split across the mag shield in a roaring burst of nebulous sparks and the *Thunderchild* drove forward through the storm.

"They're still coming!" the helmsman of the *Tigerlily* shouted the impossible.

The color drained from Commander Kristopher's face.

Then the *Thunderchild*'s heavily armored bow slammed into the exposed hull of the *Tigerlily*, tossing both crews. The Dragon's Breath continued to erupt deep within the ship. The plasma burned through the decks and then a shock wave tore deep into the heart of the ancient ship, twisting the frame. Metal groaned in agony against the impossible forces, then the *Thunderchild*'s bow broke through the other side of the *Tigerlily*. The dreadnaught had been sheared in two. The *Thunderchild*'s engines burned out and she drifted into the safety of the debris field. They were free.

Chapter XXX

The Voyage of Captain James Orson

t had been a week since the confrontation with the *Tigerlily*. Her surviving crew, including the disgraced Commander Kristopher, had drifted to the Château d'Soliel Rouge aboard the forward section of *Tigerlily*'s remains. There, they had discovered the gruesome fate of Commandant Santana and had met with his remaining guards. Their ragged, trauma-stained faces told of the horror endured during the prisoner revolt and occupation of the château. They claimed it had started with a single man, a former prisoner. They said that the Captain of the *Thunderchild* was an inhuman monster, an avenging spirit from the void. Commander Kristopher had scoffed at their fear and sent out the emergency signal to *Piety*. The rest of the fleet arrived shortly afterward. Upon the discovery of Commandant Santana's death, the Commodore of *Piety* had sworn to capture the mad prisoner-king. Then the remains of the former Keeper, Miguel Santana, favorite son of the 'o Loyos, were brought before High Father Minos, and it was said that the High Father's rage could be heard across the entire fleet. His tears had fallen like rain on the body of his oldest friend and he had sworn an undying oath to break the unbreakable man, James Orson.

Tracking signals probed the deep expanses of the debris field, and the bastion fleet sent countless ships into the scattered darkness with the impossible task of finding the rogue vessel. The *Thunderchild*'s main systems had been offline for repairs and in her low-powered state she was indistinguishable from the rest of the debris.

The remaining two spheres had been loaded into the *Thunderchild*'s hold before she had left the Château d'Soliel Rouge, as well as enough provisions to last for months out in the starsea. Grigori and his men salvaged what they could from the surrounding wreckage. This gave them everything they needed to repair the ship, but *Piety*'s hunters were ever vigilant, and the vengeance of the 'o Loyos trailed them in the dark.

While Grigori's men finished the repairs, the rest of the crew was left with little official responsibility to occupy their time, and they began to lull with boredom. A solution was found when a largely unused corner of the cargo hold, which Orson had been using to ferment beet wine for the better part of the previous month, was hastily converted into a pub, giving the former prisoners a place to relax with a quiet drink and hopefully forget for a moment what had been taken from them. Of course, as this particular corner of the hold had also been where Alazaved had set up her cot, she was forced to find other lodgings and had in turn taken Orson's bed, and Orson was once more forced to sleep on the floor.

The new pub in the cargo hold served as a ready meeting place and in the long quiet hours of their wait for repairs, there were lengthy discussions concerning their eventual destination and what was to become of the *Thunderchild* and her crew. Orson himself had often wondered. The Commandant's confession had brought back some memory of his true betrayer, a politician who had become an archinquisitor. Orson had since learned from M. Carotte that there were only six archinquisitors in the entire Kingdom of Man, and that such men possessed immense power and influence, sufficient to crush even the most powerful of the entrenched Nobility. M. Carotte knew how dangerous an enemy an archinquisitor would be, and had no desire to see his captain fall to such a foe before he could be ready. Thus, it was his belief that, with the brutal death of their common foe, the Commandant, and with the destruction of the dreadnaught *Tigerlily,* Orson's the debt had been largely repaid. But Orson was reluctant to so quickly abandon his search for revenge. It seemed to him a betrayal to the friends he had lost and the man he had become. Yet, he knew that he had avenged himself against one enemy after another and had found little peace. He felt that nothing had come from his obsessive desire for revenge. Worse, he was beginning to *feel* nothing. In the empty hours of the night, the need for destruction still burned in Orson's breast. He had begun to fear that it might always be like that. Hantalp had warned him of the all-consuming fire. The lessons of Mu had been so easily forgotten in his return the château. Still, Orson remembered the terrible fate of the Old Man.

It was Alazaved who had finally convinced her captain to put the matter of their future to a vote, and Orson called the crew to a meeting in the hold and heard their concerns. The crew responded predictably for a group of former Nobles. Some wanted to join the rebellion against the Crown, some thought they were destined to become cold-hearted mercenaries, and still others wanted to become private traders in the markets of the Burlish Tetrarchy. Orson, having good reason to distrust the rebels and having no desire for mercenary work, nor for the boring life of buying and selling commodities, had ultimately argued that they compromise and seek a life of piratical adventure(an idea no doubt spawned from his childhood fantasies). The crew had reluctantly agreed on condition that their prime targets be the ships of the accursed King Nero, and that the *Thunderchild* never target civilians or unarmed vessels. Orson agreed. Then together they raised their glasses and swore an oath to the pursuit of good-hearted space piracy.

*****

Captain James Orson stood over the large, wooden desk in his cabin. His red robes were draped over his muscular shoulders, dark stains and long swathes of stitching marred the otherwise exquisite fabric. Alazaved had asked for permission to replace his old robes, or at the very least properly repair them, while they waited in the debris field, but Orson would not part with them. He let his hand rest in the crook of his sword and took a careful sip of wine before setting his dented, old prisoner's cup down on the edge of the desk. There were deep wounds gouged across the edges of his left eye and the bloody socket was covered by a dark eyepatch. The eye was lost and the wounds would likely become one hell of a scar. The Captain was comparing several starcharts, most plundered from the Commandant's office, spread out across the table. In the middle of it all was the Old Man's own silvery chart.

Alazaved stood behind her captain. She was dressed in her own robes. The soft, deep-blue fabric clung to her thick, muscular hips like corporeal wind. Over her eye she had a scar of her own, a less savage memento of her courage. Argos lay in her open hand and she was absently petting the purring jab-bergnus.

"Hwen do we leave?" she asked softly.

Orson smiled, "Grigori said he'd finished the repairs last night. We should be ready."

Alazaved mused, "The patrol came close last night."

Orson nodded, "They've been close every night. Ever since I gave Tannhäu-ser access to the communication array, he's been torturing them. He keeps bouncing signals off the debris and sending those scout ships after each other." Then he chuckled to himself. "You know, sometimes I think he really is crazy." Orson scratched absently at his ruined eye.

"Does it hurt, Jimnes?"

Orson laughed, "No. It itches. The one in my belly hurts. Why the hell did you let me get skewered, anyway?"

Alazaved shook her head, "I did not have the choice. You are difficult to reason with hwen you are angry."

"I suppose I am," Orson answered grimly. He began to roll the Old Man's silver starchart in his hands. "Did I ever tell you that I am a count?"

Alazaved shook her head, "I do not know that word."

Captain Orson frowned in moderate disappointment before tucking the starchart away in his robes, "Oh. It's a title of nobility. It's impressive to normal people." Orson paused at the thought of his old friend, Gaston. "You know...I still feel like I should thank you."

Alazaved's face blushed blue. She shook her head, "You never have to thank me, Jimnes."

Orson kept his eye on the other starcharts in front of him. He and the girl from Arzvertun had grown remarkably close in the short time they had known one another. When they'd first met, Orson had thought she'd hated him. Then he had thought that she was merely looking for purpose. Staring down at those starcharts, Orson finally *heard* her words. Though Orson had denied it from the first moment he had seen her talking with her father in the fiery light of that dying world, he knew that she loved him, and more than that, he knew that he loved her. The realization brought him back to a night on Earth, to a restaurant famous for its meatballs. Orson suddenly felt like an idiot. There was something important that he desperately wanted to say. Instead, he chose to keep the emotion at a distance. Not because he was afraid. Not of love, any-way. He knew that the Prisoner was there, deep down in the core of him. He knew that he had to be careful. He **knew** that, now. Orson remembered the fires of Mu. He tried to shut away the emotion rising in his heart. He failed.

There was a knock on Orson's door. It was heavy and impatient.

Orson seized his chance and said quickly, "I love you, Alazaved." Then his courage evaporated and before she could say anything back, he shouted, "Come in!"

The ornate wooden door opened and a stout mustachioed man entered. There was a large eyepatch covering his right eye.

Grigori growled, "I've come for my winnings, Captain."

"You cheat at cards," Orson growled in return.

"And you are a lousy liar." Grigori countered. He looked up and raised a curious eyebrow at the panicked look on the giantess' face. His eye drifted back to his captain.

"Fair enough," Orson nodded. He walked to a tall cabinet in the corner of the room and withdrew an old, dusty bottle. "I hope you lose the other eye," Orson grumbled, tossing the bottle to Grigori.

Grigori smiled and, using his teeth, pulled the cork from the mouth. He spit it in his hand and immediately upended the bottle, taking deep swig.

"That is good," he gasped. Then he nodded to Orson. "I vill sleep very good tonight, knowing you cry in your bed...The vine vill help too."

Orson laughed. "How're the new starboard capacitors holding up?"

"Better than ve expected. I assume ve vill be leaving today."

"Very soon, in fact."

"Good. I don't like it here. It is bad luck to be sleeping in a graveyard."

Orson sighed, "Are there any Southern Burlish sayings that don't involve graveyards?"

Grigori smiled. "No." Then he asked, "Vere are ve to be going, anyvay?"

Alazaved looked down at the chief engineer and motioned to the door. Grigori glanced back up, briefly confused. She shooed him away again.

Orson's hand touched the starchart tucked away in his robes, "I know a place hidden away from the world. An island in space, orbiting a dwarf star. A place with snowy forests and high mountain halls. A place of peace and happiness where we can rest when we need. I think we all deserve some time away from the madness."

Grigori smiled, "That's sounds vonderful..." Then he nodded to the glaring giantess, "Safe journey, Madam."

And then the grim Burlishman returned to his room above engineering to enjoy the remainder of his winnings, and the Captain of the *Thunderchild* was left to face the consequences of his words. Orson tried to pretend that he hadn't said it. He turned his attention back to the starcharts. Alazaved came up behind him, and, kneeling down, she wrapped her arms around her beloved.

She said softly, "I love you, Jimnes."

Her voice was honest and full. It broke through the wall around Orson's soul and emotion burst up from his core. He'd forgotten that he could feel anything outside of anger and sorrow. He held her in his arms and pulled her tighter against himself. Happiness filled his heart, and it was a strange and alien sensation. The Prisoner was drowning. It filled Orson with strange fear. He worried that the warmth would leave too soon, so he pushed Alazaved away and straightened his robes.

He cleared his throat and mumbled, "Yeo dimg."

Alazaved smiled down to him and it was his turn to blush. Then she pulled him close and pressed her lips against his. At their feet, Argos scurried across the floor.

A while later, James Orson stepped out, onto the bridge of an ancient starship. For a moment he stood in stillness, watching his crew of former prisoners going about their duties with practiced discipline. M. Carotte was leaning over one of Tannhäuser's consoles, examining the updated navigation charts while tugging pensively on one of his tentacles. Anne Merrymore was kneeling by the door and had just finished repairing a malfunctioning sensor in the wall. Orson felt truly happy. He smiled deeply, nodding to William Von Braun as the crewman passed on his way to the cargo bay. The Captain's heart swelled with pride, and he let his thoughts drift below the surface. He let the current pull him down, to a desperate man lost in a tiny office with flaking paint. He remembered how important everything had seemed. He remembered his old coffee maker, and he remembered a cheap cat poster. He thought of Professor Cullen. He thought of himself so small and cowardly, and he saw the impossible gulf between what he had been and what he had been forced to become. Then he remembered a woman named Elizabeth, and he marveled at how the pain that was once so fresh and vibrant had faded and now merely gnawed at his heart in bittersweet notes. Alazaved stepped out behind him, and Orson was finally home. She kissed him on the forehead and placed Argos on his shoulder. The fat, little jabbergnus nestled into the thick muscle and stared menacingly at the crew. Orson sat in the captain's chair, in *his* chair. Ahead, an eager helmsman asked, "Where to, Captain?"

Adventure called to him from beyond the stars. The Captain of the *Thunderchild* squeezed the Old Man's starchart in his hand. Then the one-eyed captain of a rogue band of savage space-pirates stared out across the ancient debris of a thousand starships, beyond the roaring light of a red, alien star, and smiled.

"Second star to the right, and straight on till morning, Mr. Jiro."

Histories and Additional Content

The Houses of the First Father

The race of Man is known by the Dynastic Datahead of Man to be the most ancient and Noble race in the galaxy, and it is believed to have been the first race birthed by the Allfather at the creation of Avoromedia itself. Though often regarded as a singular collection of people, after the Great Fall the race of Man was scattered across thirteen planets and half as many star systems, until, one by one, each Old House rediscovered space travel and learned of the existence of the other survivors. There were sixteen distinct kingdoms in the Old World; but, following the chaos of the Bloodwar, these kingdoms collapsed under the rule of one house.

House Bertrum

The House of Bertrum has a long tradition of intellectual pursuit. Thought by many of the more respectful houses to be dreamers and layabouts, House Bertrum has experienced a long decline in the preceding century, culminating in the Bertrum heir's disappearance after the unfortunate deaths of his mistress and illegitimate son. House Bertrum has since returned to its roots, and has regained much ground in academia with the public opening of the previously restricted Bertrum Academy, enabling any sufficiently wealthy patron to attain a Noble education at a premium price.

House Kantos

House Kantos follows a strict doctrine of sacrifice and honor, and it is not uncommon to find Psugian servants in their homes. The sons of House Kantos have long served the armies and navies of Man, and Kantos maintains a large presence in the House of Nobles, regularly casting the decisive vote on matters of war.

House Kromm

House Kromm is among the most wealthy of the Old Houses, but, having derived the majority of its wealth from the discovery of an ancient lunar storehouse of lost technology, many regard Kromm as a useless house. The heirs of Kromm carry a reputation for ignorance and impatience, though none can question their Nobility.

House Man

The House of Man is one of many houses to have claimed primacy and has held power over the other houses for thousands of years. Despite lingering rumors of illegitimacy, paedocide, and apocryphal heresy, King Nero I has proven to be a powerful and effective ruler. Though in his later years he has begun to show signs of madness, Nero has been quick to quell all rumors of his lapsing power.

Under Nero's rule, Man has never lost a single decisive battle, and for this reason the navy of Man is widely regarded as invincible. House Man's political power is primarily derived from the nearly-indestructible ships scavenged from the Lost Fleet, a wealth of artifacts and technology from the Old Kingdoms.

House Nennius

House Nennius, much like House Bertrum, is devoted to scholarly pursuit. At best, they could be described as rivals; at worst, as bitter enemies. As far as House Bertrum has fallen in the past century, House Nennius has risen. As a direct result of services rendered to the much beloved Hundred-year King, Nero I, the alchemists of Nennius are beyond reproach and are widely regarded as the foremost philosophers of Man, despite vicious rumors of assassination and necrophilia.

House Noël

Once one of the prime houses, following the tragedy of the Winter Gates and the subsequent imprisonment of the debauched Mad Count, Gaston, House Noël has lost access to most of its lands and, consequently, most of its prestige. Were it not for the wealth and constant support of the Norlian Duchy, House Noël would have long since fallen to the ranks of the Lost Houses. Despite the increasing political presence of House Noël, dark rumors continue to surface concerning the debauchery of the Comtesse d'Noël and her connection to her former husband.

House Tiemes

Members of House Tiemes consider themselves artists above all. From poetry and dancing to painting and acting, all forms of artistic expression fall under the expertise of Tiemes. The Seventh Count of Tiemes, Grand Poet Lylliaks, is widely regarded as the singular playwright and poet of the Kingdom of Man and productions his centuries-old works are legendary.

House Venici

House Venici specializes in the transport and trading of all manner of goods, and has long been the wealthiest house in the Kingdom of Man. Venician freighters are legendary among spacers, both for their undeniable opulence and for their number of smuggling compartments.

Venician trade hubs are strategically located at the entry space of every populated system and conduct all licensed commerce. As an old saying goes, "Venici ships have silvered sails."

House Yogram

House Yogram is a manufacturing dynasty, and in most regions, century-old contracts guarantee exclusive production rights to Yogram factories. Often called the "Viper's House", House Yogram is perpetually mired in petty politics and minor intrigue. Members of this wealthy house tend to be shrewd businessmen and expert politicians. For nearly a century, House Yogram has been dominated by the shadow of Chairman Tonhg and his sons, though internal power struggles have led to great bloodshed in recent years.

The Lost Houses

According to the Dynastic Datahead of Man, there are thirteen Old Houses, from which all Nobles are said to descend. There are only nine Noble houses in the Kingdom of Man. Four others are known to be lost.

House Burles

The Dynastic Datahead has little to say on the subject of the Old Rebellion. It is known that the treacherous House Burles was expelled from the territory of Man following a cowardly Burlish attempt to destabilize the Sovereignty as a means of fostering revolution in the weaker houses and claiming the Throne of

Man for themselves. House Burles has since fallen to corruption and xenophillia. The reigning King of Man, The Hundred Year King, Nero I, has ordered a complete embargo against the Burlish traitors as punishment for their unconscionable perversions.

House Grimm

House Grimm is known to have foolishly allied themselves with the traitorous House Burles, and was subsequently exiled from Man.

House Roarie

The house of the famed General Roarie. The holdings of House Roarie, and all legitimate heirs, were lost in the Bloodwar. Tragically, many lower class merchants and thieves have taken advantage of this loss to claim Noble lineage. "Every merchant in the Hidden Mountain has a grandfather Roarie," as they say.

House Zorastros

The holdings of House Zorastros were lost in the Bloodwar, and the fates of the descendants of the once-great house have been lost to time.

The Others

The Bahrai

The Bahrai, sometimes referred to as "the sharks" or "whales", are a race of large, amphibious carnivores from the planet Bwai'i'i. The average Bahraian male stands at two and a half meters and weighs a quarter of a tonne, with the female standing at over three meters and weighing nearly half a tonne. The Bahrai have soft, rubbery skin that comes in a multitude of colors and patterns. Their small, black eyes receive only a fraction of the visible spectrum, and as a result the Bahrai rely on a series of specialized organs embedded within their skulls that allow them to detect fluctuations in the surrounding electromagnetic field. The Bahrai also possess uniquely bundled muscle tissue in their forearms which, when contracted in unison, allow the Bahrai to generate an electrical jolt sufficiently powerful to stop a man's heart.

Bwai'i'i was once a paradise world with abundant resources, which did not necessitate violent competition. Despite their coldblooded biology, the Bahrai are strict pacifists and abhor violence in all of its forms. Most Bahrai follow a form of Buddhist philosophy called the *Bahrai N'hrai*. Bahraian society is fairly relaxed with no real concept of taboo, and it is not uncommon in Bahraian colonies to see a naked Bahraian going about his daily business, though most Bahrai prefer to wear light, airy robes of woven silk. Adult Bahrai tend to have highly personal tattoos, called d'wodi, which are believed to map their spiritual essence.

The Bahrai were the first race to discover the lost technology of the Old Ones. Using their advanced science, they attempted to establish the first galactic government: the Republic of the Living Soul. Sadly, the Republic was short lived and fell not long after the Bahrai discovered K'ruukt.

The Bahrai, believing in the benevolence of all life, attempted to elevate the K'ruukta, teaching them the Bahrai N'hrai and offering them an official seat in the Republic of the Living Soul. The Bahrai were consequently enslaved by the K'ruukta for nearly a century, and their homeworld, Bwai'i'i was ravaged. The Bahrai were freed during the Burlish encroachment, which effectively cut Bwai'i'i off from K'ruukta reinforcements. Though their homeworld now lies in polluted ruin at the heart of the Burlish Tetrarchy, the Bahrai have refused member status and have rededicated themselves to enduring pacifism.

The Burlmen

The Burlmen are exiles from the Kingdom of Man and founders of the Burlish Tetrarchy. Following the tragic events of the Bloodwar, several of the Old Houses separated themselves from the philosophies of the reigning King of Man. The king, considering this to be an act of treason, demanded that the head of each house present themselves before his wrath for execution. As a show of force the king then sent his bastions into the heart of each territory. On the heels of untold death and suffering, and facing a grave, new conflict, the Burles chose to flee. A short skirmish marked the extent of what might have been another great war.

Past the confines of the Kingdom of Man, the Burles discovered previously unknown civilizations, and, recognizing their rights as sovereign people, founded the Burlish Tetrarchy. The Burlmen share many cultural commonalities with Man and, until the reign of Nero I, there was a great deal of unofficial contact between both powers.

There are three primary groups of Burlmen: the Southern Burles, whose boarder runs across the galactic divide also known as the Verge; the Western Burles, which includes the Roerian settlements; and the Eastern Burles, who are descended from members of other Old Houses exiled by Man.

The Southern and Western Burles, ever mindful of the corrupting nature of power, chose to establish a republic. One-hundred and seven senators serve on the Burlish Senate, and elect the Burlish Dictator for decade-long terms. The Dictator, in turn, represents the Western and Southern Burles in the Tetrarchy.

The Eastern Burles, similarly fearing the corruption of power, chose to found a direct technocratic democracy. Every member of the Eastern Burlish Technocracy has a single, weighted vote. The value of a vote is determined by the relevant education and life experience of the voter, such that an ignorant majority is incapable of gaining power over the educated minority. The Eastern Burles' seat on the Tetrarchy is held by the Burlish Prime Minister, who is elected by general vote every five years and is not to exceed a lifetime term limit of 14 years.

The K'ruukta

Otherwise known by the pejorative "the stags", the K'ruukta are a savage race from the planet K'ruukt. The average K'ruukta male stands just under a meter and a half tall. His body has a slender, athletic build and is covered in thin fur which thickens and darkens significantly about the shoulders and neck. K'ruukta males have narrow eyes that are shielded by thick, bone plates which grow to cover most of their brow. Males also possess a set of sturdy antlers as a secondary sexual characteristic. The males' compact bodies are adapted for ramming, and the muscle fibers in their legs, necks, and shoulders are incredibly dense. This, coupled with broad nerve bundles and thicker insertion points, allow their compact muscles to deliver truly devastating power.

The female K'ruukta differ from the males in that females typically have lighter builds with tighter thighs. The muscle fibers in their smaller legs are less suitable for sprinting and have been adapted for endurance. Lacking the male's specialized brow plates, females have large, open eyes which grant them significantly enhanced perception, and, in lieu of the males' flashy antlers, at sexual maturity females develop furred nubs which, along with small breasts, signal reproductive ability.

Most K'ruukta follow an ancient religious doctrine called *The Way of the*

Nine Paths, which establishes a sophisticated caste system and details the methods by which one may reach *N'hwir*, or enlightenment. There are three prime K'ruukta deities: B'ram, Nhristah, and K'uu, which represent the forces of creation, death, and strength respectively. The gods live in cycles, incarnating throughout every K'ruukta eon. The beginning of each eon is marked by the birth of the B'ram, and the end, by the coming of the Nhristakahn. The K'ruukta believe themselves to be incarnations of K'uu, enduring the endless conflict between the physical attachment of B'ram and the spiritual enlightenment of Nhristah.

K'ruukta fashion is dominated by caste and is brutal and utilitarian, reflecting the limited resources of their homeworld. The K'ruukta view most other races, especially Man, as decadent and wasteful.

The K'ruukta have proven to be a destructive and warlike people. K'ruukt was once a vibrant forest world, filled with endless life and bountiful resources; however, upon the discovery of Ka'ruktonhrastuunos, the lost city of the Old Ones, the K'ruukta used ancient knowledge to craft sophisticated weapon platforms and within a century had decimated their once-beautiful home.

The K'ruukta are an independent race and have few permanent allies.

The Psugians

The Psugians are an advanced race of noble crustaceans, though they have long since left their oceans. The Psugians stand at nearly two meters and have pale skin of a variety of shades depending on their emotional state. While the Psugians do have four primary limbs(a set of bipedal legs and a set of jointed arms) they are the evolutionary decedents of six-armed cephalopods, not unlike the cuttlefish of Earth, and have a set of smaller, extremely dexterous tentacles which are attached above an ape-like mandible. These tentacles vary in size from several centimeters to over half a meter. Though most Psugians no longer grow thick carapaces over their bodies, vestigial chitin does grow about their eyes and heads.

Psugian males grow thick plates on their heads, as well as their backs, along the spine, and are surprisingly hardy, possessing many redundant organs and a parallel spinal column. Psugians have two hearts and seem to have been well on their way to developing a third. The quasi-heart or 'nobility' assists the other two in times of stress. In sleep, only one heart pumps the Psugians' green blood, allowing the others the rare opportunity to rest.

Psugian females are significantly smaller than males and have only two hearts. Psugian females also lack the thicker plating present on the heads and necks of males, growing only a series of soft, down-like coverings. While physically less robust than the males, females have an enhanced metabolism that renders them immune to many common illnesses. Psugian females require significantly less sleep than the males, and often pass their nights reading Psugian romances which bare more than a passing resemblance to the Arthurian traditions of Earth.

The Psugians are a lost race. Their homeworld, Galliard, lies far beyond the Verge, in the second galactic mass. They were one of the first races to fall to the Khenosmen. The Psugians are obsessed with chivalry and their noble courts are complex, quasi-political mazes, simultaneously decrying the wasteful politics of other governments while privately fostering intrigue of their own. Psugian males follow a chivalric code known as the *Way of Uthurias*, which dictates a life of sacrifice and dedication modeled after the legendary Psugian monarch, Uthurias. Followers of the *Way of Uthurias* swear allegiance to one of hundreds of Psugian 'kingdoms' scattered throughout the Burlish Tetrarchy. Once allied with a king, the followers are given the title of Knight Errant, and are expected to leave their new homes in search of immortal honor and glory. Psugian knights are renowned for their strength, as well as their unyielding dedication to the Knight's Code. It is for this reason that many young Psugians find themselves employed as personal bodyguards, security forces, and, rarely, even mercenaries. The Psugians are a member race of the Burlish Tetrarchy, along with the Throgg and the Burlmen, and their seat is held by the Overking. The Overking is elected by an assembly of the Psugian kingdoms and is typically in the final stage of his life. Most Overkings have centuries of experience and are men of unquestionable honor and incontestable martial skill.

The Roerians

The Roerians are a race of fair-skinned giants. Despite having an average height of around three meters they have a strikingly similar physiology to that of Man. Prior to the events of the Bloodwar, Roerians lived throughout much of the territory now occupied by the Kingdom of Man. Many Roerian worlds were lost during the bloody conflict, and the surviving population was driven away with the Burlmen. The Roerians have since assimilated with the Western Burles and are viewed by outsiders, like the K'ruukta, as indoctrinated servants of an imperialistic power.

The Throgg

The Throgg are a mysterious race of short, bipedal humanoids. They appear remarkably manlike, even possessing dense, coarse hair about their heads and, in the case of males, faces; however, the Throgg come from a hot, high-pressure planet, called Throgyni. The atmosphere on Throgyni is remarkably dense and corrosive, and volcanic ash blankets the upper sky. Almost no sunlight reaches the surface, and most life on Throgyni has adapted around the planet's abundant geothermal vents. The Throgg themselves prefer temperatures in the one hundred to one hundred and twenty degree Celsius range, and find the habitable range of most sentient life forms to be painfully frigid. When away from Throgyni, the Throgg wear high-pressure thermal suits to maintain a comfortable environment.

The Throgg are fiercely intelligent and, before the discovery of the Old Philosophers' Ship, were largely industrial philosophers. The temperature and atmosphere of Throgyni made the development of most technology impracticable. As a result, the Throgg never made the necessary technological leaps to discover electric power, relying instead on an enormously sophisticated combination of steam and clockwork technology that enabled even the production of computational equipment. However, through study of the wreckage of an ancient starship, the Throgg were able learn of the potential power of a method of controlling the flow of electrons around atoms, which we call electricity. Within a decade the Throgg had developed a complex system of crystalline electronics that could operate even in their harsh atmosphere.

The Throgg bare many signs of being an engineered race and are often used by cultists as proof of the existence of a creator deity like the Allfather. The Throgg have no evolutionary ancestors on Throgyni, and have a remarkable genetic link to man, though they do share many genes with a Throgynian tubeworm. In addition to possessing genius level intelligence, the Throgg are resistant to all known infectious disease and are all but immune to the effects of aging. Most Throgg live well into their five-hundreds.

Throgg society is quite rigid and ordered, valuing stoicism and conformity. Throgg males are expected to wear something resembling a Victorian three-piece suit, produced from the fibrous membranes of local fauna, including a form of flattened top hat. Female Throgg typically wear a tight, layered dress complete with corset and hat. The Throgg adhere strictly to a religious doctrine based entirely on logic, and they typically regard the beliefs of most other races as quaint superstition.

The Throgg are a member race of the Burlish Tetrarchy, along with the Psugians and the Burlmen. The Throgg's seat is held by the Primarch, a Throgg elder valued for his wisdom and experience. Though technically a republic, the position of Primarch has been functionally patrilineal for the duration of modern Throgg society.

Creatures, Beasts, and Monsters

The Allfather

The Allfather is an anthropomorphic creator deity from an ancient, polytheistic belief system. Known by nearly every race, it is difficult to trace the origin of the myth. The Allfather is described as a titanic, primeval man. In most accounts he stands nearly three meters tall with broad, thickly muscled shoulders and a great, white beard. He is often depicted holding the great spear, Zoiradoru, and the broad shield, Upomenei. He is credited with the creation of all sentient life. In some variations of the myth, the Allfather is simply born on a great ship, while in others a dying machine god pulls him from beyond space itself and tasks him with the restoration of life in a dead galaxy. In most surviving texts, the Allfather is the eternal progenitor of man and seeds all worlds with life before being betrayed by his corrupted son, Tyran, though some apocryphal texts name Nobul as his true betrayer. The Allfather, having been grievously wounded, is thought to sleep in the darkness beyond the edge of the galaxy, awaiting the end of the world, an event known as the Ragnorisis, and the Age of the Undying Sun.

Blood-Fathers

Many myths and legends have risen surrounding these monastic warriors. Tradition holds that the Blood-Fathers were founded in the time prior to the emergence of the Old Houses, by a direct descendant of the Allfather, named Diomedes. The bodies of the Blood-Fathers are altered through a mysterious biochemical process (known only to members of the orders of the Keepers) and through the use of extensive cybernetic implantation. The Blood-Fathers forsake all attachment to their mortal flesh and devote themselves entirely to the protection of mankind. As such, they are frightful to behold: standing three to four meters tall, and weighing in excess of two tonnes, with swathes of necrotic flesh suffering from the symptoms of cybernetic rejection syndrome and bloodrot.

There were thirteen orders of the Blood-Fathers, each based within one of the surviving thirteen worldbreakers, titanic starships now called bastions. Of the original thirteen orders, only seven survive: the Ravenlords and their bastion *Vigilance;* the 'o Loyos and their bastion *Piety*; the Blackfallows and their bastion *Fraternity*; the Band of the White and their bastion *Penitence*; the Voidwalkers and their bastion *Justice*; the Houndfathers and their bastion *Obedience*; and the Heartless and their bastion *Temperance*.

Though the Blood-Fathers were founded with the purpose of reversing the tide of the Bloodwar and reducing the mounting death toll caused by the spread of the Khenosian Flood, in more peaceful times they have found themselves being used as political tools. The Blood-Fathers have since become the center of a variety of politically motivated accusations and rumors, including claims of cannibalism, necromancy, and fleshcræft.

Dataheads

In the simplest of terms, a datahead is a cybernetic computer intelligence. Lacking knowledge of the actual design and inner workings of much of their advanced technology, true artificial intelligence has long eluded the engineers of Man. Nevertheless, a solution was eventually found through the gradual implantation of powerful computer systems into the brains of skilled hackers and mathematicians.

Called "barbaric" by certain Burlish detractors, the process is slow and undeniably gruesome. Over a period of years, the implants gradually augment the memory and processing capabilities of the host, before ultimately taking over preservation and maintenance of brain tissue and function. When this is achieved the datahead is "harvested". The host's head is severed from the now purposeless body, the outer flesh is dried and preserved, and a suite of networking hardware is installed, including various input/output ports.

For millennia the Dynastic Databases of the Old Houses have been cared for and guarded by deeply encrypted dataheads, rendering the vital systems virtually impregnable. Few hackers can match the speed and skill of even the least seasoned datahead, and the oldest dataheads are thought to function at the liminal edge of reality. A good datahead can operate with minimal maintenance for more than a century, and some dataheads in the libraries of the Blood-Fathers, and in the cores of bastions, are rumored to have been in continuous operation for more than a thousand years.

Dragons

Though generally believed to be purely beings of legend, dragons are fearsome creatures, indeed. Born before the Age of Man, dragons are said to be the only creatures to remember the preceding Age of Darkness. In legend these ancient beasts are said to be portents of Ragnorisis who appear once more at the beginning of the Age of the Undying Sun, a time when the Dead God will rise from æternal Chaos and be slain at the hands of the Undying Man.

Dragons are old beyond age, and hold knowledge of the land beyond man's existence, the primordial realm, Chaos. They alone are believed to know the true name of the Allfather and the identity of the Godslayer.

Esnim

Esnim come from the lost planet, Arzvertun, and seem to be a form of large ape adapted to the frigid environment of the frozen wastes which cover most the planet's surface. The height of an esnim can vary from one and a half to well over two and a half meters. The body of an esnim is densely muscular and is covered in a thick, white fur. At sexual maturity, most esnim grow a set of black ivory tusks. Males tend to grow yellowish manes, which serve as an outward sign of virility, and their tusks tend to be more prominent, with tusks of an alpha male typically reaching nearly a meter in size. Females, on the other hand, tend to develop small breasts, and their tusks tend to remain relatively short, functioning primarily as enlarged canines. The milk produced by female esnim during pregnancy is extremely rich and calorie dense, enabling the rapid maturation of esnim young

Esnim are fierce creatures of surprising intelligence, and have been known to occupy the scattered ruins of Old Arzvertun. Some scholars amongst the subterranean city-states of Arzvertun have speculated that the esnim may have once possessed a spoken language, though little concrete evidence has been found.

Jagananth, otherwise known as The Voice in the Dark

The Jagananth is an old K'ruukta deity worshiped as a malevolent personification of the universe. Having no corporeal form, it is often depicted as a singular, dark eye encircled by a shadowed starburst. Thought by some to be a primordial dragon, the Jagananth is said to exist outside of causality, unburdened by fate.

Keepers

The Keepers are servants of the Blood-Fathers. Rarely seen outside of their temples found in the bellies of bastions, little is known about these pitied and misshapen creatures. Keepers are thought to maintain the technology and preserve the knowledge of the Blood-Fathers, functioning as a band of grotesque monks.

Khenosmen

Khenosmen are titanic monsters, standing five meters tall and weighing a full tonne. Their necrotic flesh is known to spread disease and pestilence wherever it is found. They are fiercely intelligent and all but invincible.

Little is known about their culture or their true language. According to the Arke, the Khenosmen are the dark progeny of the Lost Son, Tyran. Khenosmen come from beyond occupied space, on the other side of the galactic divide, called the Verge, and are rumored to have a complex civilization in the second galactic core. Other than second hand stories in scripture and age-worn archives, there is no record of contact with a living Khenosman. Though many no longer believe in their existence, rumors of their return continue to trickle from the fringes of known space, stirring yet more rumors of the coming Age of the Undying Sun and the time of Ragnorisis.

Nobul

Nobul is eldest son of the Allfather. Beautiful and kind, Nobul is known as the Brilliant Son, god of light and virtue. He and his brother, Tyran, were born from the forbidden union of the Allfather and his bride, Penelope. Few texts regarding Nobul have survived the Bloodwar, but in the Old Stories, he is known as the Dark Sun.

The Old Ones, otherwise known as the Forgotten Men, the Elves, and the Lost

The Old Ones were an ancient race believed to have lived before the birth of the galaxy. Almost nothing is known of this once-godlike people. Possessing a mastery of science and technology far beyond the understanding of mortal men, the Old Ones were the architects of impossible wonders which now lie in sleeping ruin, scatted across the old stars of the dual galaxy, their immortal achievements all but forgotten.

Penelope

Penelope is the wife and lover of the Allfather. Having been created from his flesh at the birth of the galaxy, Penelope's wisdom and knowledge are second only to the Allfather himself. She is known as the Blessed Lady and is the goddess of wisdom and marital love. Penelope is the first witch, and the creator of magica, which some have attributed to her study of cybernetics.

Starshades, otherwise known as Space Jellies

Starshades are massive, drifting jellyfish adapted to live in the harsh environments of space. Believed to have evolved in the celestial oceans, they are kilometer long, living nets. Though these jellies seem to lack a central nervous system, some evidence suggests surprising intelligence, and there have been numerous accounts of adult Jellies covering ships anchored too long in their oceans.

Stone Crawlers, otherwise known as Asteroid Worms

Like massive, centipedal worms, stone crawlers nest in asteroids. Stone crawlers can grow to be longer than three hundred meters. They have flat, broad bodies covered in thick, composite metal carapaces. Stone crawlers have a series of proto-eyes that run along the edge of a central nerve bundle, not unlike a spinal column. This ocular network provides the crawler with moderate visual information, but the majority of the crawler's sensory input is devoted to a line of long, electromagnetically-sensitive feelers which allow the creature to navigate the constantly shifting environment through a form of electromagnetic sonar.

Stone crawlers feed via a startling chemical process involving the digestion of silicates and iron, and traverse the space between asteroids via excretory glands that function as organic ion engines. The mandible of a stone crawler is remarkably strong and is well suited to the carving of metal rich asteroids, and there have been numerous reports of especially tenacious stone crawlers gnawing on the armor of mining ships.

Tyran, otherwise known as the Lost Son and the Dead God

Tyran is the second son of the great Allfather. In surviving texts, Tyran is born monstrously deformed and is quite hideous to behold. It is believed that his twisted body is a reflection of a dark and twisted soul. To many Bertrum scholars, Tyran is a classic example of a god of mischief and destruction. After being cast out of the Great Ship for attacking his brother, Nobul, and plotting against the Allfather himself, Tyran flees to the Land of the Dead, in the second core of Avoromedia, where he uses the power the gods to corrupt his treacherous flesh and become an eldritch horror undreamt of in the modern age. Though classically thought to be a mere nemesis construction to serve as an evil counterpart to the Allfather, certain extant texts reveal Tyran as the poor victim of his brother, Nobul's, ambition, and paint the Dark Sun as the one true God of Lies.

Tyran is often credited with the creation of the first stardrive, and spacial field generator, which he is believed to have used to cheat in a race with Nobul. The two had been tasked with retrieving a flower from Ninuette, the lost home of the Elves, with the winner to receive a kiss from the visiting Elf princess, Mezzomesta. While Nobul used his knowledge of the starseas to set his ship's course along the most favorable currents, Tyran created a shortcut. But, despite returning long before Nobul, Tyran's plundered flower did not survive the journey, and Mezzomesta awarded her favor to the handsome and honest Nobul.

Tyran's Fleas, otherwise known as the Bugs

There are many tales from the rim and edge worlds, which line the ancient borders of Man, that speak of strange insects of remarkable size that have an insatiable hunger for flesh. In most accounts these "Bugs" come from infested outland and black market freight, though older stories have them falling within meteors and asteroid fragments. Regardless of the method of their arrival, once in a population zone, these invaders form a parasitic attachment to higher organisms. In most accounts the Bugs take complete control of the host's central nervous system, though in certain lesser accounts they merely replace the host's digestive tract in the entirety while inducing a maddening sensation of hunger.

Physically, these insects vary in size from a decimeter up to more than two meters. The Bugs are covered by a thick, bone plating that resembles an arthropodic carapace. By some accounts as many as thirty-four worlds on the fringe space of Man may have fallen to an infestation of these fearsome monstrosities in the last hundred years alone. It is speculated that the Bugs may have some relation to the Khenosmen, and are listed in the records of the Keepers as Tyran's Fleas.

Worldbreakers, otherwise known as Bastions

The Worldbreakers are a frightful remnant of the Old World. These titanic city-ships span kilometers and house entire cultures. At their prime, each possessed sufficient firepower to destroy all surface life on a planet, boiling oceans and reducing all land to molten stone. Most Worldbreakers are in varying states of disrepair, and of the seven remaining Worldbreakers, only the bastion *Temperance* has retained a functioning Apocalypse Engine.

Myths, Legends, and Old Spacers' Tales

The Arke
-an excerpt from the Book of the First Father

At the end of time the galaxy was filled with death. All things had been destroyed. From eons of darkness came the **Allfather**. He came into the world upon a **great ship** and saw many things that brought joy to his heart and he knew that it was good and beautiful. He lived for many years but he was lonely and longed to share the beauty of the world. So from his flesh the **Allfather** created woman. He named his creation **Penelope**. Together they sang in joy upon the **Great Ship**.

In the **Time of Gnosis** the **Allfather** traveled the world creating life. For many years they lived in happiness and goodness but **Penelope** grew discontent and desired children of her own. So she lured the **Allfather** away from the **Great Ship** and seduced him at the bottom of the starsea.

Penelope gave birth to the twin sons **Tyran** and **Nobul**. **Nobul** was strong like his father and longed to see the world in goodness but **Tyran** was born weak and ugly. The **Allfather** was not troubled by **Tyran's** hideousness and loved him above all. To his favored son he showed kindness beyond measure. In spite of the **Allfather**'s love **Tyran** came to hate his father. As eons passed he grew vicious and cruel until in his wickedness **Tyran** attacked his brother cutting out **Nobul**'s eye and driving him from the **Great Ship**. The **Allfather** could no longer blind himself to **Tyran**'s wickedness. They made war in the **Great Ship** and **Tyran** was cast out into the void. **Tyran** fled to the **Dark Lands** where his heart burned with hatred and he seeded worlds with life of his own. The progeny of **Tyran** bore the taint of his spiteful flesh. His children grew ugly and monstrous. These are the **Khenosmen**. They populated the old worlds.

The **Allfather** weary from battle and heavyhearted from witnessing the evil of his favorite son grew wary of his creations. He left the world taking from man his immortality and power. In the place of these gifts he gave to him mortality and pain so that he might know his heart and know that he was worthy. At first man struggled with his mortality. He knew hunger and death and cursed the **Allfather**. The unworthy did not survive but mortality made man strong. In his strength he came to know his heart and the heart of his maker.

Then came the **Bloodwar**. At the **Red Hour** the corrupted children of **Tyran** fell upon the world of man in a flood of flesh and bone. Man had grown strong in his mortality and he fought the **Khenosmen**. For ages did the **Bloodwar** rage in the absence of the **Allfather**. Until at its apex all of creation was at war. It was then that a child of the **Allfather** was born. In his divine piety **Diomedes** heard the call of the **Allfather** and sought the **purity of blood**. He knew that it was the impurity of man that had separated him from the **Allfather**. Thus did **Diomedes** make his blood as the **Allfather**'s. But in so doing his impure flesh began to wither and rot. So it was that **Diomedes** wrapped himself in the **purity of steel**. Only when his blood was pure did the gifts of the **Allfather** return to **Diomedes**. At last his hands summoned destruction and he rode the **Burning Ship** through the starsea. None could stand before his might. He slaughtered the impure **Khenosmen** driving them back to edge of dark space. Yet the children of **Tyran** grew strong. They pushed back against the might of **Diomedes** and when the war was all but lost the **Allfather** returned.

When the **Allfather** saw the grotesque children **Tyran** had spawned in his exile he knew rage. In his divine anger the **Great Ship** burned all the **Khenos-men** and they were as nothing but ash. But the **Allfather**'s heart grew heavy with the death of his children. In the final days of the **Bloodwar** an envoy sent by the cruel **Tyran** breached the **Great Ship** with promises of peace. Their songs moved the heart of the **Allfather**. Thus were **Tyran** and **Diomedes** brought before him. The rebellious son prostrated himself at the **Allfather**'s feet but he had not come to make peace.

 Tyran had come to make war on the **Allfather** himself. In the corruption of the void **Tyran** had warped his flesh beyond measure and had become truly monstrous. In his hubris he struck at the **Allfather**. Mortal **Diomedes** inter-vened but the **Allfather** was wounded deeply and his left arm was severed from divinity. In his fury the **Allfather** turned his might against his favored son and smote his cursed flesh from creation.

 With **Tyran** dead man had survived the **Bloodwar** but the cost was great. Though immortal the **Allfather** was wounded. **Diomedes** carried his master to the **Black Throne**. In the moments before succumbing to the **godsleep** the **Allfather** rewarded the piety of **Diomedes** by restoring his flesh. He then tasked **Diomedes** with the protection of his children and the destruction of the last of **Tyran**'s progeny. **Diomedes** swore the **Unyielding Blood Oath** and left the **Great Ship**. Thus did the **Allfather** vanish from the world until the **Ragnorisis** when the end of the **godsleep** and the rebirth of **Tyran** marks the end of days. Thus were the **Blood-Father**'s born in **sacrifice** and **virtue**.

The Old Lady of the Verge
-An old spacer rhyme

If thou travel through the Verge,
Beware the path 'round Giddeon's Curve.
For, though the space may appear,
On ancient star charts to be clear,
No spacer old, nor diver deep,
Hast delved the seas 'round the Keep
Without the gravest loss of sleep.
For, though the seas are calm and fair,

There is a wicked spirit there.
Her name is old, her voice is dust.
Her touch is cold like winter's gust,
And when she comes upon thy ship,
Your flesh she'll prick and tear and rip.
For if thou chance that dreadful sea,
The Black Lady shall come for thee.

The Dark Sun's Song
-translated from the Black Tome, Gorgathamesh

Behold, my love, like a black tulip,
Blooms in shaded caverns cold.
Where once was lust now hunger grows,
And wraps my mind in mold.

My body lay in tortured clay
Where none that live may tread.
For primal sins and viciousness
Did Father smite me dead.

My limbs are stiff, my body aches,
I cannot feel the rain.
Immortals weep from starry skies,
While maggots eat my brain.

A soul adrift in nightmare seas,
My memories were pain.
Till, as a blessing, madness fell
To steal away my name.

But, æternal thought doth haunt me still,
And in my dreams doth lead
To The Bride, Penelope,
And godly hearts that bleed.

For untold years I loved her dear,
And so did she love me,
That when I died she came to hear
A sickly melody.

A sour note from Pathos' harp
Crossed the endless sea,
And dripped upon her weary eyes
Horrors endlessly.

For then she mourned on bended knee,
Above my rotting flesh.
In sorrow's garden did she weep,
And long for coming death

Till in her grief a bargain struck
With spirits dark and old
And made a deal, my soul to steal
From the darkest hold.
My shadow fell through chasms deep,
And swam the fiery skies,
But her sweet love did anchor me,
And bid me to arise.

And so did breath return to flesh,
And fire burn once more
Upon the rotting altar
Of my ghastly form.

I broke through stone, and tore the earth.
To heaven's touch I soared.
Until at last I gained the sky,
And mother's voice I heard:

I've wept for thee, my dearest love
Since fate stole thee away

And longed for thee my truest love
Like the coming day

While you were gone
No light did shine
The skies were
Dark and grey

now come to me
my grisly man
hold me in
your loving
arms and wipe
these hopeless
tears away
with tender
kisses

Her voice was weak, her eyes were red,
Her flesh was white as death.
But in her smile, triumph soared,
Like rapture in her breast.

In life, I was a wicked boy,
Covetous and vain.
Primeval love had saved me once.
In death, it had again.

I stood as god above my grave,
A mortal son no more.
My flesh would flee eternally
From the devil's door.

As mother watched with blissful eye,
Unruly bones gave way
To fancy lives in distant clouds
Lit along the bay.

My heart was filled with honest love.
I longed for her embrace.
But when she came in for a kiss,
I ate her lovely face.

So beauteous is truest love,
When minds are savage grey.
Yet savage beauty conquers love,
When lust our hearts betray.